EVOLUTIONARY
MAGIC

Christina Herlyn

ACKNOWLEDGMENTS

Thank you to the women of my first ever writing group who gave me the confidence to continue and the constructive criticism to improve: Kitty Carr, Lisa Ingles, and Angelique Migliore! Cover photograph of Kansas City Union Station taken by Nate Evans Productions.

CHAPTER ONE

Gritting my teeth, I ripped the manticore quill from my thigh and leaned against the wall. A tarnished hall sconce bumped my head, and peeled wallpaper tickled my neck. The venomous spine I rolled between my fingers was small, from a young manticore's tail. It would make a normal human comatose. My eyelids drooped, then I noticed the bloody hole in my already threadbare jeans and irritation drowned my fatigue.

The door beside me creaked open and a finger pointed through the crack. "It went that way, lady."

Fresh claw marks gouged the walls and viscous, dark manticore blood trailed to the hallway's exit. The stench unique to manticores hung heavy in the air. An elephant-sized hole loomed over a broken glass door that led to a rooftop pool. Of course it went that way.

"Just catching my breath, thanks." I followed the stink.

Everyone else kept their doors closed. Only idiots poked their heads into hallways when monsters roamed a building. Well, idiots and me. At least I got paid to play with monsters. Since my partner never showed tonight, I'd get all the money. Provided I took care of the manticore without killing myself.

The manticore had attacked the old Sheraton Hotel on McGee Street, now low-income housing for people who couldn't or wouldn't leave Kansas City. In the dilapidated lobby, I had cut off his spiny, weaponized tail. He had retreated upstairs, but I held no illusions that he was finished with me. He probably used the alone time to grow a new tail—or three. The abilities of manticores were still a mystery to me.

My katana ready, I stepped into the pool area. The smell of earth instead of chlorine filled my sensitive nose. In the hotel's heyday, the pool was a fancy indoor/outdoor affair, but today's tenants couldn't

1

keep up maintenance. Plus, manticores don't make good swimming buddies. The indoor half was a converted solarium filled with dirt and dying shrubbery. Outside, the rest of the cracked, concrete pool remained empty. Finances were pretty dire when people ran out of dirt.

The stars on this calm, cool evening twinkled on the purpling western horizon. I expected the manticore to jump from the darkness of the pool, but the roof stayed quiet and undisturbed—aside from overturned plastic plants and a pissed-off tomcat. He hissed at me from his perch on the wall. I hissed back. He leapt into the shadows since my fangs were bigger than his.

Halfway to the edge of the roof, the spurs of my riding boots screeched against concrete when I stopped short. There's no mistaking a manticore's voice. It resonates like competing horns in the brass section of a hearing-impaired orchestra. Shaking my ringing head, I dug a pair of earplugs from the pocket of my hoodie.

Armed with earplugs and my sword, I approached the edge. The manticore wasn't on the roof with me, but I couldn't see him despite the barred windows in the surrounding brick wall. The bars would have made interesting tan lines back when sunbathers populated the roof instead of stray cats and beast slayers.

The two-inch heels on my boots made me six feet tall—eye-level with the top of the wall. I jumped to the top. My spurs clinked on the ledge as I landed in a crouch with sword overhead and right arm out for balance. Across the street, on top of an abandoned office building, the manticore's giant blue eyes widened—I was awake instead of napping like a properly tranquilized meal. Two stories below, the street was deserted. Mythological beasts had invaded the American frontier long enough that curiosity no longer killed.

Only a beautiful, glassed-in walkway shaped like a right triangle separated us. It curved over the streets and ran along buildings to connect an area once congested with traffic. The manticore crouched, muscles rippling beneath the russet fur of his lion-like body. Claws as long as my fingers dug into the roof. He still lacked his tail, which made me smile.

He was built for pouncing, but he couldn't make it across the four-lane street. As if responding to my doubt, he roared again. His human face topped with a red mane and beard transformed into a gaping maw filled with three rows of sharp teeth. My earplugs muted the cacophony, but my chest vibrated. The decay riding his breath hit me in a sickening cloud. Half the panes in the walkway shattered, the glass tinkling musically to the pavement.

Despite my earplugs, I heard the distinct groan of straining metal joints. The roof of the walkway bent in unnaturally. The manticore had used it as a hopping point to get across. Judging by the way he eyed my appetizing self, he intended to do it again. Adding my weight to that walkway—suspended fifteen feet above the road— was not a good idea. Yet catching him mid-leap was a chance I couldn't dismiss.

His eyes focused on me. His head lowered and his front paws stretched before him. A large drop of saliva fell from his lips, and before it plopped on the concrete, the manticore jumped. All four paws briefly touched the walkway's apex at the same time. His eyes never left me. Half a heartbeat later he was back in the air, flying toward me. I jumped to meet him.

As I leapt below him, I shoved my katana into his soft underbelly, I dropped through the now glass-free roof. His traveling body did the job of disemboweling itself before I landed. My blade sliced through his abdomen like gelatin. His slimy insides dropped around me. I forced my dinner back where it belonged, dodging the biggest pieces.

The manticore's body hit the end of the walkway. It collapsed, pitching me toward the street. I lost my earplugs and my breath when I fell to the floor. Keeping my sword high, I slid on glass and manticore parts halfway to the street before I regained my footing. Then, I ran down the tilted walkway like a sailor on shore leave. Raising my katana, I used my momentum to slice off his head: standard protocol for anything but a hydra.

Smiling, I relaxed. I couldn't perfectly time such a scenario again in a hundred years. I was Andromeda Bochs: slayer of monsters and timing genius. Then Atlas broke the horizon, and my satisfaction faded. In the shape of a human heart, the radioactive rock glowed red as if true blood pulsed through the ventricles.

My first reaction to the asteroid-turned-moon that orbited Earth was always physical. My skin tingled, tiny sparks igniting in every pore and hairs reaching skyward. But my heart, just below the set of scars on my chest, dropped to the ground.

Sometimes, I wondered what the world was like fifty years ago when the asteroid hurtled through space on a path to destroy Earth.

Instead of colliding with the world, it slowed down when it entered the solar system and kept slowing until it pushed the moon out of orbit to take its place. Scientists discovered that the silica in the Earth's crust repelled Atlas, citing that as the reason it hadn't crashed through the atmosphere. They'd learned little else in the half-century since.

Tonight, I felt more frustration toward Atlas than curiosity, and I stomped my foot. "Damn it."

Atlas's magnetic flares meant that while it hovered on this side of the world, anything more complex than a refrigerator wouldn't work. The truck I had in the parking garage was now useless, and I'd have to carry the manticore to headquarters. Patrolling Kansas City brought me a paltry salary, but commissioned kills earned the real money. Without the head, I had no official credit for the kill, which meant no commission. No commission, no new jeans.

Removing a soft cloth from my pocket, I carefully cleaned the blade of my katana before sheathing it in its saya and dropping the cloth on the manticore's body.

"Hey, Evolutionary!"

My eyes sharpened on the dark entrance to the parking garage and made out two child-size forms. "What?" I sounded pretty grouchy, but then, while the name 'Evolutionary' wasn't bad, their tone hadn't been polite, either. Plus, nighttime was for monsters, not kids.

"Is that thing gonna grow a new head?"

I made a show of studying the manticore's body, placing my chin in one hand. Finally, I shrugged and looked back at the shadows. "Probably not, but I'd go home, anyway."

The kids disappeared, and the sound of running feet faded, hopefully going inside. I braided a large section of the manticore's mane into a rope then wrapped it around my hand and started jogging. At least the headquarters for the Mythical Creatures Elimination Squad was less than half a mile down the street. The so-called evolution may have given me super strength, speed, and endurance, but I still had an economical streak when it came to physical activity.

As I passed Washington Park, I saluted the bronze statue of George Washington mounted on a horse. Under the wild growth of plant life, a pedestal supported him, but he looked as though he trudged through piles of greenery instead of the snow at Valley

Forge. Even in early March, all of the city parks were overrun with lush trees, vines, and flowers—compliments of Atlas radiation. The city didn't bother maintaining parks anymore. What little money it had for maintenance went to cleaning monster messes like the one I'd just made.

I trotted down Pershing Road, the massive head bouncing behind me until I got to the circle drive in front of one of the few maintained public buildings in Kansas City: Union Station. The front of Union Station remained quiet and empty. The back of the giant, two-centuries-old building still functioned as a train station. Atlas flares and flying monsters had ruined air travel, making the station even busier. Half of the time, the train engines ran on steam, just like the First Frontier Era.

We lived in the Second Frontier Era, now, but no one lined up their wagons to head West. Thanks to supervolcanoes, desolation reigned beyond Kansas. If an adventurous person made it to the Pacific, sticking a toe into that Ring-of-Fire-heated cauldron was a bad idea. Drastic environmental change killed plenty of humans, even before the beasts arrived and inspired the Mythical Creatures Elimination Squad. The acronym was pronounced with a hard 'C,' so unofficial correspondence simply dubbed the organization 'M-kes.'

The front of Union Station housed M-kes, which employed Eliminators like me to protect mankind from all the beasts that decided they weren't mythical, anymore. The limestone structure stretched two blocks, not including the parking garage at the west end where I was supposed to haul my kill. The barriers were down and the gate station sat empty. So, I dragged the head through the main entrance set below three, forty-foot-tall arches filled with windows. Huge red banners hung over the arches. They bore the M-Kes coat-of-arms: a black severed dragon's head with a sword beneath it.

Some thought calling the emblem a coat-of-arms was too medieval, but today I felt like a dragon slayer entering the palace to bring a gift to my king. Well, if my king was a sour-faced blond woman seated at a scratched up wooden desk across the vast hall. My spurs rang as I crossed the earth-tone patterned, marble floor. I didn't usually go for spurs, but I enjoyed entering the M-kes lobby when I wore them. The manticore head slid behind me. When I stopped, its stench formed a palpable cloud.

The pale Mrs. Kress looked up from her antique desk, her mouth managing a pucker despite the tightness of the bun atop her head. "I've told you, Bochs, beast remains go straight to the west parking lot until Dr. Bennett can study them."

"The gate is shut and no one's there."

Kress' stern brown eyes and stout body had little effect on me. Being a woman myself, I recognized what she loved, and I used it. I removed three brightly wrapped chocolates from my black hoodie and tossed them onto her desk.

Kress' eyes dilated and her tongue darted out briefly before she controlled herself. "Where did you find this?" She snatched the candy and dropped it in her cleavage.

With cocoa plantations disappearing beneath encroaching jungles, chocolate was precious. Patrolling the Silent Sector one night, I'd come across an abandoned, sealed vault full of chocolate delicacies. What people hid when they thought the end was near amazed me.

I wasn't about to tell Kress that looted chocolate filled my kitchen cabinets. "Someone gave it to me."

She stared suspiciously into my light blue face with alexandrite eyes that probably glowed. If there were a way to shut off the glow, I hadn't learned it. I smiled. She flinched at the oversized incisors pushing against my lower lip. I didn't know why nature gave me predator teeth, for I had no intention of taking a beast down with my mouth, but they provided great intimidation.

Kress focused on the manticore head as tall as my elbow. One eyelid still twitched, winking at her. Most of the blood drained during the trip, but a little dripped onto the polished floor.

Kress shuddered. "Fine, leave it here." She shoved a yellow piece of paper into my hand. "Johnson and Delaney never showed tonight so this assignment is yours."

"Did they call in?"

"No."

"Did Hicks call in?" Hicks was my no-show partner for the evening.

Kress smiled. "Nope."

The paper crackled beneath my tightening fingers. As Eliminators for M-kes, we were on a short leash. Being a no-show/no-call brought Enforcers after you in a hurry. Enforcers—the bad asses of M-kes—would just as soon drag an Eliminator back dead as alive. Hicks, Johnson, and Delaney raised the Eliminator disappearances to seven this month. So far, the Enforcers had retrieved only one, very dead.

"Don't you find this rise in AWOLs disturbing?" As soon as I asked, I wondered why I'd bothered.

"No." Kress narrowed eyes that actually required the wire-frame glasses she wore. She was a Normal: one of the vast majority of humans who didn't have the E-gene. The E-gene gave physical superiority to a select few—Evolutionaries they called us, but our natural selection came with a price. The E-gene made us susceptible to the radiation of Atlas, which slowly killed us, delayed only by the silica ingots implanted above our hearts. They repelled the radiation just as silica's presence in Earth's crust repelled Atlas itself.

Most Normals despised us even though Evolutionaries died while saving them from mythical creatures. The name they chose for themselves made that clear. And all Eliminators and Enforcers were Evolutionaries; M-kes was the only job allowed us.

That all meant Kress didn't give a damn if we disappeared—not until she needed a monster killer, anyway. "When Provost Allen is concerned, I will be." She ignored my glare.

The head of the Kansas City chapter of M-kes had been in charge for six weeks, and I'd seen him twice. Provost Allen probably cared less about us than Kress. I turned on my heel, reading my assignment as I walked away.

When I got to the location description, I halted. "The Restricted Zone?"

I looked over my shoulder and Kress shrugged. "People keep going in and not coming out."

If people were that stupid, they deserved what they got. The Restricted Zone required at least three Eliminators. I looked for the order's authorization signature. "Doyen Hightower approved this?" Doyen of Defense, Josiah Hightower, didn't waste manpower on pointless assignments. Josiah was one of the few Normals worth trusting in this city.

"Looks that way, but he's not here for you to ask. Asking isn't your privilege, anyway."

So sweet, Kress. "Do I have a partner?"

She glanced around. "Guess not."

A growl began deep in my chest and burst from my throat. I knew I sounded like the animal I tried so hard not to be, but I couldn't help it. I stomped out of headquarters and back into the night. That woman would not get chocolate bribes from me again. Unless I licked it first, then wrapped it back up.

"Hey, Andee!" A sweet, almost childish voice called.

I turned upon hearing my preferred name. My parents were optimistic when they named their freak baby Andromeda. The most positive comment I'd ever received concerning my large eyes, strong nose, and wide mouth was 'bold.' I took it as a compliment, but demigods didn't line up to fight sea monsters for me. Meanwhile, I went by Andee, adding the double 'e' to make it feminine and cute, thus completing my personification of oxymoronic.

"D.J." My voice didn't mirror her enthusiasm. D.J. Chadar was everything I wasn't: short, cute, nice. Her cherubic face somehow suited her skinny, adolescent-like body that was twenty-six—one year older than me. While my skin looked hypothermic, as if I'd swum in the Arctic Ocean, D.J.'s was indigo and her eyes sparkled like amethysts. Plus, her smile contained zero fangs. None of this caused my disappointment at the sight of her.

Her dark blue hands held the reins of two massive Clydesdales, the transportation of choice when Atlas interfered. A sword as long as my arm was strapped to her waist, the end nearly touching her ankle. Modern chainmail—tiny links of titanium—covered her from neck to knee. Seeing her decked out meant one thing: she was my partner.

Ironically, Evolutionary did not always equate to finely tuned survival machine. D.J. avoided death-by-beast because she could hide in small places. While she might see a flea on a horse's ass two hundred yards away, she couldn't shoot it off. My parents, though Normals, were athletic superstars. When the Olympics still existed, my mother had twice won sand volleyball gold, and my father had played linebacker in the now mythical National Football League. I was born to be an Amazon, evolution or not.

D.J. was born to be a sharp-eyed kindergarten teacher. She handed me the reins to a horse, her cheerful eyes glowing amidst a cloud of short black hair. "Looks like we get to kill a basilisk together!"

More accurately, I got to keep her alive while simultaneously killing a basilisk. Yay.

CHAPTER TWO

The Restricted Zone bordered the eastern edge of the Broadway Bog. When ash from the Yellowstone supervolcano filled in half of the Missouri River, the current all but stopped, flooding the Dakotas and creating bogs down the riverbed. One of the most dangerous bogs was centered below the Broadway Bridge in Kansas City. It wasn't officially named Broadway Bridge, anymore, but alliteration is more powerful than the names of long-gone heroes. Filled with fire frogs, trolls, carnivorous vines, and ground that would swallow you faster than you could say, "Give me a hand," the bog was best avoided.

Luckily, one other functioning bridge crossed the bog, and it led straight to the Restricted Zone. The Kit Bond Bridge—I don't know who that was—still dazzled the eyes as our horses carried us around a bend on the deserted I-35. The dual, cable-stayed bridge stretched higher than the Broadway Bridge, avoiding deadly vines and all but the nimblest of fire-breathing frogs. At its center stood an upside down, concrete 'V' with what looked like colossal harp strings fanning out from both sides. It was prettiest at night, when solar-powered lights played on pristine cables, and the ugliness of the bog squatted in the dark where it belonged.

"Why do you think people go into the Restricted Zone?"

I studied the starlit heavens. My refusal to participate in D.J.'s last three conversation starters hadn't dissuaded her. "People don't like being told they can't do something."

"But it's so dangerous."

It hadn't been *that* dangerous until a month ago, when a basilisk took up residence in an abandoned railroad yard full of warehouses and silos. For some reason, the giant half-rooster, half-lizard monster liked the area and fiercely defended it. It sounded like a ridiculous beast that could be killed by a mutant fox, but it was surprisingly fast. Plus, its stare killed instantly and its venomous breath wilted just about everything.

Three weeks earlier, two Eliminators were sent to deal with it. They never returned. Then, another team tried and failed. Provost Allen had restricted the area so people would smartly avoid it. Some people are stupid.

"Did you ever face a basilisk on the Source Expedition?" D.J. asked.

Shit. Most people knew better than to ask me about the Source Expedition. The next time I needed a partner, I'd request Cooper. He couldn't fight either, but he'd lost his tongue to a giant black hound—I never asked how, nor did I want to know. Despite the superb healing abilities of Evolutionaries, Cooper's tongue never grew back. Quiet Cooper was the perfect companion.

Aside from the panic Atlas caused, only ocean tides and weather changed, initially. The world grew complacent with its new moon until two decades later when Atlas flared, causing technological chaos. Vehicles, computers, even guns became unreliable when Atlas traveled through the sky. Horses and swords were the new must-haves. Then, the first Evolutionary babies arrived, glowing with radiation.

Seemingly cued by Atlas, all of the world's supervolcanoes erupted, three of which were in North America. California, Washington, Oregon, and half of Arizona fell into a toxic Pacific Ocean heated by the Ring of Fire. One-fourth of the world's population expired in just days, and darkness reigned for years until the volcanic ash settled. Before survivors could enjoy the clear sky, every beast described in every ancient text—plus a few new ones—emerged to attack what remained of humanity.

Inspiration dawned for Normals: Evolutionaries—most still teenagers—were born to fight the beasts. The Source Expedition consisted of Evolutionaries sent to discover where all the mythical beasts originated then determine how to stop them. I wasn't quite twenty when placed on that elite squad and directed to investigate the Yellowstone Caldera. We learned that yes, beasts emerged from the volcano's blast zone like ants from an anthill. There was no stopping them.

D.J. watched me quietly, expecting some kind of encouragement.

"We encountered a basilisk." Two of my friends died while killing it. I tried a reassuring smile. "Just don't break that mirror you're carrying or your bad luck will last forever."

D.J. made a face and held up a large plastic bag full of what looked like the green scat of a salad-loving creature. "Is this really necessary?"

"Rue is the only plant that withstands the poisonous breath of a basilisk. The Rue paste might keep your skin from melting off." I couldn't fault her the disgusted face. Even Normals thought the smell of Rue overpowering. I nodded at the mirrored sunglasses tucked into the collar of her chainmail. "But don't bother with the shades. If the basilisk gets close enough to see itself in those, you're already dead."

Other than being exposed to its own, deadly stare, the only fabled way to kill a basilisk was with the crow of a rooster. It seemed a half-rooster monster couldn't survive in the presence of the real thing. Thanks to a recent invasion of uber-bobcats, no roosters strutted within twenty miles. A stinky mud mask and a vanity mirror were our only hope.

As we approached the Front Street exit, the interstate gently rose to the bridge. Below and to the east sat an abandoned casino built to resemble a river steamboat. Now it looked genuine, if derelict, sunk in the mire of the Broadway Bog. A fire frog the size of a bulldog sat atop a fluted smokestack, belching a flame into the night. My attention pulled from the epitome of lost money as two shadows rose beyond the concrete barriers that blocked all but a horse-sized space of interstate.

D.J. put her hand on the hilt of her sword. "Trolls?"

"Sort of; they're pa-trolls."

"This is the Restricted Zone," one of the shadows announced. "State your business."

D.J. snorted. "Oh, that's awful."

Her belated reaction to my joke offended the patrolling Evolutionaries and they menaced closer. Solar powered track lights along the concrete walls illuminated their faces, but I didn't know them. I stayed on my horse and handed the official yellow job order with the M-kes seal to the nearest guard.

He laughed—not surprising. "What did you do to piss off Doyen Hightower?"

"Not a thing. I asked for this assignment."

Shaking his head, he gave it back and waved us past. "Suit yourselves."

"We won't answer cries for help," the other guard promised as we rode away.

When we reached the high center of the bridge, I stopped and dismounted. I ignored D.J.'s choked sound when I took off my clothes. I wound my long, auburn braid on top of my head and secured it with two metal pins that I kept handy for such occasions. I shouldn't have kept my hair long, but it was thick and shiny. It made me feel pretty.

D.J. stared, mouth ajar as I opened the bag of Rue paste. The odor worked like smelling salts.

"Spread this on every inch of your skin." I instructed while she coughed and sputtered. Once smothered with Rue from head to toe, I returned to my pile of clothing. I considered just putting my boots on so I wouldn't completely ruin my last pair of jeans and my hoodie. But if the basilisk killed me and for some reason didn't eat me, I'd be found looking like a dominatrix with a Rue fetish. I decided on just my jeans and t-shirt and left the hoodie with the horse.

I studied the bog and the railyard it seethed around as I buckled my belt full of fun tools: dagger, collapsible baton, flares, chocolate. I kept my throwing knives strapped to my thighs for a quicker draw. D.J. was dressed and beside me before I had my arsenal back in place. Her chainmail clinked melodiously. The anxiety rolling off her smelled sweet compared to the stench of Rue.

"You could run at least two miles per hour faster without that chainmail."

D.J. lifted her chin. "I could die faster, too."

It sounded the same to me. "Whatever." I preferred injury to chainmail. It lessened the repetition of mistakes.

On the edge of the bog sat a warehouse at least a quarter mile wide. Beyond that, two fifty-foot-high silos rose, and behind them stood an ancient grain elevator twice as tall, stretching farther than a couple of football fields.

I pointed to the silo that still had a roof. "The basilisk defends the intact silo with a vengeance, but according to the one scout who returned, it doesn't go beyond the warehouse."

I faced her, making sure her fearful eyes stayed on me. I didn't think Doyen Hightower had sent us out on this assignment. Possibly, Kress had just handed it off to the first idiot who walked through the door. But if I survived, I would shove my baton up someone's nose. I held on to that anger and let it grow. Fear helped nothing. Panic paralyzed. Anger might keep me alive. Still, worry for D.J. nagged at me. I hated responsibility for others.

"Do not look at it. Understand?"

She nodded.

"If I yell, 'Run,' you head straight for that warehouse, hide, and don't look back. I don't care if you think I'm in trouble."

"But—"

"No. It's no good for us to both die."

She looked defiant but nodded and mounted her horse.

"Just get that mirror in its face while I keep it occupied. Do you remember the plan?"

"I circle the railyard and get to the silo while you draw it out. I climb halfway up, attach the mirror to this wire on my belt, and hang it down when it gets close."

It was a flimsy plan, doomed to fail, but I nodded approval. "We'll leave our horses at the end of the bridge, tied to the last harp string."

"What?" D.J. didn't look at the bridge and see a harp, I guessed.

"Bridge support thingy." I waved my hand at the nearest cable, bigger around than me.

M-kes horses were well-trained. Looping the reins loosely kept the horse from leaving without me, but it could still take off if a hungry griffin swooped in from the sky, or a fire frog jumped up for a taste. I wouldn't worry about the horses.

As soon as I heard a creak—like the opening of an old, heavy door—I slid my katana from the saya on my back. D.J. hopped sideways, barely missed by a flame that lit up the night. The black fire frog that snuck onto the bridge opened its mouth again. The red and gold that veined its skin glowed like embers. I stuck my katana into the mouth and the blade emerged through the back of its head, stopping the next eruption.

I used my foot to push the frog off my sword, wiped the blade with a fresh cloth, then sheathed it. "Let's go." I stepped lightly down the Bedford Avenue exit ramp into the Restricted Zone. Even little wins brought confidence. Plus, fire frog hide makes excellent boots.

About ten feet before it reached the bog, the concrete ramp had crumbled. Large pieces of it stuck out of the bog like stepping stones in a Grimm fairytale. Fog slithered through, resembling a brood of smoky snakes. Thick vines twined out from the earth and around the chunks of road. They bloomed with large purple flowers so beautiful that tempted travelers stopped to admire them long enough for the vines to wrap around their throats.

A single fire frog squatted on the last piece of concrete where the bog receded and the solid earth of the railyard began. I picked up a piece of road the size of a baby's head, threw it fifty yards, and knocked the frog off its perch. Now it wouldn't distract me while I tried not to fall into the bog. We rock hopped across, leaving a piece of concrete as soon as our feet touched it to avoid the hungry plant life. When we reached solid ground, the frog still laid there, stunned or dead.

"If he's here when we're done, you can have a pair of boots, too," I said cheerfully.

A horrible sound followed my words, and my insides dropped to my toes. The basilisk roar started like a giant, angry rooster and ended with what I imagined a carnivorous dinosaur sounded like as it chased its prey. The damn thing had already left the silo and headed for us.

I pointed to the west where abandoned railcars and piles of scrap metal made dark shapes and excellent cover. "Go!"

D.J. ran to the shadows to circle around. I rushed forward, pretending the bones strewn across the ground belonged to frogs and trolls instead of the Evolutionaries sent before me.

The nice thing about the deadly yellow eye in the center of a basilisk's forehead was that it emitted a strong light that illuminated the ground and straight up to where I shouldn't look. As soon as the edge of this convenient searchlight appeared, I stared at the ground. I wouldn't die this way, though the landscape of skeletal remains implied otherwise. I ignored the bony terrain by picturing the basilisk's lizard arms, three-eyed face, sharp beak, and horned comb.

I increased my speed, and the light strengthened, covering more of the ground as the bipedal basilisk bent forward to bring its death-stare lower. The monster couldn't get to my level without falling over, so I kept running, focused on the pair of leathery chicken legs with claws longer than my sword. I pulled a throwing knife, let the blade slip between my fingers, then threw it up. It hit nothing vital since I couldn't see my target, but the irritated beast screeched and the light bounced off the ground.

Now I had room to run straight through its legs. I passed between them with a knife in each hand, then I slashed at the poultry equivalent of Achilles' tendons—hopefully. A roar, followed by the crash of a heavy body, signaled a little success. Fighting the urge to look behind me, I ran faster.

Only a few seconds passed before heavy steps followed me, but they were slower, each one accompanied by a pained squawk. I searched for D.J. One silo was intact, but the other was roofless. A giant, u-shaped hole gaped on one side like something ten times bigger than the basilisk took a bite out of it.

A small form dashed in front of the complete silo and scrambled up the stairs that wrapped around. Another roar erupted behind me, so close that venomous breath warmed the Rue that covered my skin.

"Oh, damn, damn, damn." I increased the speed of my words and tried to match it with my legs.

D.J. stopped roughly thirty feet up the silo. The light of Atlas flickered off the bathroom vanity mirror she'd carried on her back. She lowered it from the staircase as I led the basilisk to it. It was working! We would survive!

A deep, evil laugh bounced off my bones and reverberated through the night just before half a railcar soared over my head. It smashed into the silo. The staircase separated, knocking D.J. off her feet. The mirror dropped for the longest second ever then shattered into a million pieces of glittering failure. But that wasn't what stopped me in my tracks.

Basilisks didn't laugh. They roared. Sometimes, they crowed. I'd heard rumors that they clucked. But a beast without a soul or conscience didn't laugh.

"Andee, watch out!"

I lunged to the side. Massive claws raked a gash across my ribcage. Fire ignited in my side. I barely remembered to close my eyes before I rolled away from the bloody bird feet beside me. Face down, I opened my eyes then hopped up, but I had no chance.

D.J.'s voice rang out again. "Stop!"

Even my heart obeyed her as it briefly stuttered. Time froze. Next to me, the basilisk didn't move.

"Andee, run!"

My feet worked again. Time started, faster than before, as a crazy idea entered my head. I sprinted to the half-destroyed silo, fumbling with the tools on my belt until I found a flare.

"Hide, D.J.! Don't look!"

When I stepped on the first rusty silo stair, the basilisk huffed close behind me. I scrambled, up, hoping the three inches of rain last week created a big enough collection of water in the roofless silo. Reaching the point where the ruined wall ended, I squeezed my eyes tight and turned toward the basilisk. I slammed my spurs into the wall and let the backs of my knees touch the torn metal. I broke the flare in my hand and hinged backward at the knees, holding onto the silo wall with my spurs and calves.

The rough metal bit into my hamstrings as I squeezed to hold myself upside down. My head banged against the inside. Sparks from the flare sizzled on my rue-covered hand, but I ignored all that discomfort when the venomous breath of the basilisk blew over me. Half of my jeans burned off and my shirt vaporized. It was so powerful that despite the Rue, my skin burned. My eyelids glared red as the basilisk stared beyond them.

The monster roared for just a second before cutting out. The glow of its eye, the heat of its breath, the shadow of its presence, all disappeared. Even when I heard the body fall, I feared opening my eyes.

"Andee! Andee, you did it!"

I cautiously slit my eyelids. My reflection rippled in a pool of water at the bottom of the silo. Light from the flare filled the round chamber. The sound of sparks sizzling in the water mingled with my giant sigh. I let the flare drop, threw my hands over my head, and swung upright.

"Ow." I felt those cuts in my legs and side, now.

On the ground, D.J. kept a safe distance from the fallen basilisk, casting nervous glances between the two of us. I descended the rickety metal stairs; glad I'd been unaware of their state when I used them to save myself. I'd just touched the ground when it trembled and the basilisk convulsed. I put my arms over my face and a cloud of grime hit me with an audible puff.

Slowly, I lowered my arms. A giant pile of red ash replaced the basilisk. D.J. and I approached it together. She shook so hard that her chainmail sounded like wind chimes.

"Did you hear it laugh?" she asked.

"Yes."

"Was it supposed to turn to dust?"

"No." I pulled a small plastic bag from my belt and scooped up some of the dust. At least this proof of kill was lighter than a manticore head. I put the bag in my pocket, which peeked out below the bottom of my jeans, burned into Daisy Dukes by basilisk breath.

"What's that?" D.J. pointed to the other silo where the flying railcar had torn a hole. Pieces of debris escaped into a pile on the ground.

I bent down for a closer look. Small, shiny cylinders of solid metal clinked as more constantly fell onto the pile. I picked up a half-inch-long piece. Silica ingots: replicas of the implants in a circular pattern above my heart. I dug my hands in, feeling sick as the pile clattered. I stood, my stomach whirling and head reeling.

I leaned against the silo wall. "Stupid basilisk."

"What in the—" D.J.'s breathless voice didn't finish. Her indigo face lightened to periwinkle. Her eyes rolled up and she fell in a heap.

CHAPTER THREE

"I can carry those things. I'm okay."

"No." I kept my eyes on Main Street, though at 3:00 a.m., even monsters had called it a night. Nothing scuttled between the brick buildings and occasional high-rises of downtown. After dragging D.J. away from the silica silo and slapping her awake, I'd taken a few more samples. Then, I'd gotten the hell out of there.

D.J.'s pride smarted as she rode beside me. "I was just lightheaded. Stop treating me like a sick child."

Please. For the first minute, I thought she was dead. Those silica ingots stayed tucked in the bag attached to my saddle. "Look, D.J., everyone likes you. If I let you die, they'll be mad at me. I can't deal with that negativity right now. I'll let you die another time, okay?"

As we turned our horses onto Twelfth Street, my weary body lightened a bit. I was so close to my bed on the thirtieth floor of One Kansas City Place. My boots had melted to the Rue on my legs. My jeans hung in tatters at a length strippers thought indecent. I didn't wear a shirt or even a bra under the hoodie I'd kept out of the basilisk's reach. I wanted to cut everything off, soak in my tub, then fall into bed.

"Do you think the ingots are tainted?" D.J. worried. "Someone might use them to make Evolutionaries sick."

"I'll take them to the lab tomorrow and find out. Maybe they just look like silica." We'd both received regular silica implants since birth. The thought that these ingots that made us nauseous were the same as those in our chests made me nervous, too.

Finally, we arrived at the front of my apartment building and I hopped off my horse. D.J. lived closer to headquarters, so she would take both horses back. I let her do that, at least. I removed everything from my horse. D.J. kept her eye on the plastic bags full of dust and ingots that I transferred to my hoodie pockets. She opened her mouth, and I glared at her.

"Fine." She sniffed. "You know, you pretend not to care about anyone else but you're awfully protective. I think there's a soft heart under your tough skin."

"Wow, I didn't know they handed out psychology degrees to Evolutionaries. You should use that education to get a lower risk job."

She left in a huff, finally insulted enough to go away. I entered my fancy, high-rise apartment building with relief. Normally, fancy doesn't suit my style or budget. My parents bought the condo for me, and I gave in with little argument. Letting your parents feel needed was important. They wanted to know that I resided in a place that wasn't condemned, quarantined, or on anyone's places-to-avoid list. I wanted sleep. I didn't fear local thugs or nighttime intruders, but killing humans was frowned upon. Thus, parent-purchased condo accepted.

One KC Place hadn't always been residential, but realty and brokerage firms weren't widely used anymore, so the office space had been converted into fortified apartments. A law firm and an energy company still occupied the bottom floors. I passed their darkened lobby windows on my way to the elevator. Jason, the security guard, waved at me from behind his desk. He no longer acknowledged my physical state after a night of dragon slaying.

A true elevator wouldn't have worked half the time. Instead, a system of weights and pulleys engaged after the gate closed. The design might have come from the notes of Leonardo da Vinci. I had to stay awake and keep track of the passing floors so I could stop at the thirtieth.

Only three other Evolutionaries lived in the building. We had the thirtieth floor to ourselves—separated from the Normals below and the posh penthouses of wealthier Normals on the top ten floors. There used to be forty-two levels, but a confused flock of griffins had fought itself in the mirrored glass, destroying the top two floors. I suspected my parents had paid a lot more than Normal tenants for the same floor plan, but I was usually too tired to take a stand for equality.

I reached my floor, pulled a lever, and got out. The trash bag I carried fell to the plush, burgundy carpet and I dragged it to my door. On the southwest corner, my window-filled apartment gave me a killer view of a downtown Kansas City made peaceful by distance. Those on the other side of the building had a picturesque scene of the Broadway Bog, lit up at night by heartburning fire frogs.

My vision of a relaxing bath dissipated three feet from my steel door—paneled with wood for aesthetics. If I'd been on alert, I would have smelled the intruder in the elevator. The door easily opened, no key necessary since he'd unlocked it with his own. My weapons stayed sheathed, for now, but I had a bone the size of a basilisk femur to pick with Josiah Hightower.

I didn't have friends with apartment keys. Friends required a lot of time and emotion. Plus, as soon as I got attached, they got themselves killed. D.J. had been closer to the truth about me than I liked.

Josiah Hightower wasn't my friend, but he'd been my warden before his promotion to doyen. He had a key in case he ever needed to let my parents into my apartment to collect my things before the landlord snooped around. He'd abused the privilege repeatedly, but this was his first visit since he became Doyen of Defense for Kansas City.

As I stepped into the foyer and pushed the door closed, his voice rang out from the living room. "That's you that stinks of dead frog and manticore with a hint of Rue? I smelled you enter the building."

When I'd met Josiah nearly a year ago, that comment would have made me laugh. Josiah was a Normal. He looked Normal. He smelled Normal. If asked, he would have said, "I'm a Normal." I'd since learned that man was anything but normal. It's possible he did detect my stench from thirty floors up.

I deposited the trash bag and stopped at the living room entrance. Leaning one shoulder against the wall, I noticed how comfortable Josiah's big body looked in my oversized, black leather recliner. Beyond his hawkish profile, my windowed walls provided the décor of a clear, starry night.

"You're not directly responsible for me, anymore. Should you be seen socializing with the commoners?"

His head, with its slightly spiked, midnight black hair stayed bent as he pretended to read the book in his lap. Even seated and disinterested, Josiah looked hard. His intense, blue-gray eyes and almost sharp cheekbones implied a face of granite. The only trait that marred the effect was the wide, soft mouth that twitched at the corners. "No one knows I'm here."

He intended to offend me. The smile gave him away. I wondered why he didn't grow a beard and cover that damn mouth. "Here to finish me off since the shit assignment didn't work?"

Josiah finally looked at me. The book fell from his hands. "Where the hell have you been?"

I'd never seen him rattled. My dirty, bloody, half-clothed body must have looked pretty bad. And unless he was an excellent actor, he hadn't sent me to the Restricted Zone.

"When Johnson and Delaney didn't show up tonight, Kress gave their work to D.J. and me."

Josiah stood in a blink. I knew he had better speed and reflexes than some Evolutionaries, but it still surprised me. I'd seen him fight when he had learned that the complaint I went to handle wasn't just two harpies invading a nursing home but an entire flock. He'd shown up with a crossbow and taken out half of the creepy, clawed bird-ladies. He'd beaten two more with the bow when he ran out of arrows.

That day was why I still hadn't attacked him in the middle of my living room tonight. Well, that and the man stood four inches taller and outweighed me by at least thirty pounds. I'd never win a hand-to-hand fight with Josiah.

But anger toward me didn't flush his cheeks. "You and D.J. went to the Restricted Zone?"

Oh, that counted against him. "You knew where Johnson and Delaney were supposed to go tonight?"

"No! I mean, yes, I authorized the assignment, but I knew they wouldn't go."

My eye caught something shiny and I momentarily forgot his words. I gasped, taking in so much air that Josiah fell back a step. I marched over to the wood and glass coffee table to point at three candy wrappers. "You can send me to the Restricted Zone. You're the boss. But coming into my home and taking my chocolate is completely unprofessional. It's beyond the pale!"

He had the nerve to laugh. "Are you reading Regency romances again?"

I unstrapped my katana saya and laid it on the table. Then I removed my dagger, sat down in the chair he'd vacated, and started cutting off my melted boots. "No."

I only had the one romance, and it happened to be what he chose to read one morning when he'd let himself in while I slept. That he'd entered my apartment and I'd slept through it was insult enough, but he wouldn't let the romance thing go. I hadn't even liked the book. At all. Mostly. "The fact that you know it's Regency is highly suspicious," I muttered. "Ouch." Nicked myself.

"You're going to ruin that nice chair."

"Leather wipes off. That's one of its selling points." I'd tested it, many, many times.

Josiah made a noise similar to an air compressor valve releasing. "Is D.J. okay?"

"Yes."

He took my spot against the wall. "How did you kill it?"

I smiled at his assumption that I'd succeeded. "With a flare, a pool of water, and strong thighs."

He was quiet while I worked off my boots. Most of the Rue peeled away with the boots, along with a layer of skin. Leaning back and letting my head rest on the chair, I closed my eyes. I didn't know if I still trusted him, or if I just couldn't keep my eyes open anymore.

"Are you injured?"

"Geez, I hope not. I'd be sitting here dying while you talked about romance novels." True, I already felt better. The bleeding had stopped before I left the Restricted Zone. My body burned up energy to repair my wounds, causing my lethargy. Even the claw mark on my ribcage would close by morning and be smooth in a week.

"I'm sorry you got sent to the Restricted Zone, and I apologize for questioning your taste in reading material. I would apologize for the chocolate, but I'm pretty sure you stole it anyway; and you've got nothing else worth eating in this place."

True. "You owe me." I felt bolder with my eyes closed.

"Yes."

Keeping my eyes shut, I pointed in the general direction of the front door. "Take that trash bag to Connor's Tannery in Parkville. They have my measurements and preferences."

"You think I owe you fire frog boots?"

"Well, yeah." He'd sounded flabbergasted. Weird. Fire frog boots were tough and—naturally—fire retardant. I bet they wouldn't have melted to my legs.

"Okay."

That was easy.

"But I want you to make me a promise, too."

Ah-ha. "What?"

"Fire frog boots are worth more than you getting sent to the wrong assignment and me taking a few pieces of chocolate."

"What." I opened my eyes and turned my head to meet those slate irises.

He hesitated; an oddity that made my sleepy body sit up.

"I want you to leave town for a few days."

I stared until his eyes narrowed with irritation. "Sure. Are you going to tell the Enforcers not to hunt me down? They listen to Doyen Graves, not you."

As Doyen of Defense, Josiah oversaw patrols, outposts, and the wardens who managed Eliminator units full of Evolutionaries like me. Richard Graves was the Doyen of Discipline, direct supervisor of the Enforcers: elite Evolutionaries who didn't care about solidarity and supporting their own kind. They would hunt me down like a beast and hope I resisted.

Josiah crossed his arms, probably trying to distract me with intimidating biceps. "Look, strange things are happening, and I want you to stay out of it. You have four days off in a row coming. Take a vacation."

Though he was no longer my warden, he knew my schedule. I doubted my current warden, Cash, even knew where I went this evening. Josiah had seen the state of my kitchen cabinets, though. I had no money for a trip.

I stood up. "Is that what you told Johnson and Delaney? Because I think the Enforcers hunt them just like the others who have disappeared. Do you know what's going on?"

His face closed off. Even his pretty mouth hardened. "Why do you think I know anything?"

"Because I haven't spoken to you since you got promoted to doyen last month, and now you're in here trying to be my warden again. I have a new warden."

Josiah's upper lip curled. "Have you seen Cash since he became your warden?"

"Once." I'd walked into his office with a gash down my arm, dripping blood onto his desk. He'd reached into a drawer and given me a tissue. "Cash is a hands-on warden with my best interests in mind."

"Cash is an incompetent asshole. I doubt he knows your name."

"If you care so much, why did you stop being my warden?" Whoa, why had that left my mouth? I clenched my teeth together to contain any more damning words. I knew why Josiah took the promotion. Any man with brains and ambition took a promotion.

"Do you miss me?"

Yikes—danger ahead. "I'm just trying to understand you. I'm a people person."

Strong white teeth flashed as he laughed, but his eyes made my breath catch. Something dark and predatory gleamed there before he shut it down. One more item to add to the 'Not Normal' list. Unfortunately, that list never revealed the truth about Josiah. He just grew more mysterious.

He turned, grabbed the trash bag, and opened the door. "If you want boots, get out of town." He stepped into the hall then paused. "And stay away from Allen."

"Hold on." I hurried to the door. "Provost Allen? You want me to avoid the head of KC M-kes?"

"Yes." He didn't turn around as he added, "and Sophia."

I sidled out to scrutinize his back. His long legs moved him down the hall with their standard grace. Some might mistake him for a dancer, but he was a martial Artist. Capital 'A' required. I'd heard rumors that he and Dr. Sophia Bennett were friendly. "My tastes don't run that way. Your girlfriends are safe from me."

He kept walking, holding the bag of dead fire frog over his shoulder like a light jacket.

"This promise is suddenly covering a lot," I called as he reached the elevator.

"I know how much you love boots." He disappeared.

I placed my hands on my hips and tapped one foot. "Damn it." I did really love boots.

CHAPTER FOUR

Volcanic rock dug into my elbows and knees as I crawled to the lip of a mile-wide crater. The hot, dry air licked up my sweat as it left my pores. A red light emanated from the hole, proof that magma still flowed in the depths of the Yellowstone Volcano. But not only lava moved inside the glowing cone. A line of beasts exited the caldera as if riding a conveyor belt from Hell. Beside me, Jun gasped. Grant squeezed her hand.

The three of us had to get back to the rest of the team before any of those creatures got a whiff of us. We scuttled backward in unison. I counted eight lion-like beasts and five winged monsters before the wall of black rock obstructed my view.

We ran, me at point with Jun and Grant flanking. Each black mountain and ash dune looked like the next until I worried that we made circles. My legs shook, and my lungs screamed as they tried to salvage decent oxygen from the toxic air. Then, a yellow light brightened the ground ahead of me.

"Andee, don't turn around. Keep your eyes on the ground!" Jun's voice cut to that spot below my heart where fear breeds.

A screeching roar shook me. I gazed at a black lava flow frozen in time, washed yellow by the glow of a basilisk's stare. A basilisk was one of the few monsters we'd been told to avoid not engage. My limbs stiffened in terror as Jun and Grant yelled, trying to keep each other out of danger. The urge to act consumed me until it hurt.

I turned my head, raising my eyes to a giant, scaled pair of legs. Jun scrambled behind them, the tip of her katana flashing in and out of my vision. Grant's sword entered the scene, delivering a wound that brought the beast to its knees. I darted my eyes to the ground, trembling with fear that the basilisk eye would reach me. It happened so fast. And I did nothing.

A victorious shout from Jun filled the air, then the yellow light slid away from me. I risked a look. Jun stood on the beast's back with her katana raised after slicing its neck to near severance. But the light still glowed.

"Jun!" Grant and I both screamed as the monster's head tilted up.

The glow lit her shocked face. Grant moved as her limp body fell to the earth. He leapt over her, stepped on the basilisk's shoulder, then thrust his sword right through its eye. It still caught him.

His lifeless body dropped beside my best friend.

I screamed, but heard nothing. The monster's head dropped to the ground, Grant's sword protruding from the deadly orb. I closed my eyes tight before the world exploded with light, washing over me, burning me. Finally, my scream found voice: a piercing, insistent screech.

I woke on a gasp and blinked at the sunlight glaring through my windows. I slammed my hand on the top of my beeping alarm clock, then brought my arm across my face. My pulse drummed through my head. My chest shook with labored breaths.

"Damn it, D.J." I brought trembling hands to my face and rubbed my temples. D.J.'s Source Expedition questions weren't at fault, though. Facing the basilisk had ripped the scabs off my wounded memories.

I let my arms drop to my sides and watched the midmorning light reflect off my fish tank to play on the ceiling of my bedroom. I maintained the tank though I'd never bought a single fish. The bubbling sound soothed me, and I figured someday I'd hide something tiny and important in the little treasure chest at the bottom.

I peeled myself off the bedspread I'd collapsed on last night. A layer of Rue, blood, and basilisk dust roughly shaped like me soiled the pale blue and green striped cotton. I really had to stop passing out before bath time.

I removed the pair of underwear I'd slept in, dropped them on the ruined boots and jeans, then kicked it all toward the trash can on my way to the bathroom. Keeping my head down, I studied my injuries. The gashes behind my legs were now itchy, red lines. The claw mark on my ribs still ached, but it was healing. Looking in the mirror before I showered proved a poor decision.

My almond-shaped, light purple eyes glowed softly in the midst of chaos. Half my hair hung in tangles at my bare shoulders while the other half stuck out of my bun, creating a spiky crown. Rue and basilisk dust had dried in a grayish, leprous mess on my periwinkle-colored skin. I looked like the last zombie on Earth.

Good thing I didn't have a man to come home to last night. Oh wait, I had come home to a man. He'd told me I stunk, exclaimed at the sight of me, and ordered me out of town. Perfect. As a result of my genetic make-up, men didn't come around much, anyway. Those that did expected excitement, but I had enough of that outside my bedroom.

My eyes lowered to my chest and the circle of magenta-colored scars that looked like tubular flower petals. My scars were the final reminder that I wasn't Normal, should I ignore everything else. I couldn't remember not having the silica implants. When their effectiveness lessened, a surgeon replaced them. I really wanted to know about those ingots I'd brought home.

"Damn." I'd forgotten to tell Josiah about the silo and the basilisk turning to dust. He'd gotten me all worked up with his orders and his promise of boots. He'd have wait for my report like a typical boss.

After a long shower, I was ravenous, but I had to make a stop along the hallway before visiting my poorly stocked kitchen. Some people converted their second bedroom to an office or a storage room. I called mine The Dungeon.

Blackout drapes smothered the sunlight in front of the floor to ceiling windows. One of the walls held an array of weapons, each of them loved, though none of them as important as the katana I carried in with me. Of all my weapons, it had cost the most, yet I'd paid no money for it. My friend, Jun, had made me promise that if anything happened to her, I would use her katana to continue her tradition of defending the helpless.

I'd taken it from her still warm fingers. Grant's hand had lain beside hers, their fingers not quite touching. I'd taken his sword, too—right out of the basilisk's eye. I hadn't made any promises to Grant, but it seemed right to keep the two weapons together.

The helpless wouldn't need so much defending if they had the sense to stay out of the way. But I'd loved and respected Jun, and I honored her memory by fulfilling her wishes. Honor and memories had been big with Jun Tekada.

After turning on The Dungeon lights, I sat on my knees in the middle of my practice mat. I pulled the katana from its saya and placed it on a low table. I retrieved a wooden box from beneath the table and removed cloths, a small bottle of oil, and a short stick with a silk bag attached to the end called an uchiko ball. Taking a cloth, I rubbed the blade to remove oil, dirt, and blood.

I gently tapped the uchiko ball up and down the blade forged of rain drop Damascus steel. Fine powder puffed out of the bag and coated the pattern of concentric circles which looked as if water droplets froze in the metal as it cooled. The powder was ground up polishing stone, and it soaked up anything I missed before I wiped the blade again. Last, I put two drops of choji oil on a clean cloth then rubbed the blade until it shined.

Keeping my katana clean was important, but I valued the methodical, purposeful process most. It helped center me after a night of reliving the worst day of my life. I sheathed the katana and left The Dungeon.

I didn't need to open my cabinets to know what sat inside them: two cans of soup, a box of stale crackers, and roughly forty pounds of chocolates. I spent most of my money on weapons and boots. Either one could give out at a bad time if cheaply made.

Just in case I'd forgotten about some bacon or eggs, I opened my fridge. Nope. The same shriveled apple, pile of fuzz, and half gallon of milk greeted me. The milk had 'Genuine Cow' written on the container in letters so large that it was likely a lie. It contained some kind of animal protein, though, and mixed with melted chocolate, I tolerated it.

With my championship breakfast out of the way, I had a new dilemma. All of my jeans had been ruined in the past month, but sweatpants seemed a lazy alternative. One answer hung in the back of my closet, so deep that even the two dresses I owned were more visible: a pair of tight, red leather pants. A few weeks ago, my favorite tanner gave them to me as a token of appreciation for my business. Probably, he couldn't sell them, but I accepted them and promptly hid them.

I fingered the soft, quality leather. I hated clichés. A 5'10", sword-toting, monster killer with fangs shouldn't be clad in leather. "Screw it." I wriggled into them. Maybe they would help me catch a ride to headquarters since I'd left my truck in the Sheraton parking garage.

*****

By noon, I settled at my desk within the bowels of the limestone and marble monstrosity that was M-kes. A night of beast slaying always equaled a stack of paperwork the next day. The reports posed questions like: Did I recognize and classify the creature? Did the creature appear enhanced or adapted in any way? Did the creature eat any human whose family might file a complaint against my lack of timeliness?

Luckily, the answer to the last was 'No.' A 'Yes' led to a whole new set of forms and a performance evaluation from my warden. My reports finished, I rose from my uncomfortable chair with a spine-cracking stretch. I adjusted the bags of evidence in my pockets, then grabbed my paperwork and walked down the hall.

My boots didn't ring on the marble floor like the destroyed pair from last night. They were soft, black suede and shapeless until I zipped them up to my knee. The wedge soles of thick but pliable rubber served great for running and—I thought—stealth. Someone around the corner still heard me.

"Hey there, Bochs."

Despite my negative opinions of Thomas Waya, my heart always fluttered when he spoke. The treacherous organ reacted to his velvet tone and come-a-little-closer smile no matter how often I ordered it to stop. At least I had the chance to compose myself before he came into view.

I rounded the corner and kept walking past his tall form leaning against the wall. "Hey, Waya."

A low whistle sounded behind me. "Love the pants."

"Thanks." I tried not to think which part of my anatomy he stared at, but my ass heated up.

"If you wore those more often, maybe Hightower wouldn't use you for monster feed."

I wanted to defend Josiah because I still trusted him. However, my irritation with him had yet to fade. I said nothing as I turned around with polite inquiry on my face.

"D.J. told everyone about your performance last night. I wish I'd been there." There was that smile, simultaneously tugging at the corners of his mouth and an invisible string attached below my bellybutton. Damn, Waya could make me think about sex more often than a teenage boy. I blamed the fact that I hadn't participated in that activity for over a year. I really hoped my cheeks weren't turning the same color as my pants.

His gaze dropped. "Are those your reports? I can take them up for you."

My hand automatically rose to hand them over. What the hell was wrong with me? I whipped them behind my back. The reports contained information that Josiah and Provost Allen wouldn't want others to read before them. "No thanks. I have to go that way, anyhow."

Waya pushed off the wall and stepped closer. I smiled, proud of myself for not moving backward. Then he returned my smile, complete with fangs longer than mine and a twinkle in his deep mauve eyes. I thought the devilish points of his dark brows and goatee were natural, rather than a conscious effort to appeal to the bad girl hidden inside every woman. Either way, it worked.

Waya was the only male Evolutionary that Josiah banned me from partnering with, citing the no fraternization rule. He wouldn't partner Waya with any women. I'd put on a big show of offense, but not for long. Waya could talk me out of my pants in a heartbeat and convince me it'd been my idea. If he'd been with me last night, I would have drooled as I watched him fight then dropped dead from a basilisk stare full in the face.

Just looking at that lean body, wrapped with corded muscle barely disguised by a tight black t-shirt and jeans, caused palpitations. My mind suspected Waya could show me a good time, and my body knew it. The no-fraternization rule was the most frequently broken at M-kes. Unfortunately, Waya never had fun with the same woman twice. I refused to be his toy.

Now, he looked expectant. Which meant he'd asked me something while I wrestled my hormones back into their closet. I shrugged—always a good cover.

"That's what I like about you, Andee, so indifferent."

Yep, that sounded like me.

"It would piss me off to nearly be wasted on a basilisk." He leaned closer and inhaled my scent. "You're the Golden Girl of the Eliminators. Why did Hightower hang you out like that?"

Golden Girl? I'd had saltines, chocolates, and milk of questionable origin for breakfast before catching a ride to work on the back of a moped. "Maybe he holds a higher opinion of my abilities than the rest of you."

"Oh, I know you're talented."

I didn't touch that one.

His eyes hardened and his mouth lost its kissable appeal. "We have to be careful. Now that Johnson and Delaney disappeared, I'm on high alert. I last saw those two speaking to Hightower."

That brought my attention back to its proper focus. "What? When?"

"Yesterday morning," he whispered, looking around before continuing. "Hightower is dangerous."

Not a secret. "Message received." I turned on my heel. One nice thing about long legs was I could appear leisurely while quickly eating up ground.

I made it to the end of the hall before Waya called, "You should just apply to be an Enforcer. Then Hightower can't control you anymore."

And there was the other thing I disliked about Waya. Aside from his love of one-night-stands, it didn't bother him to be an Enforcer and treat his fellow Evolutionaries like animals. "I prefer to hunt monsters."

"Evolutionaries are still monsters, sweetheart. We're just more challenging to hunt."

I ended the conversation by disappearing around the corner, but his comments circled in my head. A dangerous Josiah was no revelation, and he and Waya had been at odds from the beginning—like two alpha wolves in the same pack. Right after Josiah's promotion to doyen, Waya applied to be an Enforcer, effectively putting himself out of Josiah's jurisdiction. I knew Josiah had communicated in some form with Johnson and Delaney, but I worried where they were. Life had been easier when I'd kept my head down and ignored people.

No one else talked to me as I hurried through the hall of Enforcers to get to the administration hub a floor above. I suspected half the Enforcers hunted for Hicks, Johnson, Delaney, and anyone else they hadn't found, yet. I took a wide marble staircase, passed a theater with an eighty-foot movie screen now used for monster briefings, and headed into a large office where three women sat: the assistants to the doyens and provost. They reminded me of Norns with pens instead of scissors.

The box for assignment reports sat on the desk of Josiah's assistant, Missy Colyer. She was a younger, shorter version of Kress but a little nicer. She probably ate more fiber.

I dropped my report into the box. "Is Doyen Hightower in?"

She glanced up with the same disinterest as Kress but without the sour mouth. Yep, somebody had a bran muffin for breakfast. "He's out."

"Thanks." He could read about the ingots and basilisk dust instead of hearing it in person. Next stop, the lab, where I had to avoid the detail-oriented director who had her nose in everything, Dr. Sophia Bennett.

A marbled hall floor with fifteen-foot, brick walls and floor to ceiling windows led to the M-kes lab. I passed through the middle of a trio of giant doorways and into the sun-lit atrium that filled almost the entire western half of headquarters. It was a two-level courtyard of spiral staircases, weird tunnels, and catwalks. Long ago, the top floor had been renovated to mimic the building fronts of a European village. The giant space resembled a vaulted, marble capitol building more than a laboratory.

Directly across from me was a mini-helicopter pad that had once given children hours of make-believe pleasure. Now, it was a catch-all for discarded lab equipment and sealed tanks of cloudy liquid that probably held monster parts for Sophia's experiments. I never ventured close enough to look inside. If not for the area outside her lab where she kept jars full of floating beast remains and a couple of cages with small, live creatures, I would have loved the laboratory atrium.

Just a short sprint across a cobblestone walkway was a non-functioning glass elevator. A metal staircase went down half a level on the right to access the helipad, but I needed to go all the way to the bottom. I passed to the left of the elevator and put it between me and Sophia's top floor lair before she caught sight of me.

On the southern end of the lab I descended a staircase that spiraled around a fake tree. More fake trees and rough stone walls filled the lower floor which had once opened onto a lawn. Now, the glass doors were chained closed. Weeds and debris filled the area outside, surrounded by a sagging fence high enough to imprison baby monsters. The floor in front of my destination was covered with a faded pinwheel that still showed the lines of an old maze. I'd mastered it years ago but stopped to maneuver it every time I visited. Somebody told me it had been designed for children over a century earlier, but I still felt accomplished.

Beyond the maze sat a giant sphere: the domain of head chemist, Dr. Jeff Trotter. Jeff was quiet, quirky, and probably the smartest man in Kansas City. Entering his lab was like walking into a model of the Death Star. I once asked Jeff why he loved his round room of a lab so much, and he'd said something about being the nucleus of the atom that was M-kes. I hadn't found much humor in it, but he'd laughed at himself for a full minute.

He didn't look up from the Bunsen burner at his work station, but he grinned. "Hello, Andromeda!"

Jeff always said my full name with such pleasure that I didn't cringe when I heard it. "Hi, Jeff." I skirted the railing that circled the center of the room. "I have some interesting items for you to study when you have time."

"Of course." He picked up a test tube then turned to truly look at me. The tube clattered to the table. "Wow." He cleared his throat. "New pants?"

"Yes." I pulled two of my sample bags out of my pocket and handed him one. "A silo full of those ingots made D.J. faint, and I almost followed her. I thought they were just silica, but I wondered if something was wrong with them."

Jeff hefted the ingot bag then lowered his eyes to my pockets. "They fit in there, huh? And still warm, too. Isn't that something?"

Between Jeff and Waya, I doubted my wardrobe decision. I dangled the bag of dust in front of his face until he focused on it. "This is what the basilisk turned into after I killed it."

For the second time, Jeff dropped what he held when he saw something more interesting. "Really?" He took the bag and pulled a magnifying glass from his lab coat pocket. "It's a fine powder. No bones or anything?"

"Not even a claw." I'd dug in the basilisk pile up to my neck.

"Hmmm." Jeff's summer sky eyes pondered the dust. He reached up and grabbed a handful of sandy hair. "This is more a biology thing."

I tensed. Sophia ruled the biology department. He looked up and smiled. "But there's no way I'm pushing this off on someone else. I might need a different lab for the dust, though. Let's take a look at the ingots, first."

I sat on a stool and focused energy to the parts of my body that still ached while Jeff scraped, measured, liquefied, and performed other tasks I knew nothing about. I was semi-comatose an hour later when he pushed his microscope aside with a sigh, rested one elbow on the table, and put his chin in his hand.

"They're the exact chemical make-up of the ingots in your body." He sounded depressed.

"Maybe D.J. and I just have a virus or something." I tried to cheer him up.

He rolled his eyes. "You've never been sick."

True.

Jeff sat up straight and faced the row of ingredients he'd been adding for his tests. "We'll do biology testing, instead." He reached toward a small, reddish rock then jerked his hand away at the clack of high heels.

A petite, bronze-skinned woman with raven hair pulled into a high ponytail entered the lab. Behind her wire glasses, intelligent brown eyes observed everything before her toned legs passed it. Jeff shrank away.

She flashed her smile at me. "A social call, Miss Bochs?"

Damn it. I just broke one-third of my promise to Josiah in less than twenty-four hours. "Work, Dr. Bennett; it's always work."

CHAPTER FIVE

In my six years with Kansas City M-kes, Josiah was my fourth doyen and Allen the second provost, but Sophia Bennett had been here the entire time. I'd avoided her lab until today. Just one order from my doyen to stay away and I found myself cozied up beside her on a lab bench built for two. She smelled of peaches and spice, which should have given me happy thoughts about cobbler, but it didn't suit her, so I didn't like it.

After taking me to her lab and offering the bench, she sat beside me. Shocking. Sophia looked at Evolutionaries like furry creatures who shed—completely opposite from the likable Jeff who invited us to his Christmas parties. Since she answered only to Provost Allen, most of us treated her with respect; but she intimidated Jeff, which made me mad. If she bothered to look up from the whirring centrifuge and microscope, she'd see my eyes glow with menace, just for her.

She sat back from the microscope. "Well, Dr. Trotter was correct about the ingots."

"Hmmm." She made it sound as though I'd questioned Jeff's expertise and she'd had to take over. One look from her and Jeff had relayed everything. She'd grabbed the evidence, said, "I'll take it from here," and instructed me to follow. My other bag of ingots poked my hipbone inside my pocket, but I refused to reveal its existence.

The centrifuge stopped. She removed the test tube of basilisk dust and solution spun at high speed. "And now for this . . . dust?" Her little nose wrinkled as she separated the solution into smaller tubes.

I investigated the room while she worked. A row of bright lights hung over her table, but most of the lab remained shadowed, hiding her secrets. It felt warmer than it should, given all the cool darkness.

Against the nearest wall, a large glass case stood with a bulky object inside. Sophia stiffened when I rose, but otherwise she ignored me.

Faded signs still hung on the room's brick walls, citing facts and suggesting science experiments for the kids who visited these rooms long before Atlas arrived. That Sophia's lab had once nurtured learning and childish discovery felt wrong. Trusting her with children would be a mistake. I strolled over to the glass case and regretted the decision.

Inside, a repulsive hodge-podge of a monster floated in a gelatinous substance. One arm appeared human but clawed, the other was shorter and sheathed in reptilian skin. Its legs looked like the hindquarters of a dog, and its disproportionate torso had thick, gray pachyderm skin. There was no head. Yuck.

I leaned in for a closer look and something twined around my ankle. Jerking my foot up, I freed myself then stomped. A green tendril of a plant wriggled beneath my boot. As I stared at it, three more tendrils crept into view.

"Stop that," I ordered. They shrank back. I lifted my foot, and the trapped vine retreated nearly six feet to a niche with a UV light.

"Are you talking to my pets?"

"Just teaching them some manners."

I expected a sneer, but Sophia looked thoughtful, like she'd heard I was interesting but couldn't figure out why. Finally, she said, "I'd come back where it's light, if I were you."

No persuasion needed there. Men found Sophia desirable with her snug lab coat, too-short skirts, and too-high heels. I thought of her as a reject for a porno called 'Sexy Scientist.'

When I asked men if they wanted to come to my Dungeon and see my weapons, I meant it—though some were disappointed when I showed them a bunch of swords. Sophia's Frankenstein lair took her farther into freak territory than I could ever go. I returned to the table, but I didn't sit down.

Sophia tapped a test tube with one bright red fingernail and pressed her lips together. "This is just magnesium, iron, a little aluminum: vermiculite, basically."

"And that is?"

"Clay."

"So, the basilisk turned into clay?"

She leaned back and glared at me. "No. The substance you're trying to pass off as dead basilisk is clay." She grabbed the slides, tubes, and bag with remaining dust then walked to a drawer in the middle of the far wall. Light glowed around the drawer. "Really, Miss Bochs, I'd heard better about you. This will have to be reported. I can't let you receive a commission you didn't earn."

"Hold on."

She stepped on a lever. The drawer opened, and a tongue of fire rose as she dropped everything inside. She slammed it shut with her foot. Holy shit, she had an incinerator. Her lab really was Hell. She crossed her arms and narrowed her eyes. "We're done here, Miss Bochs."

The fact that I hadn't strangled her proved me more human than most Normals. My controlled voice belied my anger. "I killed that basilisk. I'm happy to take you on a tour of the Restricted Zone and show you how safe you are *there*."

Her arms dropped. "Are you threatening me?"

"I don't bother with threats. Monsters never listen to them." I strode to the door and yanked it open. "And we're not done."

I only saw red as I seethed back to my office. Even Waya's masculinity didn't distract me when we bumped shoulders outside the lab. "Bad day, Bochs?" His fangs flashed in a smile.

I waved him off and kept walking. Sophia had to be wrong about the basilisk dust. D.J. would back me up. Josiah, might, too, though he had warned me—sort of. If he really played bedroom tag with that female Frankenstein, he'd be lucky if she didn't kill him and use him for parts. Fortunately, I had another bag of dust tucked in my pants that Jeff could study after hours. I'd just have to remove it early so my body heat didn't addle him.

I leafed through a stack of papers on my desk in order to calm down. Most of them were copies of reports that I needed to file. I smiled a little at a petition for changing the name of M-kes. I'd signed the first petition months ago. It called for the title of Mythical Creatures Elimination Squad to change to Apparently Real Creatures Elimination Squad. Made sense. The acronym ARCES would—of course—be pronounced 'arses.' I signed it again.

Next was a receipt for the manticore kill, but nothing for the basilisk. Sophia worked fast. I heard a low, grating noise, realized I ground my teeth, and tried to relax my jaw. I'd only beat an angry tattoo against my desk with the hilt of my dagger for a minute when Cash, my warden, walked into my office.

Well, if he'd walked 'in,' he'd be standing on my desk, so he simply lurked in my doorway. Josiah thought Cash was an indifferent jackass. Indifference implied a conscious choice to ignore, and I didn't think Cash had the brains to make choices. Cash's ineptitude led me to believe he was the son or beloved nephew of someone high up. Josiah couldn't appoint his own wardens; not even Provost Allen had that power. All warden, doyen, and provost appointments came straight from the chancellor of M-kes in Chicago. Chancellor Galegi held more power than the U.S. president, now a symbol instead of a true leader—like a European monarch.

The country had been in a state of emergency followed by martial law for two decades. The president's cabinet dissolved long ago, but the secretary of defense still existed as the only leader more powerful than the chancellor of M-kes. I didn't think Cash actually related to Galegi, but someone close to the chancellor was missing a dumbass.

Cash never remembered rules—or names—and I often reminded him of protocol when his hazel eyes glazed over. Not once had it occurred to me to call on Cash for help with the Restricted Zone. Now, his shaggy head tilted to the side, and his brow wrinkled in confusion. "Ummm."

"Bochs." I sighed.

He pointed at me like a star pupil. "Right."

Yay, for me.

He scratched his head, then the chest of his stained polo shirt. Cash definitely belonged in a basement, just that of his parents, not M-kes. "Ummm, oh!" His face brightened, and he raised his other hand which held a dark red piece of paper. He dropped it on my desk, and my heart dropped with it. "Here you go!" He was always cheerful. I'd give him that.

Cash vanished, oblivious to the bomb he left behind. My vision blurred, but I knew what the heading of the paper read: From the Desk of Provost Robert K. Allen, Kansas City Chapter of the Mythical Creatures Elimination Squad.

I had an appointment with Provost Allen in less than an hour. "Arses."

*****

A brisk spring breeze pushed against me as I passed the empty fountain in front of Union Station and headed east toward the parking garage where I'd left my truck. My braided ponytail whipped around my neck. The end slapped me in the face, adding another item to the 'things-I-want-to-cut' list. I kept walking while I wound the offending hair into a bun and stuck a pin in it. Near Washington Park, footsteps followed too fast for a leisurely stroll.

I wasn't running away to avoid Provost Allen, though it had crossed my mind. However, moving my truck to the M-kes parking lot might prove convenient in the near future. The scurrying behind me increased. Pulling my dagger, I whirled about to face my stalker. Jeff jumped backward with a yelp and a hand to his heart.

"For God's sake, Jeff." I sheathed the dagger. "Call out next time. A simple, 'Hey, Andee,' could save you some stitches."

"What? No!" He grabbed my arm and pulled me behind a blooming pear tree surrounded by lilac bushes. Scents heavier than perfume filled my sensitive nose. I pinched my nostrils together to ward off a sneeze. Jeff retrieved a handkerchief from his pocket and wiped his brow. It was sixty degrees, tops; not sweating weather.

I wrinkled my nose a few times to work out the itch. "What's wrong? Is Dr. Bennett giving you trouble?"

He put his hand over my mouth. "Shhhh!" He looked into my eyes glaring over his hand and dropped it. "Do you have more of the ingot and dust samples?"

"Yes." I reached into my pockets.

"No, no." He put his hands on me again. "There's no way I can run any tests with her breathing down my neck. She's on high alert, now. But I know a guy, someone with a lot of experience about things . . . things like this."

"Basilisk dust?"

Jeff glanced around and whispered. "Weird things. Keep the samples hidden. Don't bring them back inside! Take them to him. If anyone can help you figure it out, he can." He shoved a piece of paper into my hand and started toward Union Station.

"Wait." I stepped out from behind the tree.

He growled and made a waving motion behind his back while he picked up speed. That man did not want to be seen with me. He passed a woman pushing a stroller. She looked from him to me, then hurried across the street. I usually ignored this typical behavior, but my mood had plummeted.

"I just killed a manticore here, last night," I yelled at her retreating back. "You're welcome." I turned and nearly knocked over two teenage boys, their faces still round with youth and innocence.

"We don't mind you," one said. He didn't look at my face. Though in his defense, he was eye-level with my chest.

His friend's mouth opened and closed like a fish a few times. "N-nice, uhm, sword."

And these were the typical reactions from the public. Either males who'd yet to learn what it meant to be a man drooled over me, or adults who should know better feared me. "Take a few years to practice eye contact." I jogged to the parking garage.

Thanks to the meetings with a mad chemist and my fan club, my old blue pick-up rumbled into a parking space with little time to spare. I started to jump out when I remembered Jeff's instructions. I needed to hide the sample bags before I went inside.

Before I routinely cut off the head of every kill, I'd earned a row of gashes in my leather seat from a chupacabra that turned out to be very alive in the bed of my truck. I removed the duct tape covering the holes, shoved the evidence bags inside, then replaced the tape. I sprinted all the way to administration.

I slipped into the suite right on time. Provost Allen's door stood open, but his assistant blocked my way. "You can't take that inside Provost Allen's office." She nodded at the katana handle above my right shoulder.

I eyed her from her glossy brunette bob to her sensible black pumps. "I'm not comfortable leaving anything with you." Josiah's door was still closed. "Is Doyen Hightower in, yet?"

"He's gone to San Antonio," Josiah's assistant said from her desk.

So, he left town, too. San Antonio was a legitimate place for him to go, though. It served as the southernmost outpost for M-kes, but every day the Tex-Mex Jungle grew closer to swallowing it. Josiah had been down there several times the past month, helping them relocate to a new post in the inhospitable but less dangerous Texhoma Desert. A person could see danger from miles away in the desert. Unless it was a dune dragon. A quick trembling of ground served warning before the dragon burst from the sand and swallowed its victim whole. Or maybe bit them in two. Sometimes I loved Kansas City.

I still wasn't going around weaponless. I crossed my arms, leaving my katana where it belonged.

"You can't take it in."

"Karen, Karen." A melodic voice sounded from the provost's office. "Let the girl bring in whatever she likes. Her sword does not bother me."

CHAPTER SIX

A slight man with pure white hair brushing the tops of his shoulders appeared in the office doorway. I'd never seen Provost Allen up close, and I'd avoided the Provost office until today. His face was plain and middle-aged, but his hair and dark eyes seemed ancient. He smiled and my insides warmed, like I drank a mug of hot chocolate.

"Please, come in, Andromeda." He had a bit of an accent, putting emphasis on the third syllable of my name and lengthening the 'e.'

Karen the Watchdog grudgingly moved aside, and I entered an office dominated by the color red. From a decorative sense, it should have led to angry, violent emotions, but the textured scarlet walls were warm and comfortable. Plush rugs, swirled with every shade of red from rust to ruby, softened the marble floors.

Allen's silk shirt matched the walls, and his tailored black dress pants had probably cost more than all the pants I'd ever purchased put together.

"We are not to be disturbed," he said as I passed him. Then he shut the heavy, polished wood door.

I faced him, hoping my expression didn't show the disbelief topped by worry that I'd already failed to keep two parts of my promise to Josiah. Since I needed all of the money I'd made last night for jeans and groceries, I wouldn't leave town, either. I could make manticores disembowel themselves and kill basilisks with water, but when it came to avoiding a couple of Normals, I completely failed.

"You seem distressed, Andromeda. Are you alright?"

I also failed at hiding my emotions. "I'm fine, thank you, Provost Allen."

His eyes crinkled at the corners, then he nodded at my katana. "You are left-handed, how delightful. I am, as well."

Knowing that the handle protruding over my right shoulder meant that I fought left-handed showed he already know more about weapons than his predecessor. Allen pointed to a set of shiny sabers mounted on his wall. "It would give me pleasure to practice with a fellow left-handed opponent someday."

Sparring with the boss. I didn't need Josiah to warn me away from that one. "I haven't kept up my sword-fighting skills. Monsters aren't much for dueling."

Allen smiled briefly before he moved to four red leather armchairs arranged around a low table of dark wood. "Perhaps you haven't met the right monster."

"I think all monsters are wrong. That's why I kill them."

He chuckled as he sat. "Please, sit down. We have much to discuss."

Not a quick chat about killing basilisks and threatening lab directors, then. I eyed the chair opposite him, imagining the impossibility of sitting with dignity on leather while wearing leather—not to mention clashing with the shade of the chair. Slowly I sat and placed my hands on my knees.

"When I was young, many thought me evil because I used my left hand. My parents tried to force me from it, but I never relented."

"Where the hell did you grow up?" I blurted, then clamped my mouth shut. As a kid, Normals didn't even look at me as evil, just unnatural.

He grinned. "It's all right. You would be surprised how much darkness existed in the world before Atlas arrived. My village was remote, in the mountainous Wales, an . . . archaic place."

I didn't question him, but I knew a couple of Brits and they sounded nothing like him. He must have crossed the pond before the Leviathans multiplied in the Atlantic Ocean. Atlas ruined satellite signals, and just one Trans-Atlantic cable still functioned—sometimes. Traversing the Atlantic was extremely risky, and communication with any other continent besides South America rarely happened. I only knew the location of Wales because of a childhood love for old maps.

"Being left-handed was unusual and no one understood it," Allen explained. "They feared what they did not understand, much like ignorant people fear you."

Ah, I'd heard this speech many times—mostly from my dad after some idiot kid tried to hurt me and I kicked their ass. Next, Allen would tell me to be more understanding and patient with people like Sophia. I smiled politely and waited.

Allen leaned forward, clasping his hands. "Dr. Bennett is very protective of M-kes. She's a mother hen."

"Really." I tried to picture it, but only saw a basilisk in heels.

"When she doubted your accomplishment, you of course became defensive. While Dr. Bennett's scientific mind cannot grasp what you did, I can."

I stared at him until his words sank in. The leave-Normals-be speech just took an unusual turn. "You believe I killed the basilisk?"

He held up his hands. "I went to the Restricted Zone and saw no basilisk. Either you killed it, or you convinced it to leave. Both scenarios make you very skilled."

I'd never heard of a provost travelling to a restricted area to see the handiwork of his minions. "I wasn't alone."

His lips quirked as he leaned back in his seat. "I already spoke with D.J. Chadar. If I told her that you killed three more basilisks on your own, she would believe me. And she was most unhappy with Dr. Bennett's accusations."

I squirmed. He needed to bring on the punishment instead of tiptoe around it. "I'll apologize to Dr. Bennett. She's safe from me." I sounded sincere enough that I nearly convinced myself.

But Allen waved a hand with an amused noise. "I will handle Sophia. Do you have any more of the clay or ingots?"

My insides lurched. If I gave the samples to him, they'd go straight to Sophia. No matter how much sugar Allen coated her with, she was still rotten. If he wanted more, he could go back to the perfectly safe Restricted Zone and get them.

I kept my trust in Jeff for the moment and lied. "No."

His sigh seemed relieved. "No matter. You have a commission check for the basilisk with my assistant."

Allen was my new favorite Normal. I wondered why Josiah had a problem with him. I tensed my legs to stand, assuming the meeting had ended. Allen's dark eyes met mine, and his hand lowered, palm down in a silent order to stay. "Now that the misunderstanding is cleared away, I have a proposition."

I cautiously leaned back. "Okay."

"First, I would like you to answer a question. Why are you not an Enforcer?"

I didn't have the courage to run from M-kes and live a free but short life. At the same time, I refused to hunt any Evolutionaries whose only crime was a desire to be free. "I like my role as protector of the public." I gripped my hands together, waiting for him to tell me that corralling my fellow Evolutionaries—sometimes killing them—*was* protecting the public.

Allen tilted his head in acknowledgement. "It is a role at which you excel. You never fail."

"Here. I had plenty of failure before I came to Kansas City." A familiar ball of lead filled the pit of my stomach. I did not want to go where this conversation led.

Allen's brows rose. "The Source Expedition was successful! You returned with knowledge of where the beasts came from and strategies for battling them." He leaned forward, his eyes bright. "You, still a teenager, escaped the pits of Hell."

He understood the Yellowstone Caldera. But he didn't understand success. "Twenty of us went in and seven returned. That is not success."

Allen settled into his chair again, and rested his elbows on the arms as he clasped his hands in front of his chest. "But that is not why you choose to stay an Eliminator. Come, Andromeda, you can admit that you do not wish to kill your own kind. I will accept it." His eyes warmed with his fatherly smile.

"May I?" I indicated the handle of my katana, not wishing to alarm him by drawing it.

Amusement crinkled his eyes again. He nodded.

Slowly, I drew the sword and laid it on the table as I brought my knees to the floor in front of it. The flinch I'd expected from him when I drew my weapon didn't come until I rested my right hand beside a fist-sized, black rock on the table. It must have been one of those ugly, expensive things that wealthy people buy because they can.

"This katana belonged to my friend, Jun Tekada."

"A member of the Source Expedition."

He knew names. That surprised me. He dropped gracefully to the floor across from me and brought his intense gaze to my level.

"Yes. Jun's katana passed down to her from her father who received it from his father, and so on. It is a sword that demands possession by a person who vows to defend the helpless. Jun entrusted me with carrying her katana out of the Yellowstone kill zone and using it as she would. I don't think Jun and her katana would consider killing fellow Evolutionaries a noble endeavor."

He could have told me to use a different weapon or scoffed that the katana didn't know any differently, but instead he nodded. "I agree with you."

A charged silence fell between us. Not much information about Allen's personality floated around. I hadn't expected understanding and support. Normals—especially powerful Normals—didn't care about the plight of Evolutionaries. Yet now, one sat on the floor in his expensive pants and reflected my standards.

Allen smiled slowly, reading my disbelief. "What if I told you that Enforcer does not have to be as high as you can go? What if you had authority? Power to make changes?"

Despite my doubt, a thrill sparked inside me. "How?"

"I want to show the world the potential of Evolutionaries. Some of you are so talented, so gifted, yet you are stifled. But I need help, and I fear someone plots to stop me. I spoke with two of your peers recently, and now they are gone."

Dread replaced my growing enthusiasm. "Johnson and Delaney?"

Allen frowned and looked down at my katana. "Yes. I think someone with power knows what I attempt. They want you under their thumb. That is why I want you to tell no one of what I have said. When the time is right, I will ask for your aid. Until then, silence is key."

Considering he hadn't told me much, silence was also easy. A little disappointed in the meeting's anticlimactic end, I prepared to leave. I grabbed my katana with my left hand, but as I moved to sheath it, my right hand brushed against the black rock.

I stuck to it. Warmth spread from my fingers to my elbow, and my skin lost its blue tint as the heat intensified. I jerked away with a gasp and held my hand to my chest where my heart thumped wildly.

"My apologies!" Allen jumped to his feet with youthful agility. He grabbed a decorative blanket from his chair and dropped it over the rock before picking it up. "It is a trick rock that reacts to body temperature. It can be shocking. Are you alright?"

My skin tingled, and I was breathless, but I felt fine, so I nodded.

"Did it make you cold?"

"No." I finally found my voice again, but I stayed on my knees.

"Warm."

Curiosity replaced the concern on his face. "Interesting." His eyes shifted to my katana, which I hadn't realized I pointed at the rock beneath the blanket.

"Sorry." I sheathed it and rose to my feet.

"Before you leave—if you do not mind." Allen stopped to clear his throat, looked down at the blanket, then placed it on his desk. "I have a different rock—they are a fascination for me. I am curious to see how it reacts to your touch."

I hesitated and felt foolish. He was just an eccentric old man who wanted me to touch his pet rock—which would sound weird out loud, but in my head it seemed harmless.

"If you like, I will touch it first." He grabbed a small glass case with a rock similar to what Jeff had in his lab. Allen held the case before me with one hand and reached in with the other to touch it. The porous, rusty surface shimmered slightly, then flooded with red as bright as his shirt.

"Does it reflect your appearance?"

"I am not sure." He removed his finger, and the rock went back to normal. "I have not figured it out, yet, so I like to test it on visitors. Do you mind?" He pushed it closer to me.

I lightly touched the rock with my left hand and expected a shock but felt nothing. The surface flickered between dark green and black several times, as if confused. I wore red and black, and my skin was blue. I broke contact and stepped away. "Maybe it's broken."

He kept it in front of me, and I thought he would ask me to touch it again, but he put the case back on his desk with a shrug. "Thank you, Andromeda, we will speak again, soon."

*****

Barriers didn't block I-35 at the Kit Bond Bridge, anymore. A couple of cars sat along the bridge, holding what I called bog-gawkers. They hoped to catch sight of a dead basilisk but lacked the courage to go down to the railyard. It would have been a wasted trip, anyway.

I drove my truck all the way to the pavement's end before getting out and surveying the Restricted Zone in daylight. It was like turning on the bedroom light to discover that the monster in your room was a jacket hanging on your dresser. The deadly vines lay limp, and not a single fire frog lounged in the sun. Even the bog looked more likely to bounce if I stepped on it instead of swallow my boots, which had happened, once.

I'd rushed to finish paperwork, cash my commissions, and do my shopping so I could pay a visit to the Restricted Zone before dark. Sophia had destroyed the ingots and dust, Jeff had ordered me to hide them, and Allen had asked if I had more. Collecting extra sounded like a good idea. I rock hopped across the bog and headed for the silos.

Thirty yards from my destination, I halted. The giant pile of basilisk dust was gone. There had been some wind today, but the silos protected the area in front of them. Maybe Provost Allen had failed to mention cleaning up while he had investigated my achievements in the Restricted Zone.

I studied the ground, then drew my katana when the sound of metal clanging against metal reverberated through the abandoned railyard. I moved toward the intact silo. Movement on top drew my eye just before a dark head disappeared over the roof. Running feet pounded atop the grain elevator that extended behind. I rounded the silo and hurried up the rusty ladder.

I wouldn't get hold of this guy unless he had the speed of a sloth, but I might catch a glimpse of him. When I reached the top, he was halfway down the quarter-mile-long elevator. Long, jean clad legs ate up the distance between us, and a broad pair of shoulders lowered in preparation for a leap off the four-storied elevator.

"Wait!" I yelled just as he disappeared over the edge.

He was dead. I continued running, needlessly, fear pushing me faster. I only made it a hundred yards when a flash of light blinded me. A rumble of thunder hit me in the chest like a sledgehammer. Darkness surrounded me.

When I woke, pain radiated through my chest in sync with my pulse which raced like I still sprinted. Slowly, I sat up. I'd kept hold of my katana through the brief blackout. I half-laughed, then winced with my sternum's protest.

I pulled the v-neck of my sweater down to assess the damage and saw nothing but unmarred blue skin, save the implant scars. Phantom sledgehammers left no mark. I stood with a groan, then cautiously walked to the roof's edge. Only railcar tracks and scrap metal covered the ground.

My legs gave out, and I dropped to my knees. A relieved sigh escaped me and the pain in my chest eased. Most of my pain had been panic. I'd expected to see his broken body four stories below. His scent hovered in the air. I inhaled the smoky sweetness of it before cursing Doyen Hightower with words my mother still hoped I didn't know.

At least alive, Josiah could answer some questions. The first of which would be how he'd survived a jump off the roof while knocking me flat. He didn't have to know that I'd recognized him by his butt. His spiky black hair was distinctive, too.

"San Antonio, my ass." I rose to my feet and went back to the silo, both dreading and hoping to find why Josiah ran from me. I found more questions and zero answers. Completely cleared of the ingots that had been piled eight feet high last night, the silo stood empty. In its center, the soft earth had a deep indentation from something heavier than thousands of ingots. The shape was irregular, but someone with better math skills than mine might calculate its size and weight if they knew the soil's composition. Feeling more like a scientist than a monster killer, I scooped yet another dirt sample into a bag. I made some rough measurements using my hands and feet, then explored the deserted railyard.

Including the lack of basilisk dust, the area was free of tire tracks, footprints, and even broom marks. A sick dread filled my chest: what if it had regenerated? For the second day in a row, I got the hell out of the Restricted Zone.

CHAPTER SEVEN

I stood before the wall of windows in my apartment and contemplated the city skyline as I took a long pull from the tepid beer bottle in my hand. To my right, farther down Twelfth Street, the golden cupola of the Cathedral of the Immaculate Conception glowed rose in the light of Atlas. To the south, the four concrete pylons of Bartle Hall stood proudly. On top of each column, metallic spheres and rods resembled satellites or antennae, reflecting the red glow of the risen Atlas. The artwork atop the pillars appeared so alien that many misguided individuals had tried to climb them and wait for Atlas to take them away.

Just beyond the pylons, the Kauffman Center shone. If the Bartle Hall columns served as beacons to aliens, then Kauffman Center was the command center. If someone wrapped a potato longer than a football field in aluminum foil then sliced it, the effect would be similar to the side of the Kauffman Center that faced me. The other side sparkled with glass like the inside of a geode. On a cold night, when the air was thin, I could hear the KC Symphony, which still played in the building. Music proved resilient through the Atlas Apocalypse.

No surprise that cult fanatics took pilgrimages to Kauffman and Bartle in the early days of Atlas. Those two buildings had fared better than the squat, massive blot of darkness that was the Sprint Center, aka the Mother Ship. In a time of mass hysteria, unspeakable rituals and crimes against humanity occurred within the walls of the former entertainment venue. Just looking at the abandoned building brought a chill to my skin.

Somewhere in the dark, interspersed with cold steel and sharp glass, hid Josiah Hightower. I stared into the mouth of my second beer but found no insight into Josiah's game—or why he would run from me when he'd just made himself cozy in my apartment last night. After leaving the silo, I'd tried to return the favor, but he wasn't at his modest home in Brookside. A little frustrated, I'd lodged a throwing knife in his front door in lieu of a note. Headquarters still claimed he was in San Antonio. At least I knew more than they did.

I downed the last of my beer on the way to the kitchen and quit for the night. Alcohol didn't affect me long, anyway, since my body burned it up so quickly. I felt the past twenty-four hours warranted a treat, and I liked this particular brew made with barley and berries. Due to farming and exporting difficulties, former staples like coffee, tea, and cow's milk were now indulgences, but just about anything could ferment.

I pulled out the contents of my leather pockets, tossed it onto the granite countertop of my kitchen island, and sat on one of the stainless-steel stools. I leafed through receipts for jeans and groceries; bags of ingots, basilisk dust, and silo dirt; and a piece of folded legal pad paper.

I put my elbows on the table, placed my chin in one hand, and pushed the bag of basilisk dust around with a finger. Light caught flecks of something reflective inside, but it never looked like more than fancy potting soil. So why did Provost Allen care if I had it? Sophia's destruction of it implied it had value beyond the simple clay she claimed. Something strange and shadowy stirred at M-kes, and the clay felt key. But until I found the lock, the key was worthless.

Rubbing my temples with a sigh, I turned my attention to the ingots. If Josiah had emptied the silo of ingots, he would have needed a sizable truck and manpower. He certainly didn't drive a truck when he left. No, I assumed Provost Allen ordered the clean-up.

Josiah had been investigating like me and had perhaps found something he didn't want to share. I wondered if his assistant believed he was in San Antonio, or if she'd been instructed to tell me that. And why order me to stay away from Allen, the most helpful, understanding provost I'd known? My lips turned down in disgust. Josiah's trustworthy status wavered, and few people ever made that list let alone got scratched.

I picked up the piece of paper Jeff gave me, reading a name, phone number, and address followed by a footnote: CALL FIRST!

I ran my finger under the name. "Charles MacDuggan."

Until the Restricted Zone visit, I'd planned to blow off Jeff's suggestion. But he was uncomfortable helping me, and I wouldn't go to Sophia. Josiah didn't trust me, which made me question my continued trust in him. This MacDuggan probably couldn't help me, but meeting an expert in what a strange man like Jeff called 'weird things' might prove amusing.

*****

Not many people lived outside the safety of metropolitan areas after the mythical beasts arrived. My parents—who retired from professional sports to grow corn—were exceptions, and so was Charles MacDuggan. I left my apartment at nine in the morning and nearly two hours later found the entrance to MacDuggan's place, obscured by heavy foliage and large rocks that had rolled down the bluff backdrop to settle perfectly on the roadside.

I'd driven for miles along the Missouri River, past abandoned farmhouses and a maintained railroad. I'd performed a U-turn three different times, but I hadn't crossed the riverbed, which meant I remained in Missouri, not Kansas. Road signs were either destroyed or covered along the cracked highway that was a rainstorm away from complete envelopment by bushes, trees, and wildflowers. So as my truck rumbled up a packed dirt drive, I pegged MacDuggan as a man who valued his privacy.

I emerged from a line of trees into a nineteenth century watermill compound of three rugged brownstone buildings: a two-level house, a smaller outbuilding, and a mill complete with a ten-foot, wooden water wheel painted red. A stone wall fronted the property and disappeared into more trees. I eyed the bright red numbers painted on the stone wall and double checked the address Jeff gave me.

"Finally." I drove past the mill and stopped at the end of the dirt drive where a lush lawn sprawled before the double wooden doors of the house. I made sure the slamming of my truck door announced my arrival before I shook the kinks of travel from my legs and rolled my shoulders. A low, feline growl interrupted the cracking of my neck.

A giant black panther on the roof greeted me with a mouth full of sharp teeth. My fangs bared instinctively, but I wouldn't win a pissing contest with this cat. I'd seen panthers in Texas and the parts of Louisiana not swallowed by the Gulf of Mexico, but none even half the size of this beast.

It leapt at me. I jumped up, landing in the bed of my truck as claws screeched against metal. Its head snapped up, and glowing green eyes met mine. Damn, even standing in the truck, my knees were level with its head. My katana in hand, I judged the distance between the panther's jugular and my blade. Its hindquarters tensed, and I bent my knees. Behind the panther, the double doors of the house flew open. A tall, angular man ran out.

"Stay back!" I yelled.

"Boar! Boar! Down, girl!"

"This is a panther, idiot! Get back!"

He halted just a few feet away. The panther sat back on its haunches, snarling one last time before lying down and resting its head on massive paws. Even when the man chuckled, I didn't take my eyes off the suddenly docile beast. He strolled up and scratched behind its ears until it closed its eyes. A raspy purr filled the air.

"She's not a 'boar,'" he explained. "She's the Beast of Roslin, B-O-R. She's never responded to other names."

I finally looked directly at him. He grinned with an abundance of teeth. His chestnut hair grayed at the temples, and he wore it a little long. A natural wave made it crest above his high forehead and away from his rather large ears. "You can put the sword away. She won't hurt you."

Cute. "Actually, I was about to kill it. I'll put the sword away when I'm done."

Green eyes snapped open like it understood me. A snarl curled the panther's lip. I matched it.

The man laughed again. I wondered if my ass-kicker face had stopped working. "Come now, if you wanted to kill my pet you would have tried by now. And you can quit looking at me like that. I know you won't hurt me, either."

I let the tip of my katana fall. I reluctantly found his Scottish accent charming. Though not very thick, it emerged in the slight rolling of his r's and the occasional dropped "t." It reminded me a little of Provost Allen, but Allen's accent was darker, heavier.

I gave the panther—or whatever—one last look before I sheathed my sword. "My name is Andromeda Bochs. Are you Charles MacDuggan?"

He looked momentarily surprised, then his face closed. "And here

I thought you were lost."

"Jeff Trotter sent me."

A slight smile returned. "Ah, Dr. Trotter, this should be interesting. Did he tell you to call first?"

"I did. Three times. If you don't want visitors eaten by your beast, you should answer your phone."

MacDuggan chortled and held out a welcoming arm toward his house. "She was just playing with you. She ate this morning."

Fed or not, I kept my eye on her as I hopped down from the truck. "I'm not familiar with the species Beast of Roslin."

"I suspect there are many things you're unfamiliar with, Miss Bochs."

I had the same suspicions.

*****

"Would you care for tea, Miss Bochs?"

"You have tea?" I drew my eyes away from the farmhouse tabletop where a latticework of sunlight played through large, cottage-style windows. I hadn't had tea since visiting my grandmother two years earlier. Even before Atlas' arrival, she grew Camellia bushes to make her own tea.

MacDuggan leaned against a kitchen island with a wood-plank top scarred enough to be a giant cutting board. The island counter hit him mid-thigh, making him six feet, four inches, at least. "I have an adventurer friend who found a few Rose of Winter bushes for me. I lost one, but the others flourish in my garden."

Rose of Winter was a beautiful Japanese plant introduced on the continent hundreds of years ago. My grandmother's plants came from India. I smiled at the memory of her instruction on the care and harvest, while my restless, juvenile self had been sure I didn't care and wouldn't remember.

MacDuggan returned my smile, though he couldn't know my thoughts. Even owning the plants, his tea should have been precious to him. His hospitality surprised me, especially since I'd tried to kill his pet beast.

"I've never had tea from the Rose of Winter. I'd love to try it."

"You're in for a treat, then." He filled a tea kettle with water and rummaged about the modern kitchen nestled within the old stone walls.

I investigated my surroundings from a comfortably padded chair. I sat at a large, heavy table made of dark wood. In the wall across from me was a stone fireplace with an elaborate, wrought iron screen. Tiles the color of wet clay covered the floor, and the cheery yellow walls amplified the sunlight streaming through a multitude of windows. Along the bay window at the end of the table, ran a line of potted plants: aloe, rosemary, mint, clove, and an oregano plant that looked sick.

Leaning sideways, I ran a finger along a yellowing vine that needed pruning, then poked into wet, spongy soil. "Your oregano needs to be re-potted, trimmed, and watered less often," I informed him as I sat straight again.

MacDuggan glanced over his shoulder. "Is that all? Have a green thumb, do you?"

I shrugged and placed my chin in one hand as I watched him scoop loose tea leaves into an infuser. "My grandmother is a botanist, my parents are farmers, and I have an unfortunately good memory."

He chuckled: a sound already familiar to me. Placing a tray of tea paraphernalia on the table, he sat across from me. "So, did Dr. Trotter send you here with a problem of yours, or have you come to rescue my plants?"

I studied his very normal face, slightly lined at the corners of observant, dark blue eyes. Aside from harboring giant, woman-eating panthers, he didn't seem weird, at all. "Are you a scientist?"

"I am a biologist." He tilted his head toward his plants. "But not a botanist."

I put a hand inside my hoodie pocket and touched one of the plastic bags. "You don't have to help me." I frowned. It sounded like a promise not to kill him if he told me to go away. Despite my skills, I wasn't a killer—not of humans, anyway. Even if he threatened to report me to M-kes, I wouldn't hurt him. Hell, I probably wouldn't hurt his cat. I placed a lot of trust in Jeff by confiding in the man across from me.

MacDuggan patiently waited, watching the struggle play across my too-open face. I grasped the three bags, pulled them out, and placed them on the table before I could overthink any longer. "I'm sure you've guessed that I work for M-kes." I paused with another frown. My genes were obvious. MacDuggan had invited me, an armed Evolutionary, into his home. I met his expectant eyes, and he bit into a cookie. "Two nights ago, a co-worker and I were sent to the Restricted Zone to kill the basilisk."

MacDuggan choked a little on crumbs, but said nothing.

"I—we—succeeded, but afterward it exploded into a pile of that." I pointed at the bag of clay dust. Then, I moved my finger to the bag of ingots. "It was guarding a silo full of those which made me sick, though this small amount doesn't bother me. When I returned to the scene, the basilisk dust was gone, and all of the ingots were gone, but there was a large indentation in the ground, as if the pile had been hiding something. I took some measurements and a sample of the soil." I finished by indicating the last bag of dirt.

MacDuggan grinned. "I see your grandmother taught you the basics of scientific inquiry."

"She was persistent." That was an understatement.

He leaned back and laced his fingers together. "Well, you've presented quite a pile of mysteries. Dr. Trotter couldn't help you?"

I pressed my lips together and kept eye contact despite my desire to look away. "He's afraid."

"I see." He looked down at my evidence bags, pulled his fingers apart, and tapped the tips together rhythmically as he worked his mouth. "If Dr. Trotter is afraid." He slowly reached a hand toward the bags. I held my breath as his hand hovered over the samples. He looked up with twinkling eyes and grabbed the bags. "This must be very interesting, indeed."

I sipped excellent green tea and nibbled a not-so-excellent cookie while MacDuggan held the bags up to the sunlight. He studied them with a narrowed gaze that was probably just as responsible for his crow's feet as laughter. Eying his strong profile and the firm skin of his neck, I wondered about his age.

He lowered the final bag and glanced at the half-eaten cookie on my plate. "I'm not much of a baker. My apologies."

"I'm saving it for later."

He flashed his toothy grin. "Let's get to work, then, shall we?"

He escorted me to the top floor where it appeared that several walls had been knocked down, and everything had been renovated to accommodate lab equipment as sophisticated as Sophia's. I looked closely at MacDuggan's soft sweater and well-tailored khakis, then down at his sturdy but expensive leather boots. Either he was funded—in which case I needed to be very careful—or he was independently wealthy.

"Nice lab," I said casually.

"It is, isn't it?" MacDuggan pulled his sweater over his head, revealing a pristine, white undershirt, then he slipped into a protective lab coat. After buttoning up, he raised his serious face. "My parents come from old money, as people say across the pond."

He waited, but I didn't know what he expected. Maybe no one took him seriously as a scientist when he revealed his background. I was relieved to know he wasn't backed financially by someone he might report my problems to.

I raised my shoulders and replied, "Mine are rich, too."

He politely refrained from mentioning my beat-up vehicle in his driveway and just accepted my statement with a smile. Rubbing his hands together, he sat on a stool. "Now, I want to hear exactly what happened that night—and I mean everything. Did Jeff investigate the components of these ingots, already?" He held up the bag.

"Yes. He said they were silica ingots, exactly like those above my heart. He didn't get a chance to try any biological tests. I'm sorry, Mr. MacDuggan—Dr. MacDuggan."

He shook his head. "Call me Mac, please. I'll work while you talk."

I relayed the entire battle with the basilisk while Mac moved about his lab, never hesitating, knowing exactly what he wanted and where it was. He paused to look at me when I mentioned feeling paralyzed after D.J.'s shout. Then I had to pause after I described the kill because MacDuggan laughed so hard.

"Oh, I'm sorry," he wheezed, dabbing the corner of his eye with a fingertip. "A flare and a puddle, that's fabulous."

Pleasure warmed my cheeks. Josiah hadn't even acknowledged my quick thinking. I gave an absurd little bow. "Thank you."

By the time I finished with what Jeff and Sophia had discovered—or claimed to discover—Mac sat with crossed arms and a thoughtful face. He reached up with one hand and tugged on his lower lip as he stared at the toes of his boots which moved side to side a few feet in front of him. "Clay makes sense if it were a golem," he muttered. "But a basilisk golem? Hmmm . . . did you see his forehead, by chance?" He looked up at me.

I had no clue what he mumbled about. I shook my head.

"No, I suppose you wouldn't, what with the eye and all." He glared back at his toes but they refused to give answers. Finally, he sighed and stood. "We'll come back to the basilisk clay. I'll show you what I've found in the ingots."

He seemed normal again, but I walked to his side with caution. What the hell was a golem? I'd come upon the 'weird things' Jeff referred to yesterday.

Mac picked up a case enclosing a reddish rock just like Jeff had in his lab. After closer inspection, I realized the second rock I'd touched in Allen's office resembled it, too. "I'll be damned."

"Ah." Mac smiled. "You know what this is, then."

"No."

"Oh." He blinked twice. "Well, it's a piece of Atlas. When the asteroid first arrived, pieces of it broke off, and there were meteor showers almost daily for months. Look through the lens." He pointed at the microscope in front of me.

As a child, I'd been obsessed with biology for obvious reasons. I never discovered anything important about myself, but I knew how to work a microscope and understand what it showed me, thanks to my grandmother. I made myself comfortable and looked through the lens. A pile of metallic shavings lit up on the slide.

"That's a sample from one of the ingots," Mac said. "Now watch what happens when I place a little crushed Atlas beside it."

A magnified, blurry scoop appeared and dropped a fraction of ground up rock on the slide. The rock immediately disappeared. I raised my head and Mac pointed to a small amount of dust on the table beside the microscope.

"Look. The ingot shavings repelled Atlas completely off the microscope's stage," Mac said.

"Well that makes sense. That's why they're implanted in my chest—to keep Atlas' radiation from mutating the E-gene and killing me." Even Evolutionaries uninterested in science understood the facts of their survival on Earth—and why they appeared freaks to the rest of the world. The side effects of silica in our chests were blue skin, purple eyes, and sometimes fangs.

Mac frowned so deeply his brows nearly touched. "Right. But watch this." He took a clean slide, placed a small amount of ingot shavings on it, and put it on the stage. Then he shocked me by taking a tiny needle from a sterilized package and pricking his finger.

"What are you doing?"

"Just look."

I bent to the eyepiece and saw a drop of blood squeezed onto the slide. For a moment, nothing happened. Then, his blood bubbled and darkened to nearly black.

"The ingots poison your blood?"

"Yes. If they were simple silica that shouldn't happen. In large amounts, of course, silica would be bad for anyone, but it shouldn't immediately kill my blood."

I responded with silence, not sure if he meant these particular ingots were poisonous, or that I somehow survived poisonous silica in my chest.

"Would you like to see what happens to your blood?"

I stepped away from the microscope and offered my finger. If the ingots in the silo poisoned my blood, then D.J. was right, and someone intended to hurt Evolutionaries through the tools meant to save them. My heart beat a little faster at the thought of witnessing the poisoning of the life that pumped through me.

Mac guided my finger to the microscope slide while I looked through the eyepiece. To begin with, my blood didn't seem as bright as Mac's. I thought I saw a few specks of black on the surface, but they disappeared. "I see nothing."

"Now, let me magnify."

After he adjusted the turret, I looked again. Whoa, it was on a cellular level almost too great for the amount of blood on the slide. Now I saw tiny pieces of silica migrating to my blood. They crossed the membranes, then my cells enveloped them. Some of my cells took on a spiky appearance, which meant they were dead, destroyed. Most of the them, though darker, remained intact.

"The E-gene eats the silica," I whispered. "It's like when I'm weak for a couple of days after an ingot replacement, because my blood has to adapt to the higher concentration of silica. The doctors compare it to chemotherapy."

"I know what they say," Mac said tightly. "But there's a problem with your theory."

I sat back to see his face flushed and his lips compressed. "What? Your blood was destroyed because it couldn't withstand the silica. Mine adapted because I have the E-gene. Really, Mac, I thought you were a biologist."

He didn't smile at my barb. Okay, maybe our new relationship wasn't ready for banter. "The problem," he answered, keeping his bright eyes locked on my face, "is that I have the E-gene, too."

He looked so serious. I tried, but I couldn't hold down the laughter that burst from my throat. "No, you don't. Look at you." It wasn't the obvious that made me doubt his words. Without the silica ingots, I'd look Normal, too. However, Evolutionaries tended to glow, and we couldn't live past ten without the silica's protection. "You're what, forty-years-old?"

"I'm thirty-three."

Yikes.

I glanced at his graying temples and lined eyes which proceeded to roll in the first immature action I'd seen from him. "My life has na' always been easy. You try being a nervous four-year-old as you cross an ocean full of sea monsters, why don' you."

He meant it. Mac believed he had the E-gene and had likely run tests to prove it. "Okay, let's say you have the E-gene. Maybe Atlas is aging you, killing you, and you refuse to see it."

"I feel great," he insisted, his Scottish burr thickening with his agitation. "You're the one who's sick, and you don' even realize."

"I could kill your beast and simultaneously kick your ass with no effort. I'm fine."

"Such violence," he mumbled, searching his lab table. "I bet you're a shifter. They're usually volatile."

"What?"

He held up an ingot. "I'll show you sick, Andromeda Bochs."

With his other hand he pulled out a pocketknife and popped open the blade. I jumped back, flexing a hand over my dagger and hoping he wouldn't test my earlier boast. His blade flashed, and blood flowed from a deep gash inside his forearm. Grimacing, Mac shoved the ingot inside his wound.

"No!" I moved to him.

He sat hard on the stool, holding up his other arm to bar me. "Watch." He spoke through clenched teeth.

I'd watched it poison his blood. "This will kill you!"

His laugh was more of a pant. "Just watch."

I moved my eyes from his sweating face to his arm. Black lines streaked from his wound in paths of literal death as his blood was destroyed. Around the wound, his skin turned blue. The color spread in every direction, steadily covering his once-beige arm. I nervously looked back to his face, even more strained and pale. He opened his eyes, and I fell back in shock. His irises were a deep, vibrant purple. His lids fluttered, and his breathing stuttered.

I grabbed his shoulders. He slumped and half of his weight fell into my hands. "I believe you, I believe you! Get it out!"

He raised a hand and weakly brushed against the wound before slumping farther. "Can't."

I put an arm around his shoulders, holding him in the crook of my right arm as I stuck my left thumb and forefinger into the cut. I pulled the ingot out and flung it across the lab, probably contaminating everything on his tables. I tried to move him to the floor, but he pulled away from me.

"I'm okay," he whispered, leaning on his good arm and stretching his wounded one out before him. "Watch what happens, now."

"I'm tired of watching." I looked anyway. The black lines faded, and his skin returned to its natural shade. "This only backs up what you showed me through the microscope. Why do this?"

"To prove that if I had been introduced to the ingots as a babe, I'd be just like you. You haven't built up an immunity to Atlas, Andromeda, you've built an immunity to the ingots. You saw how it changed me in a matter of minutes. That can't be mere silica." He closed his eyes. "Now, watch how I change myself."

He murmured a few words I didn't understand. Gradually, his face glowed, as if golden blood flowed beneath his skin. The light spread down his neck and arms, brightening around the bleeding gash. It intensified until I had trouble looking at it without a pair of sunglasses. The glow receded, and unmarred skin was left behind.

I had fantastic healing abilities, but I'd never done that. His face showed none of the strain it had moments earlier. This was freaky—frightening, even. "What the hell is going on?" Unaware of moving, I stood several feet away from a Mac who barely looked ruffled.

He smiled at my shock. "What if I told you that we're not Evolutionary, you and I? We're magical. Those ingots inside you don't block radiation. They block the magic Atlas tries to give you. My body reacted violently to the silica because those ingots are magically cursed. Since I'm an adult, my magic has matured, rooted inside me. Losing the magic was like losing my life."

Well, damn. I'd wondered what the 'weird things' were, so I'd asked for it. "It was nice to meet you, Magic Mac." I turned on my heel and headed for the door.

"Wait! Where are you going? I can save you!"

I rounded on him. He leaned heavily on the table, probably feigning weakness to earn more of my compassion. "I don't need saving, you idiot. Atlas has aged your brain, too. If you truly have the E-gene and this isn't some parlor trick, you need to seek medical help before Atlas kills you."

A puzzled frown replaced the indignation on his face. "Parlor trick? A fan of historical romance, are you?"

"No!" I stormed out. He'd been so smart and likable. I couldn't believe what a disappointment the day had become.

"This is no trick!"

The wooden stairs made a satisfying racket below my stomping feet.

"Just look at my beast at the bottom of the stairs, then. Explain that, will you?"

At the word 'beast,' I drew my katana and skipped the last three stairs in what I hoped was a surprise entrance. Beside the kitchen entryway, on a corduroy pet bed, slept a black cat—slightly larger than the typical domestic. The only similarity it had with the Beast of Roslin was a dark, nearly indiscernible, spotted pattern on its fur.

"Dumbass," I snarled and sheathed my sword. "Insulting my intelligence gets you nowhere."

Mac's voice sounded from the top of the stairs. "She's sleeping to renew the vast amount of energy it took to transform. It's the same animal, I tell you!"

"She's sleeping because she's a cat." Now I felt sorry for him, so I clamped my mouth shut and kept walking. I needed to get out before I did something out of pity that I would regret.

Footsteps on the stairs sounded while I entered the kitchen to reach the only exit I knew. I heard him stumble and glanced over my shoulder. He knelt on one knee, his hand gripping the frame to the kitchen entrance. My protective instincts screamed. I stuck my fingers in my ears in an absurd attempt to ignore them.

"You don't believe I or my beast are magical, fine! But what about you? Look at my oregano. You touched it, didn't you?"

I reached the kitchen island, my back to the windows. Since they hadn't worked, at all, I removed my fingers. Giving in, I looked at the plants. The oregano that had been on the verge of death was lush and green—literally thriving. I had no words for what I saw, just a chest tight with fear and feet ready to run.

Mac stayed in the doorway. "You healed my plant without thinking. The blocking curse on your ingots must be fading. I bet you're due for a replacement soon, aren't you?"

"No." Next month wasn't that soon. Most Evolutionaries got their ingots replaced every five years, but mine wore out faster than most. The longest I'd gone was three years.

"Liar."

Practically running from the kitchen, I ignored him. I opened the double doors, halting when he finally made it to the front foyer.

"I'm begging you, don't let them replace your ingots. If I'm Normal, those ingots shouldn't have changed me like they did. If I'm Evolutionary, the accepted science says I should be long dead. Please. Please, just think about what I've said—what you've seen. I'll be here."

I left without looking back, but I waved an acknowledgement. As my truck rumbled past the stone wall, a black cat jumped on top to watch me leave. In my rearview mirror, sunlight glinted in a pair of eyes greener than the oregano leaves before it jumped off and disappeared.

CHAPTER EIGHT

I strolled past a boarded-up restaurant boasting mass-produced cheesecake and crossed a deserted Forty-Seventh Street. Luckily, mythical creature activity was low on my last night of duty. My mind wasn't on dragon-slaying as I patrolled the area officially named The Country Club Plaza, now called the Silent Sector. The abandoned specialty shops and restaurants that filled the sector were useless to the inhabitants of Kansas City, and beasts rarely made an appearance. Maybe a semi-benevolent administrator had taken it easy on me before my four days off.

As my feet crunched through the litter of broken, Spanish roof tiles, I reviewed my options. It only took a few steps to finish the list. I could go to my parents' farm in Illinois or hide out in my grandmother's cabin deep in a dark forest beside a monster-infested lake. Money was still tight, but Josiah's order to get away for a while seemed a good idea regardless of his motives. I just hoped that Doyen Graves didn't catch wind of my disappearance and put his Enforcers on my tail.

You could go to MacDuggan, the crazy part of my brain whispered.

"Wrong," I answered aloud with complete confidence in my sanity. I needed a place to think, to plan. That strange man at my shoulder spouting nonsense about magic wouldn't help.

A picture of a healthy oregano plant flashed through my memory. I kicked a roof tile and it skittered into the street. My brain wouldn't let up, forcing me to relive Mac changing to Evolutionary then healing in front of me. I shook my head and jumped on a storm drain grate repeatedly until the sound of metal grinding against concrete echoed through the streets and filled my head. I needed a better distraction.

The Silent Sector fully lived up to its name tonight, not even harboring a brave scavenger searching for any chocolate I had missed. Josiah lived in Brookside Park, less than two miles away. If I left the sector, I'd be leaving my patrol, but I could be at Josiah's in eight minutes. Who better to be with when you're breaking the rules than your boss? Then, I could amuse myself by questioning him, annoying him, or—if he was still gone—raiding his fridge. I hadn't bothered calling headquarters again, so I didn't know today's story of his whereabouts.

An Atlas-lit jog past the abandoned mansions of Ward Parkway and into the inexplicably maintained Brookside felt cathartic. Brookside homes were fairly old and thus should have been avoided when people looked for real estate. Most homebuyers wanted reinforced steel and thick glass, not to mention locations near M-kes headquarters or at least within Eliminator patrols. Brookside had none of those perks, but beasts never attacked it. To reinforce the eccentric nature of Brookside's inhabitants, two of them gave me a friendly wave from their porch swing where they drank a midnight glass of wine. No resident of Brookside had ever crossed the street to avoid me.

Josiah's brick and white-siding Colonial house on Grand Avenue had been remodeled several times in its more than one hundred years of existence. I assumed he'd added a few defensive touches of his own, though I'd never noticed them. Slowing to a walk in front of the quaint, black iron fence that would keep out nothing, I saw disappointing darkness behind the large windows of both floors. Large windows were another rarity in this world of scary creatures, yet every house in Brookside had them.

I pushed the gate open with one finger and snorted at the lack of a basic lock. The sidewalk that curved gently through his lawn on a meandering path to his porch was free of plant life. Someone maintained his yard and garden, because this time of year plants had to be trimmed and grass mowed every few days, or the rampant vegetation took over and hid the front door. The brick porch was clean, and the mortar cracks free of weeds.

I stopped in front of the crimson-painted door, noting the absence of the knife I'd left yesterday. A rustle in the flower bed made me tense. Normally, I'd think of a cat or squirrel, but with the Beast of Roslin fresh in my mind, I immediately drew my katana. I caught a whiff of formaldehyde just before white roses the size of my fist exploded, and a blurry, compact body flew from the bushes. I dropped to one knee. As my attacker sailed over my shoulder, I sent an elbow into his midsection.

The thing—a kind description—rolled across the lawn. The head and torso were human, though the eyes bugged out like a strangling victim, and the skin had a corpse's pallor. Stitched to the body were furry, wickedly clawed arms similar to the front legs of a lion.

The legs brought kangaroos to mind with their reddish fur, muscular hindquarters, and large feet. They would barely bring the head to my shoulder, but I'd better avoid a kick. A dirty loincloth hid whatever tissue connected the legs to the humanoid torso. For the sake of my gag reflex, I appreciated the attire, though it struck me as pathetic.

Something else struck me between the shoulder blades, and I soared. My back screamed with pain, and spots raced before my eyes faster than the grass passed below me. I tried to tuck and roll, but the landing knocked the breath from me. I couldn't move more than my head to see what came next.

The first human/lion/kangaroo hopped up laughing—as unpleasant a noise as I could imagine coming from a hu-li-roo. A second one had ambushed me from the flowers while I tried to categorize the first. A third hu-li-roo jumped out of a tree.

I played weak on the ground to see what happened; and because I'd just been knocked across the yard by a freaking kangaroo man. I'd dropped my katana in the middle of the lawn, but I didn't want to cut these things to pieces just yet. I needed to know what they were and why they staked out Josiah's house.

Number One desired payback, evident in his smile just before he leapt at me. He jumped so high, I had time to grab my baton and extend it as I brought my feet up to meet his torso. I took his weight—the damn thing outweighed me—and lowered my knees to my chest. We looked like kids playing superman as he swung his claws a few inches from my face.

I heaved Number One away, using my momentum to jump to my feet and swing a fist into the solar plexus of Hu-li-roo Two. I crouched, and Number Three flew over my head from behind. He collided with Number Two in a tangle of lion and kangaroo limbs.

Number One hopped up, and I took the offensive, whacking my baton across his nose then his torso. His kangaroo feet weren't built for retreat, and he fell trying to back away. I felt another one coming. I squatted, nearly touching the ground with my hand before I exploded up to punch him in the face. The jolt traveled to my shoulder, and I'd feel it tomorrow, but I knocked him out.

The last one was smarter than the others, bouncing off a tree and flying at me with claws swinging. I rapped my baton on the back of one paw, veering him off course before I head butted him in the nose.

Ouch. We both staggered backward.

The broken nose didn't slow him. This time he jumped high, trying to land on me from above. I rolled under and popped up just as his feet came straight at my face. I dodged sideways, sticking out my right hand and grabbing one foot. His body kept going, pulling my arm to the absolute limit of my joints as I bent my knees. At the end of the jerk, I used my entire body to swing him in a circle and let him loose toward Josiah's house. Falling forward at the release, I expected to hear a broken window or at least a few loosening bricks.

All I got was a human's gasp, followed by the crackling of a giant bug zapper. The hu-li-roo was suspended in the air, spread eagle. Blue light pulsed away from him and rippled across the entire front of the house. The light flared red, and the hu-li-roo convulsed. Trails of smoke curled away from him, then he dropped to the ground. Josiah's house blurred for a moment, like it sat behind rippling water. It cleared, and silence fell.

I turned, expecting an attack from behind, but one hu-li-roo still laid on the ground, and the other was gone. He must have watched what happened to his partner and fled. I was tempted to run myself, but curiosity made me retrieve my katana and walk to the house. I'd knocked on Josiah's door many times last night after seeing him at the basilisk silo. Nothing had happened then. Still, I hesitated to reach for the knocker while the fried hu-li-roo stayed in my peripheral vision.

A strange idea occurred to me—probably a result of all the blood talk from Mac earlier in the day. I traded my sword for my dagger and nicked the inside of my arm, letting the blood smear on the blade. Gradually, I pushed the dagger toward the front door. Two inches from the house, resistance met the blade. Blue light sparked again. I tried to pull the blade out, but it held fast. The handle warmed as the light formed a bubble that enveloped my hand.

"Shit." I couldn't let go.

I squeezed my eyes shut, prepared to be electrocuted. Following my death, my name would likely be synonymous with 'idiot.' "Don't pull a Bochs," would become popular words of warning.

Though my entire body tingled, I felt no pain. I risked opening my eyes. The light shimmered to bright white just before the hold on my dagger released. I fell against the door with a sigh of relief. It opened easily, but the lack of locks no longer surprised me. Josiah had a hell of a defense system.

"Josiah," I called, mainly out of house-entering protocol. A lit-up hu-li-roo outside his front room window would not have gone unnoticed.

Inside the foyer, a small table with a bowl for keys stood with a mirror above. I glanced inside the bowl and found my throwing knife. "Hmmph." I sheathed it in my boot.

From the doorway on the left, I searched his front room full of comfortable, masculine furniture in earth tones. A grandfather clock announced the passing of time throughout the silent house. On the other side of the hall was his office, furnished with cabinets, a desk, and even a highly unreliable computer. They always dropped files or translated typing into an alien code, if they even powered up.

At the front window, plants drooped on a staggered tier stand. I should have left. Instead, I went over and touched each one while thinking happy plant thoughts. I also watered them with the half-full watering can on the floor. I waited a minute, but nothing happened. Either I was a moron, or MacDuggan was crazy. Probably both.

I went to the back of the house and inspected the spotless kitchen, clean from its dark hardwood floors to the bay window of the breakfast nook. No lights brightened his backyard. The yard was darkness with trees marked by deeper shadows. I continued on, glancing in a sparsely decorated guest room before reaching the garage door. The garage smelled of oil, fertilizer, and all the other things that a man kept in his garage—except his car.

Sighing, I closed the door and contemplated the staircase. I'd never been invited upstairs, and Josiah probably wasn't here. Then I recalled how he let himself into my apartment, sat in my favorite chair, and read my books while eating my chocolates.

I went upstairs.

A gasp of pleasure escaped me when I entered my dream room. It boasted gym equipment, a sparring mat, and an interesting array of weapons that numbered twice as many as mine. It only lacked a bed.

With its spacious floor plan, large bathroom, and walk-in closet, it had to be the master bedroom. I wondered where the man slept.

I sauntered across the hall to a jack-and-jill bathroom connecting two bedrooms. One bedroom was empty. The bedroom at the front of the house had a loft and two giant windows with a view of the lawn. Cautiously, I climbed the loft ladder, not sure what I feared to find. Josiah with a lab coat wrapped around his neck and Sophia's stiletto heel through his eye, maybe. Other than a giant bed with a pile of twisted sheets and blankets, there was nothing suspicious. I'd pegged Josiah as a make-the-bed-every-morning type, so maybe he'd left in a hurry.

I'd just descended the ladder when the pop and sizzle of the alarm sounded. Blue light exploded into the room. Dropping to the floor, I elbowed my way to the window and peered through the bottom corner. A slim throwing knife suspended in the air like the hu-li-roo fifteen minutes earlier. It fell to the ground, and the light disappeared.

A lanky man about my height with short gray hair stood on the sidewalk a few feet in front of the house. He wore khakis and a blue polo, but his stance shouted military. Four Evolutionaries flanked him, wearing more hardware than Josiah had in his master bedroom. Doyen of Discipline, Richard Graves, and his merry band of Enforcers had come calling.

Graves still stared at the house when I backed out of the room and went down the stairs. His voice boomed through the halls. "Doyen Hightower, we've detected a disturbance at your residence. Please, come out!"

I didn't think he meant the 'please' part. He sounded like a negotiator humoring an armed criminal with hostages. I hugged one wall of the foyer and crept toward the door. In the office, the ailing plants were a riot of vines and blooms. Damn it, I was as crazy as MacDuggan.

Shaking my head, I slid to the corner of the foyer and eyed the response team through the front door transom. The Enforcers behind Graves consisted of Waya, a stocky man named Carter, and two others I didn't recognize. Graves's eyes sharpened on my hiding spot. The man didn't miss much. He'd been a high-ranking soldier before his appointment to Doyen of Discipline a year ago.

"I need to speak with you, Hightower. If you don't come out, I'll be forced to send a man inside."

Good luck with that. I retreated to the corner. Graves was a jerk with far more authority than he deserved. If I could ignore him until he left, I'd avoid a lot of trouble.

He didn't wait very long. "Waya! Go to the door."

Not a jerk then, but a complete jackass. The fried hu-li-roo was visible in the flowerbed, and since Graves had been smart enough to throw a knife at the house, he knew exactly what had happened. I watched Waya approach. His body moved with confidence, but sweat beaded at his hairline.

I held my breath, hoping Graves would change his mind. My hand gripped my dagger like a security blanket. I licked my lips. Waya got to the porch and stopped to look over his shoulder. Graves nodded without a twitch.

"Son of a bitch." I threw the door open to glare at Waya a foot in front of me.

His eyes widened, then he relaxed with a smile. "Hey, Bochs."

"Doyen Hightower isn't home," I announced for Graves to hear.

The Doyen of Discipline stalked up the sidewalk. "And just what are you doing here, Miss Bochs?"

"Watering his plants."

Waya snorted.

It was half the truth, at least. "I can't let the English Ivy wither while he's in San Antonio."

"He never made it to San Antonio," Waya said. "No one knows where he is."

"Waya." Graves barked. "Stop giving intel to the skirt."

Wow. I leaned against the door jamb and crossed one jean-clad leg over the other. "What the hell's a skirt?"

Waya chuckled, taking in my stance with his blood-warming smile. "I miss the leather."

"Retreat, Waya. I'll handle this."

"Yes, sir," he drawled and joined the others.

Great. Being handled by Graves was one of the many reasons I didn't want to be an Enforcer. He'd requested an Enforcer application from me three times in the past year. I'd declined each one. Not that he would have liked me anyway, but it wouldn't help me here.

Graves stepped onto the porch, shoved his hands in his pockets, and rocked back on his heels to look over Josiah's house like a prospective buyer. A man with his personality shouldn't have eyes the color of smooth, dark chocolate. When they met mine, nothing warmed their depths. "I need you to come to headquarters and have a chat, Miss Bochs."

I stayed put. Graves had no direct authority over me, and as no warrants for my apprehension had been issued, I didn't have to acknowledge his request. Unfortunately, I was curious. "Why is the Doyen of Discipline investigating an incident at the Doyen of Defense's house? Doyen Hightower has a hundred Eliminators on hand to deal with his problems. He doesn't need you and the Enforcers." An idea occurred to me. "In fact, it's why I'm here. Everything is under control, Doyen Graves. You may go."

Graves' head fell back, and the sound of rocks on a cheese grater came out of his mouth: his version of laughter. "Hightower told you how to pass his defenses? Right."

"I'm inside and you're not. Explain that." Actually, I hoped he could, because I was stumped.

Then his square jaw lifted. An unpleasant smile stretched his mouth, making me sorry I'd issued the challenge. "I intend to; but first, I'm going to explain you. When you refused my application request the first time, I thought you might be nervous. The second time, I decided you were arrogant. But the third . . ." He stepped so close I felt the energy of the defense field charge. "The third time I realized what your problem is. So, I'm confident you'll come out here when I tell you that I'll send each of my Enforcers in to get you. One at a time. Until you come out."

He held my gaze, and I felt my pulse quicken as my anger neared its boiling point. "That's a big waste of manpower just to talk to one arrogant Eliminator."

His smile widened. "We'll start with Waya."

He would. He'd go through each of them, then call headquarters for more. The fault for the deaths would be his word against mine. My heart would feel the blame, regardless. D.J. wasn't the only person who'd figured me out.

I moved forward quickly, treating the barrier as if it didn't exist and pulling the door closed behind me. My skin warmed. Resistance pushed against me briefly before white light flashed. Graves stumbled off the porch, barely staying on his feet. It was petty of me—causing all that energy to ignite in his face—but he deserved it.

While Graves recovered his eyesight, I marched up to the Enforcers, all of them built like efficient killers. Waya stayed put, wearing his cool smile. Carter took a hesitant step toward me then backed off. The other two circled me slowly and stood behind my shoulders.

"What the fuck is that?" Waya jerked a thumb at the hu-li-roo I'd punched.

I felt a twinge in the general location of my heart. I'd never killed anything resembling a human. I hadn't meant to. "Not sure. Maybe you should bag it up and take it to Dr. Bennett."

"I'll give my men their orders, Bochs," Graves said behind me.

The slightest flicker of disdain fluttered between Waya's long eyelashes before he held a hand toward the street where five horses stood. "Did you bring a ride?"

"Nope." I'd driven my truck to the Silent Sector where it was stuck, thanks to Atlas—again. I didn't have much patience for horses, preferring to drive or run wherever I went. A vehicle with a mind of its own wasn't ideal transportation.

Waya grinned. "You can ride with me."

I shrugged it off and followed him. Surely I couldn't get myself into trouble with so many witnesses—not the Waya kind of trouble, anyway. I wasn't quite out of hearing range when Graves muttered, "Carter, bag those two things and bring them along."

None of us reacted to a door opening across the street. A couple of curious neighbors already stood on their porches, shifting their weight in a manner that said they would jump inside at any moment. When the newcomer walked down his sidewalk, I expected a demand for information. The sawed-off shotgun he removed from beneath his bathrobe shocked me.

Waya tried to push me behind his horse. I jerked away, preferring to take my chances with an unreliable firearm over getting kicked by a Clydesdale. Aside from alleged military prototypes, guns malfunctioned constantly. On the off chance a gun didn't explode when fired, the bullets disappeared—and not into targets. The theory was that the magnetism of Atlas disrupted bullet trajectories. In short, the bald man squinting down the barrel wasn't likely to hit me. The horse was.

"Hands off the lady!" The man shouted.

Ah, how sweet; and no one touched me. Graves moved to the front of our group, his hands placating. "Sir, I assure you she's in no danger from us. This is just a standard M-kes operation. We all work together."

"I saw the whole thing! She fought those weird creatures, then Hightower's house let her right in." The man motioned toward me with the rifle, and despite my knowledge of firearms, I cringed. "I've seen her here before. *She's* okay. But not you. I know she doesn't want to go with you."

Oh, boy. I cleared my throat and stepped forward, but Graves shooed me back. "Stay out of it, Bochs," he snarled without taking his eyes off the neighbor. I crossed my arms and stifled a sigh. If I hung out with the antiquated Rifleman and Graves much longer, I'd be using my katana to make home-cooked meals and cut out patterns for my dresses.

"Then she doesn't have to go with us." Graves sounded pretty convincing. "We'll get on our horses, and if she chooses not to accompany us, we'll leave. Is that acceptable?"

Even across the street, I could see the glint of his eyes swiveling between Graves and me. I smiled reassuringly. Or I thought I did. He pivoted the rifle toward the horses and fired. A spray of broken asphalt pelted the horses, which reared and screamed. Two of them took off down the street.

Graves and the Enforcers jumped Josiah's black iron fence just as another shot splintered the tree branch above their heads. They disappeared into the foliage. Waya's head emerged but quickly dropped down when the man fired again. His voice called to me, muffled by leaves. "Bochs, get the hell out of the street!"

I stayed on the curb through the entire scenario that lasted a minute, at most. A Normal who challenged a group of Enforcers led by a hardass like Graves should have been nervous as hell. Rifleman stood relaxed, his face calm, his eyes on the prize—in this case, a cluster of trees where he'd sent an elite force running, tails tucked. Either he was an absolute nutcase, or he acted the bumbling neighbor. Considering he had a functioning rifle, I went with the latter. I crossed the street.

He never looked my way, but he smiled. "You can leave now, darlin'."

"Nice. Who are you? Josiah's personal henchman?"

"Just a concerned neighbor who doesn't care for bullies."

I studied the cluster of trees where not a single leaf rustled.

"Graves is a bully, but if I don't go with him now, he'll have his entire force after me by dawn. And he'll get Provost Allen involved."

For the first time, Rifleman's brow wrinkled. "Here's what I know. Josiah's house accepted you. This Graves fellow knew it wouldn't let him in, which is highly suspicious."

"What kind of alarm system is that, anyway?"

"It's special."

"As in, not Normal." I couldn't bring myself to call it magical, though MacDuggan's presence was so thick in my mind that I expected him to materialize.

Rifleman smiled. "You should use extreme caution before you knock on any doors in Brookside."

I took in his shaved head with its hint of stubble, his shiny effective gun, and his suede slippers. "You're not very Normal, either."

"Now, that's just mean."

"I have to go with them, though I appreciate your effort." It was a shame for him to go to all that trouble, but he'd enjoyed it.

"Consider yourself warned, then." He kept his rifle trained on the trees. "I'll just keep them pinned until you mount a horse."

"I have one question before I leave."

"Shoot." He didn't even guffaw. Impressive.

"Do you know how long those creatures have been around Josiah's house?"

"I saw the first one this afternoon. I think Hightower put his defenses up last night or early this morning, but I haven't seen him in days."

If Josiah didn't want to be seen then he could easily arrange it.

"If I were you, I'd find out who made those unnatural beasts," Rifleman suggested.

"Made them?"

For the first time, his eyes left the trees to look into mine. They were a kaleidoscope of green and brown. "Those things are man-made. I'd stake my gun on it."

His face became fuzzy as I focused on my memory of the hu-li-roos. Pieces of the last two days locked together, and realization dawned. "Son of a bitch." I laughed a little. The hu-li-roos really were sons of a bitch. No wonder Josiah had told me to stay away from Sophia Bennett.

CHAPTER NINE

With my hands free and my weapons still on my body, I wasn't technically a prisoner. No one gripped my elbow and propelled me down the hall. If I made a move Graves didn't care for, that would all change.

Graves hadn't even issued a warning to Rifleman when the neighbor backed into his house and closed the door. Shocking, considering the size of Graves' ego.

"This way, Bochs." Waya poked me in the shoulder and nodded to the stairs going down when I started toward the Admin offices, instead.

"We're not going to Graves' office?" I asked.

"Nope. Enforcer interrogation."

I paused mid-step and met Waya's innocent gaze. The interrogation rooms were for captured Eliminators who went AWOL or those suspected of helping them. "All I did was kill a hu-li-roo and water some plants."

Waya smiled wide, showing his fangs. "Don't worry, Bochs, we won't hurt you."

Then his hand covered my elbow, squeezing constantly as we descended deeper into M-kes. My chances of getting out gradually lessened. The hallways in the Enforcer division of M-kes were narrow, dark, and laid out like an intimidating maze. As Waya escorted me farther into the labyrinth, each echoing footstep seemed to toll: you'll never leave.

Graves had gone ahead, leaving the Enforcers to ensure my deliverance to the small room where he waited for me. Since he smiled, I decided to, as well—just to shake things up. The Enforcers stopped at the door, but I sauntered inside.

Without an invitation, I took the wooden chair across the table from Graves. "You wished to speak with me?"

He kept his affable expression, lowering his forearms to the table and clasping his hands. "I always knew you'd end up here, Bochs."

"Interrogating you? I'm a little surprised myself."

An amused noise escaped Waya who stood in the doorway.

Graves scowled. "Leave us and close the door."

Waya straightened from his slouching pose. His eyes focused on me with an expression I couldn't decipher.

"Now," Graves snapped.

Waya's lips pursed. He sent one more glance my way, then followed orders.

My palms moistened, and I tried to take a deep, calming breath. Waya wasn't the chivalrous type. If leaving me alone with Graves made him nervous, then it made me nervous, too. "Does Provost Allen know I'm here?"

Graves' arms jerked an inch off the table, then he squeezed his hands until his fingers whitened. "I'm not breaking any rules, Bochs. You, on the other hand, left your scheduled patrol area tonight."

"I told you, Doyen Hightower asked me to check on his house and water his plants. If he ever bothers to contact you, he'll back me up." Provided he was interested in my welfare and not hiding from me because I killed his pet basilisk and discovered his silo full of deadly ingots.

Whoa . . . the thought had been a shadow in my sub-conscious, but I hadn't acknowledged it until that moment. The evidence pointed Josiah's way more than anyone's. I couldn't think of another reason for him to be at the silo and knocking me flat before I discovered it empty. He'd even tried to keep Eliminators from confronting the basilisk which could have been for the basilisk's safety instead of the opposite.

Graves found his smile again, which didn't put me in a feel-good place. "I do love the arrogance, Bochs. Usually you have the talent to back it up, but you don't look too sure of yourself."

"I'm here at your request, Doyen. I've never failed to report for a shift. There are no disciplinary actions against me."

"There's Dr. Bennett's claim that you falsified proof of kill."

I relaxed, despite the sparks her name ignited inside me. If Graves had something solid against me, he'd have brought it out by now. "That was a misunderstanding that has since been cleared up to my satisfaction."

"Not to hers." Graves leaned away from the table and let his hands rest on his stomach, looking like an amiable conversationalist. "If I were you, I'd watch out for her. Sophia holds a grudge."

I smiled. "Is that why I'm here? Dr. Bennett's hu-li-roos couldn't take care of me so she put her muscle on the job?"

"No." Graves' scowl could have melted a frost giant. Nothing annoyed a male chauvinist more than implying he answered to a woman. "What are hula-whats-its?"

"Those creatures at Doyen Hightower's house: part human, part lion, part kangaroo—hu-li-roo. They're more unnatural than a chimera." Quite a feat, since a chimera had the body and head of a lion with a goat's head protruding from its back and a snake for a tail.

Graves stilled. "You think Dr. Bennett *made* them?"

"Have you seen the shit she sews together in her lair? I can't think of anyone else with the materials and knowledge for such a thing." Well, many scientists might have done similar experiments, but Sophia had pointed her dominatrix fingernail at me so I returned the favor.

"I try to avoid Dr. Bennett's lab." Graves looked genuinely uncomfortable. "But I'll look into it."

This unexpected promise struck me dumb. Graves was quiet, too. His eyes stayed on me as his bushy, steel gray brows wriggled up and down. Finally, he sighed and leaned forward again, closing the distance between us by half. I tilted forward, too, waiting.

Graves cut his eyes to the door then back to me. "Do you know where Doyen Hightower is?"

"No."

He kept staring with his shake-down look. Eventually, he appeared satisfied yet disgusted. He settled back in his chair and rubbed a hand down his face. Technically, I'd told the truth. Josiah could have gone anywhere after I watched his backside disappear over twenty-four hours earlier.

Graves looked tired and a little defeated: not his typical arrogant doyen self, at all. "Look, Bochs, you need to—."

I never learned what I needed to do because voices rose in the hallway then the door swung open with authority. Provost Allen stood on the threshold, fiery in a crimson shirt and a garnet silk tie with a ruby the size of my eyeball pinned to it.

But his eyes chilled. "What is this?"

I'd never been fought over by two men. Considering they both ignored me and neither was younger than fifty, the effect wasn't quite the stuff of dreams. Allen stormed in, and Graves stood to meet him. I surreptitiously vacated my chair and went to stand against the wall. From Allen's hissing accusations and Graves' amusing sputters, I gathered the provost expected to be informed when an Evolutionary went to interrogation, no matter the situation.

"I thought that was why you were here, Provost. Didn't Carter find you?"

Allen snorted. I didn't believe it, either. I kept my eyes on Graves who never once looked or signaled my way, so I was surprised when a hand gripped my bicep and pulled me from the room.

"What?"

Waya's palm covered the lower half of my face. He pushed me against the wall of a now empty hallway. "Shhh," he whispered, his lips brushing my ear. "I'm helping you. Come on."

Thinking straight proved difficult with his body pressed against mine. I gave him a shove, more for my hormones' benefit than as a display of independence. He stepped back and tilted his head toward the end of the hall before striding away. Clearly, he expected me to follow like a lovesick Evolutionary.

I went. Curiosity would be my downfall.

Our steps synced, echoing through the empty, marble tomb of M-kes. Eliminators on duty patrolled; Enforcers hunted; and Normals got to go home at the end of a regular work day. I paused, wondering why Provost Allen stayed after midnight.

Waya grabbed my hand and jerked me deeper into the Enforcers' hall. I let him lead me while I speculated how the argument in interrogation progressed. Allen had been as red as his shirt, and though Graves never lost his stoic demeanor, I'd caught fear in his eyes. I was so lost in contemplation that I didn't realize we entered cold storage until a wave of freezing air cooled my skin.

I pulled from Waya's grasp and stepped away from the open steel door. Dead Eliminators and Enforcers stayed here until their autopsies—done by Sophia, of course. The thought of her having custody of my remains encouraged me to stay alive more than anything.

"I need to show you something, Bochs. This is why we showed up to Hightower's house so fast. Why we need to find him."

No one who risked their life daily wanted to see solid evidence of their mortality. It depleted the confidence required to do the job. Shaking my head, I motioned him in first. He calmly complied.

Despite the refrigerated air, an unpleasant smell assaulted my nostrils. Waya unzipped the first of seven body bags placed on metal gurneys, and I wrinkled my nose. An emaciated, gray body lay inside. The skin pulled so tight against the skeleton it looked like nothing was between it and the bones.

"What is that?"

"That's Johnson."

"What? How?" Johnson was a twenty-two-year-old blond with dimples and biceps the size of my calves.

"He's bloodless. Practically all of his tissue is just gone." Waya swept a hand down the line of body bags. "The rest of the Eliminators we've found are exactly the same, except for one thing." His mauve eyes pierced mine. "Johnson was found in Hightower's backyard this morning."

I bit back a string of curses and shook my head. Josiah wasn't stupid enough to leave a dead body in his yard. Yes, he pissed me off, and I suspected him of something I might not approve of, but he protected by nature. Unless I'd judged him poorly, Josiah would never kill an Eliminator in his care.

"Wake up, Bochs. Hightower is missing, and he's leaving a trail of mummified Eliminators behind him." Waya grabbed my upper arm, but I was too stunned to protest. "Where is he?"

"Why does everyone think I know where he is?"

"Because he's always had a special interest in you." The sneer in Waya's voice put ugly emphasis on his claim. "Everyone knows he visits your apartment all the time."

I pushed him away. If he placed any more nastiness into his words, I'd need a shower. "Our relationship is, and has always been, professional. Some men have a handle on their libidos."

I stormed out, satisfied with the dark tint of Waya's cheeks after I accused him of no control. I headed for the Admin hub and the quickest way out of the building.

Waya caught up with me. "Andee wait. I'm sorry."

I didn't know why I stopped. Probably because he used my first name, and it threw me. I certainly didn't believe his apology.

He did achieve a look of remorse, though, right down to the puppy dog eyes—if puppies had purple eyes. "I didn't mean to accuse you of anything. I'm just worried about you, that's all. And maybe I'm a little jealous."

I cocked a brow.

"Hightower earned your trust, which I know is hard to do, because I've tried. I wish you would believe me when I tell you I just want to help. They've got orders to stop you at the front. Come this way."

He was completely pathetic. So was I, because instead of doing it my way, I let him lead me like a dumbass sheep. I thought we headed for the train station running behind the labs and across the back of the building. I didn't come to my senses until he turned me up the sloping walkway to Sophia's lab.

I dug in my heels. "Oh, no. I'm not going to Dr. Bennett's Experiment Palace."

"Andee," Waya chided. He pressed his muscled chest against my shoulders and firmly gripped the railing to my left. He couldn't completely cage me in because the walkway was too wide, but I felt his strength. And I knew his speed. His warm breath tickled my neck. "Bennett couldn't hurt you if she wanted."

At the risk of sounding arrogant, Waya was my male counterpart: quick, strong, and smart. I could probably get away from him, but it would cost me a lot of energy and maybe some blood. After that, I'd have to run. Fast.

I angled my chin over my shoulder and our eyes locked as I weighed the odds. His smile widened. Then Sophia's voice reached my ears and traveled to my stomach where it curdled like sour milk. "Bring her up, Thomas."

I'd already decided to wait, so I just widened my eyes at Waya. "So, you're Bennett's muscle? Does she call you 'Thomas' while she whips you with her lab coat?"

Waya moved forward, forcing me to walk or get pushed over the railing to the unforgiving concrete twenty feet below. "Ours is a professional relationship." His mimicry of my voice didn't flatter.

He wasn't capable of professional relationships with women. Josiah had kept other female Eliminators away from Waya, too. He didn't like Josiah for many reasons, but I think the chess game with female Evolutionaries burned his pride.

Sophia stood in her doorway, looking fresh despite the hour: lipstick applied, hair in place, lab coat wrinkle-free. Her eyes looked hungry, and they focused behind me. I couldn't sneer—I had trouble controlling my thoughts around Waya, too. I wondered what kind of magic Mac would claim Waya had.

"Why are you doing this, Waya?" I asked before we reached the cobbled landing.

"I'm still helping you. Dr. Bennett realized that you need your ingots replaced. She believes Atlas affects your brain."

I'd accused MacDuggan of the same thing just hours ago. I stopped at the top of the ramp, ignoring the push of Waya's hand on the small of my back. The very asteroid in question glowed through the atrium walls and ceiling, washing the lab in a suitable, sinister red. I snorted and crossed my arms.

"Why else would you be so trusting of Hightower?" Waya asked.

Sophia smiled, her teeth reflecting Atlas light like the ghost of blood. "See, Miss Bochs? I knew you behaved oddly. You're innocent of wrongdoing, and I can get you back to normal tonight. We want to help you."

"Were your hu-li-roos after me or Josiah?"

Her pretty brow wrinkled. "My what?"

I hadn't really expected an answer. I gripped the catwalk railing with my left hand, right in front of Waya's. "Since when do you perform ingot replacements instead of surgeons? Thanks for the offer, but I'll wait."

When Waya pushed harder, I resisted then rolled to the right. My sudden move put him off-balance and he pitched forward. Using his back as a springboard, I vaulted over him. As he got an up-close view of cobblestone, I belly-slid headfirst down the railing. My awkward dive roll at the bottom ground my shoulder into the floor, but I jumped up sprinting. Running down the marble hallway to the front of the station would attract too much attention.

I reached the derelict glass elevator when Sophia shouted. "Get up and catch her, you imbecile!"

A snort of laughter escaped me while I splintered the plywood across the elevator opening with a push kick. Sophia made an excellent villain. I didn't turn at the sound of Waya's steps on the ramp. I jumped in, angling my left foot toward a metal brace in the glass wall. I pushed off to do the same with my right foot. Pinballing all the way down the shaft slowed my fall, but my landing still sent a shock through my ankles.

"What the hell, Bochs." Waya's voice echoed from the top before I kicked out the bottom and took off.

He'd expect me to go through the dark subway tunnel that led to the train station, so I ran toward Jeff's lab and the locked glass doors instead. I weaved through the lab tables of lesser scientists, grabbing a stool before running across the pinwheel maze. Beyond the glass doors, darkness, abandoned buildings, and monsters would hide me. I threw the stool at the glass.

Before it reached its destination, Waya's form appeared, flying across the night sky. He grabbed it, landed, and spun, releasing it right back at me. It was such a pretty move that I forgot to duck.

The stool hit me square in the chest and knocked me across the maze. He leapt for me and I rose just enough to jump on a lab table. My body broke tubes and equipment in musical accompaniment as I performed an ugly backward roll. Clutching my chest, I landed in a crouch behind the table.

"Come on, Bochs. This is a waste."

I had no breath to respond. My chest ached like a manticore stepped on it.

His movements were barely audible. I peeked around the corner of the table and saw his back in the windows. He prepared to leap over my hiding spot. I picked up a microscope. Drawing a real weapon would be the equivalent of throwing down the gauntlet. I wasn't ready to challenge Waya like that.

When he jumped, I rose and swung the microscope, catching him in the ribs. He landed on the table and rolled away before I could land a hit to his abdomen. Dropping my weapon, I tried to jump on his back, but he moved too quickly. His elbow caught me in the throat. He twined one leg behind both of mine, taking us to the floor where he won top position.

Waya smiled triumphantly as his legs squeezed mine together and he trapped my right arm. He couldn't grab my left, though, and he didn't notice the dropped microscope within my reach. I grabbed it and swung a glancing blow at his temple.

His eyes rolled up, and he collapsed on top of me.

I enjoyed a half-second thrill, then shoved him off. "Sorry." I ran, hoping to be far away before he woke up.

I took four steps toward the glass doors. Squat shadows dropped from the helipad above, bouncing up like the floor was a trampoline. A line of them bounded into place to block my way. Atlas reddened their corpselike pallor. Hu-li-roos.

I drew my katana. Waya didn't fall into the category of Sophia's creatures—yet. Killing the hu-li-roos didn't bother me anymore.

Their grating laughter ground against my eardrums, but I kept smiling—even when three more dropped down to total seven. Sophia's heels clacked against the spiral staircase to my left. She emerged from behind the fake tree. "Keep her here!"

The hu-li-roos scooted on their kangaroo feet, trying to edge around me. I backed up. An alarm blared, bouncing off the cavernous lab walls, and I realized my mistake. The hu-li-roos weren't there to attack me. Sophia wanted to keep me busy until Enforcers answered her alarm. I couldn't escape a group of Enforcers.

Sheathing my katana, I turned toward the brick and concrete subway tunnel.

"Stop her!"

Only two hu-li-roos were close enough to answer Sophia's command. They stirred the hairs on the back of my neck as they both leapt for me. I squatted into a duckwalk and they collided above my head.

"Idiots!" Sophia's heels stacattoed across the cement floor.

Inside the dark tunnel was a large steel tube that children had once slid down from the top floor. I hopped into the open bottom then shimmied up and out of sight just as more hu-li-roos entered the tunnel. They hopped past, heading for the hallway that led to the restrooms and the train station.

"What the hell?" The startled voice of D.J. carried down the tunnel.

Sophia's firm steps passed my hiding spot and stopped. "Miss Chadar, which way did Bochs go?" There was a beat of silence before she asked, "Are you sure?" Her suspicious voice barely rose over the alarm.

D.J.'s voice warmed with assurance. "Yes. She ran that way when I left the bathroom. Do you need her? Better hurry, Dr. Bennett."

I had an urge to slide down the tube and go wherever D.J. told me. Sophia's steps faded along with hu-li-roo laughter. I slid out of the tube, hands ready to grab any flying, furry feet. D.J. stood at the base of the tube with her arms crossed.

"Thanks." I smiled. "Which way?"

She jerked her head backward, pursing her lips. "I sent her to the trains."

"Perfect." I rolled out and ran the other way, past a brick column.

Halfway up a set of stairs, D.J.'s whisper reached me. "What is going on?"

"You'd better stay away, D.J." I hurried up the stairs then ran to an all-but-forgotten door beyond Sophia's lab. Behind it, wood, tarps, and hardware piled beneath layers of dust. Two by fours blocked a door on the far side of the room. Beyond the door was an old footbridge that spanned the railroads before descending into a district full of shadowy, abandoned buildings perfect for hiding.

I'd had to make a fast choice between running and giving myself up to the right person.

I had no clue who that would be. Even if Provost Allen understood as he'd led me to believe, he supported Sophia. Graves didn't seem fond of Sophia, but he liked me even less. If Josiah were here, he might be the first in line to lock me up.

I kept prying boards from the walls when D.J. entered and stopped behind me, forbiddingly silent.

"Either help or go away," I said.

She grabbed a board and ripped it off.

"You better hope Sophia doesn't catch you in the lie, or she'll put you under the knife, next."

D.J.'s shocked face briefly filled my vision as I turned for another board. "She was going to operate on you? Was she going to turn you into one of those—those—things?"

That stopped me short. It hadn't occurred to me that I might be an experiment. "I don't know. But you need to be careful, ok? Don't let Dr. Bennett touch you or convince you to replace your ingots."

D.J. sniffed. "I'm the one who can talk people into things. Did you hear how fast she believed me?"

"About that." I pulled off another board. "When you get someone to do something they normally wouldn't, does it feel—I don't know—magical?"

D.J. stared, then she grabbed my head and pulled my eyes level with hers. "Are you okay? Did they hurt your head?"

I slapped her hands away and started working again.

"Are you about to go missing, too?"

I just gave her a disgruntled look and kept moving.

"At least I'll know you did it willingly. Did you hear? Three more Eliminators and two Enforcers are missing."

I paused. Now Enforcers entered the tally. This was bad.

Shouts and running steps echoed in the cavernous lab below. I picked up the pace. "Are you coming with me?"

"What?" D.J. seemed surprised. "No, I can't keep up with you. Besides, I'm not even sure why you're running. Are you in trouble?"

I didn't answer, having pulled the final board away and kicked the door open. From my belt, I grabbed a small pouch full of dried green leaves. I handed it to D.J. "Shut these doors, spread this through the halls, then do your best lying."

She opened the bag and frowned. "Mint? We've always been told that the stories of its effects aren't true."

Early Atlas fables claimed that min inhibited the olfactory nerves of creatures with a preternatural sense of smell, Evolutionaries included. I'd used it a few times to gain an advantage over monsters. I wasn't dead, so maybe it worked. If it hid my scent trail from the Enforcers, I'd carry it forever. "I've recently decided to challenge everything I've been told. I'll start with mint and see what happens."

"How recently?"

"About five minutes ago." I stepped onto the bridge. An ominous creak spread from beneath my boot. "I have some things to figure out, but I'll be in touch. Be careful. Don't trust anyone but Dr. Trotter."

She closed the door and I started running. The quarter-mile long footbridge was the size and shape of an Amtrak passenger train with a glass roof and walls. Concrete pillars supported it, and the trappings of an old freight-train bridge surrounded it for aesthetics: repurposing at its finest.

Stars and Atlas lit my path. I glanced down to miles of train tracks and stationary engines softly illuminated with red light. Hu-li-roos hopped over tracks and through train cars. The clatter of several different locomotives filled the yard, covering the pound of my boots across the creaking bridge. They never looked up.

A brief wave of relief tickled my senses when I reached the end without Enforcers swarming the bridge. After descending the stairs into an empty parking lot, I stopped long enough to study headquarters hundreds of yards away. Beams of light flickered and crossed each other at the front. They moved away from me instead of coming closer.

"There's a point in the mint column."

I couldn't count on my luck continuing, so I ran through the broken asphalt and sporadic plant life of the parking lot. The shadows of abandoned restaurants that had once been abandoned warehouses hid me. I stuck to the darkness, following a set of freight train tracks no longer in use.

Slowing down, I filled my lungs with cold night air, trying to get my brain out of survival mode and back into decision condition. I'd already had a run earlier that night, plus two fights. I was tired and hungry, and a north wind bit through my hoodie, making me wish I'd dressed with vagrancy in mind.

A good, two-mile run would get me to my apartment. Then I could say, "Hello," to the Enforcers who probably waited there. Until I knew my allies, there was no going home. I'd have to make do with my belt of gadgets, the thirty dollars in my pocket, and three chocolates. I unwrapped one and popped it into my mouth then climbed the screeching metal rungs of a fire escape. On top of the brick building, I surveyed the Kansas City nightscape.

My eyes were immediately drawn to my apartment building, the tallest in the city. Solar rods on its roof winked mockingly at me as I thought of the kitchen I'd stocked with food and of my favorite fleece throw draped across my couch. I tore my eyes from what I couldn't have and looked elsewhere.

Slowing down gave me time to plan. It also gave me time to notice the aches and pains of an active evening. My chest throbbed where the stool hit me, and I probably had bruises on my back in the shape of kangaroo feet. My body needed transportation, which meant a horse until Atlas set in a few hours and cars worked again.

My wandering eyes caught site of a fire near Bartle Hall, a few blocks away. At first, I thought a fire frog had snuck away from the nearby bog, but this fire held steady and stationary. I headed for it.

Not many homeless people lived in Kansas City. The brutal truth was that they provided easy meals for things that went bump in the night. Anyone who survived the streets of a beast-riddled city was tough. I hoped that one would also be a helpful survivor and point me in the direction of food and a horse.

It took me nearly ten minutes to get to the barrel fire. I spent the time wondering if D.J. was okay; what the Enforcers were doing to my apartment; and if I'd ruined Waya's face with the microscope. My stalking skills never failed, but one of the figures huddled around the barrel looked up before I reached the halo of firelight.

"Who's there?" She was she shortest of the three, but the bravest as she moved toward me. The other two slid behind the barrel. The girl looked like a pre-teen, but given the circumstances of her life, she might have been older.

I stayed in the shadows, stretching my empty hands in front of me. "That's a nice fire." I didn't know anything about starting conversations with kids.

"You want by the barrel, it'll cost you," she replied.

She wore short sleeves and jeans, and stood far enough from the fire now that she should have been cold. She didn't show it. Usually, vagrants didn't make fires in the spring. They saved fuel and kindling for the bitter cold of winter.

"You don't look like you need the fire. Why are you wasting it?"

She tossed her dark ponytail and snorted. "I can make fire whenever I want." She held her hand open, and a tiny flame erupted from her palm as she grinned. She probably frightened strangers away with that trick on a daily basis.

A couple of days ago, I might have jumped. However, I'd since seen MacDuggan turn into an Evolutionary; been convinced that I somehow had a magical green thumb; and been favored by a house that fried what it didn't let in. I entered the light completely, and her smile disappeared.

"I'm not interested in your fire, kid. But I'd be careful with that talent. There are others nastier than me who would be very interested." Sophia came to mind. "I just need a horse and maybe a sandwich. Know anyone?"

She let her hand drop by her side. "You're an E-freak. They don't give you a horse?"

E-freak was a derogatory term for Evolutionary that no one had used in my face since I was thirteen. I took a deep breath and reminded myself that I wanted something from this kid. If it turned out she had nothing, then I could scare the shit out of her. "They're fresh out."

"Collie," she called over her shoulder.

A teenage boy came out from behind the barrel, looking like he'd much rather go back. The firelight reflected in a large pair of sad, brown eyes, and I knew how he'd gotten his name.

If I didn't have crazy hearing, I would have missed his soft words. "There's a man down by thirty-five has horses. I don't know 'bout sandwiches, but Ol' Nita roasted a tatzelwurm her son killed last night. She'll sell you a kabob or two."

"Collie!" The girl glared at him. "If she wants info, she got to pay."

I might not have been hungry enough for roasted tatzelwurm— basically a stubby serpent with the head and front paws of a cat. Then again, no other offers had materialized. "How much?"

"What you got?" she asked.

Right. "Ten bucks."

She cut sly eyes to Collie. "That means she got twenty."

Saw that one coming.

"You give us ten, Collie will take you to Old Anita's and the horse guy." She stuck out her hand.

I pulled a ten from my pocket and dropped it in her palm. I didn't mind handing over ten of my last thirty dollars to homeless teens. I just hoped they'd spend it wisely.

CHAPTER TEN

Collie's fear of me gradually lessened as I followed him down a dark Broadway Boulevard. My spine radiated anxiety as much as his when we headed toward Union Station, back the way I'd come. Sunk in the hood of my sweatshirt with my saya tip tucked into the hem, I did my best to match Collie's strides. His shoulders relaxed and his scent changed once we reached Eighteenth Street. He wore faded brown corduroys and a shirt with holes at the elbows. Every once in a while, he'd cross his arms with a shiver then straighten his spine and pretend he wasn't cold.

We walked one of the oldest areas in Kansas City, full of brick buildings once renovated and revived only to become run-down again. The market for quaint tea houses, essential oil suppliers, and Bohemian boutiques had been overshadowed by retail more necessary to survival. The pillars of Bartle Hall with their shiny beacons stood as sentries behind us.

We advanced on a small group of young people who didn't look like they searched for legal activities while they sauntered down the weedy brick sidewalk. Collie slouched and veered toward a building front, away from the group. The leader sized me up. I smiled. He turned on his heel ninety degrees and ushered his followers across the street.

Convinced they'd cause no trouble, I focused on my guide, once again. "Do you have any talents like the fire starter?"

Collie only jumped a couple of inches when I spoke to him. "Nah. Spark's the only kid I ever met could do something like that."

Spark? That disappointed me. "Does she always call the shots?"

"Yeah, I don't mind. She watches out for us—me and her little brother, Josh. He's my friend."

We stopped at a small brick building set up like a diner. A hand-painted sign announced *Old Anita's Twenty-Four-Hour Kitchen*. Collie opened the door and stood back for me. It felt more like a gesture of respect toward a dominant adult instead of a woman. I nodded at him.

"So, does the menu consist of whatever her son killed the day before?" I asked casually as we approached a chipped tile counter.

"Pretty much. A couple days ago she had manticore stew."

"Really." The cat-headed tatzelwurms weren't all that difficult to kill: lure them with a ball of yarn, then cut their heads off. A manticore would swallow the yarn whole and the hunter with it. "I don't suppose her son found it by the old Sheraton on McGee?"

"Yeah! It knocked down a whole walkway, glass everywhere," Collie answered enthusiastically. No matter how much the world changed, boys still loved destruction.

"Hmmm." You're welcome, Old Anita. I fed more than myself when I made a kill.

I was relieved the manticore stew was gone, even if the tatzelwurm kabobs disappointed. Tatzelwurm did *not* taste like chicken. It was stringy, with a vinegar aftertaste, and I nearly choked on a tiny, fishlike bone twice. However, I finished three kabobs of the stuff by the time we reached I-35. They'd been a dollar a piece, and I'd bought three for Collie, too. The kid couldn't finish his, but he saved the rest for later.

Six dollars for a tatzelwurm meal might have been frivolous, but I couldn't have bought a horse for twenty dollars any more than I could fourteen. I planned to make an offer for the horse and keep the rest of my cash at the same time.

Landon Cates' stable wasn't just near I-35, it sat beneath it on Twentieth Street. An overpass served as the roof of the building made of bricks, broken pavement, and railroad crossties. The stable proved that city government no longer cared where or what you built so long as it was out of the way. Building inspections were clearly a thing of the past, too. I forgot the sagging walls and dripping "roof" when the smell of rotting hay, rodent shit, and horse piss overwhelmed me.

"You should hire Collie as a stable boy," I suggested.

Cates' crafty little face wrinkled in confusion. He'd been asleep when we'd arrived, so I might have had an advantage.

"A few dollars a day and that kid will make your place clean and inviting." I looked around and shrugged. "You'd get more business. Do you rent or something?"

Cates yawned. "Yeah, give me something down, and I'll give you a ride for two hours. Prices vary. I'll need a retainer."

Two hours would barely get me out of the city. I walked down the line of wobbly stalls to study a mule, a large donkey, a decent brown mare, and the biggest, most muscular black gelding I'd ever seen.

I nodded at the mare. "I'd rather buy her."

Cates laughed until his eyes watered. He was awake, now. "I ain't sellin'. It'll cost you sixty to rent her."

"Do you have any vehicles to rent when Atlas is gone?"

"I got a car."

"What if you had a truck?"

Cates frowned, unconvinced.

"With a truck, people can haul things: stuff that won't fit in their car or that's too heavy to carry by hand. You could put an advertisement on its windows, then people would bring business to you even as they rented from you."

I saw a spark of interest in his eyes, but he pretended indifference. "I got what I need."

"I have a truck parked in the Silent Sector. We can ride over there to see it. I'll trade you the key for the mare."

Cates violently shook his head. "Not the mare. She's my best. You want a trade, it's got to be the gelding."

"The gelding?" I'd expected the donkey as the counter-offer, or at best, the mule.

"That thing costs me more to keep than he makes me. Last week I had to give up an entire down payment plus rental money because the customer got maimed by a griffin. The damn horse runs straight at things he should be afraid of. No one wants to rent him anymore."

I pretended indifference this time. A horse that didn't buck at every roar was more than I'd hoped for. "He sounds like trouble. Maybe I can find something else."

I turned and walked out to where Collie waited for me, making sure I got what I needed. He was a good kid. I hoped Cates would consider my suggestion.

"Wait!" Cates followed me out. "Someone like you can control Buster, easy. He's strong, fast, healthy. I'll throw in a bag of feed."

"Buster? Can I rename him, at least?"

"Sure. Give me a truck, and you can call him 'Cates'." He stuck out his hand for a shake.

I hesitated, then nodded at the boy beside me. "Give Collie a job?"

Cates pursed his lips. Collie stilled.

"Would you like to clean stables for a few dollars, Collie?" I asked.

His eyes widened. "Okay."

"Fine," Cates said and moved his outstretched hand toward Collie. "You get here every morning and do good work, or you're gone, kid."

"Yes, sir." They shook.

"Better get some rest so you can show up," I told Collie. He started to leave, but I put my hand on his shoulder. "I owe you a tip for your help. Here." I removed my hoodie, immediately missing its warmth. It was dark green, made of sturdy cotton, and lined with fleece.

Collie gasped when I handed it to him, but he didn't argue. He had it on in a flash, then rolled the sleeves up twice for a better fit. "Thanks."

"If you ever run into trouble, come to One Kansas City Place and leave a message for me, Andromeda." Of course, I might never set foot in my building again. That caused a tiny hitch of panic in my chest.

"Okay."

I nodded at Cates. "Let's get your truck."

*****

I left Cates with his new truck and headed out of the Silent Sector before he remembered he couldn't drive it, yet. Normally, I would use Broadway and face the bog with its well-known dangers, but it was obvious. My comfort zone coincided with the Enforcers' comfort zone, so I needed to break out into the unknown. In this part of the country, going west equaled going nowhere, so that's the direction I took.

In an unusual moment of sentiment, I named my new horse Pegasus. He didn't notice the change, ignoring me no matter what I called him. For a few miles, we were on the same page. He took me the direction I wanted and never stopped, not even when a carriage full of carousing Normals veered dangerously close. My pleasure with him changed just before we crossed into Mission Hills, Kansas. A roar shook the loose concrete riddling the highway. Pegasus stopped, his ears twitching.

I dug my heels into his side. "Go." I had no time to chase down random monsters.

Another roar sounded, followed by shouts and screams. People streamed out of an apartment complex a couple hundred yards off the highway, most of them dressed for sleeping. Some of them didn't wear much for pajamas.

Pegasus galloped toward the apartments. Unless I wanted to walk out of Kansas City, I had to go with him. I sighed and went along for the ride. A large retaining pond with a dike cutting it in half separated the highway from the apartments. Pegasus dashed across the narrow strip of earth, sending rocks flying into the dark water and nearly bouncing me out of the saddle.

"Holy shit! I bet you gave Cates panic attacks."

Pegasus snorted, then leapt over a parked motorcycle and landed in the parking lot. My teeth clinked together, and my ass slammed back into the saddle. That was enough of that.

I jerked his reins, muscling his head around and shocking him into standing still long enough for me to jump off. "Idiot horse."

"My son! My son! He's not out here!" A blonde woman in a fuzzy pink nightie ran up to me, terror in her eyes. She whirled around twice, shivering with more than cold. "Daniel! Daniel!"

"What's in there?" Preparation made up ninety percent of the work with monster killing. Most Eliminators focused on the other ten percent: don't die. It was the reason they died anyway.

The woman pulled on her hair. "My son!"

A tall man came beside her, and I looked to him for help.

"Three tunnel rats," he answered. "Big ones. You got here fast."

Great. M-kes had been called, which meant the people I ran from would be here soon. "Can you get everyone to move over there?" I pointed across the parking lot to another apartment complex with a working Koi pond.

"Yes, ma'am," he answered.

He put a restraining arm around the woman who wanted to run inside, and used his other to wave at the crowd as he shouted. His polite address surprised me. I knew not all Normals supported the suppression of Evolutionaries, but the sensible were usually drowned out by the idiots. Respect wasn't familiar to me.

After he got the group moving in the right direction, he turned back. "You need anything else?"

"Save my son!" The woman screamed, tears streaming down her cheeks.

"I will." Then I answered the man. "I'm going to herd them to the retaining pond, if I can. Try to keep everyone away."

"Yes, ma'am."

Water killed tunnel rats, but not the Wicked Witch of the West kind of kill. It had to be a body of water. Submersion paralyzed them, causing them to sink and drown before turning to water themselves. It was strange, like—well, like magic.

Another roar ripped through the night, followed by the frightened cry of a child. I ran into the foyer, vaguely noticing the hoofbeats followed by an irritated horse whinny when Pegasus couldn't fit through the door. He both frustrated and fascinated me.

The thumps and growls came from above. I drew my katana, but turned before I ascended the stairs. Pegasus filled the complex doorway, stomping and snorting like a fabled horse of the apocalypse.

"Wait here. I'll bring them out," I promised. I ran upstairs, shaking my head as I realized I'd just given instructions to my horse.

All three tunnel rats gathered around a closed door. The quadrupedal, giant rats only stood three feet tall so they preferred to hunt in packs. Their teeth and claws were two inches long. Sharp, bony protrusions ran the lengths of their whip-like tails. Beneath their fur, the thick skin was difficult to penetrate with anything less than a sword.

Whiskers twitching, all three stopped ramming the splintered door and turned their heads toward the delightful smell of Evolutionary on the landing. Blood dripped from their yellow teeth and pooled around the two torn bodies in the hallway behind them. It didn't matter if their victims had died before I heard the commotion, I still cursed myself for hesitating. Dunking the rodents wouldn't be enough, anymore. I wanted to sink my katana into their flesh.

"Hey, Daniel," I called.

"Y-yeah?" He didn't sound terribly young, but not adolescent, either.

"Push as much furniture as you can against that door. I'll take care of these rats then send your mom in for you. Don't come out until you hear her, okay?"

"Okay."

I had no more time for talking. The rats opened their mouths and a collective roar filled the hall. They managed high decibels through synchronization. Swiveling as one rat, they scampered toward me.

Despite their size, they scurried as fast as a normal rat. The middle rodent headed straight for me, while the other two climbed the walls. They were as smart as normal rats, too.

I dropped to one knee, making myself as tall as the leader. Angling my katana behind me to protect my back, I grabbed a throwing knife with my right hand and shoved it into the leader's nose. It reared back, slicing its claws across my chest. A second rat landed on my katana point. The force punctured it but not deep enough. It wiggled off, gouging my back as it shoved against me.

The other wall rat toppled me from the side. I dropped my katana to grab its snapping mouth with both hands, just inches from my throat. Holding it off, I swung my legs toward the stairs and swept one rat down them. Then, I jerked my legs up and over my head, beating back the rat with my knife in its nose.

My hostage methodically shredded my arm with its claws, trying to free itself. I rolled on top of it, and shifted my grip to clamp the mouth shut. The spiny tail reminded me that it existed by wrapping around my thigh and tearing my flesh. I shoved my other knee into its diaphragm, and its entire body relaxed just long enough for me to hop up and swing it by the nose.

It slammed into the wall, then fell to the floor with a pile of plaster. The knife-nose rat leapt at me. I roundhouse kicked it into the other wall. I grabbed my katana and shoved it through the rat's neck, right behind the head. It took all my body weight to force the blade through. The rodent convulsed and squeaked, pinned to the floor by my sword.

The last rat shook plaster from its eyes, saw what I did to its buddy, and took off down the stairs. I started after it, but from the top step I saw Pegasus blocking its way, standing over the pulverized body of the tunnel rat I'd sent downstairs earlier. My horse reared slightly, showing off his rat-stomping hooves. The surviving rat turned and ran down the hall, out of sight.

Putting my foot on the now-still body, I pulled my katana free. I thought the thing was dead, but I nudged it down the stairs, just in case. Pegasus kicked it in the head for good measure while I skipped stairs to the bottom. The emergency door at the end of the hall clicked closed behind the survivor.

Damn. Damn. Damn.

Out in the open, I was faster than a tunnel rat, but the Normals weren't. I busted through the door, sprinted around the corner of the brick building, and halted. Two Eliminators stood over a decapitated rat body lying beside a freshly churned mound of earth: the tunnel rats' point of entrance. One Eliminator held a wicked, horseman's ax dripping with fresh blood.

"Oh, well, good then." For everyone but me. I forced a smile, praying that these particular Eliminators didn't recognize me any more than I did them.

"Hey, Bochs," the ax-wielder said. "What are you doing over here?"

Well, they already recognized me. I could only hope they knew nothing about me as I lied. "My parents live in Mission. I was just headed over there after my shift."

"Mission?" The other one snorted. "Brave people." Mission wasn't patrolled as much as it should have been. Some called it The Edge of Death. If my parents really lived there, I probably wouldn't visit.

"Is that your horse guarding the front?" axman asked. "He's wicked."

"Yeah, he's great." He'd been helpful, but he still annoyed me. "Well, I better get going." I walked by them, my lips moving in silent thanks that Atlas ruined communications. These two didn't know of my trouble with M-kes.

"Hold up."

I stopped, struggling not to let my shoulders droop. "Yeah?"

"You're bleeding all over the place. Let me patch you up a little." The shorter Eliminator already had a bandage roll out.

"Oh, you don't have to."

The axman slid his weapon into a leather strap on his back and grabbed a tube of ointment from his jeans pocket. It took them five long minutes to wrap up my left thigh and my right arm from shoulder to elbow. I'd bled a lot, and I was hungry again. This would be a long night on the run.

The axman tied off my final bandage when the pink nightie lady ran up to me. She opened her mouth, but I cut her off. "He's fine. Go get him."

"Oh, my God, thank you! Thank you!" She knocked axman backward to get her arms around me in a hug that set my torn back on fire.

"Sheesh," I wheezed. I didn't meet many grateful Normals. Right now, that didn't feel like such a bad thing. I pulled her arms off. "He's scared. You better go."

Axman chuckled as he watched her run away. "I can't remember the last time a Normal woman hugged me."

"Probably never," his partner offered.

"What are your names?"

"I'm Lajani," axman answered.

"My name's Valdez."

"Thanks for the help, Lajani and Valdez." I stepped away from them and backed toward the parking lot. "There are two dead tunnel rats at the front door. You guys are welcome to the commissions. I just want to go home and eat my mom's lasagna."

Lajani's fangs flashed with a grateful smile. "Wow, thanks, Bochs."

"Yeah, thanks." Valdez sounded suspicious.

I made it less of a sweet deal. "The rats killed at least two people before I got here."

They didn't thank me for that part.

*****

Instead of growing lush and green like the countryside should, the outskirts of the city looked like a giant tornado had ripped the leaves from every tree and plucked the grass. West of Kansas City, everything was gray, just like Kansas in the Wizard of Oz. No vines reached for us, and no eyes watched our progress, awaiting opportunity. We approached the edge of the Dead Plains, no longer Great.

The Dead Plains was the overlap of the kill zones of three supervolcanoes: Yellowstone, Valles, and Long Valley. An excellent place to hide, it was also the easiest place to die of thirst, hunger, and exposure. Pegasus basically galloped into Mordor. I'd already taken one quest into that hell, and I had zero interest in another.

So, I convinced my horse to head north once we reached I-435 which veered toward the Missouri River and back to civilization. It was a crook-shaped journey: the staff moved west from the Silent Sector, then the hook curved northeast, into Missouri again. Somehow, I stayed awake—probably from anxiety. I sure as hell didn't have the kind of horse that felt his sleepy rider slipping and politely stopped moving.

Streaks of purple and pink colored the eastern horizon when we reached our destination. Pegasus walked up the quiet drive and through the stone-wall entrance. I slid from the saddle and immediately landed on my numb ass. Pegasus snorted amusement. I jerked on a stirrup to help me stand, and he side-stepped out of my way.

I was so exhausted that it didn't occur to me to test for defenses before I knocked on the door. I didn't smell burning flesh, so I assumed I hadn't fried when the door opened. A wide-awake Mac smiled at me. The Beast of Roslin in cat form draped across the back of his shoulders like a magic stole.

"Oh, good! You'll be interested in the basilisk dust analysis."

My hazy mind couldn't fathom what he meant. I yanked the collar of my ruined shirt down to expose tunnel rat gashes along with my ingot scars. "Take them out."

CHAPTER ELEVEN

A creaky floorboard invaded the peaceful silence. I saw nothing but black until I realized my eyes were still closed. With a deep sigh, I nestled into the softest bed ever and lifted my lids. Mac sat beside me, holding a tea tray. "Where on Earth did you find your majestic Percheron?"

All of my weapons were under the bed. I lifted the blanket. I'd slept in my t-shirt and a pair of fleece pants I barely remembered Mac handing me. Nothing majestic there. "What's a Percheron?"

"Your horse. You don't even know what you ride? Percherons were the war horses of the Middle Ages. He should be carrying a knight into battle."

I rubbed my eyes with the heels of my hands and relaxed against the pillow. "He feeds his riders to griffins and stomps on tunnel rats."

"Well then, he's perfect for you, isn't he? What do you call him?"

"Pegasus."

"That's awful. Besides, Andromeda never rode Pegasus. Well, I suppose she did when Perseus rescued her, but—."

"I know, I know." I didn't need a lesson about the original Andromeda. No one had pointlessly studied Greek mythology looking for positives more than I had. "But I'm the heroine here, and I'm tired of being the only Greek freak. Someone should suffer with me. I chose the horse."

"I happen to love your name, but then, I'm boring old Charles. Here." He stood and set the tray on the table beside me. "You slept nearly eight hours. Eat up. I'll be back."

I bolted upright. "Eight hours?"

Mac flipped a dismissive hand. "You'd been up all night. I couldn't make any sense of your talk about flammable vagrants, magic houses, and evil hula hoops."

I had to think for a second. "Hu-li-roos."

"Oh." He paused then shook his head. "Still not sensible. I stuck you in the guest room, closed the door, and left you be."

Oh God, I was so behind. I should have looked Normal and boarded a train by now. I hopped out of bed, felt a rush of malnourished faintness, and promptly sat. "We have to get this done so I can get out of here. You can take them out, can't you?"

"What, the ingots? I suppose."

"Suppose? Enforcers hunt me. They'll find your place, eventually. If your theory is correct, then I can pass for Normal once the ingots are out. Even if you're wrong about their purpose, and Atlas will kill me, I'd rather die that way."

Mac held his hands out. "Slow down. Don't worry about Enforcers. If I don't want them to find me, they won't. And Atlas isn't going to kill you, I promise. But we can't just pull the ingots out then suddenly you're Normal. I hate that term 'Normal,' by the way. Let's just say, 'you'll be whole.'

"It will be quite an adjustment. I'll have to teach you how to control your magic and the outward signs of it. Plus, I'd rather remove them when Atlas isn't on this side of the world. The intensity of the magic flooding your body will be high if Atlas is near, and it rises in a couple of hours. We've got to put it off until morning."

I crossed my arms toddler-tantrum-style. Mac's sigh made me feel more like an annoying child, but I couldn't help myself. I'd made the crucial decision to get the ingots out, and I wanted instant satisfaction. I still doubted that I possessed this magic he feared would overwhelm me. I came here to lose the ingots and look Normal so I could evade the Enforcers. "I told you I'm a wanted woman, right?"

"And I told you not to worry about them. You came to me, and I intend to do things my way, on my schedule." I must have looked a little pathetic because his face softened. "You heal plants with a thoughtless touch, lass. I've no idea how much power you really have. If I don't teach you control, you'll be more obvious than you are now."

I threw myself back on the bed, now acting like a frustrated teen instead of a toddler. At least I grew up. "Waiting is brutal."

"Eat your tea then come to the lab. I have plenty to show you that might pass the time."

"Eat my tea?" I discovered a plate of tiny sandwiches and scones with the teapot and cup. Beside the plate sat a small bowl of something that looked like lumpy sour cream.

From the hall, Mac replied, "It's the most important meal of the day."

After eating all of the tasty cucumber sandwiches and half of the scones, I went to the lab. Mac's back was to the door as he sat in front of a computer. In the minute that I stood there, the screen turned black with wavy white lines three times. Mac growled each time.

"Why do you bother with it?" I stood beside him.

With a sigh he tapped a couple of buttons, and the screen went black permanently. "Because there are still calculations and applications that would take me a hundred times longer without it." He turned to me, his face thoughtful. "Before we talk about you. Would you like to know exactly what I am and why I'm here?"

"I don't know. Are you going to ruin my image of you as an intelligent, nice, though slightly eccentric, human?"

He tilted his head as his brows came close to meeting. "I don't think so."

"Okay, then."

"What I am is simple. Do you feel all those horrible wounds you walked in with this morning?"

I hadn't even wondered why I felt so good this morning. Light lines on my arms and chest replaced the gashes the tunnel rats had delivered the night before. My back and thigh had burned the entire ride before I'd gone numb in Mac's hallway. I squeezed my leg, but felt no pain. "No," I answered slowly, wondering what he'd done.

"I am a healer. While you slept, I sped up your body's healing. Some of the bruises might still sting, and you could have a few more hours of weakness from blood loss, but you're much better than the mess who walked in a few hours ago."

"Wow." Convincing me that magic existed might be easy. "Thank you."

"You're quite welcome. Now, for why I'm here. Follow me." Mac walked to a wall with a four-foot wide map of the United States full of red, yellow, and white push pins. Some were in clusters, others solitary.

He studied the map, waved his hand at it, and turned to face me.

"We'll get to that in a minute. I'll start with telling you that the E-gene is quite real, but it's not an evolutionary gene. It's a magical gene. One or both of your parents have it and passed it to you. Atlas activated the gene nearly two decades after it established orbit around Earth. The gene is dormant in any carrier born before that, which is why your parents and mine have no symptoms, no magic. Atlas is a new magic source that awakened dormant magic. Follow me?"

Maybe. I nodded.

"Once upon a time, the moon was the source of all magic. Around the year 1000, magical humans realized the moon was dying. It moved farther and farther away from Earth, making it harder to tap its magic. It took over a century for the moon to die. My ancestor, a healer, was one of the last mages to draw power from it. He wasn't strong enough to put himself in stasis like some magical beings, but he kept vast records—knowledge—that passed through generations all the way to me."

"Stasis?"

"A deep, magical sleep. There are warlocks, witches, and other Magics out there who just awoke from a thousand plus years nap. Not many managed it. Some probably died centuries in because they just didn't have enough magic to sustain them until Atlas arrived. It was a guess that the moon would be replaced, and no one could predict Atlas' arrival; not even the most powerful seer." He stopped, a question in his eyes.

"Got it. Please continue."

"Did you know that North America has, by far, the largest population of Evolutionaries?"

"Yes. I've heard it's because three of the world's six supervolcanoes erupted here. The massive outpouring of mythical beasts required the largest number of Evolutionaries to battle them."

"A sensible explanation." Mac nodded. "It's tripe."

"Is that like shit?"

Mac wrinkled his nose. "Yes."

I tucked my lips in to avoid smiling.

"Here's my theory. When magic died, North America hadn't been colonized, yet. Over the centuries, most people who immigrated here looked for new lives, and a lot of them wanted to forget the past. Where many magical traditions stayed intact in the Old World, much was lost on the voyage to America. The Indigenous Peoples had Magics, but their eighteenth and nineteenth century uprooting and genocide nearly eradicated their oral tradition and ethnic memory of magic. There are still pockets of Indigenous Magics but I found them with great effort.

"In short, a large percentage of parents in the rest of the world had the knowledge to recognize magic in their glowing babies. Most Americans didn't have that memory. Thus, it was easy to convince them that something was horribly wrong with their children, and they accepted the miracle treatment offered."

"Are you saying this wasn't a misdiagnosis or scientists reading results incorrectly? Parents of Evolutionaries were tricked?"

"Yes." He turned to his map. "Even before I earned my degrees, I studied the statistics of Evolutionaries: where they were born, what age when they were reported, what hospitals performed their ingot implanting. It troubled me as a child. My parents, both in scientific professions, encouraged my investigations. While I believe that Evolutionaries are magical just like me, my parents—and many others—suspect that Evolutionaries are black magic gone wrong: a product of another magical being."

I held up my hand. "So, you think I'm magical because of Atlas, but your parents believe that someone magical *created* me?"

"Manipulated your genes would be more accurate. You're definitely human, born of humans. Don't ever think you're unnatural." He faced me, his blue eyes intense and his voice firm. I once read of something called A Crusader's Fire to describe the passion in one look. Today, I understood it. Mac hated the thought of me or any other Evolutionary being an outcast. He really did despise the term 'Normal.'

Warmth spread through me, starting with my ingot scars then tingling to my fingers and toes: the comfort of acceptance. "I won't."

"Good." He shook himself. The intensity faded. "Now, where were you born?"

"Chicago."

He picked up a yellow push pin and stuck it in the middle of at least fifty covering Chicago. "And in what city did you receive your implants?"

"Chicago."

Red pin. "Do you see how there are no yellow or red pins in

lesser cities or rural areas?"

"Yes, but there are hardly any people there, anymore, and no hospitals."

He nodded. "True. According to this map, all reported Evolutionary births and implanting occur in metropolitan areas. However, I've found evidence of many unreported Evolutionaries throughout the continent. I did this through news, interviews, travel, and investigation. Most of them are in their teens to mid-twenties, with skin that occasionally glows and abilities that no one can explain." He raised a strong finger in the air. "But, they are also a part of close-knit communities—mostly relatives—that protect them from testing, discovery, and implanting. Some avoid the ingots because of their religion, while others simply don't trust science. They are the white pins that you see, none of them near a metropolis."

He waited quietly as I stared at his map and absorbed his words. I'd never paid much attention to the Evolutionary population outside my own little sphere. Since the resounding message had been 'your child will die if you don't get them implanted,' parents had wanted their babies tested, wanted them saved. White pins strung out from Canada to Mexico. Most of them were east of Kansas City; but nearly everything was east of here since Death reigned between the Missouri River and the Pacific Ocean. One cluster of white caught my eye.

"You found people in Western Oklahoma?" It wasn't quite as desolate as say, Colorado, but no one wanted to live there.

Mac nodded. "A unique group. They thrive in the location and weren't particularly pleased when I found them." He paled, and I thought that might be a story worth hearing another day.

"Have you kept track of these Evolutionaries? Of their health?"

"Yes. They are all quite healthy, none of them dying or even ill. The oldest is thirty-two, like me . . . and she had twins last year."

He dropped the last like the bomb he knew it would be. My eyes jerked from the map to meet his. Evolutionaries were sterile. Plus, no recorded Evolutionary babies had been born to Normals for nearly a decade. I expected to fight off beasts into my golden years because I had no replacement. The government forced Evolutionaries to rid the country of dangerous creatures before we all died off.

I sat down hard on the stool behind me and brought my knees up for an elbow rest. The official word claimed that Atlas' radiation sterilized Evolutionaries. My hand to my heart, I rubbed the scars beneath my shirt. "The ingots make us sterile?" I whispered.

Mac's voice was just as quiet. "Yes."

A torrent of emotion rolled through me: anger with no target. Being sterile because of Atlas was dumb luck, an ironic price for evolution. I never railed against an inanimate object in the atmosphere, blaming it for my situation. Things suddenly became personal.

Someone had decided to make my skin blue. Pressing my palms against my abdomen, I felt ill at the knowledge that people, not Atlas, stole my choices. Someone had put silica inside me, knowing what it would do to my body, knowing that I didn't need it.

I dropped my head into my hands, wishing Mac would leave the room for a while so I could process. I heard him come closer, then felt a firm hand on my shoulder that made my body shudder with the emotion boiling beneath my skin.

"I don't know if removing them will change that part." His voice comforted. "But I will fix everything else, I promise. We'll get you whole, then we'll help the others. We'll show them the truth, and set them free."

"Whoa." I sat up, dislodging his hand and holding out my own. "I'm a fugitive with my own problems, not some crusader."

He stepped away, and his cheeks flushed. "Sorry. Sometimes, I get carried away with my mission to save magical humanity." Turning his back, he walked to one of his lab tables. "Let's focus on you and your problems."

Sarcasm tinted his voice, but he couldn't make me feel guilty. He'd just inundated me with a flood of information that destroyed the foundation of my entire life. I felt no shame in my selfishness. "You've been working on this for decades, and just told me all of it. Maybe give me more than thirty seconds to adjust."

Mac sighed, and his stiff shoulders relaxed. "I'm sorry." He gave me a small, repentant smile. "I need to tackle one project at a time. Right now, that's you."

I stood. "I need a break." Actually, I needed to get the hell out of there before I started screaming. "Do you mind if I get a little exercise outside?"

"You spent an entire night on the run and you need exercise?"

"It's my version of tea."

"Ah." He nodded to the window nearest him. Night had completely settled about his house, and the surrounding forest looked like an army of shadowy monsters waiting to greet me. Perfect.

"I own the surrounding eighty acres, and beyond that there's really nothing, anyway. BOR keeps the woods pest-free, and she won't bother you, now that she knows you."

I had my suspicions on that, but I could handle an oversized housecat if she gave me trouble. "Thanks."

*****

My chest heaved as I leaned against a giant oak at least three centuries old. It had been awhile since I'd run through nature. That it took so much out of me disappointed. Kidney shots from hu-li-roos and furniture to my sternum hadn't helped. Maybe Mac had only healed the visible wounds.

Mac's forest was quiet. Creepy quiet. He hadn't exaggerated 'pest-free.' If I wanted an uber-cougar or two to break up the monotony, too bad. I trotted a few more yards to the clearing around the house then drew my katana, ready for some practice after my warm-up.

Stars lit the yard, but Atlas hung so low in the horizon that the forest blocked it from view. I still felt it: a persistent squeeze in my chest, all the more irritating now that I knew its secrets. Fueled by frustration, I moved my katana in fluid figure eights as I lunged across the yard. When I reached the edge, I pulled my dagger. I sidestepped right, slashed back left with my katana, then lunged forward with my dagger.

Methodically, I worked my way to the other side, lunging backward as I sliced, stabbed, and dodged in mock retreat. I didn't even smell the cat before I turned and came face to face with the green-eyed pain in the ass. I brought the katana up defensively and stepped back, keeping the dagger loose and ready.

She was in beast form, giving me more of a closed-lip growl than a snarl. I glanced at her paws: claws sheathed. I looked back into her glowing orbs. She blinked.

I straightened and let the tip of my sword drop slightly. "You want to play?"

She stretched back until her belly touched the ground and her paws pushed three feet in front of her face. A rasping noise came from deep within her chest. She blinked twice more.

Of all the weird things dumped on me the past forty-eight hours, sparring with a beast topped them. She snorted when I put my weapons away to avoid accidentally killing Mac's pet. She didn't think I could hurt her with my sword, anyway.

I bent my knees and left my hands hanging loose but ready. "Alright, BOR, let's go."

She leapt, aiming her head into my abdomen. I jumped, tucked, and flipped, using my hands on her back to catapult myself over. I twisted before I landed so I'd be facing her, but she wasn't there.

A rush of air warned me soon enough to evade a rib-bruising blow. Her paw still caught me in the hip, twirling me like a dancer. She immediately pounced, but I dropped into a ball as she sailed inches above me. I grabbed one of her back legs before she landed.

She jerked it, shaking me like a toy, but I held on. Squatting deeply, I seized the other leg out from under her and swung her through the air. She outweighed a hu-li-roo by a hundred pounds, so she only sailed a few feet, but she was off-balance when my jump-kick nailed her under the chin.

While she shook the stars from her vision, I jumped on her back, driving my feet into her ribs with all my weight. I sat and squeezed my thighs, expecting her to shake me off. She rolled instead. I couldn't adjust before her weight crushed me to the ground.

I gasped for air as she got to her feet and crouched for another pounce. Coming to my knees, I caught her mid-leap with a double-fisted punch to her feline diaphragm. I heard the breath rush from her lungs, and she flipped behind me.

"Right back at you."

She tried to circle around me, and I countered with a smile. She didn't snarl, so I decided we still played. Unfortunately, not everyone saw it that way.

Pegasus shot around the corner of the house: darkness galloping from the shadows. He headed straight for BOR just like the rats last night. BOR switched her attention to him, fangs bared and claws out.

"No, Pegasus!" I shouted, wishing I knew how to train a horse. I sprinted on an intercept path and hoped one of his massive hooves wouldn't hit anything vital. Just as I shoved my shoulder into his side and sent him off course, Mac appeared.

He put his arms around the panther's neck. "Stop, BOR." He

crooned in her ear with a heavy burr. "It's alright. He's protecting her. Relax, girl."

The cat's eyes snapped, but she closed her mouth and laid down to let Mac pet her.

"That horse doesn't give a flying fire frog about me. He's a lunatic."

Pegasus whinnied in offense then stomped in agitated circles.

"Jackass," I muttered.

"No, that's a horse, lass."

"Funny."

"How did he even get out?" Mac wondered. "I had him shut in the stable with Gael—a fine name for a horse, by the way. You should consult with me next time."

I looked at my horse, standing proud and innocent as if he hadn't just tried to run over a giant panther. "I think this is my last horse."

"What did you pay for him?" Mac cleared his throat. "If you don't mind the question."

"My truck."

He left BOR purring on the ground and circled around Pegasus. "Normally, I wouldn't take you for a savvy business woman, but I think you won in that deal."

"I don't."

He stepped up to Pegasus and rubbed his neck. "Do you suppose he's magical?"

"I think fanatical more likely, but sure, why not. Everyone else here is."

Mac squinted at me through the darkness. "Get a little grouchy with hunger, do you? Are you finished working out your emotions through violence, or should I keep supper warm?"

Since the first response that entered my mind was to call him a jackass, I decided on food. "I could eat."

After securing Pegasus with Mac's chestnut gelding in the stable—the old millhouse—we went inside. I sat with a sigh, then immediately jerked back up when BOR rounded the corner in housecat form. She'd been a panther when we walked through the front door. I rubbed my tired eyes and sat again.

"We were just sparring. I wouldn't kill your BOR."

Mac laughed. "No one is worried about that, lass."

His back was turned so he didn't catch my glare. The lack of faith in my abilities around here really irritated me. I hoped he cooked meat. My fangs needed to sink into something more substantial than cucumbers. Maybe my need for violence wasn't quite satisfied.

CHAPTER TWELVE

"I'd like to do a before test of sorts, if you don't mind."

I sat in the guest room, surrounded by whatever Mac needed to remove my ingots: scalpels, gauze, tongs, gloves, and things I didn't recognize. "Before test?"

He pulled a glass box from his pocket. "Pieces of Atlas will change color according to the magic of the individual touching them. Would you mind?" He held the box out and opened the lid.

I blew out a sigh: been here, done this. The rock flickered between green and black when I touched it.

"Good," Mac said as he pulled it away. "I think the ingots confuse the Atlas rock so that it can't detect your brand of magic. The same happens when a Magic with perceiving skills tries to read an Evolutionary. It's why so many Magics think you're a product of magic instead of magic yourself. Look what the rock does when I touch it."

The rock shimmered and transformed to look like molten platinum though it kept its shape. "That's the color of healing magic," he informed me. "I suspect yours is a form of Earth magic given what you've done to my plants. You're probably an Earth mage or maybe even a fairy."

"A fairy?" I craned my neck to look between my shoulder blades. If I wrecked more clothing by sprouting wings, Mac would buy me a new wardrobe.

"Only sky fairies have wings. You're definitely earthy."

I raised two fingers and tapped my pointy incisors. "And these?"

"There are accounts of fae with fangs. As I've told you, the magic source is different which means the magic is different. Plus, I doubt every account handed down through the ages remained uncorrupted."

Hmmm, I ran my tongue across the points of my fangs. "As long as I'm not a vampire."

"Vampires don't exist."

"Neither did fairies five minutes ago."

Mac shook his head like a frustrated school teacher. "A being whose heart has stopped yet needs blood for survival isn't sensible."

"Of course not." I wriggled all of my fingers in front of me. "It's magical."

"You'll see," Mac promised. "Now finish that tea. It contains a sedative you'll be thankful for."

I took a sip, and its bitter warmth made me cringe. "So, how deep are these things?"

"Just in the first layer of muscle. It's their location over the heart that's the important factor."

I drained the cup in one fast gulp. "Bleh."

"Now relax. I have plenty of healing power to take care of the incisions. Plus, your magic will help you heal."

I laid back on the bed and closed my eyes. My limbs sank into the soft mattress. That tea did quick work.

The last words I heard were "Of course, if I nick an artery, you're in trouble."

Ass.

*****

Sometimes an ingot replacement gave me a fever for a few hours, but never heat like this. Fire licked the inside of my skin, searching for an exit but finding no freedom. The source swirled deep in my core, sending out more energy, more heat, until a scream ripped from my throat.

The sound shattered in my skull, slicing my mind with sharp fragments. Bursts of green and yellow light blinded me. I tried to cover my eyes, but immovable strength held my limbs. Lungs full of fire struggled to bring in air. I thought I was on the Source Expedition again, running through toxic air and stumbling across desolate lava plains. My heart raced at an alarming pace, and my limbs ached with the exertion of a five-mile run to nowhere.

Then darkness came. Slowly it rolled from my belly, replacing fire with ice. The light in my head intensified, flickered, then disappeared beneath shadows. Whispers in a foreign language swirled through my broken conscious. Then one word I recognized pounded with my heartbeat: free, free, free . . .

The price was excruciating. I tried to shake the web of whispers from my head, but movement brought waves of pain that filled my ears and pushed against my eyes. Creeping, oozing shadows slithered through me. I slipped below the surface, drowning in darkness. The cold left me weak and heavy. I couldn't remember why I struggled. The abyss extended an invitation. I relaxed, and it consumed me.

*****

Death should be a peaceful event without growling and thudding. I dared open one eye, slowly, expecting a burst of light or a flood of suffocating darkness. I saw the guest room.

It looked different. The doorknob, window, everything loomed higher, like I'd shrunk. Oh God, I turned into a fairy, or a pixie, or some tiny, weak being. I sat up. A wave of nausea rolled to my head, and I laid back with a thud. "Ow." Double-ow. My throat stung, and my voice croaked.

The noise stopped, and curiosity practically radiated through the wall. Then the door rattled with banging more forceful than before.

I stared at the ceiling and slid my hands away from my sides, feeling the wooden planks of the floor. I had no clue why I laid on the floor, but at least I'd stayed normal size. I rolled to face the bed, and my hand met resistance. A warm spark like static electricity shocked my fingers. I drew back.

My skin was lightly tanned with a rosy glow that lit up the tiny hairs on my arm. Faint white lines marked rat claw gashes. I held my arm in front of my face, turning it to marvel at the tiny pores and the light blue veins. I took stock of my body, trying to note anything different. It just hurt, as if every punch, claw, tooth, and blade that had ever hit me had come back at once. I sighed, and my throat burned.

On the floor, a white substance formed a line where my fingers had been shocked. I cautiously sat up again, and the nausea stayed at bay. The white line completed a circle around me.

Something heavy hit the door, shaking the hinges and reverberating through the floor. A feline growl rolled from the hall. I ignored BOR and looked at the place I last remembered. Now Mac sprawled on the bed, face down with one arm hanging off and his fingers brushing the floor. His clothes were wrinkled, and his white shirt stained as if he'd sweat a gallon. Half his hair plastered to the back of his neck, and the rest stood straight up from his scalp. The lashes of his visible eyelid fluttered. Another thud shook the door, and his eye popped open.

"Morra, miff, arrghh." He spoke around a mouth full of blanket. His eyes squeezed tight, and he rolled onto his back.

Thud. Shake.

"BOR! I'm fine. Go away."

A low growl, then silence.

I kept my eyes on Mac, watching his chest rise and fall with deep breaths for at least a minute before he looked at me. "How do you feel?"

It was a simple, polite question, asked with a calm voice. But apprehension filled his eyes, and his hands fisted.

I felt like I'd been beaten by a herd of trolls, then had a flanged mace shoved down my throat. I managed a whisper. "Sore."

His body relaxed. "I'll get something for that throat, lass. You sound terrible." He stood with hands out. "Just stay there a moment. I had to contain you, so don't try to go past the salt circle."

Unexpected rage burst from my belly in a nauseous wave. The effort to subdue it left me shaking. I should be free, not trapped more than ever. "Contain me?"

He looked frightened again. "It's temporary, I promise. You nearly killed me. But now that you're conscious, we'll get you out in a controlled, safe manner. Sound good?"

Now I was frightened. I nodded, and he left the room. I couldn't have assaulted him while experiencing that horrific assault of my own. Impossible. I couldn't even lift a finger as the fire and darkness fought to control me. My weapons remained on the large cedar chest at the foot of the bed. Yet, I'd alarmed Mac so much that he'd magically imprisoned me.

I sat cross-legged in a meditative state when Mac returned carrying a tray with—what else—a pot of tea. He'd combed his damp hair and changed into a crisp pair of khakis with a light blue golf shirt. As he walked to the bedside table, the cups rattled in their saucers.

He poured two cups without spilling, then squeezed half a lemon into one, followed by a spoonful of honey. "The lemon and honey will help your throat."

He sat outside the circle, facing me. When he passed his hand through the invisible barrier, it glowed like mine. He set a cup in front of me. "You did a lot of screaming. I'm sorry I didn't realize how painful this would be for you."

I studied my own softly glowing hand before I picked up the cup. The sip burned slightly, then soothed enough for me to whisper. "It was worth it." Probably.

He appeared doubtful, too, but he nodded and drank his tea. His face completely relaxed, and he quietly sighed. The man loved his tea. "The other mistake I made, was believing that removing the ingots when Atlas was gone would take care of the overwhelming magic issue. Instead, you took magic from everything else, myself included. It was odd."

He shook his head and looked out the window where the soft light of dusk barely penetrated. "I'm no perceiver, but I could see colored waves of magic flowing from all directions through the walls, coming straight to you. I was afraid you'd explode, but you just kept absorbing and screaming. BOR ran off into the forest, but I don't know how far she had to go. You sucked magic from the trees. I gave you another sedative, and it slowed you down. It had to be fast, so I injected it. Sorry."

I looked down at the inside of my left arm and a green bruise with a bandage across it. Despite the disturbing details, I smiled. "You stopped to give me a bandage?"

Mac was offended. "I am first and foremost a healer."

I drank more tea. "Thank you."

He inclined his head. "I had enough power left to get you to the floor and make a containment ward. Then I collapsed and slept as long as you did." He gave me a long, serious look. "You've got tremendous power, lass. This is going to require time and great care."

"I understand." I did. It didn't keep my hands from itching for my weapons, or my heart from beating wildly. Wild. That's what I was: a wild animal trapped in a circle. I closed my eyes and forced deeper breaths.

Mac's voice pierced my panic with the assuring comfort of a

healing professional. "We'll start by gathering information, then together we'll decide how to move forward. Okay?"

I opened my eyes to him holding the Atlas rock again. He placed it in the circle with me, and it vibrated slightly. "Am I doing that?"

"Yes, but don't worry. You'll have that under control by sunrise. Just touch it, so we can know exactly what we're dealing with." He pulled a giant white binder from the nightstand behind him and opened it. "This is a catalog of magic colors down to the very shade. It will tell us not only the Earth part of your magic but the precise brand."

"Well, we already know I'm not a fairy. I'm still big."

He snorted, then cleared his throat. "Sorry. The fae aren't all small. Some of them are bigger than humans and quite ferocious. But I think you're right. If you had fairy blood, your family would have protected and passed the knowledge over the years. Just touch it, lass. It won't feel any different than before."

I reached a cautious finger toward the rock. If I could fail a rock-touching test, I would. The Atlas rock did nothing for seconds while my finger rested on top. Maybe I didn't have magic, after all. Then, it rattled beneath my fingertip. The surface turned the deep green of a mountainside forest.

I breathed a sigh of relief.

"Hold on," Mac ordered as he turned pages. "Keep it there a moment."

I did, thinking the green beautiful and peaceful. Then the change began. "Mac."

From beneath my finger spread a net of black lines across the green. It formed an intricate pattern that looked like old-fashioned, black lace overlaying the green.

"Huh." Mac paused with a page in his hand and stared at the rock. He slammed the binder shut and set it aside before jumping to his feet. "That won't be in there." He opened a drawer to rummage through it, saying, "Don't break contact. Keep touching it."

I couldn't stop. I twitched my finger, and the rock twitched with me, melded to my skin at my increasingly warm fingertip. "Should I feel heat running up my finger?"

Mac sat in front of me with a sketchpad and a pencil. "Perhaps . . . a little. I need to draw this pattern before it disappears. The green is the color of Earth magic; Celtic Earth mage, to be precise. I've never heard of a pattern appearing, or even more than one color."

"Did you test the rural Evolutionaries you found?"

He drew quickly, sticking his tongue out a little as he kept looking back and forth. "Mmm-hmmm."

My finger glowed white hot, then it spread to my hand. The rock trembled beneath me. "I think you better hurry."

"Yes, yes." His pencil flew over the paper. "Okay, you can stop."

I tried to pull my finger away, but it stuck. Somehow, the small rock had become so dense that I could barely drag it. "I can't." The heat built. It didn't flow through me, burning me from the inside out like before, but it was intense.

"What?" Mac was perplexed. "Just pull it off."

I took a deep breath, tensed my muscles, and jerked my hand. The rock exploded into glittering dust, pushing me against the circle's shield. I hung suspended a brief moment. Tiny shocks traveled through my body, then I fell on hands and knees. Mac's ward must have been a lot weaker than whatever Josiah had around his house, because it didn't scramble my brain.

Mac stayed put, his mouth slightly ajar and his eyes wide. A layer of rock dust covered the floor inside the circle. "You broke my Atlas rock."

I sat on my heels, dusting off my arms and face. "Sorry."

He looked down, and childlike disappointment filled his face. "It's in your tea."

I stared at the cup, wondering if I should apologize for the tea, too.

Mac shook himself and stood up to pace. "We need to document all of this." He pointed a finger my way without looking. "Don't move. I need a sample."

I couldn't handle the circle much longer. Energy and frustration steadily grew within me. Mac continued walking, mumbling, and rubbing his chin.

"Why don't you take the sample, now, and grumble after?" I suggested.

He dashed out of the room. I stayed cross-legged, closed my eyes, and purposefully tensed every muscle in my body while holding my breath. Slowly, I released the air and relaxed, picturing myself sinking into the earth. Peace gradually replaced frustration. I smelled fresh cut grass and rich soil.

Cautiously, I opened my eyes. My attempts at relaxation were usually lame and fruitless without my katana to clean, but it worked fairly well this time. My skin no longer glowed. The constant vibration of the floor disappeared, too.

Mac rushed back in carrying tubes and tools. He reached into my circle and collected his samples.

When he finished, I said, "Look at me."

The distraction of the destroyed rock left his eyes as he truly studied me. A satisfied smile stretched his mouth. "I knew you could do it." He felt the floor. "Very good, lass. Would you like out?"

I considered barking and running in a circle, but he probably wouldn't appreciate my joke. I settled for nodding.

"It's almost dark and Atlas is close." He warned. "When I break the circle, you'll feel the magic rush in, trying to balance, like osmosis. Don't fight it. Let it in, and it will balance itself. All you have to concentrate on is controlling your reaction like you did within the circle. It will be a little harder because there will be more magic. Understand?"

"Yes."

I waited, expecting him to speak some spell or begin a complicated process. He simply put his hand in and swiped a section of the salt away. Sparks ignited my pores and warmth coated my skin like body armor. It was the same reaction as always to Atlas, except stronger and without silica implants pulling me away from the magic. Magic sank into my blood, searching for my heart, my brain, my nerves.

"Control the glow, lass," Mac whispered.

I closed my eyes and focused on breathing, relaxing.

"That's it."

The sparks receded, leaving a pleasant tingle along my skin. Life like I had never felt it pumped through me. The air smelled sweet, earthy. When I opened my eyes, a new brightness intensified the colors around me. I focused on Mac. A hint of magic glowed beneath his skin and shone in his eyes. I'd never noticed the electric blue lining his cobalt irises.

"I see your magic."

He nodded. "And I see yours, but it's subtle, nothing a non-magic will notice. You're doing very well."

Raising my hand, I touched the soft skin just below my eye. "Could I . . . see myself?"

"Lord, I'm thoughtless!" Mac jumped to his feet. "Just a moment."

While he was out of the room, I stood. My muscles trembled, but energy hummed through me. A rumble filled my stomach. With a little food, I'd be back to normal.

Mac returned with a handheld mirror. "Sorry, I wasn't thinking." He offered the mirror to me with a slight bow.

I raised the looking glass. My long, silent study of myself must have made him nervous because he couldn't stay quiet. "What do you think?"

"Well, it's me," I replied around a growing lump in my throat. I probably just needed more tea.

Simply seeing my arms and hands hadn't done the change justice. Both my parents showed in my face, now, where traits of them had been hidden by blue skin, fangs, and crazy purple eyes. I had my mother's eyes, green as summer grass. My hair hadn't changed from the auburn many shades darker than my mom's; but my dusky skin was somewhere between that of my fair mom and my swarthy dad.

No longer shaded by periwinkle skin, my cheekbones stood out like my handsome father's. Somehow my long nose and wide mouth looked more like his, though they hadn't changed. They looked good on him. On me . . . I couldn't decide.

I parted my lips to see a row of strong, white teeth. I ran my tongue under the even set. An unsettling thought wrinkled my brow. "If I'm just a mage, why did I have fangs?"

"I've thought about that." Mac took the mirror. "It's possible the fangs were a side-effect of the ingots and whatever magic they were cursed with, having nothing to do with your specific magic."

"But I know Evolutionaries without fangs. Why wouldn't it happen to all of us?"

Mac shrugged, less concerned than me. "Earth magic is broad. It's possible that since animals are sometimes involved with your magic, the fangs showed up. Or, maybe Atlas' magic determined that Earth mages require fangs whereas the old moon magic didn't. If they pop out, we'll deal with them. It's easier to walk around with your mouth closed than your eyes."

"Have we met?" I asked.

Mac chuckled. The pleasant sound made me smile.

If he had no worries, then neither did I. "Okay."

"The Atlas rock doesn't lie, which means you're an Earth mage. A powerful one, judging by the way you disintegrated my rock before I even broke the circle. I think the little piece tried to give as much magic as it could because you were still inside my ward which blocked magic from Atlas itself. The rock exploded with effort."

"How many Atlas rocks are there? Yours is the third I've seen in a week."

"Countless. Many non-magics have even collected them."

I remembered Provost Allen's confusion about how his worked. "Do they react to Normals, too?"

"Not usually. I saw it happen once, when a non-magic had been in prolonged contact with a powerful mage. She had residual on her skin."

"The M-kes Provost doesn't know how his rock works."

"That's not a surprise." He stilled. I sat on the edge of the bed while he seemed to weigh words in his head. "You do realize that M-kes is full of Magics posing as so-called Normals, yes?"

"I figured." Now I knew Josiah really wasn't Normal; and when I found him, he could explain why he never bothered to clue me in on the truth. A sliver of betrayal knifed through my heart, depressing my spirit. Josiah didn't trust me.

"Provost Allen could be magical, pretending to be naive."

One glaring characteristic made me doubt this. "He's older than my dad."

"Hmmm, it's true that the oldest Magics—or Evolutionaries, as you call them—aren't over forty; except the sleeping Ancients, and I've never met one of those rarities."

Allen's words and actions replayed in my head. "He was cautious of the Atlas rock. Plus, it wasn't the only weird rock he had. He may have been afraid of the other one. Instead of touching it, he threw a blanket over it to pick it up."

Mac moved in front of me and lowered his head, like a grown-up about to communicate serious words to a child. "What did this rock look like?"

"Black and porous."

One hand slapped his forehead and slowly moved down his face until it stopped to squeeze his chin. "How big?"

"Barely the size of my fist."

"Did you touch it?"

A lump of fear filled the space where I'd wanted food a few minutes earlier. "Yes."

"What happened?"

"It turned my skin the color it is now. And it made me warm. He was surprised by that part. I think it must make him cold when he touches it."

Mac stared at my hands and without looking up asked, "Are you sure it made you warm?"

Uh-oh. "Yes; like when I touched the Atlas rock earlier. Only it didn't explode."

He studied my hands like a difficult puzzle.

"Is it dangerous?"

Mac bit his lip briefly before answering. "In the wrong hands, yes, very dangerous. It's a *malus molaris*, and there aren't many of them about. Mainly because a person has to travel to the heart of a supervolcano to retrieve one."

"The heart?" My pulse quickened with just the thought. I'd been on the perimeter of a supervolcano with the bravest people I'd ever known. None of us would have dared go inside. "Why would someone do that?"

"Power. A *malus molaris* was formed with the same black magic that incubated monsters within supervolcanoes until Atlas arrived. Atlas didn't just activate the magic genes of humans. It also triggered the balancing dark magic inside volcanoes. When the monsters were ready, the volcanoes erupted and released them. A *malus molaris* sat at the heart of that magic, feeding on it. If a strong enough Magic gets hold of one, they can store and save an incredible amount of dark magic."

I wanted to scoff, but I'd seen the line of terrifying creatures leaving the Yellowstone Caldera. I believed Atlas had fed the volcanoes until they erupted and destroyed much of the world. I *knew* volcanoes made beasts to finish the job. "Provost Allen might not even know what he has. He had the rock sitting on an office table like a conversation piece. Is he in danger?"

"If he's not a Magic, the rock just makes him uncomfortable. It creates cold and a strong, illogical fear."

"That explains the blanket."

Mac studied me, willing me to look at something I ignored. I dropped my gaze to my hands, now permanently the color that the *malus molaris* had turned them a few days ago. "The rock made me warm because it fed on my magic, right? My black, terrible magic."

He squeezed my hands with one of his. "I don't think so. All accounts claim that the rock makes everyone cold and afraid whether it's taking magic from them or not. I think, maybe, your magic fought the rock, causing the warmth and the physical change." He gently tipped my face up to look into his. "Don't worry, lass. You'll be fine. But tell me this, and think hard, were there any bigger rocks in Allen's office? Something like a small boulder?"

"No. Why would someone keep a boulder in their office?"

"It has to do with what I found out about the silo and the basilisk."

Pounding vibrated the floor beneath my feet. Mac sat back on his heels and tilted his head. "You're not glowing. Are you afraid?"

"That's not me."

The noise continued, followed by muffled shouting.

"Oh . . . Oh!" Mac ran to the hall. "That's my door!"

I followed him downstairs. "I hope BOR is sleeping and not trying to eat your visitor."

He turned with a huff when he reached the front doors. "BOR doesn't eat people." He opened one side to a petite woman whose posture appeared old, though her dark hair was free of gray and pulled into a tight bun. She wore a black coat with a white-feathered collar over her hunched shoulders, making her look like a giant vulture. The beady eyes and hooked nose helped, too.

I'd never seen as fake a smile as the one Mac wore. "Mrs. Holt, lovely to see you."

I quietly opened the other door and leaned out, looking for her companion. Nope. A large, shiny black car sat in the drive with not a soul inside. The small woman shook the whole house by herself. I sidled back into the doorway to find her dark eyes burning a hole in me. A line of gold glowed around irises so black they nearly merged with the pupils.

I smiled. Damn, now I missed my fangs.

The gold intensified slightly, then her eyes widened. She stepped backward off the porch. "What is that?" she hissed.

Not the grand re-entry into the world that I'd envisioned.

Mac stepped in front of me and with his height, shielded me completely. "Did you have a reason for visiting, Mrs. Holt?"

I backed into the house and leaned against the foyer wall. Hiding behind men and walls wasn't my nature, but I floundered. I knew nothing of this new world or its rules and etiquette. Instinct told me she was rude, but she might be the Grand Empress of Magic who could order my death if I told her to bite me.

Her sharp voice carried into the house. "Her magic is wrong. It's shadowed."

"Her magic is perfect. It's the silica poison inside her that's wrong, and I'm taking care of it. Anything else?"

"Yes. Whatever experiment you performed this morning drew the attention of everyone in a two-mile radius. It looked like the Northern Lights. I finally tracked it down to you because the residual still glows all over your house and *her*. You'll likely have company, Mr. MacDuggan. You can't do these experiments and expect your neighbors to sit idly by in ignorance."

"Thank you, Mrs. Holt, you've been surprisingly helpful. Now, you'd best get home before Atlas rises and you have to leave your lovely car."

Mac shut the doors and leaned his head against them, closing his eyes. He took several deep breaths, reminding me that I held mine. I released it in a rush when a car door slammed and an engine started.

"What did she mean?"

Mac kept his eyes closed. "She could see the remaining darkness of the ingot magic. I suspect that's why the Atlas rock had black lines. When your blood regenerates, it will purify."

"Can you see it?"

He shook his head. "Mrs. Holt is a perceiver—a strong one. She's like a walking, talking, offensive version of an Atlas rock. She can see the exact magic of a person or thing, and she can track it. However, perceivers can only see the ingot magic when they look at an Evolutionary. That's why so many Magics believe that Evolutionaries are products rather than true Magics themselves." He sighed and looked at me, keeping his forehead on the door. "She's right, though. Others will have noticed and want to know what happened."

"I can't stay here, Mac. They'll find me." Panic gripped my chest. I didn't even know my capabilities, yet. Facing a group of Enforcers could be disastrous. "I'm not ready."

"Right, then, change of plans." He stood tall. "We're taking a trip."

CHAPTER THIRTEEN

I sat at a laboratory table and watched Mac pack up print-outs, folders, binders, even sealed containers, into a giant duffle. My jeans were clean—though they had new holes thanks to a tunnel rat tail. My current possessions consisted of jeans, boots, belt, and weapons. Judging by the size of my borrowed, yellow t-shirt, it belonged to teenager Mac or an ex-girlfriend.

Mac talked the entire time he moved about his lab. Some of it I heard, the rest passed by me as I pondered my recent life choices. "We'll take the train from Leavenworth."

I nodded acceptance before I registered his words. "What? I can't do that." I'd given him a summary of my escape and the events that led up to it. He knew I fled from M-kes.

"Why not?"

I stood and swept one hand from head to toe. "I'm an M-kes fugitive, Mac. Soldiers will be looking for me in Leavenworth, plus, that train stops at Union Station. You know that's M-kes headquarters, right? Doyen Graves could look out a window and see me sitting in the train, twiddling my thumbs."

His eyes followed the same path as my hand had. "You don't look Evolutionary to me. Everyone else will see it that way, too. They don't know what we've done. We just have to make a few minor adjustments."

He went back to work, and I watched with a growing lead ball of dread in my gut. Leavenworth was one of four military posts on the western edge of the country: the final defense before the Dead Plains. No individual branches remained on the military tree. It was just one, all-encompassing entity. The Leavenworth base existed almost solely because of M-kes.

Sure, the military could step in during an attack from a full-fledged beast army that M-kes couldn't handle; but the true purpose of Leavenworth's troops was to keep Evolutionaries in line. Kansas City boasted over two hundred genetically evolved freaks with weapons. The close proximity of the military served as a metaphorical cattle prod in case any of us decided to change the status quo.

I suspected that by now, my picture was posted at three-foot intervals in every Leavenworth bunker. "It's not a good idea."

Mac zipped a bag then gave me his full attention. "Follow my reasoning, lass. In Kansas City, it will be fellow Evolutionaries looking for you. People who know you. In Leavenworth, soldiers will merely be looking for a rogue Evolutionary. They won't recognize your walk, your voice, your mannerisms. They'll see a Normal woman and move on. Plus, we'll be on an already searched car when we stop in Kansas City. If the Evolutionaries are searching, they'll only bother with those who board at Union Station. They won't waste their time with a car covered by soldiers in Leavenworth."

He made sense, but I still worried. Aside from no fangs and Normal skin, I didn't look much different. "What minor adjustments?"

Mac seemed overly interested in the test tube rack in his hand. "Well, for starters, we'll have to cut that hair."

I grabbed my braid with both hands.

"It's lovely hair. That's why it has to go."

It would grow back. "What else?"

He looked down at my boots. "Definitely new clothing. Something you'd never wear."

"If you say 'dress,' I'll punch you."

He snorted. "It's too cool for a dress. I thought a business suit."

He'd managed to come up with something worse than a dress. "Why?"

"You're clearly most comfortable in pants. Do you wear jeans and boots every day?"

"Yes." No point in lying.

"A business suit won't be obvious for you. Plus, a dress would show those legs, and they'll get attention."

I looked down at my legs, long with muscle that stretched the flexible denim and poked through various holes. "Because they have claw marks?"

"That, too." He lazily rolled an empty test tube back and forth on the table. "And you can't wear the katana."

The air around me disappeared. I tried to breathe in a black hole, no oxygen to be found. "What?" I choked.

"Normal women don't walk around with swords strapped to their backs. It will be a defining trait on your 'wanted posters.'" I hardly noticed his use of air quotes. He was skeptical about wanted posters.

"No, no, no." Black leaked into the edges of my vision. My chest tightened to the point I thought my ribs cracked. My knees weak, I blindly reached behind me for the stool.

"Andromeda?"

I bumped the stool with the backs of my thighs and sat hard. If I left my katana behind, I might as well leave my heart with it. My vision rippled like ocean waves, and I saw a blurry Jun smiling sadly. A forehead touched hers, then Grant turned to look out at me from my ocean of memories. His disappointed eyes pierced my soul. I clutched my chest.

Their weapons were all that remained of their doomed love: a love annihilated because I couldn't kill a monster. No katana meant no memories, and no memories meant no purpose. I'd die quickly without a purpose, then I'd be floating in a surreal sea with my friends. I felt myself falling.

"Good lord, she's having a panic attack over a sword." Hands gripped my shoulders, pushing me upright. "Breathe, lass, breathe. Look at me. Look at me."

Two blue sparks ignited before me. Air rushed into my empty lungs. My hands ached from gripping my katana to the point of pain.

"It's part of me," I gasped. "I need it."

Mac massaged my shoulders. "Alright, alright, just relax."

He used his healing magic on me. The pain in my chest lightened with each squeeze of his fingers. My glowing hands released my sword. Closing my eyes, I took a deep, calming breath. "My katana represents everything I stand for." My words hitched in something dangerously close to a sob. "I can't forget."

*****

My hair barely reached my chin. A slight wave caused the ends to flip out in a flirty, feminine way. I was adorable. I thought it might not be me, but the mouth in the bathroom mirror definitely moved when

I said, "What the hell have you done to me, Mac?"

"Cute and sweet." He appeared over my shoulder, grinning. "Look at it this way. Now, when you punch someone they're just as likely to fall down from surprise as from the hit. You're guaranteed victory."

"Hmmm." I narrowed my eyes at him in the mirror. "Keep calling me cute and sweet. You'll be the first test subject."

His grin never faltered. "The last train leaves at 10:30. We need to go."

All playfulness left my face. I hated that I'd brought trouble to his door. He shouldn't be going on the run with me, dodging danger and looking over his shoulder.

"I told you I'm going," he said, reading my thoughts as they crossed my face. "This is just as much my fault as it is yours, and I'm fixing it. Besides." He stepped into the hall and picked up two duffle bags. "I'm buying the tickets."

I sighed and turned away from the mirror. "I might never be able to repay you, Charles MacDuggan, but I will always be grateful."

The kindness I'd noticed in his eyes on the day we'd met glowed, warmed by his smile. "Then I'm repaid."

I started toward the hall, and the sole of my flip flop caught on the vanity rug, ruining my stride. "These shoes have got to go," I said for at least the third time.

"We'll be in El Dorado Springs by morning. You can get a pair of tennies."

"Aside from the name, they sound great."

I picked up a backpack full of essentials Mac had scraped together for me. Attached to one side of the backpack was a rolled yoga mat with a riot of straps at both ends disguising—sort of—the katana handle protruding from the top. Mac assured me that I only thought it didn't work because I knew it was there.

At least my over-attachment to my sword led to no business suit. Instead, I wore a pair of black yoga pants a couple inches too short. I didn't ask where he got the pants, but the Cornell sweatshirt I wore belonged to Mac. He claimed his mother left the flip-flops on her last visit.

In order to coordinate with my casual attire, Mac had traded his khakis for jeans and his golf shirt for a bright red tee with a bagpipe-playing dog and a claim that "Scotland is Heaven on Earth." It had that crisp, creased look of a gift that had gone straight to the back of his closet. He wore a navy jacket to block the brisk March breeze.

Mac opened the doors to complete nightfall, and for the first time I saw the ward of his house. It shimmered like a silver, gossamer curtain. Beyond it, the horses waited, saddled by Mac while I had stared at myself in the mirror.

I caught up with him at the doorway and studied the starlit yard. Pegasus jerked against the tree he was tethered to, and Gael stood stiffly, staring into the trees like a pointing bird dog. My enhanced sight discerned individual leaves twitching in the woods, concentrated in one spot.

Mac's foot went through the ward as I said, "Wait."

He descended the porch before turning around. "Forget something?"

Two human-shaped forms dropped from the roof and landed behind him just as three more burst from the trees across the yard. I couldn't make out details, but their torsos appeared disproportionately large. They ran like apes, long arms reaching for the ground. At least they weren't hopping hu-li-roos.

"Damn it! Duck, Mac!"

He didn't question me before dropping to all fours. I kicked off the flip flops and leapt through the ward, planting my feet solidly into one shape as something sharp sliced through my shoulder. I hit the ground and rolled, trying to pull my katana free of the yoga mat. My wrist caught in the straps, and I yanked so hard, I spun myself in a circle. The spin gave me a panoramic view of the yard. The three from the forest closed in quickly.

"Son of a bitch!" I screamed as I tried to free myself and simultaneously grab my tactical knife with my right hand. I forgot about control as my frustration mounted. The pressure of magic built within me, making me glow so bright that a halo formed on the ground.

"Just use it!" Mac yelled behind me. He was tangled with one of the roof attackers, his long legs winning the fight for the moment.

The one I'd knocked down got up to help his partner. I ran toward them, my left hand still stuck over my shoulder. I had no clue what an Earth mage would do in such a situation, so the magic was useless. Fortunately, I knew what I would do.

Shrugging the backpack off my right arm, I dropped my upper body until the left strap slid to my hand. I kept the movement continuous so that when I twirled with a jump, a hell of a weight behind the backpack connected with the ape-man's head. He flew backward. A jolt traveled up my arm from my numb hand.

I let the backpack hang, trying to work my left hand free as I found my knife with my right. Mac kindly shoved a beast my direction, and I sliced its hairy abdomen. The ape-man caught me in the shoulder, knocking me off balance. I fell back to one knee and slashed his hairless inner thigh, cutting the femoral artery. Formaldehyde-infused blood splattered my neck.

He was dead. He just didn't realize it yet as he swung a long arm at my head. Dodging, I caught him below his point of gravity and grabbed one scaled calf to flip him. The three from the woods were seconds away. I formed a fist around my knife handle and punched him in his hairy face. Sharp teeth snagged my knuckles, drawing blood.

Finally, the backpack fell off my wrist. I caught it on the top of my foot and kicked it to Mac. "Get my fucking sword out!"

A pair of hairy arms lifted me off my feet. I cursed the time I'd wasted with the backpack. Strong hands whipped me around, and I managed to free my left arm. A cloud of dog breath hit me in the face. Dark gray fur covered a large canine head with a mouth full of fangs. A wolf head on an ape's body with scaly reptile legs: no mystery who sent these guys.

My right arm still trapped in the ape thing's embrace, I leaned back and swung a left hook into his sensitive nose. Yelping, he dropped me between his legs. I shoved my knife into the sensitive flesh behind the knee. He bent to grab me again, and I punched him in the throat.

As he staggered back, one of his friends grabbed my feet. For a moment, I was a kid playing with her dad in the yard as he spun me in a circle. BOR entered the scene with a leap, pinning the third remaining creature to the ground. That was all I saw before I continued my revolution, but she clearly had things under control.

Squeezing my glutes and abs, I let my arms swing over my head and vaulted up. As I rose in my aerial crunch, I bent my knees to come face to snout. Momentum pushed my blade straight through his eye into his brain where it stuck. I fell to the ground with no weapon.

"Andromeda, here!"

I hopped to my feet and caught my saya in my right hand. Pulling the katana free with my left, I whirled to meet the last creature standing. The sudden appearance of my sword surprised him, and I easily removed the arm reaching for me. On the backswing, I turned the blade and sliced off his head. The arm and head dropped a second before the body, sounding like coconuts falling just before the tree. Silence followed. Even the horses stopped their frantic activity.

I kept my katana raised, studying the dark woods but sensing nothing else headed my way. BOR released a bloody wolf head from her jaws and cleaned her paws with a long pink tongue. She was growing on me.

"You cussed at me." Mac had what I'd come to think of as his stern teacher face.

"Sorry. I was very tense." I pulled the sweatshirt up and used the red "Cornell" letters to wipe blood off my face and neck.

Mac's disapproval relented slightly. "That's understandable. I really don't like that word, though. It's ugly."

It wasn't my favorite, either, but more because of its historical meaning and the distracting images it brought to mind than the actual sound of it. "I'll remember that. We need to move."

"Really?" Mac looked down at his watch. "It's only been four minutes." His eyes scanned the scene in front of his house, and his face went slack. "You killed everything in my yard in four minutes."

I reached for my pockets to find a cleaning cloth and realized I wore yoga pants. "To be fair, BOR took care of one." I went to my backpack. "And that one by your feet is still breathing."

Mac took two giant steps to the side. "That's still one minute and twenty seconds per monster."

I found a cloth and wiped my blade. Apparently, Mac's analytical side took over when he was flustered. "Well, I hadn't killed anything for nearly two days. It'll come back to me."

He paled and I almost regretted teasing him. "Your reflexes are—" He studied the pile of body parts where I'd killed the last one. "Phenomenal. You did say your parents are farmers?"

"Yep." I sheathed my katana and slipped my feet back into the horrid flip flops. "These things were sent to find me and keep me busy until the Enforcers get here. We've got to go."

"Yes, of course. We'll take care of your sword and yoga mat issues when we get to Leavenworth. I think it was rolled too tightly." He looked about. "I don't suppose I have time to collect some samples? These creatures are quite—umm."

"Unnatural?" I put my saya strap over my shoulder where it belonged and finally felt comfortable. "If you can get samples in half the time it took to kill them, go for it."

He pulled a handful of plastic baggies from his back pocket. "Two minutes, right then."

While I re-rolled the yoga mat, he muttered. "Farmers. Farmers? Farmers . . ."

I walked to Pegasus and tied the mat to his saddle before I finally enlightened Mac. "They only became farmers after I was born. Before that, people paid Mom to spike volleyballs on the beach and Dad to tackle running backs and intercept footballs."

"You're mean."

"That's for calling me cute and sweet." I untied Pegasus and rubbed his neck where it was likely sore from trying to free himself. He nudged my shoulder, and I raised my chin to put my mouth closer to his ear. "Who's a good horse? Is Peggy a good horse?"

He snorted offense, and I laughed. "Don't like that name, Peggy? Good. Now I can annoy you half as much as you do me."

"BOR!" Mac called his beast and detached an oversized pet carrier from Gael's saddle.

The giant panther settled at his feet, purring deep and closing her eyes. Her skin rolled, knots in her muscles bubbling up and down. Her huge paws twitched, shrinking a little with each jerk. A soft green aura surrounded her as her limbs shortened. In less than a minute, she became a twenty-pound housecat. Her fur glistened with sweat and her ribs rapidly rose and fell. Mac picked her up and put her in the carrier.

"Wouldn't she rather stay here and hunt in the woods?"

"She can't." He slid the carrier into a customized slot on the back of his saddle that kept it suspended above Gael's backside. "She's bound to me. Legendary beasts like BOR tend to be tied to a place or family. In the moon era, they had nearly limitless magic, but they didn't all have the skills or intelligence to go into stasis. My ancestor helped BOR sleep when the moon died. Shortly after I was born, she found me, and has never left. I don't think she can stay more than a mile or two away."

"Huh." I absorbed the fact that the cat riding above Gael's ass was

130

over a thousand years old, then I mounted Pegasus. "I'm bound to chocolate, but it fits in my pocket."

"Chocolate will melt in your pocket."

"Not the kind I can afford."

We started down the gravel drive where the stars and Atlas threw deceptive shadows over our path. My anxiety grew, but pushing too fast could result in a horse with a broken leg. I kept the reins tight on Pegasus and myself. The roads would improve closer to Leavenworth, then we could let loose. Once we left the woods regulated by BOR, we might have a few beasties to contend with, but the night remained still and quiet.

We made it to the highway before the air shifted. I inhaled a familiar, spicy scent with undertones of leather and musky male. We hadn't been fast enough.

I turned to Mac riding beside me. Scenarios rapidly played through my head for two precious seconds before I made a decision. "Yell at me."

He leaned back with a frown. "I'm not even mad at you."

I lowered my voice to a fierce whisper. "Pretend I'm stealing your horse."

He shook his head. "There's an old word that suits you perfectly. Daft."

For God's sake. I stood in my stirrups, then swung my right leg over Pegasus' back and threw a punch into Mac's face. Since I dismounted as I hit him, the blow glanced off his jaw, looking more violent that it was.

"I'll take the damn horse if I want, you stupid bastard!" I slapped Gael's rump, and he galloped away.

Mac slumped in the saddle, but I had no time to worry before Waya dropped from the trees beside me. I kept my arms out to my side, turning so that he stayed in my peripheral vision while I waited for his partners to surround me and Pegasus. Despite my orders, the dumbass horse wouldn't budge.

No one else showed. I took a deep breath, smelling nothing but nature, horse, and Waya. He casually leaned against a boulder as high as his hip, his usual smile in place.

"You're alone? Graves knows that if you manage to kill me by yourself, you'll be damaged, right?"

"Relax, sweetheart, we don't want you dead. You didn't have to send your friend away. I won't hurt him."

"Not a friend. He wants to go north, but I'd rather not, so I sent him on his way." I doubted he'd fall for the say north because I knew he'd think south, so I was really going north ploy, but it was worth a shot. I almost confused myself.

Waya stalked closer, and I knew the moment he saw me clearly because he lost his smile. "What the hell have you done?"

"Freed myself." I motioned him closer. "Come see what I can do."

Shaking his head, he circled me about ten feet away. "Why won't you let me help you? If you don't want Sophia doing the implants, we'll work something out. I'd hate for you to die because of jealousy."

I countered, turning his circling walk into a stalking dance. I ignored the jealously barb—which might have been a little true. "I can't go back to the ingots, even if I wanted. Now, they'd finish the job they started when I was a child."

Waya halted. "What?"

"The implants poison Evolutionaries, Waya. They don't keep you alive. They keep you chained."

He scoffed and held his arms wide, letting his long-sleeved, spandex shirt stretch across his muscled biceps and torso. He looked like a martial artist out for an evening run. Strong white fangs flashed as he asked, "Do I look chained?"

"No." I smiled, slipping off my shoes and feeling the soft spring grass cushion my soles. I knew he'd wait while I removed my katana and sweatshirt. This was a civil sparring match—for now. I tossed my sword and sweatshirt to the side.

My betraying cheeks warmed as he admired the close fit of my white, stretchy tank top. "After we compare notes you might change your mind. I'm not going with you, Waya. Let's get this over with."

I let magic slip from my core, and more surged into my body as my skin glowed bright. The light of Atlas entered each pore, boosting energy deep into my body where the magic churned. I gloried in the feel, its vibrancy bringing a smile. Waya took a hesitant step back. I bent my knees and let my hands hang loose.

"Fine." He growled and charged.

Pegasus took off. I thought Waya was scarier than tunnel rats, too, but I stood my ground. Too smart to be caught mid-air with nowhere to go, Waya wouldn't leap. His movements seemed slow as I easily dodged the long leg sweeping at my feet. Before he rose from the crouch, I hammered my foot into his pretty face. He rolled away and jumped to his feet with a snarl that gurgled at the end when blood from his nose rolled into his mouth. He had a green bruise on his temple where I'd hit him with the microscope.

"You should stop leaving your head wide open."

His dark eyes snapped, and he bit the air with his fangs. If I could keep hold of my control, this fight would quickly end in my favor. Waya jumped, performing a handspring intended to bring his legs around my neck. I dove beneath him, but instead of completing his flip, he brought his full weight down on my back.

Air vacated my lungs with a whoosh as my chest met the earth. I struggled against the panic that reigns when there's no breath to be had. Waya hopped off and landed behind me. I did a push up, swinging one foot between his legs and nailing him in the spot he loved even more than his face. He flipped from the impact, barely landing on his feet.

I did a quick roll in the opposite direction, coming to stand near the boulder. Waya's face darkened: a shadow surrounding eyes that glowed like rubies lit by fire. Well, if I'd wanted him pissed, mission accomplished.

He charged me again. I jumped back onto the boulder and shoved off to deliver a double fisted punch into his solar plexus. Magic exploded from my hands in a flash that knocked me backward. Shit, I hadn't meant to do that. Waya flew across the clearing and landed spread eagle.

My mind was relieved when he sat up, shaking his head, but something deep inside me roared disappointment. I didn't remember running to him. I just knew a primal need to take him down. Before he could gain his wits, I flipped him onto his stomach, pinned his arms with my legs, and crossed his throat with one forearm. Darkness twined through the magic glowing inside me: a toxic stain fed by Waya's struggles beneath me.

"Stop fighting," I whispered, straining to speak through my desire to conquer him.

"Bochs." He gasped.

Tears pricked my eyes, but I squeezed tighter, cutting off his air. My other hand shook as I brought it to rest on his head. I was losing a battle, and I didn't know my opponent. Waya's soft hair against my palm brought a connection—some thread of humanity that tugged at the darkness which controlled me. It was a brushstroke of sunlight on an overwhelming canvas of violence. I latched onto it.

"Relax, Waya. Feel my strength, my power."

I pushed against the insistent need inside me, appalled when it became a visible black web across my skin. Darkness filled my veins. My control slipped. Magical light and shadow twisted before my eyes in a cloud. Beneath me, Waya stopped moving, and his eyelids fluttered closed. Something sinister lurked behind the shadows in my mind, and it thirsted for his blood.

A chokehold was painful, brutal. I wouldn't do it to my worst enemy. I had to gain control. Gritting my teeth, I shifted my forearm off his windpipe and slid it to the pulse at his neck, changing from chokehold to stranglehold. The names didn't sound much different, but a victim would always choose strangle.

He gasped, gulping the air he'd been denied. The sound touched the seed of compassion shouting for my attention. I opened myself to more magic, trying to smother the dark yearnings. Two green sparks lit up Waya's cheek: my eyes, glowing with a magical build-up that pressurized my brain. I focused on the grass, amazed when it shot up four feet to hide us in a magical copse.

I brought my lips to his ear. My voice wavered with restraint. "You can have this, too, Waya. You can be stronger, faster. You can be free. Take the silica out."

I felt his pulse against my skin. His heartbeat moved through my body to meld with my own. The moment the flow to his brain ceased, I let go of everything: the magic, the primal desires, and Waya.

It took all I had to squelch those desires. They tore at me, like a beast clawing its way out of my soul. Nausea rolled through me, burning the back of my throat. I collapsed on my side, crushing the thick grass.

Considering what I'd done to him before I came to my senses, he'd be out for a few minutes. My hand slid from his head, the backs of my fingers caressing his peaceful face. "I'm sorry."

I rolled out of the grass prison, and held one arm above my face. First, the twin green lights disappeared, then the black lines faded and the glow of my skin flickered out. Hopefully it was the last of the ingots' poisonous black magic leaving my body. I let my arm drop to the ground and stared at the night sky. My breathing returned to normal, and the magic condensed back where it belonged.

Hooves clopped on the highway, then rustled in the grass before a pair of leather reins hit me in the nose. Horse breath ruffled my hair.

"Where the hell have you been? You've stuck your dumb nose into every fight until this one, when I nearly killed a man. You couldn't throw a distraction my way when I needed one?"

Pegasus snorted and shook his head, dragging the reins across my face. I knocked them out of the way and sat up to ponder Waya, nestled in the thicket. Even asleep, he looked capable of killing me or seducing me, however the spirit moved him. I noticed the flattering fit of his jeans as I shifted him to get to his favorite weapons: two wickedly sharp Fixation Bowie knives sheathed on his belt. I couldn't help smiling a little, imagining him awake while my hands slid along his hips. After I removed the knives, I placed them on the boulder twelve feet away.

I found a length of light rope on my saddle and bound his hands behind his back. He was still in BOR's territory, so nothing predatory would come by before he woke up, made his way to the boulder, and cut himself free.

Mac wasn't far down the road when I found him, rubbing a sore jaw and fuming over the insult of being called stupid. The entire trip to Leavenworth he lectured me on manners and common courtesy. He never mentioned 'bastard,' so I assumed that part was okay.

CHAPTER FOURTEEN

I stared at her scowl, mouth open just enough to show two fangs protruding below the upper lip. It was a black and white drawing with the blue skin implied. I vacillated between victory that my wanted posters existed and disgust at the artist's rendition of my face.

"I do not have a uni-brow."

Mac stood behind me. "Right you are, lass. That looks nothing like you, anymore."

I glared at him. "Anymore?"

"Well, you might try smiling a little. You don't see many glowering yoginis. They tend to be peaceful."

I forced a wide smile.

Mac flinched. "Maybe without teeth; and your eyes glowed."

The call to board our train sounded over the intercom, and I relaxed a little. We'd be out of Leavenworth soon. Just before we crossed the bridge into Kansas, Mac rolled my katana back inside the mat with the promise that I could pull it free much easier next time. There were no livestock cars on late trains so we'd stabled the horses with a friend of Mac's. On the way, we'd passed at least a dozen soldiers. None of them had looked my way twice, but it only took one spark of recognition to bring my downfall.

We made our way to the boarding platform and joined the light, Friday night crowd. A few casually dressed people like Mac and I waited, though they were likely off for a weekend of fun. Most of the travelers were tired men and women who worked in Leavenworth all week, and now they headed home.

Soldiers patrolled, clad in the drab gray and black of the military. All young and strong, the soldiers' bodies contributed to the tally of weapons they possessed. Below their caps, their sharp, observant eyes flashed as they moved on the perimeter of the boarding crowd.

One soldier stood beside the conductor who studied tickets and directed passengers at the top of the steps.

"Damn."

"You've no reason to be nervous. Just be normal," Mac said with only one corner of his mouth moving. "Quit acting like it's an issue, and it will no longer be an issue."

I nodded, focusing on deep breaths and smiling without teeth. We mounted the steps, and Mac handed over our tickets. The conductor's hand shook a little as the soldier peered over his shoulder. I watched the soldier through lowered lashes. He glanced at Mac then me before moving his attention further down the line.

I was two feet past him before he said, "Wait. She can't go in first-class."

Slowly I turned, squelching the desire to challenge him with a fist. He wasn't looking at me.

I'd been so wrapped up in myself, I hadn't noticed an Evolutionary teen with her parents in the line behind us. On the short side, with dark blonde hair and skin the color of blueberry milk, she stood half-hidden by her father. His eyes sparked, and he raised his chin. Her mother placed her hands on the girl's shoulders.

"This is our last trip before she goes to The Academy." Her father argued. "We paid for a first-class sleeper. No one else will even be inside with us."

Evolutionaries entered The Academy at fifteen. I met the girl's eyes, a dark purple dulled by resignation. Her spirit already waned, and she hadn't even started. She'd probably die with her first monster.

I grabbed the pet carrier and raised it to head height, earning a sleepy growl from BOR. "This smelly cat can ride first-class with us, but she can't?"

Mac pulled my arm down. The conductor cast a hesitant look at the soldier suddenly interested in me. "It's a safety issue," the soldier said.

Mac stepped in front of me, and I took the hint, breathing deeply before magic lasers shot from my eyes. "What my wife means," he began, and I was glad no one saw my surprised face behind his back. "Is that we don't mind the girl in our car. We just purchased our tickets, and we are the only occupants of car number five. Why can't the family stay there? Or do you not need their first-class fare, seeing as the train is so full."

"It's against the rules." The soldier insisted.

I badly wanted to stare him down, but Mac's shoulder was eye-level. A green sheen bounced off his navy jacket. Hiding my eyes was probably best.

"Actually, it isn't," Mac replied in his lecture tone. "The military has no rules for railroad passengers, nor does it have the authority to interfere with the railroad without a direct command from the Secretary of Defense. The soldiers are here for support and protection.

"The train authorities reserve the right to deny someone—anyone—passage if they deem necessary. I doubt that includes a harmless girl traveling with her parents. So, it is up to the conductor." He turned to the awed conductor. "Do you think your superiors wish to refund three of what is likely just a handful of first-class tickets?"

Score for Mac. I dared rise on my toes and peek over his shoulder. Mac received a full-out glare from the soldier, but the conductor smiled at him. He raised a clipboard, produced a marker, and made some notations on a print out. Then he took the family's tickets and wrote on them, too. He handed them back to the father with a smile. "Car number five, sir, compartment C."

The father looked like someone who had expected to be arrested and instead got a pat on the head. "Uh, thank you."

Mac faced me, grabbed my upper arm, and propelled me toward the train like a disobedient child. "Way to avoid attention. I think we need to review basic vocabulary. That was in no way normal."

"It was to me."

Mac answered with a growl as his hand moved to my back and pushed me onto the train. We turned to enter the corridor, and I glanced back. Luckily, the soldier's eyes attempted to burn a hole through Mac's head instead of mine. If he'd looked into my eyes, he might have grabbed a weapon.

The dark carpet lining the narrow sleeper hall was clean, but old and worn. Coal-powered bulbs offered dim, almost blue light that flattered the shabby train car. Windows made up the opposite side of the hall, looking out on a stunning view of another train. Of the three compartments in car number five, we were in A. Mac guided me through the door, slid it shut, and locked it.

He dropped both his bags with a sigh and stood in front of the closed blinds of the window with hands on hips, as if he could see through to the platform. I placed BOR's carrier against the wall, quietly watching Mac's back. He still radiated frustration, but his shoulders drooped, and I'd noticed circles beneath his eyes. Atlas in the sky meant the train was in steam mode, making for a slower trip. We could both use the time to rest and recover.

Mac sat in a blue armchair reduced to child-size to make it look comfortable and appealing in the small area. The door to a tiny bathroom stood on one side of the chair. A small table was attached to the wall on the other side, then a matching chair sat on the other side of the table. A set of narrow bunkbeds lined the wall opposite the chairs. They didn't appear long enough for either of us. I could still collapse on one and sleep for days.

Mac rummaged through one of his bags, continuing with his unbearable disappointed-silence-mode. Pulling a couple of things out, he put them in the tiny square fridge under the window. Nothing else would fit in there.

I moved away from the door and practiced removing my katana from the yoga mat. After a while, I noticed Mac flinch every time the blade sang through the air in the small space. I quit and completely removed saya and katana from the mat, placing them under the pillow of the lower bunk. I kicked off my shoes and plopped down on the bed.

"I haven't fought with one hand in a while," I said, trying to fill the silence. Usually silence was my favorite companion, but Mac exuded something that put me on edge. "That was good practice."

He didn't respond, so I looked over to find his token frustrated look.

"What? It was almost disastrous, but it worked out. I definitely need some shoes that can hold a knife or two. Or . . ." I sat up, a little excited. "Could we fashion sheaths for my arms? Then I could cover them up with this sweatshirt." I looked at the shoulder where one of the ape-things had cut the material and given me a gash. A decent amount of dried blood decorated the sleeve. On the front, the once placid Cornell bear looked like he'd recently killed a hiker. "Maybe not this sweatshirt. I suppose it will draw attention in daylight."

Mac finally spoke, and he didn't sound happy. "The solution isn't more accessible weapons. The solution is using your magic. You had all that power at your disposal, and you didn't use it."

"To do what?" I jumped up, automatically stifling the glow that rose to my skin with my emotion. That part was easier, at least. "The magic didn't come with any instructions that I suddenly found buried in my brain when I needed them. I felt power, but my only instinct was to deal with the threat the best way I knew how. Weapons are what I know, Mac." I stopped before I mentioned the instincts that bubbled to the surface during my tussle with Waya. I couldn't describe them, anyway.

"You felt no connection to the Earth? You were even barefoot! It should have been filling you with power through the soles of your feet."

My anger deflated a little. "Well, my feet were off the ground a lot. When I said, 'Wait,' in your doorway, I could see the slight disturbance of the trees across your yard. Was that Earth awareness?" I couldn't help the touch of sarcasm with the last two words. It was just too alien to me, still.

"Yes, but with the power you gather you should hear the trees calling warnings, the Earth offering help."

"Did the magic turn me into a fairytale princess? Will animals come to my rescue?" Full sarcasm on that one.

Mac threw his hands up and leaned back in his seat then crossed his arms and closed his eyes. He looked ridiculous with his lanky frame folded into that chair; like a father at a tea party in his daughter's bedroom furniture.

I sat in the chair opposite him. It bothered me that I didn't feel this connection he thought should be naturally present. Even worse, I'd felt the pull of darkness deep inside me, instead. It had been as intoxicating as the world's best lover dipped in chocolate: a temptation I might not resist if it happened again. I'd had no such desire when I fought the wolf-apes. Then again, I hadn't held back to avoid killing them.

Studying Mac's tired face, I knew he'd stay awake with worry if I told him about the remaining black magic's influence. He'd said it would disappear, eventually. I had to wait it out. Too bad my few and simple characteristics didn't include patience.

"Sorry," I said, no longer able to stand the guilt that his silence heaped on me. "I get rude when I'm frustrated, or nervous, or scared, or . . . breathing."

A puff of laughter escaped him, and he waved dismissively,

keeping his eyes closed. "We're both frustrated. I know I could use a nap." He smiled then opened his eyes. "It will just take time. The ingots worked against you for over twenty years. Once we have the proper environment, I'm sure we'll manage."

I nodded to humor him. I knew they still worked against me.

*****

I slept through Kansas City. All of the anxiety I'd built up over the stop there hadn't kept me awake for it. For all I knew, Graves had walked the corridors while I'd dreamt of soldiers with wolves' heads chasing Evolutionary children as I sat beside a life-sized chocolate Waya.

"Mmmm." I blinked at the barred pattern flashing on the floor: starlight breaking through passing trees and the blinds on the window.

The announcement that woke me, an approaching stop at Nevada, Missouri, sounded again. In Nevada, the tracks split, one leg going south to Fort Smith, and the other southeast to El Dorado Springs before veering straight east toward the heavier populated parts of the country. Residents of the West and half of the Midwest had either died or fled when the supervolcanoes erupted. Repopulation was a slow process.

The U.S. had taken little time to change from an airplane and car dependent society back to railroads. Most of the tracks were pre-Atlas freight tracks. Some engineering wiz had developed a way to modify passenger trains with little need to change thousands of miles of tracks, opening the entire country to railway travel.

We wouldn't disembark in Nevada. I considered going back to sleep, then the second reason I woke up gurgled from the bottom of my empty stomach. I studied Mac's motionless bare foot hanging off the bunk above me. He hadn't incapacitated four ape-wolves followed by Waya. He probably wasn't hungry.

I rolled off the bunk and slipped on my flip flops. The small clock on the stationary table showed 2:00 a.m.—perfect time for a dining car trip. Two green eyes glowed within BOR's carrier.

"Would you like out?"

A raspy purr answered me.

I opened the cage, and she sauntered out, radiating offense as if

I'd been the one to shut her inside. She performed an investigation of the room's perimeter before curling into a regal feline pose in the middle of the floor, facing the door.

"I guess you're on guard duty."

Her eyes narrowed, and her whiskers twitched.

"I'll bring something back for you. Do you like chicken?"

Purr.

"Right."

Before I opened the door, the screech of a pissed bird sounded through the car which shook on its tracks. I ran to the window and lifted the blinds. A powerful beam of light blinked on from below the window, shining straight into the sky.

Pressing my cheek against the glass, I saw more lights running the entire length of the train to brighten its perimeter. A dark form swooped into view, flapping large wings and keeping pace with the train a few cars down. I saw the outline of a giant beak. It had a set of large, deadly talons in front with feline paws and a tail hanging behind. A griffin.

Of all the beasts blessed with wings, the half-eagle, half-lion griffins were the dumbest. The missing top floors of my apartment building testified to that. They'd take on anything in their path. Sure, they could carry off a person and devour them in a few minutes, but they'd never win in a fight against a train.

The griffin rammed its head against a car window, shaking the train again. Griffins weren't huge, roughly the size of my horse with a twelve-foot wingspan, but they could ram on the fly, literally. That was reason number eleven why commercial airlines no longer existed. One hit from a griffin in a vital spot, and a plane would plummet to the earth in a fiery plume. Even if a train derailed, survival chances were decent—especially with slower steam engine speeds. Only private planes flew anymore, with people looking to commit spectacular suicide.

Another shake and a screech announced a second griffin on the other side. While the beasts would wear out before they did serious damage, they might break a window and make off with a victim or two, first. If they coordinated, they'd knock the train off the tracks, but they were griffins, sooo . . .

A line of trees growing close to the track flashed past our window. The griffin rose out of sight, cleared the trees, and dropped back down—right beside me. A large eagle eye glared at me with raptor glee. I smiled back.

I hadn't decided how best to goad it when an arrow pierced its furry back followed by two more in the neck. It screamed and fell back, out of sight. I put an eye against the glass to see the griffin drop its back legs and spread its wings like parachute brakes. Half a dozen more arrows pierced its wings and neck. It crashed to the ground and rolled into the dark countryside.

"One down." I ran for the door.

"No sword," Mac mumbled. He hadn't even raised his head.

I frowned at my hand, wondering when I'd picked up my katana. Panic constricted my throat, but I fought it. It was just a little trip to kill a griffin. My sword wouldn't go anywhere. "Fine." I dropped it on one of the chairs.

"And don't glow," he called as I slid the door closed.

The lights in the corridor flickered with another shake of the train. Griffin number two was still alive and flying.

"No need for alarm, ma'am." A porter hurried toward me with a strained smile, clearly not believing his words. "We have two ballistae, and our personnel are the best. They'll have these beasts taken care of shortly." He held a hand toward the compartment side of the car. "If you'll just sit tight?" The questioning accent sweetened his order with politeness. I ignored it.

A ballista was a Medieval archery weapon modernized as a more effective defense than unreliable firearms. Two modern ballistae could shoot twenty to thirty bolts a minute. The griffins should have been long gone.

"Actually, I'm headed to the dining car."

He paused, one foot literally suspended above the floor. "Oh, uhh—"

Another jolt ended with the complete loss of lights. Mild exclamations sounded throughout the train. I darted out of the car before the porter could turn on a flashlight. I sped through three cars to reach the dining car which happened to be the griffin's point of interest. Maybe it smelled the food.

The lights flickered back on, illuminating long cracks in the windows that covered one side of the car. Quaint, built-in booths lined up beneath the windows. A sharp beak snapped beyond the glass. Napkin dispensers and condiments littered the floor. On the opposite wall sat a glass case full of sandwiches, wraps, salads, and chocolate cake.

"Yum." I stepped toward the case.

The griffin shrieked for my attention and rammed the windows again. Half a pane shattered onto the booths and floor. It shoved its eagle head through the hole, got raked by broken glass, and jerked out. It pecked away pieces of glass, making the hole bigger.

Right. Kill the griffin now, eat cake later. Unfortunately, the throwing knives strapped to my calves beneath the yoga pants wouldn't do much to a griffin. I scanned the room for cutlery and spotted a knife block behind a stainless steel, diner counter with stools bolted to the floor. I jumped onto the counter and startled the dining attendant huddled behind it.

"You should leave," I suggested as I studied the cheaply made options the knife block offered.

"I'm not allowed." The small woman tried to push into the corner under the counter. She hugged herself, convulsing with fear.

"What, are you supposed to protect the food at all costs?"

She nodded.

I chose a boning knife for my right hand and a butcher for the left: one to stab, one to chop. They'd both break before I finished. "I tell you what." I tried for a reassuring, toothless smile. "I'm really hungry. So, I'm going to take care of this problem for you, then you can sell me a sandwich."

I turned my attention to the thrashing beast. The griffin had made the hole big enough for its head and one talon to fit through, so had pushed inside. The top half of one wing made it, while the rest flailed outside. Stupid griffin.

I jumped to the middle of the car, then catapulted toward the one-armed, sitting griffin. My right foot caught its neck, pushing the head away as I landed with my left foot on the floor. I swung the boning knife down, pinning the griffin's shoulder to the booth table underneath it. I probably had seconds before the blade broke.

I lifted my right foot, willing the massive beak to come closer. It tried to bite my right arm, but I jerked back and swung the butcher knife at its throat.

"Damn it." I missed the throat, but a five-inch section of its tongue fell to the floor. That would distract it for a minute. It reared away from my pain-inducing butcher knife and broke free from the table.

The handle and half of the boning knife blade protruded at the base of its wing. It forced the rest of the wing through the window and swept me toward razor-sharp talons. I back-flipped out of reach.

Finally realizing its tactical error, the griffin tried to wriggle out the window. I leapt for it. Just as the head and claws slipped outside, I landed on the bottom half of its wing. Wrapping my arms around the appendage, I hooked my legs under the stationary table. Muscle and bone writhed beneath me, and I squeezed tighter. Feathers tickled the sensitive skin inside my arms. I choked back a giggle. The bolts of the table groaned, and the screech of claws against metal filled the car as the griffin pushed against the train to break free.

Slowly, the wing pulled me toward the window until my face crossed outside. Wind hit me with breathtaking force. The bloody beak bit inches from my nose, and an eagle shriek filled my ears. I faced the wind, looking up the tracks. Then I smiled.

One, two, I let go of the wing. The back half of the griffin collided with a giant oak tree. I made sure I wouldn't suffer the same fate before I stuck my head and shoulders through the window. A powerful searchlight caught the griffin struggling on the ground. The train completely passed it before a cloud of ballista bolts finished it off.

I snorted. "Griffins."

Shouts and running steps approached from both ends of the train. I threw the butcher knife out the window, ran to the counter, and sat between two stools, hugging my knees. If I got caught in beast-slayer mode, Mac would yell at me again.

I called out to the hiding woman. "All clear. Stand up and tell them it got caught in the window and hit by a tree."

Simultaneously, both doors of the car banged open. My porter friend with two others charged in from one end, and three men brandishing long knives and cross bows entered from the other. All eyes went straight to the broken window and the bloody, destroyed booth.

"It's gone." The attendant's wavering voice cut through the silence. She moved around the end of the counter, one hand on top for support. "It was stuck in the window and got hit by a tree."

The porter studied me. "Are you alright, ma'am?"

"I'm fine, thank you."

His face tilted down, and his lips moved in a silent count. His foot pushed along the floor toward me, nudging my flip flops. Hmm, kicking them off were automatic. "Thanks."

He opened his mouth then compressed his lips, turning to the armed men. "What happened?"

"The left ballista broke a spring," one answered. "We couldn't shoot on this side."

"Are we sure it's dead?" The porter looked so tense he could have replaced the broken spring.

The woman locked gazes with me, clearly panicked by the thought of a simple lie. I heaved a sigh and stood. "I stuck my head out when it disappeared. Your other ballista took care of it after we passed."

"Okay, we are five miles from Nevada. I'll inform the conductor that we need repairs. Everyone back to their stations." The porter turned on his heel and ushered his lesser colleagues out. Once they were gone, he kept his hand out, looking pointedly at me. He should have known better.

"I'm still hungry."

Shaking his head, he left. Clearly, I didn't fit his cooperative passenger definition. At least all this magic hadn't changed my personality. Hmmm. I surveyed the carnage where I'd tussled with a griffin. I couldn't recall feeling any magic. It had just been a faster, stronger me doing what I'd always done. No surge of power from Atlas. No glow. No shadowy monster crouching inside me, roaring for blood. Maybe the ingot magic had disappeared.

A cleared throat shook me from my musings. The attendant, still pale and wide-eyed, stood behind the counter. "You want something to eat before we stop?"

I chose a few sandwiches, potato salad, and two big slices of cake. Patting my hips, I discovered that my yoga pants hadn't developed pockets. I'd grabbed my katana for a trip to the dining car without thinking, but had failed to bring money.

"No charge," she said, eying me. "I'll say the griffin got it."

"Oh, that's okay. I can bring some money back."

She shook her head. "I saw what you did. I owe you."

Well, that was unfortunate. I'd expected her to hide behind the counter like a good innocent bystander. She pushed the pile of food toward me, and I picked it up. "I would appreciate you not telling anyone what I did."

She stared, zero comprehension.

"I'm traveling incognito."

Her brows rose, and I tried to think of a good reason, but not the actual truth. Leaning across the counter, I whispered, "My ex-husband taught me to fight. He doesn't like being an ex."

"Ohhhh." She held her hands up. "I never saw you."

My step bounced on the way back with the victory over a griffin and the promise of food improving my mood. The door to Compartment C stood wide open, and the Evolutionary girl loitered there, silent and watchful.

"Hey." My teenager communication skills hadn't improved since the vagrants.

The girl tilted her head and made a face like a mute who acknowledged a greeting.

"Did the griffins wake you?"

"I think so." This kid had zero personality. I wondered if her magic bored, too.

"Well, they're gone now. You can go back to sleep." I started to open my door and paused. The conversation felt incomplete, and I knew why. Sighing, I faced her again. "Look, I know The Academy seems scary, but you'll be safe there. I think change is coming, soon. You might . . ." I tried to avoid false hope. "You're stronger than you think."

Her wrinkled brow cleared, and she smiled. "Thank you." She backed into her compartment and quietly slid the door closed.

CHAPTER FIFTEEN

"You just can't help yourself, can you?" Mac asked. "Violence draws you like a moth to a flame."

I was a little shocked that he glared at my chest, until I noticed the griffin blood splattering my white tank top. No wonder the porter and the Evolutionary girl had stared at me. I shrugged and sat cross-legged in the middle of the floor, depositing the food. I ripped open a chicken salad sandwich and gave half to BOR who sat beside the woman with food. "I prefer the magnet to metal analogy. It has a happier ending."

Sighing, Mac joined us, folding his long legs like a crane. "Normals let other people handle beasts for them while they hide. Our goal isn't for you to draw attention."

I finished my half of the sandwich, thinking carefully before I spoke—maybe magic *was* changing me. I liked Mac, and I'd never be able to repay him for what he'd given me. If we stuck together, we needed to understand each other.

I reached over to the chair where I'd dropped my katana and grabbed it, laying it across my lap. Looking Mac in the eye, I asked a simple question. "When you look at me, what do you see?"

His lips twitched. "Putting your sword in your lap won't force the answer you want from me."

"You already knew the answer."

His exhale sounded like defeat. "Fine. I see an ass-kicker. Satisfied?"

I got him to say 'ass,' so it satisfied a little. "Magic won't change who I am, and I don't want it to. I happen to like myself—usually. When I came to you for help, my goal wasn't to become Normal. I want to be free.

"I know Normals wait for someone else to take care of the

monsters. Since seventeen, that someone has been me. Eliminator is my actual title, Mac. It's my job, and I do it well. That doesn't mean the same thing as it does to Normals. Failing doesn't mean I get passed up for promotion or fired. It means I'm dead.

"So yes, I attack beasts without hesitation and with everything I've got, because I can't watch someone else do it when I know I'm better. If I'd sat in here and waited, and someone had died before the griffins were dealt with, it would have bothered me because I could have prevented it. I'm arrogant. I'm stubborn. When something weird and scary drops in front of me, I cut its head off. That's who I am. Can you accept it?"

Mac hesitated. I understood, but it still hurt, deep in my chest where my emotions wound tightly. He smiled. "Of course, I can. I just want to help you learn to use your magic. I want to find the right way so I can help others in the future. You don't have to change who you are for that."

I opened another sandwich, and Mac took one for himself. We ate in silence until I started the decadent chocolate cake that would have cost half of my money. Mac had already eaten his, but I chose to savor.

He reached behind him and pulled a duffle bag forward, then removed a giant book that belonged in a dusty, Victorian library. A leather-bound journal followed the book. "While we're sitting in Nevada awaiting repairs, let's discuss what first brought you to me."

It took me a minute as I cleaned the last crumbs from my fork. "The basilisk?"

"No." Mac pointed a finger at me, scientific excitement lighting his eyes. "Which is precisely the crux."

"I didn't understand any of those words, not even no."

He grinned. "It was not a true basilisk."

"Well, it was made of clay, so . . ."

"And blood."

"Blood?" How had the top-of-her-field Dr. Bennett missed that? Wake up, Andee. She hadn't missed it. She'd lied. She *was* trying to use me for Frankenstein parts, after all.

Mac leaned forward and whispered, "Human blood. *Magic* human blood."

I smiled at his exuberance. Science brought him to life like violence did me, but I kept the observation to myself. He wouldn't appreciate the parallel.

"I had to do some research." He opened his journal, set it down, then leafed through the book. "The clay points to a golem: a creature, usually humanoid, made with clay and magic. It performs specific tasks willed to it by the creator until the tasks are completed or the magic runs out. But the blood mystified me until I found this."

He laid the book out in front of me. Boldly drawn sketches and archaic looking script filled the pages. Some words were familiar but most weren't. "What is this language?"

"Old English. This is a copy of an ancient tome kept in my family's library. I didn't even know I had it until my mother told me what shelf she'd placed it on when she brought it one visit. I've spent my entire adult life studying current magic and Evolutionaries. I had to call Mum when the basilisk dust stumped me, and she steered me here."

He pointed to a picture of a cloaked figure beside a thigh-high rock. One hand touched the rock, and the other he held out with a red ball suspended above his palm. A hood completely hid his face, and the tip of a sword showed at the cloak's bottom. The figure's boots trampled broken, emaciated bodies.

"Why is he stepping on old, dead men?"

"They aren't old. They're shriveled because he removed their blood and magic to make beast golems that he controlled. Turn the page."

I couldn't. When he said 'shriveled,' Johnson's body in the Enforcers' vault burst into my mind and paralyzed me. This would be bad. If I didn't turn the page, maybe I could ignore it.

"Andromeda?" Mac nudged me.

Without looking up, I took a fortifying breath and turned the page. The same figure stood with his hands held before him while particles floated up from a pile of dirt at his feet. The ball, now red and black, swirled between his palms. A stream of red connected the ball to a red outline of a creature with wings. The next page depicted a solid dragon with red eyes, bowing to the cloaked man.

"The original book is over a thousand years old, and in that one, the red color is rusty brown because the scribe used real blood. When the scribes did that, they meant business. Blood mages are often considered unsavory for obvious reasons, but they're not all dark. Only one blood mage in history ever had the ability to make blood golems, and here he is."

I tried to read the name scrawled beneath the cloaked figure: Cynddelw. "Sin-dual?"

"Pronounced KUN-thool."

"Kun-thool? Kun-thool . . . English is weird."

"Cynddelw is an old Welsh name derived from—never mind." Mac waved himself away from his own tangent. "Cynddelw was defeated by Merlin a century before the moon died. So, either Atlas created a blood mage with similar abilities, or the real Cynddelw didn't die. He just went to sleep early and reinvented himself across the pond after he woke."

I held up a hand. "Merlin was real?"

"*Is* real, lass. Just before my family left England, he woke up and relocated to southern France. But even if contacting Europe were easy, he probably wouldn't help."

"Why not?"

Mac's brow wrinkled as he shrugged. "It's complicated. Those of the Old Magic are disoriented and anxious. Some of them have amnesia, and almost all of them want nothing to do with magic in what they call the New World. Only indigenous tribes and a few enterprising Vikings knew about this continent before the moon died. Many believe there is no true magic here because they're . . ." He quirked his lips.

"Magic snobs?"

"Precisely. My parents came here because they feared for my safety as a young boy with magic in a land where powerful Ancients awakened. They thought I'd be safer here. I've told you before they don't want me interfering with New Magic, either. Mum just helped me with this because she can't resist a chance to lecture."

"Well, you can be sure she's your mother, then."

"Ha."

"So, we're on our own?"

"I have friends. The good thing is that magic is always balanced. Everything can be defeated. We'll figure it out."

I studied the broad shoulders and long, powerful legs of the blood mage. His cloak fortified him like a layer of confidence while he held out a sure hand full of stolen magic and shaped a monster. He wouldn't be a man easily fazed by a sword-wielding woman named after a Greek princess.

Mac stayed optimistic. "I think we can cross off the possibility of this being a new blood mage because of the soil samples and dimensions of the depression in that empty silo."

"Why?" I'd forgotten I gave him that stuff.

"Its irregular shape led me to believe something natural hid under the pile of ingots. I studied the soil samples and found traces of volcanic ash that isn't North American, at least, not with the recent eruptions."

"Ash is different?"

"Just like soil, ash is particular to location. Factoring in the recent rains, the natural composition of the soil in the silo, and the rough dimensions you gave me, the most likely cause of the depression is a volcanic rock. An *old* volcanic rock."

"Like a *malus molaris*?"

"The mother of all *malus molarii*." Mac turned back a page and pointed to the small boulder Cynddelw touched. "*Roc Fuil*: literally 'blood rock.' When the moon's magic activated eons ago, volcanoes reacted just like they did to Atlas. *Roc Fuil* is the largest, oldest, most powerful *malus molaris* known. Cynddelw used *Roc Fuil* to transform and taint the magic he stole in order to shape his blood golems. The ingots in the silo would have shielded the rock from magical detection."

"So the basilisk was guarding the rock that helped make it."

"Yes."

That was why the thing had been so attached to the Restricted Zone. It was created to stay there. The events of the past week played in my head on fast forward. I'd been wrong. This wasn't just bad. It was devastating. "This is what happened to all the missing Evolutionaries. Their shriveled bodies are lying in the M-kes basement. I killed a basilisk made with their blood."

Mac laid a hand on my shoulder. "They were already dead, lass."

"I know." My skin didn't glow with anger at myself. That son of a bitch had tried to kill me with a beast made of my colleagues. When that hadn't worked, he'd tried to send me away and separate me from the protection of M-kes. Sophia served as his sexy little pawn, chasing me down with her weird creatures.

I stared at the picture of Cynddelw. He was confidence clothed in power and mystery: Josiah Hightower's prominent characteristics.

My core roared with heat. Maybe my blood literally boiled. I would coat my katana with Josiah's blood. Let him try to make a golem as his own magic spilled onto my boots.

A vengeful smile stretched my lips, then I noticed Mac. His face was as bloodless as the bodies in the book, but something in his eyes crackled—blue sparks of magic. They were two magical pools of water that made me unbelievably thirsty. Heat built beneath my skin and parched my throat. I needed one little drink.

"Andromeda!" Mac scooted backward.

I blinked.

"Look at your skin!"

I was on my feet, legs tensed for a leap and arms reaching out for Mac. Beneath my skin, a reddish glow emanated like a hand closed over a flashlight. Gray lines webbed over every visible inch.

"You look like you're burning from the inside. Are you hot?" Mac cautiously crawled toward me.

My tongue swelled, crowding my mouth. I nodded, forced my sandpaper lips apart, and rasped, "Thirsty."

Mac's eyes met mine, still full of cool, delicious magic. They held what I needed. I inched forward. A growl rolled through me then stalled in the dry heat of my throat. I would die of thirst.

The blue sparks flared. "Stop that."

I smiled and fangs pushed against my lower lip. BOR dropped between us, transforming into a beast with an explosion of light and fur. Her body filled half the car, shoving me into the door. She blocked Mac from view, showing me her teeth. Mac's magic pulsed brightly behind her, just out of reach. I locked eyes with the cat. I could kill a panther.

"Andromeda." Mac's voice was muffled by panther fur. "Use your calming breath technique. Your body craves magic. Stop blocking Atlas and let its magic fill you."

His words pierced a haze that I recognized as lust. I rested my back against the door and slid to seated even though my muscles vibrated with need. Closing my eyes, I imagined the air was tinted blue and watched it flow into my lungs. I held it, willing the blue to saturate my blood and reach my fingers and toes before I exhaled heat and angst.

I repeated several times and my pores opened, letting light from Atlas soak through my skin. My body cooled, and the hum vibrating my core felt lighter, healthier. I grabbed one of the water bottles from the dining car and downed half of it. "I'm okay."

"Are you certain?"

"Yes." I took another deep breath, focusing on balance. "The evidence is pointing to Doyen Hightower, a man I trust and respect. I got angry, then really hot. I think my magic recognized your healing power and wanted me to take it from you. I'm sorry."

There was silence behind BOR, but she relaxed, sitting back to give me space. I waited anxiously. Maybe I'd scared him so bad he'd tell BOR to keep an eye on me while he escaped. Maybe I wanted BOR to keep an eye on me. "Mac, are you okay?"

"What? Oh, yes." Paper rustled, then he skirted BOR, holding his journal and a pen. "This is fascinating." And he was back. "Do you remember exactly what you were thinking?"

"Uhmmm, yes."

His pen remained posed above the page, then he looked up. "That bad?"

"I was really mad."

He only looked mildly sick as I described the vision of a defeated Josiah bleeding at my feet. "And that seemed to suck the moisture from your body?"

"It felt that way."

Mac tapped the end of his pen against his teeth. "I learned control so young that I've forgotten what it feels like to forget to balance with Atlas, to essentially deny yourself magic. You were a quick learner with blocking, but maybe you're too good. In a way, doing without magic is like dehydrating. Your cells need to be saturated with magic or they'll crave it and make you crazy. Is this the first time it's happened?"

So much for the black ingot magic disappearing. "No. I had to fight a strong urge to take the life of Waya. It felt like I wanted to kill him, but maybe it was his magic I wanted. The black lines were on my skin, and I had to contemplate the stars before I settled down."

Mac tilted his head thoughtfully. "What about the ape-wolves?"

"Nothing."

"The griffin?"

I shook my head.

"Did you have skin contact with Waya before this desire manifested?"

I couldn't remember. "Maybe. I don't know if the fangs came out, either. And." I hesitated. This might kill Mac's magical dehydration theory. "I used magic when I fought Waya. I wasn't magic-starved or whatever you want to call it."

"Interesting." He made a note and turned the page.

"That's it?"

"I'm not going to make any wild hypotheses, but we already know the magic of the ingots lingers in your blood. I suspect it will clear up on its own. Right now, I want to talk about Cynddelw while it's fresh. Are you calm enough to tell me why you think he's your doyen?"

This felt clinical. Mac couldn't look more like an inquiring scientist if he put on a lab coat and perched on a centrifuge. "That depends. Are you going to tell me to lie on my bunk and recall my childhood?"

Mac grinned and sat on the floor in front of me. "There she is."

Well, he seemed confident that I wouldn't try to devour him again. BOR wasn't as sure, judging by the intensity of her stare. She remained in beast form, ready to pounce.

"The desire took you by surprise. Now that you know the signs and what to do, I think you'll manage control. And I'll pay closer attention, too. Now, tell me the clues that point you to Doyen Hightower."

Sadness weighed on me, and a thread of doubt bothered. I wanted to curl up on the bed with my katana instead of talk, but I answered. "Josiah never felt Normal, even before you put magic ideas into my head. He could easily be an Ancient who put himself in a position to feed on ignorant Evolutionaries. The Eliminators began disappearing when he became Doyen of Defense, and though privately he led me to believe that he's investigating, he hasn't made public attempts to find out what's happening."

"As your doyen, didn't he give you the assignment to kill the basilisk? Why would he call attention to the blood rock's hiding place?"

"Because he's a devious son of a bitch." Mac looked doubtful, but I'd thought that part through. If I made Josiah the bad guy, I had to go all in. "He couldn't just let a basilisk control part of the city and not attempt to eliminate it. He's *in charge* of Eliminators. But he admitted to me that he'd signed the basilisk order intended for Johnson and Delaney, then made sure they wouldn't show up. At the time, I thought he meant he'd protected them and was genuinely pissed that the job was given to D.J. and me. Maybe he was just mad that I killed his basilisk."

"It would take several Evolutionaries and a lot of power from *Roc Fuil* to make a basilisk," Mac conceded. "I'm sure you angered its creator. Whoever he is."

"The missing Eliminators, Johnson and Delaney, were last seen alive with Josiah. Then Johnson was found dead—shriveled and bloodless—in his backyard. That part makes him look less guilty." Doubt tugged at me, again, but I waved it off. "Maybe Sophia left it there." I liked the idea of her as an idiot sidekick. "Anyway, Josiah is missing, hunted by Doyen Graves. I last saw him at the silo where he managed to knock me out without touching me. When I woke, the ingots and this *Roc Fuil* were gone."

"Are you certain they weren't gone before?"

"No, because he distracted me into chasing him before I could look inside. Very convenient."

Mac worked his lower lip between two fingers and tapped his pen on the journal. "This is damning evidence, but I have problems with your theory. I know that Dr. Trotter trusts Doyen Hightower. He claims that Hightower is a champion for Evolutionaries. Of course, it's possible Dr. Trotter has been fooled, but you trust the doyen, too. You call him 'Josiah,' are you close?"

I squirmed. "He was my warden before he became doyen. He probably knows me well, but I can't say I know him."

"If he's a Magic and he's spent much time around you, at all, he knows you're powerful. You'd be first on his list to suck dry before you became a threat. Plus, if you passed through a ward on his house, it means that he held no negative thoughts toward you—and vice versa—when he set it. Provided he's the one who set it."

I rolled that around in my puny brain as I placed my chin on a fist. "I wasn't very happy with him when I crossed his ward."

Mac shrugged. "But if you had no intention of harming him, you were still worthy of passing through."

Interesting. Wards knew my feelings better than I did. "You say Dr. Trotter spoke to you of Jo—of Doyen Hightower. Do you think he's told Hightower about you?"

"Maybe." Caution elongated the word. "But I've given Jeff no revelations concerning magic. He believes I'm a scientist interested in helping Evolutionaries escape the restrictions the government has placed on them. Which is true."

"Did he know of your desire to remove the ingots?"

"Yes."

"What if Hightower wanted to know what I was first? You said that perceivers only see the ingot magic when they look at Evolutionaries. When Hightower told me to stay away from Sophia, he knew that I would go to Jeff." And with the promise of fire frog boots, he knew I'd try. I really needed to change my materialistic values. "He probably guessed that Jeff would send me to you. Josiah's watched me for almost a year. He'd suspect that I'd get the ingots removed and take my chances with Atlas.

"The hu-li-roos at his house may have been waiting for me, not him. When that didn't work, Sophia tried to get hold of me while I was in Doyen Graves' custody. I'm almost positive those ape-wolves were Sophia's creations, too. Wait. Could they be golems?"

Mac shook his head. "Golems return to dust almost immediately. When I put the blood and tissue samples of the ape-wolves in the mini-fridge, they were still intact."

Eeww: don't use the fridge.

"Why would Hightower tell you to get out of town and stay away from Allen?"

"He probably told Johnson and Delaney to get out of town, too. Hell, I bet they told him where they were going. We all trust him. I might have only evaded him because he's concentrating on Graves. Or, he might be on this train waiting to dramatically bust in."

Mac flinched and glanced at the door. Ha.

"As for telling me to stay away from Allen . . . Allen knows something is going on. He confided as much to me. He also confided in Johnson and Delaney before they disappeared. My guess: Hightower didn't want Allen and I comparing notes. It can't be a coincidence that Waya dragged me away to Sophia just after Allen showed up in the interrogation room.

"I'd say Waya is Sophia's muscle. He showed up after the ape-wolves, and he was alone. Alone! Graves wouldn't send Waya by himself. I'm not sure where Graves fits in. He's always struck me as a by-the-book kind of guy."

Mac clicked his tongue at me. "Slow down. Graves could even be Cynddelw. I'm not convinced of Allen's innocence, either. Don't fall in love with a theory so deeply that you try to force square assumptions into round facts. You have a lot of suspects, right now, and you've got a couple of them working together in your mind."

"But you have to admit that Jo—Hightower is up to something."

"Something, yes, but for now we'll treat everyone like Cynddelw."

Now was the time for Josiah—damn it—Hightower, to knock the door down and vacuum the magic from my veins. There were a few shudders and jerks of the car, then the floor vibrated, but the door remained firmly closed.

A disembodied voice from the hall speakers announced that we'd converted to electric engines. That meant we'd sat in Nevada so long that Atlas had completed its vexatious trip through the night sky, and dawn approached.

Mac rubbed his eyes and stretched out on the floor just a few feet from a bed. We'd talked through an excellent sleeping opportunity. Putting his hands behind his head, he closed his eyes. "Wake me when we're close."

El Dorado Springs was less than twenty miles away. "We're close now."

A dreamy smile touched his lips. "Fifteen minutes."

Shaking my head, I grabbed my katana from where it had fallen out of my lap. Odd that I hadn't reached for it when contemplating going through BOR to get to Mac's magic. Instead, I'd wanted to use my hands, my magic, but I didn't know how.

That I'd nearly attacked Mac still tugged at the thread wrapped around my conscious, making me too anxious to sleep. I sat in a chair and faced the door, just in case Josiah actually showed. I decided to keep the familiarity in my mind. It helped maintain a healthy anger—provided I remembered to breathe. So, I watched the door while Mac watched his eyelids. And BOR watched me.

CHAPTER SIXTEEN

"Should I have just purchased it, you think?" Mac asked.

I tossed my backpack into the bed of a small, once red pick-up that might have fought with a triceratops and lost—many times. Large rusty holes and dents covered the body, but after checking under the hood, Mac declared it sound. No horses meant we needed transportation, and the truck was the only vehicle we could rent to head into the wild Lake District. Charging us three times its worth just to use it four days meant the owner didn't expect happy returns.

I lifted a deluxe cooler full of food, guaranteed to last a week without ice replenishment. "If we'd gone in looking to buy, yes, but you asked to rent first which meant you needed it soon. We wouldn't get a good deal, no matter what."

The cooler dropped beside my backpack with a loud thump. BOR's carrier followed, and she growled a protest of my rough treatment. I was familiar with the drill of heading out of El Dorado Springs, and I'd told Mac to buy, not rent. He hadn't listened. At least he'd wasted his money, not mine.

El Dorado Springs was the last sizable community in south-central Missouri. Springfield, Branson, and West Plains had all been swallowed by the affectionately named Enchanted Forest. Home to the people—and their descendants—who had fled once ideal real estate surrounding the numerous lakes nestled in and near the Ozark Mountains, El Dorado Springs tripled in size after Atlas.

El Dorado Springs also served as a stopping point for crazy people like us to buy supplies before we hacked our way down dilapidated highways covered by the Enchanted Forest just to reach a monster-infested lake. The closest body of water, Stockton Lake, had been my grandmother's favorite vacation spot as a child. When frightened land owners fled volcanic eruptions, she rushed in and bought two-hundred acres. For years, her botanist's brain studied the Atlas-fed forest. She tested theories until she figured out how to build a home that the Enchanted Forest would ignore, believing it belonged.

Others followed her example, so hers wasn't the only home on the lake, but most people couldn't handle the beasts that crept through the trees or slithered beneath the dark lake's surface. My eighty-year-old grandmother no longer lived in her lake house full-time. However, once a week a family of lake lovers like her cleared out encroaching plants and wildlife so she could find her driveway when she visited. If Gram's house wasn't an ideal place for me to practice Earth magic, then no place was.

We stood at the edge of town, in the parking lot of an old military surplus store brought back to life by the Atlas Apocalypse. Gram's house was twenty-five miles southeast, beyond rolling hills covered in dense vegetation. I could literally see where the local government's road maintenance ended. Two miles outside of town, the highway simply disappeared. We would need the two machetes Mac had balked at buying.

I performed a few calf raises, breaking in the pair of camouflaged sneakers I'd added to the machetes. Mac questioned my fashion choice, but I welcomed any shoe that neither flipped nor flopped. Plus, I was in a hurry to leave town. It would take us half a day to travel that twenty-five miles—longer if we ran into trouble.

"Will The Academy break her?"

I looked questioningly at Mac who had come to stand beside me. He nodded at the diner across the street where the Evolutionary girl and her family left after Saturday brunch.

"No. M-kes is running out of Evolutionaries, but the mythical beasts haven't slowed down. It's in their best interest to keep Evolutionaries alive until trained. Plus, most kids in The Academy have families that keep close tabs on them. A high rate of accidental death or suicide would bring unwanted attention."

Mac worked his lower lip with one hand in the thinking posture I'd come to recognize.

"What?"

He shook his head. "Observations like that make me wonder what the mastermind behind the ingots is trying to achieve. Why eliminate people who are vital to the safety of everyone else? They're both anti-magic and anti-nonmagic. It makes no sense."

If Mac didn't have an answer, I knew I wouldn't find one. I shrugged and went to the driver's side of the truck. Mac didn't argue. When it was time to chop away at truck-eating vines and trees that had issues with humans, he could drive. The truck started immediately, a major plus. I steered out of the parking lot and onto the highway.

"So, why is there no outrage from families when Evolutionaries die on the job? Don't your parents still keep tabs on you when you work for M-kes?"

On my list of conversation topics, my relationship with my parents didn't make the cut. It involved uncomfortable emotions. After killing anything with sharp teeth and claws, compartmentalization was my greatest talent. I kept my voice neutral, staring at the empty road. "There are waivers and other legal documents we sign as adults. Families no longer have authority concerning our welfare after seventeen."

"It shouldn't matter." Mac's voice vibrated with emotion, but I chose not to look at him. "Every time an Evolutionary dies fighting beasts, families should protest at the doors of M-kes. Why do they stop caring?"

The steering wheel creaked, and I loosened my grip. "Eliminators and Enforcers eventually lose contact with their families. It's easier that way."

"What? How?"

"Because answering 'How are you?' or 'How was your day?' is stressful. You don't want them to worry, so you lie. Lying takes a lot out of you when you're not accustomed to it, so you avoid it. Your parents sense your reluctance, so they quit calling, and just wait for you to contact them when you want, which is rare. Eventually, calls only happen on birthdays and holidays, after you've worked up a list of positives that have happened over the past few months. You can tell them about those instead of telling them your best friends died right in front of you, or you spent the past week recovering from a chimera nearly goring your heart through your back.

"Parents don't want to hear those things. Unfortunately, those are the things that happen to Evolutionaries. I wasn't born a closed-off loner. I keep my parents in the dark and I have no friends because that's how I deal with life."

I'd said far more than I'd wanted, and my eyes stung accompanied by a lump in my throat. Even so, a small part of me felt relief from sharing what I tended to keep locked inside. Plus, exposing my feelings stopped Mac's questions. We sat in blessed silence until the forest edge loomed before us.

Up close, it didn't look so bad. A living tunnel enclosed the highway, like a secret passage through the hedge of a garden maze. Two thick vines with thorns as long as my fingers crossed the entrance. I opened the door to get out and clear them away, but Mac placed a hand on my arm. "Did those things really happen to you?"

I concentrated on his tightening fingers instead of his face. Carefully removing his hand, I answered as I walked away. "Yes."

After dealing with the vines, I hopped into the back of the truck, holding a machete—my katana would *never* be raised against dulling vegetation. I knocked on the rusty metal roof, and Mac took the steering wheel. We slowly entered the dark tunnel. Hacking away at choking vines and reaching tree limbs appealed to me more than continuing Emotion Hour with Mac.

The tree canopy wove tightly together like a rain forest, so that little light filtered into the tunnel. Less than a mile inside, Mac turned on the headlights, illuminating impossibly ancient trees. Their giant trunks sheltered thorny bushes and brambles that would engulf my leg to the hip if I stepped in them. For the first five miles, the road itself was clear, with the exceptions of a few wandering vines and fallen branches.

Occasionally, a clearing the size of a car opened on the roadside. Metal fencing pushed the foliage away from dark drives leading to the hidden homes of people who desired both seclusion and the benefit of a nearby city. These forest dwellers kept the road clear for a few miles, but eventually the woods became too dark and deep, even for them. We bumped along at a good forty miles per hour until the private maintenance ended and our first obstacle stopped us.

"Thank, God." Machete in hand, I vaulted out of the pick-up. One more minute rattling around in the bed of that truck and I'd have stress fractures in my jaw.

A trio of dark green vines, each one thicker than my thigh crossed above the road, too thick and high for the truck to drive through. I warmed up my wrist, standing in the middle of asphalt cracked and warped by underlying roots. The truck door opened.

"Wait." Mac came beside me, his eyes on the natural barrier. "This is the perfect opportunity to practice."

I studied the stalwart vines, silently daring me to pass them. "Well, they're not trying to eat me, but sure, any chance to swing a blade can be practice."

Mac closed his eyes and shook his head. "Practice your magic, lass. Put the sword away."

I'd known what he meant the first time, but I didn't want to practice. I wanted my magic to stay safely confined inside me where it couldn't do things like kill companions. BOR, back in domestic cat form, snoozed inside her carrier. If I lost control, she couldn't rescue Mac.

"You can do it," Mac insisted. "When I use my healing magic, I picture the wound, the injury I want to heal, and I feed it with my light. Touch a vine, force your magic into it, and imagine it shrinking."

Right.

"Go on."

I handed Mac the machete. "Just in case."

Stepping forward, I took a deep breath and touched the smooth skin of the top vine. The dew that shimmered in the headlights shifted as the vine shook beneath my fingertips. I let my magic escape, concentrating it where my fingers connected with the plant. When my magic pulsed against it, the vine recoiled. Heat tingled from my fingers up my arm, then all three vines glowed fluorescent green and trembled. They fled from my touch, receding off the highway and melting into the quiet trees.

"Wonderful, Andromeda, you did it!" Mac walked up with a grin. "That was far better than I expected."

I kept my eyes on the point where the vines disappeared into the safety of the forest, my hand still raised to touch them. An urge to follow niggled me. I shook my head, letting my hand drop to my side. "It felt wrong."

"You did exactly what I told you, and fast. It was completely right."

I looked about at the trees, wondering if I imagined the branches and brambles pulling into themselves like animals preparing for a storm. I couldn't explain how I knew I hadn't used Earth magic to control the vines. Their fear at my touch felt like hot needles of anxiety pushing against my fingers. The vines were magical—no doubt everything in the Enchanted Forest was—and they'd fled from my power while they'd had the chance. Mac's pleasure with my progress convinced me to let it go. He knew magic, not me.

After that, nothing rooted in the ground blocked our progress. Maybe the vines sent a warning down the road, and everything moved. Aside from a few giant adders and a troupe of flying monkeys, nothing got in our way.

I'd dealt with the monkeys before. Once I cut the first one in half, the rest flew to the forest ceiling and burst through the canopy, out of sight. As leaves and twigs fluttered onto my upturned face, Mac called from the open window. "If we come across a lion chewing his tail, I'm going to carry a bucket of water around the forest."

I snorted. "When you kill one, they always take off. Gram taught me that, years before I went to The Academy."

"Really." Mac peered at me as I passed to my spot in the back. "I'm beginning to think your violent nature isn't magically induced, at all."

I'd already told him that.

*****

We reached Gram's driveway at dusk: record time. I rapped on the back window, and Mac stopped the truck, sticking his head out. "We're here."

His brows shot up. "That was easy."

"Boring." I said at the same time.

He laughed, withdrew his head, and turned into the foliage tunnel leading to the house.

The driveway, made of smooth flagstones cut from the gray limestone cliffs surrounding Stockton Lake, caused less bumps than the highway. Large boulders of the same rock lined the drive, keeping the forest at bay. A century earlier, a quarter-mile driveway paved with stone would have cost a fortune, but area artisans and contractors struggled to stay in business twenty years ago when Gram completed her house plans. Only the price of materials and the architect had been exorbitant, and she'd considered them vital to the success of her house.

Every time I stopped in front of the rock and timber structure set at the back of a high bluff overlooking the wild lake, I agreed that the architect deserved whatever he'd received. Local stones chiseled to fit together formed the foundation of the house. Timber from the surrounding forest made up the rest of the house, and the roof comprised of tightly woven vines from the forest floor, treated with a waterproof coating. Anything emerging from the wood saw itself and the surrounding trees in the reflective glass of the windows.

I got out of the truck, seeing the house with new eyes. "This shouldn't have worked. She used magical materials from these very woods. Wouldn't the surrounding forest attack instead of accept the building?"

Mac swept a glance from the balconies to the carport where four living trees served as the corners. "This is your mother's mother? The botanist?"

"Yes."

"Did she do any of it herself?"

"A lot of it."

"My guess is that the Earth magic gene in her blood established a connection with the materials and the surrounding forest when she touched them. Amazing, really. I wonder if she remembers feeling anything at the time. Can I ask her? She's here, yes?" He nodded at the shiny black SUV under the carport.

"No."

I'd noticed the SUV, too, but I knew its owner. I considered getting back in the truck to leave, then the front door opened. The light from inside fell just shy of our feet at the base of the stone steps, keeping us in shadows. A tall, broad shouldered figure stood in the doorway.

I sighed and walked up the steps, facing the scowling man with graying black hair. Though he was sixty years old, his six feet, four-inch frame looked able to run me over, topple Mac, then take on a few forest beasts as an encore. His eyes remained shadowed and dark, but I knew in the light they sparkled a bright, golden brown. Josiah had always reminded me a little of him. Maybe that's why I'd foolishly trusted my secretive doyen.

A riot of red curly hair rose over his shoulder, followed by large green eyes. It took one second for those eyes to widen. "Oh my God, Nash, it's Andromeda! Move!" She shoved him aside, which couldn't have been easy. She was two inches shorter than me, with a lean build. She got close and stopped with a gasp. Her hand covered her mouth, and she shook her head violently before turning away from me and stepping into him. He kept his unreadable eyes on me as one arm circled her shoulders.

"Hello, Mom, Dad."

Mac might have choked behind me. I didn't look to make sure.

"What are you doing here?" Dad sounded genuinely curious, but it wasn't the greeting of childish dreams.

"I could ask you the same," I said, easily slipping into the role of rebellious daughter. "Isn't planting season around the corner?" They should have been in Illinois, preparing their land to seed.

Dad opened his mouth, but a keening wail rose from his shoulder where Mom had buried her face. Her head tilted back and Dad looked into her face. "What is she doing here? It's obvious! Just look at her skin! Her eyes!"

God had withheld drama from both me and Dad and thrown it all into Mom. She skirted him to go inside, and I knew her destination. Dad followed her, with me behind, and a bewildered Mac bringing up the rear. Just off the front door, a small sitting room contained a special piece of furniture that Gram had purchased with her daughter in mind. Mom already half-reclined on the beige leather fainting couch, her feet touching the floor but her upper body leaning against the side. One forearm covered her eyes.

Dad and I spoke at the same time.

"Shanna, calm down."

"Mom, just listen."

She sat up, tears flowing down her flushed cheeks. As a redhead, it never took much for that pale skin to blush under the mass of freckles she'd acquired from choosing two professions in the sun. "She's dying, Nashoba."

Dad flinched. Until Mom, his grandmother had been the only person to call him Nashoba more than once. It meant 'wolf' in a language no one spoke anymore. In his football days, sports commentators enjoyed revealing his full name and its appropriateness. Even they had called him Nash to his face, though.

Mom railed on. "Those ingots aren't working anymore, and now Atlas is killing her! She's obviously come here for a final weekend with—with." She waved a hand at Mac. "With whoever he is."

"Whoa, whoa, stop the crazy conclusion train. I'm not dying, Mom, okay? And I'm definitely not here for a last hurrah with Mac."

Mac sat down hard beside my mother. "Lord, no."

That stung a little. "Nice to know we're in agreement, I guess."

"No offense, lass, but I'm certain you'd kill me."

I hadn't realized I came off as so sexually aggressive. No wonder Waya always had a smile for me. Speaking of aggression, my father, King of Testosterone, looked ready to kill someone. I didn't know if he thought Mac and I were lying, or if Mac basically calling me a dominatrix made him angry. Actually, I didn't want to know.

"Mac is a scientist," I said, trying to placate the entire room. "He discovered that the ingots weren't really helping me, and I let him remove them. Now we need a quiet, unpopulated place for me to be while I adjust. I'm his experiment."

Dad's dark complexion turned rusty. "Your entire life you complained of being that very thing."

Oops, placation failure. "I'm helping others." I paused, realizing this had become true. Somewhere along the line I'd decided to help other Evolutionaries find freedom. "When I learn to control my—my talents, I can help other Evolutionaries control theirs."

Dad relaxed, but his whiskey colored eyes sharpened. "Talents?"

I glanced at Mac who nodded. When they didn't believe me, I could just show them. "It turns out that the E-gene isn't an evolutionary gene. It's a magic gene."

A full five seconds of silence passed as my parents stared at me. Mom threw her hands up in the air and leaned against the fainting couch once more, squeezing her eyes shut. "She's insane. It's probably the first symptom of death by Atlas radiation."

I locked eyes with Dad, and for a moment I was fifteen again, pleading with just a look for him to intervene with sensibility. Although, this time I asked him to accept magic, so sensibility might have been the wrong word. He sat down in the oversized leather recliner across from Mom's couch. After rubbing his eyes with both hands, he leaned back with a grim face. "What kind of magic?"

Mom sat up. "Are you serious, Nash?"

"Relax, Shanna. What kind?"

"Earth magic." At the least, I expected ignorance with my answer. I hadn't even known what Earth magic was—still didn't, really. The brief relief that crossed his face as he sank deeper into his chair surprised me. What had he dreaded hearing from me?

"Okay," he said, resignation clear. "Let's go outside and have a demonstration so your mother can calm down enough to eat supper."

*****

I stood beside one of the Camellia trees that Gram planted in her garden behind the house two decades ago. Many varieties thrived in this magical environment. She loved tea as much as Mac who gasped with pleasure at the sight of them. A dozen Camellias already bloomed pink and white amidst lower lying, lushly green hostas.

"Bless your grandmother," Mac said, touching a delicate white flower.

I loved the tea trees, too, which influenced my choosing them. Thoughts of tea and cookies with Gram filled my head until my skin glowed with warm pleasure. Surely my magic would be positive with my mind's example.

Closing my eyes, I pushed the memories of my loving, accepting grandmother forward and touched the tree. It shuddered beneath my finger. A unified, sharp intake of air sounded from my parents. I opened my eyes. The tree had grown up and out a foot, and the blooms—now gently glowing—had doubled. I removed my finger, and the magical light faded from the blossoms.

"Well, I'm satisfied," Dad announced from the growing darkness in the backyard. He pulled Mom by the hand, toward the house. Not much kept Dad from a meal.

I frowned at the thriving tree, then shifted my gaze out. Through the gently shifting boughs of evergreens, oaks, and ash, Stockton Lake glittered like a dark jewel. Atlas peeked over the landscape, its red light dying when it met the dark water. Rugged, gray cliffs towered on the opposite side, mirroring the bluff where I stood. Flowering redbuds clung to the rocks, their finger roots losing their grasp the more they grew.

"Well done, Andromeda. I hear BOR growling. I'm going to let her out to roam before she gets too mad at me. I'll retrieve our cooler and bags."

I nodded to Mac, keeping my eyes on the lake. An eagle appeared, soaring low over the water, dipping its talons in and coming up empty. Rising, it built speed and dropped again, this time winning a fish for its effort.

The water beneath it bubbled. A large head with silvery scales and glowing yellow eyes erupted from the lake and snapped massive jaws at the bird, missing it by a feather. The serpentine body undulated above the water before diving back into the lake. The surface returned to a glassy, deceptive calm.

I should have been happy with my tree experiment, but it hadn't grown from my love, my memories. Along with my magic, I had shared my image of Gram, and it had grown for her. Another tree, a tree she'd never touched, might have reacted like the vines across the highway, shrinking away in terror. I studied the dark, deadly lake, fearing my monster waited beneath the surface, too.

CHAPTER SEVENTEEN

Supper was a quiet meal—to Mac's obvious discomfort—but I loved it. I read once that heated discussions while eating had an adverse effect on digestion. Plus, we'd only stopped for a quick sandwich and an apple during our forest journey, so Mom's roasted chicken and vegetables disappeared into my mouth at a record rate. Thankfully, she always made too much.

The kitchen was at the back of the house, providing a panoramic view of the lake and surrounding forest. Full of windows and cabinets, only a fraction of the pale-yellow walls showed. The back wall had a bay window, French doors in the middle, and cabinetry filling the rest.

Flowers from the outside filled the house in various ways: thriving in pots, dried and framed on the wall, or pressed between window panes. Gram's method kept some of the outside in so that the rest of the outdoors would overlook her alien house. Now, it made me wonder if she suspected the presence of magic or at least something more than an Atlas-induced super-forest. As quickly as my parents accepted magic, they likely harbored the truth inside them, too.

I tugged at the collar of the shirt I'd borrowed from Mom. It needed to be a size bigger, but she refused to let me sit at the table wearing a shirt stained with griffin blood. In between bites, I discreetly studied my parents. Dad looked tired, his eyelids heavy above dark circles. A weariness in his movements made me think he'd been struggling with fatigue for weeks. Mom shot anxious looks my way, as if she expected me to sprout tree branches from my head.

Mac disrupted my visions of turning into a rosebush by pushing away from the heavy farmhouse table. "That was excellent, Mrs.

Bochs, thank you. If you'll excuse me, I'll just take Andromeda's bag upstairs. That couch in the den looks more than adequate for myself." He talked as he left through the wide, arched opening between the front of the house and the kitchen.

"Wait!" My mother called, jumping up. "I need to change the sheets."

The upstairs loft that spanned the front of the house only had two bedrooms. The same sheets from the last time they and Gram had been here together were probably still on the guest bed.

"Don't worry, Mom," I said, following Mac. "I'll change them."

My hair ruffled as she ran past me and up the lodge-style stairs made with knobbed, roughly carved logs. She approached her sixtieth year, but she hadn't slowed down much. At the door, she cast a worried glance over her shoulder to see if I followed. I quietly climbed the stairs, listening to the frantic sounds of her stripping the bed.

When I made it to the doorway, she already had the pale green comforter on the floor and the sheets in a pile. She shook a case from a pillow, a frown wrinkling her freckled brow.

"What's wrong?"

She jumped before smiling. "Nothing, sweetheart. I'm just so happy to see you. I want the room to be perfect."

True, my mom always went overboard to welcome me on the rare occasions I visited. I thought it was a guilt trip for not visiting enough. This looked different.

She moved to the carved cedar chest at the foot of the oak, sleigh style bed. As she removed clean sheets, I studied the room. French doors filled the far wall, flanked by two windows, with a balcony beyond. A large cream and green rug covered most of the wooden floor, and the bed sat on it. The nightstand held a lamp, a newspaper, and an empty glass.

I picked up the glass and little drops of water rolled at the bottom. The paper was from St. Louis, dated four days earlier. Holding the paper, I looked down at a pair of large slippers under the bed. Mom stopped.

Slowly, I raised my eyes to hers and kept my voice neutral. "Dad's been sleeping in here?"

She bit her lip. Her eyes teared before she looked away and jerked the fitted sheet into place. I waited, but she remained silent as she shook out the flat sheet and kept working. My dramatic, over-reactive mother wouldn't talk.

All my childhood years, my parents were so in love that it sometimes embarrassed me. Yes, Mom could be crazy, but Dad balanced her out, and he never complained about the job. He was born to keep her sane, and she was born to keep him busy. I'd often felt like the third wheel on their romantic bicycle built for two. Before the reality of being an Evolutionary hit—when I was young and naïve—I'd longed for a love like theirs. I couldn't fathom what had happened. "What did you do?"

Mom gasped and turned on me with a glare. I wasn't sorry. It had to be her fault. Dad had finally tired of her irrational anxiety and put space between them before he went crazy. I raised my brows, dropped the paper, and crossed my arms. In my peripheral vision, Mac entered the room and set my backpack on the floor. He took us in and walked out.

"It's the nightmares," Mom finally answered through clenched teeth. "I didn't do anything."

"Nightmares." Great. "Did you stop taking your anxiety medication?"

She looked down. "I haven't needed meds since you quit calling."

Having what I'd said to Mac that morning thrown back at me hit with bite. The blood drained from my head. Mom raised her eyes and paled beneath all the freckles. She reached toward me. I recoiled, acid rising from my churning stomach. It quickly turned to anger. "I stopped calling because if I really told you about my life, you'd overdose to calm your nerves. You can't handle having me for a daughter, so I relieved you of the burden."

"Stop." Dad's quiet order from the doorway filled the room.

Mom's look for him was full of pleading—or maybe apology—before she busied herself with the bed, again.

"It's not her nightmares that are the problem," he continued, watching her back.

She stopped, staring at the sheet in her hands. "Nash, it's all right, you don't have to."

"No, Shanna." His tired eyes met mine, and I saw a vulnerability in my strong, invincible father that scared me. "They're mine. I'm the one with the nightmares."

I was speechless. Dad stood, waiting for me to reply. When I came up with nothing, he left. Mom silently worked in that calm, accusing manner that only a mother achieved. I didn't realize I ground my teeth until my jaw ached.

I relaxed enough to say, "There are two couches. Dad can sleep in here."

She shook her head. "You know he won't. Just take it."

I knew. It was a shock, and probably a sign of his fatigue, that he'd admitted as much as he did. He wouldn't accept an acknowledgement of what he considered a weakness.

Mom never turned around, keeping her spine straight and proud. For a second, I had an urge to hug her, but I shook it off. She'd gasp or stiffen in response which would completely ruin it. Instead, I just sighed. "Sorry, Mom."

I was at the doorway when she softly called, "Andromeda?" She faced me, wringing her hands. "I'm sorry, too."

"Why?"

"I should have questioned them." She choked on a sob, and shook her head. With a deep breath, she looked me straight in the eye. "I just accepted what they told me when you were born. If I'd tried to understand you, maybe we would have learned the truth sooner. So." She held her arms wide, looking defeated. "I'm sorry."

Well, damn. In two steps, I reached her and squeezed her in a hug that forced the breath from her lungs. Her arms circled my waist, and her tears soaked through the shoulder of my t-shirt. I couldn't remember the last time I'd hugged my mother—or anyone, really. I'd forgotten how therapeutic a sincere embrace could be. All the distance I'd worked to put between us suddenly erased with two apologies and a hug.

Keeping my face between her head and shoulder, I whispered, "It's okay, Mom. We were all fooled. It wasn't your fault."

She shook slightly, her voice muffled. "Are you going to fix it? Help the others like you?"

I had to. Anytime I thought of simply running off to live my own free life, I saw D.J. and the girl from the train. Even Waya needed me. "I'll do my best."

She pulled away to look at me, sadly smiling. "You have to be careful. This couldn't have been an accident, could it? A scientist's mistake?"

"Mac doesn't think so."

Sniffing, she rubbed my arms and picked some piece of fuzz off my shirt that she spied with her super Mom-eyes. "Then someone very powerful tricked an entire generation of parents for reasons that can't be good. If they catch you interfering . . ." She didn't finish.

A seed of regret grew inside of me for easily letting the walls fall and giving her a glimpse of my dark, dangerous world. I wouldn't be able to keep her out, anymore. "I'll be careful. Don't worry."

Her eyes rolled playfully, but they still brimmed with dread. "I've heard that before."

Lead filled me, weighing my heart to my feet until I ached to be held again. One hug and I was an addict. Forcing half a smile, I denied myself the contact and laughed at her words; ignored her fear.

*****

Night settled around the forest like a velvet blanket, and Atlas glowed high in the sky, radiating magic. The hum of the hydraulic dam had ceased, reminding me it existed in the first place. The half-functional dam provided power to those living in the forest and a few towns north. Sometimes, service paused for days when an adolescent lake monster or something equally large got trapped in the turbines. Atlas provided power of a different kind as it forced electrical silence.

I sat on the built-in bench of my bedroom balcony, watching the trees bask in Atlas light. Tired as I was, sleep eluded me, so I'd left the bed and come outside. Dropping my guards, I let the magic enter. It sparked on my skin like magical fireflies. My sight sharpened, and I heard the soft sounds of everyone else sleeping beyond the walls and closed doors.

With my magic running hot, I saw a silvery white line marking the ground ten feet from the house and disappearing around both corners. A transparent wall shimmered and rose from the line, sloping until its sides met to form a dome a few feet over the house. Mac had set a ward before going to bed—a big one, too. No wonder he'd snored as soon as he hit the couch.

I reached out and pulled the tarp that covered a bulky shape on the balcony. It dropped to reveal a shiny, well-maintained ballista loaded with arrows. Chuckling, I pushed it side to side, and it soundlessly glided on a well-oiled wheel.

Gram had bought a ballista for her cabin and asked my parents to install it. She practiced daily at the archery range two miles from her house in St. Louis. I had no doubt she ran it better than any of the crew on that train last night. I threw the tarp back on and stepped up to the balcony railing.

It started as a flutter in my chest, as if I'd sprinted after drinking too much tea. The feeling intensified, growing into a heavy awareness that something familiar watched from the forest. I scanned the ground, but saw nothing until my eyes moved higher.

Perched in the groove between a large branch and the trunk of an evergreen, sat a creature I'd never seen. It drew in the shadows around it, making itself a dark outline. Ears pointed past the top of the head, and the body had long arms and legs that bent sharply past the shoulders as it squatted in the tree like a small human. I should know it.

Imagining my magic as a spout of water, I focused and pushed it past the ward, straight at the shadowy beast. My magic hit it like a flashlight, illuminating gray skin pulled taught over a skull comprised of bat and human features. Ribs and ropy muscle stood out in the surrounding darkness. The creature bared fangs in a hiss, and my fangs grew in response.

Control. Show it control.

My magic surrounded the beast, recognizing the shadowy contours of the creature even if my mind didn't. The darkness within me growled, and the low rumble escaped my lips. The tiny red dots in the creature's eyes brightened and grew. I felt its realization that I was familiar. Familiar and dominant. Its fangs disappeared, and the head dropped, followed by the shoulders in a bizarre bow.

My inner beast howled in victory, and my control of it slipped. I drew my magic away, pulling it into me with an effort that made me tremble. Breathing deeply, I closed my eyes until the calm returned. I dared a glance at the shadowy creature. It reverted to the dark, space-eating form. The eyes dimmed, and the body stilled, keeping its position in the tree.

Without my magic, I wouldn't have known it was there. The owl that lighted on the branch by the creature sensed no danger. It tilted its head and focused on me, instead. The attack came brutally quick. With a flutter of feathers and a distressed squeak, the owl disintegrated in a swirling cloud that flowed straight into the creature's mouth. Red eyes flared with satisfaction, then it leapt from the tree and disappeared into the night.

I stared at the peaceful spot of the owl's demise, unable to remember the last time a beast had shocked me—aside from the basilisk. BOR in beast form patrolled the ward perimeter and continued on, never looking at the tree where the shadow beast had inhaled the owl. I hadn't come in contact with plenty of creatures and phenomena in the world, I knew that. This thing identified me, though, and deep inside, I had recognized it, too. I'd come to the balcony to get my mind in a better state for sleep, but Morpheus didn't even tease me, now.

A cry from my parent's bedroom pierced the peaceful silence. I jumped from my balcony to theirs in panic. I'd never heard such a sound from Dad. Without hesitating, I kicked in the curtained French doors. Mom screamed, but I ignored her as I scanned the room for danger, finding nothing. Dad thrashed on the bed, crying out again.

"Nash." Mom shook his shoulder. "Nashoba, wake up."

"The nightmares?" I walked to them. Until this moment, I'd doubted their claim.

Mom nodded, tears flowing down her cheeks. Dad's face contorted with fear and pain. He gripped the sheets that twisted around his struggling legs. This had to be horrible for him. Being attacked by something he couldn't punch in the face was probably his greatest fear.

My magic rose to the surface with my anxiety. That my skin glowed bright barely registered when I touched his shoulder. A shock jolted from my fingers straight to my chest, and an invisible bond melded my hand to him. I gasped as my vision blurred. The floor disappeared, and I spiraled down a gray vortex.

I hit the bottom of a canyon formed by glistening black rock and darkness. Shadows rose around me, whispering and twining between my legs, around my waist, through my fingers. I stood in a black and gray world. My skin was a few shades lighter than the shadows that surrounded me. The only color glowed red in the swirling clouds of an endless sky. A distant, insistent thumping vibrated the earth, and my heart hurried to meet its anxious pace. The more I tried to calm my pulse, the faster the beat raced, like a frenzied drumline rallying me to war.

It pushed me to run. My feet flew over jagged fissures and

boulders. I saw no destination, but my heart would explode if I didn't arrive soon. Finally, I came to a cliff and leapt onto it. I barely found holds for my fingers before they let go to reach higher. Slowing down was impossible as the ever-present shadows rose with me. Just when I thought the beating pressure in my head could get no worse, I landed on the top, and the beat halted.

I didn't realize I held my breath until the drum sounded again—this time a slow, steady pace. A deep crater of darkness spread out below me with gray mist rising like tongues of smoke. At the edge of the cliff knelt a man, his bare back gray and glistening with sweat. He gasped and hugged himself, his body trembling. A low moan full of anguish floated back to me.

"Dad?"

He didn't answer. I came to stand at his shoulder, positive of his identity when I saw the '54' tattoo with my mother's name below his football jersey number. I reached toward him, then remembered that our last contact had landed me here.

"I can't stop it." His voice was harsh and raw, like he'd screamed for hours. He turned his head toward me, and fear crackled like static up my spine. His face had lost any softness, now only hard planes and shadows. His eyes were completely black—no whites, no pupils, just pools of darkness framed with lashes that stood out against his stark, gray cheekbones.

"Help me," he whispered. "Make me stop."

"Stop?" Dad never asked for help, and to imply that he needed it insulted him.

"Please." Black liquid leaked from his eyes, rolling down his cheeks to drop on a chest so gray and defined by shadows it looked like marble. Dear God, he cried.

Then the heart drum rolled, bringing thunder that built beneath my feet until it crashed.

"Please. Please!" The anxiety in his voice built like the drums.

The mist in the crater darkened. Slowly, the vapor became black, swirling into human shapes then solidifying. Dozens of obsidian statues stood before us, like the terra cotta warriors in ancient tombs. Silence reigned, heavy and pregnant until a crash shook my bones. The statues glowed. White cracks in the obsidian grew and widened, then exploded so brightly I had to close my eyes.

When I could look again, there were people. People I recognized:

177

my mother, my grandmother, two uncles, an aunt, and countless cousins. Behind them stood others I didn't know, but I suspected the man beside me, trembling with expectation, knew them. Their skin shone ghostly white. They moved toward us, walking but not quite touching the ground.

Every mouth whispered. It seemed they said the same words but at different times: a twisted, insensible round that caused my head to ache.

"Stop! Stop!" Dad put his hands over his ears and bowed low, trying to push himself into rock.

They advanced, chanting with cavernous mouths and staring with empty eyes. I backed away. "Just wake up. Wake up, and they'll go away."

He convulsed, struggling to hold a weight I couldn't see. Suddenly, he shot to his feet and flung his arms wide. A unified scream from a hundred mouths ripped through the air, and my family turn to ash like Pompeii victims. A massive gray cloud filled the crater as each body disintegrated. Then, the cloud rushed my father in a tidal wave.

He shook, absorbing every last particle through his mouth, his eyes, his pores, each part of his body that the cloud touched. His skin darkened, and his veins stood out black, pulsing wildly like the frenzied drum. With a hoarse cry, he collapsed on the ground.

"It's just a dream, it's just a dream," I said, dropping beside him and rolling him to his back. Over his heart, his skin was black as tar, like the leathery skin of a bat. The patch grew, covering his chest and shoulders in seconds. This was magic—black magic that my father's body couldn't handle. It would kill him.

"Give it to me," I whispered.

His eyes fluttered open. No recognition hovered in their dark depths, just pain and despair.

"I can free you." I grew frantic as more than half of his body changed. He'd be lost if the transformation completed. This wasn't a dream anymore.

I placed my hands on his head and closed my eyes, opening myself wide to everything churning within him. Shadows rushed my mind, eagerly wrapping themselves tightly, making a home deep inside me. "More," I demanded. "Give me all of it."

A glorious wave of darkness slid through me, filling the empty spaces I hadn't been aware of, fortifying invisible weakness. My bones turned to steel as my body feasted on the shadows that had weakened my father. What poisoned him was ambrosia to my cells. When I sucked up the last of it, I released his face with a joyful shout.

Euphoria enveloped me, exhausted me, so that I fell on my back, gasping for air. I opened my eyes to see Mac's troubled face over me, his blue eyes a shock after so much gray.

"What did you do?" His voice bounced inside my head.

I smiled lazily. Sleep crept into my weary mind, and his face blurred. "I satisfied the beast."

CHAPTER EIGHTEEN

Birds chirped, and leaves rustled. Light glowed beyond my closed eyelids, but I turned away from it, burrowing deep under my blankets. I didn't know what nature was so pleased about out there, but I wished it would shut up.

As far as I recalled, last night's activities consisted of sulking on my balcony before eating my father's nightmare. My body ached like I'd run for miles carrying a monster on my shoulders.

"Awake, are we?" Mac's voice invaded my cozy cocoon.

I might not be able to send nature packing, but I knew how to scare him away. "I sleep naked."

"Nice try. I'm the one who put you in bed."

That news had me pulling the covers off my face to stare at him. He sat in a stuffed armchair in the corner, his clothes rumpled and hair standing on end. Stubble shadowed his jaw and smudges of purple marred the skin beneath his eyes. "Did you forget to put yourself to bed, afterward?"

Mac frowned, his tired face gaining a few more lines. "It seemed prudent to keep watch over you. BOR and your mother are with Mr. Bochs."

I sat up. "Dad needs watching?"

Mac yelped and put a hand over his eyes. "When did you manage that?"

"I warned you." No matter how I went to bed, I tended to work my clothes off. Not every night, but definitely when anxiety ruled my mind before bed. It was the reason I'd gone through three roommates at The Academy until Jun Tekada had shown up. She'd just laughed.

I raised the sheet to my armpits and held it in place, a little annoyed that my bare breasts alarmed him so much. They were about the size of grapefruit and a decent shape, in my opinion.

Anything bigger would get in the way. "You had to see my boobs when you took the ingots out." A light pattern of white scars over my left breast was the only physical reminder of the silica ingots.

"Purely clinical."

"Okay, your sensitive eyes can look again."

He dropped his hand, looking sheepish. "Sorry. I mean, you *were* wearing a shirt when I laid you down, and I haven't left."

I wasn't exactly light. He'd probably had to carry me over his shoulder like a sack of BOR feed. BOR probably ate deer or mountain lion, maybe baby manticore. I wondered if she ever left dead tunnel rats at Mac's door. I relaxed back onto my pillows, waiting for my brain to completely wake up and stop worrying over BOR food. "What's wrong with my dad?"

Mac rubbed a hand down his face. "As far as I can tell, he's simply an exhausted man finally getting the sleep he needs. However, it's been almost twelve hours."

Whoa. I stared at the faded yellow paisley pattern on the sheets. Even after my roughest nights of monster-slaying, I didn't sleep more than five or six. Mac's sedatives after the ingot removal hadn't even lasted twelve hours.

"It would help if you could tell me what happened," he said.

I hesitated. Whatever he'd seen had concerned him, but I remembered feeling fantastic—perfect, even. Sure, my muscles ached now, but a few other nights in my past had been well worth the next day's discomfort.

"Your mother told me about the nightmares."

He thought I worried about revealing Dad's secret. Fine, I'd give him the basics. "I touched his shoulder, and found myself inside his nightmare, I think. In his dream, our family and other people he cares about—." I paused. My statue, my image hadn't been with the group of my Dad's loved ones. I swallowed past a heavy lump in my throat. "These people floated before him, like washed-out zombies. They exploded into some kind of dark cloud that he absorbed. It made his veins look like yours did when you stuck the cursed ingot under your skin. Then his body started turning black. I thought he suffered from dark magic."

Mac pursed his lips. "In his mind, maybe, but he never changed outwardly. You, on the other hand." He stopped to stare at me like he didn't understand me, anymore. "You were floating off the floor and shining like a supernova. Your mother tried to pull your hand off your father's shoulder, but you wouldn't budge. Something dark, like smoke, did escape his mouth. It was like an exhale into cold air, except gray and substantial. Then you breathed it in and your skin swirled with the same dark lines as before. They looked like spider web tattoos and stayed there for hours."

I held an arm out before me, trying to imagine tattoos covering my skin. I'd attempted a tattoo when I was sixteen. My body had completely absorbed the ink and nearly healed the wounds before the artist was half finished. He'd been kind enough to just charge me for the ink.

"Before you passed out—"

"I went to sleep."

Mac's lips twitched, finally softening that weary expression I didn't like to see on him. "Right. Just before you went to sleep, you said, 'I satisfied the beast.' Was there a beast in your father's nightmare?"

Uh, that would be me. "It's just an expression."

Mac's brows raised. He remained quiet, not buying the excuse.

I tried to keep my voice light. "It means that the monster—" I used air quotes, and nearly lost my sheet—" the monster inside me swallowed my dad's nightmare, and now it's quiet and happy."

Silence dropped between us, so thick I might touch it. Finally, his blue eyes sparked with incredulity. "There's no expression for that." He jumped up and waved his arms, cutting through all that heavy air. "That's not a thing!"

"It is now."

"No." His hard voice shook me. He stepped close and pointed a finger that came inches from my nose. "No, that would require repetition, and you can't do this anymore. We have to learn what it does to you, first—what it even *is* that you did. We don't yet know what it's done to your father."

Of course I shouldn't have told him what I thought had happened. Now he worried, and he couldn't do anything. This was internal—a problem deep inside me that he couldn't see or understand. I had to take care of it on my own. "I'm going to get dressed and see Dad. You have five seconds before the sheet drops."

He was gone in two.

★★★★★

Dad looked peaceful lying on his back with his arms at his sides, palms up: Corpse Pose. I opted not to divulge this Yoga knowledge to Mom as she sat beside him, looking twice as haggard as Dad had yesterday. Bad situations quickly took their toll on Mom. Unfortunately, the resident Shanna Whisperer was in a coma, though Mac had refrained from using that term.

When I left my position in the doorway, Mom tensed. BOR stood and left through the open French doors, then jumped off the balcony. At least the panther trusted me to behave. "I won't touch him," I promised.

Mom relaxed, leaning one elbow on the bed as her other hand smoothed Dad's thick, salt and pepper hair. "I'm grateful he's finally resting. I just—I don't know what." She pressed a fist to her mouth so hard that her lips turned colorless. The love and fear in her eyes brimmed until a single tear slipped down her cheek.

"I understand." I sat on the heavy cedar chest at the foot of their bed decorated in blues and greens like the rest of the room. She needed to get out of there, at least for a few minutes. "If I promise to stay right here and yell if there is a change, will you get something to eat and a little fresh air?"

She grabbed Dad's hand as if I'd threatened to carry him off into the forest, instead. "I'm fine. We're fine."

I wasn't surprised she didn't trust me, but it still hurt. "Mom." I hesitated. Dad would put an arm around her shoulders and stroke her hand. Obviously, that wouldn't work for me. Sighing, I gave it my best. "When Dad wakes up—and he will—he'll need you to be at your best. If you don't refuel yourself, you'll have no strength when he leans on you. You'll both collapse."

She shifted, glancing doubtfully at my father's face.

With a tight chest, I played the card that I knew would show her hand. "That will leave me to help you both."

The horror of that flashed across her face before she hid it. Growing up, the fear that I would catch in her glances concerned my welfare. Now, it was fear of what I might do. Even more irritating, I feared the same thing. The distance I'd closed between us last night was easy to replace, after all.

"Okay." She stood, caressing Dad's face one last time. "I'll send Dr.

MacDuggan in to—to help."

I didn't argue.

She paused in the doorway. "Can I bring you a sandwich?"

I shook my head. After she left, I watched Dad for a few minutes before shifting my gaze out the French doors which let in an abundance of light and fresh air. Mac wouldn't join me for a while since he currently stood at the edge of the woods, shaking a stout stick. He tossed it in the air, and BOR in beast form leapt from the branch of a giant oak to catch the stick in her mouth. She landed lightly beside him.

"You've got to be kidding me."

"Cats don't fetch." A hoarse voice agreed from the bed.

Dad had his face turned toward the forest, able to see through the large spaces between the balcony balusters. My first instinct was to childishly leap onto the bed and grab him in a bear hug. I rose off the chest and tensed for a jump before I forced my ass back onto the cedar lid. I'd said I wouldn't touch him. No family discord would be struck by my broken promises. "Mom just left to eat. I'll go get her."

"No. Close the door. I need to talk to you."

I hadn't had a private conversation with Dad since I left for the Academy at fifteen. I also couldn't remember the last time I hadn't done what he told me to, so I shut the door.

"And these damn French doors. She knew I was sleeping, right? Nobody needs sunlight for sleeping."

He continued to complain about nature while I closed the doors and pulled the shades until the light no longer touched his bed. Dad loved the outdoors, and he'd yet to reach grouchy old man status so he built up to something. My guess was it would make us both uncomfortable. I returned to the cedar chest and waited.

His eyes were bright and refreshed, the weary sag gone from his features. Those topaz eyes studied me a moment before he sat up and propped all the pillows behind him. He crossed his arms and frowned. "Do you ever have nightmares?"

"Often."

He pondered that a minute before continuing. "I'd never had any before, at least, not any that stuck with me. These—these were." He fidgeted. "Always with me. Even when I was awake I could feel the pressure in my head, like knowing I couldn't do anything was a physical weight. The nightmares were all I could think about. My memory of anything else became shadowy. Those shadows." He cleared his throat and took a drink from a glass on the bedside table. "The shadows made me realize what was happening. That and the fact that you weren't there until last night. You remember what you saw? All our family?"

"Yes." I bit my lip. Not *all* our family.

"You were never there."

I pressed my lips together.

"I mean with the rest of them. I remember exactly where you were last night."

I flinched at his death toll tone. "Dad, I didn't mean to—"

"Never mind. What I'm saying is that it bothered me you weren't with the rest of the people I care for in these nightmares. Because I do care for you." He made sure my eyes locked on his so I could see his sincerity. "I'll always love you, Andee, no matter how little you contact us. It killed me that you wouldn't become a dependent and stay on the farm where it's safe, but I understand why you didn't."

When I was young, Evolutionaries only avoided working for M-kes one way. If an Evolutionary were claimed as a dependent by an *acceptable* guardian, that Evolutionary could then stay on their property after signing an oath. If the Evolutionary ever disappeared, the guardian was deemed responsible. It was basically house arrest with penalties for the wardens. Given my physical skills, Mom and Dad would have been deemed unacceptable guardians, anyway, so that M-kes could use me. The government no longer allowed the dependent loop hole. The dying Evolutionary breed had to be used to its fullest capacity.

Dad had never said much when I decided to go to The Academy and train for M-kes. He'd held Mom back and told her my path was my choice. "I love you, too, Dad."

I glanced away as he pretended to rub sleep from his eyes, and I sniffed loudly. If we kept throwing our feelings out, we'd get off course, and Mom would show up before he told me what really bothered him. "What did you mean by the shadows and my absence from the nightmares told you what was happening?"

"It reminded me of a story Noni—my grandmother—told me and my cousins when we were young. She died when I was thirteen, and my mother never cared much for stories, so I haven't heard the tale for decades. It was Noni's favorite, though."

"An indigenous story?" Dad's Noni had thrown tales and native history at her grandchildren regularly. Most of it had died with her.

"It's kind of our family history. We always liked it because it promised we'd be strong, fast, and resilient."

"Prophetic." Dad's uncles and cousins were phenomenal athletes just like him. His mom had been strong and healthy, too, until she'd fallen to her death on a mountain climbing exhibition a few years before I was born. He barely remembered his German father who died when Dad was six years old.

"But like all Noni's stories, there was a catch." He stopped and watched me, silently asking.

"Mom won't stay away long," I said. "Bring it."

With a nod, he closed his eyes and leaned back onto the pillows. Noni's story went like this:

Long ago, monsters roamed the world. They were beasts formed by magic, and by magic only could they be destroyed. As with all powerful things, they became arrogant and bold. Magic was a delicate balance of light and dark, but the beasts threatened the balance. With regret, the Great One took magic away, because its abuse increased, and the people were fearful.

Without magic, the monsters expired; some of them quickly, but others lingered. One day, a young man named Kiliahote came upon Nalusa Falaya—a shadow monster. He tried to eat Kiliahote and make him the final meal for a fading monster. The young man cried out to the sun which came free of the clouds and chased Nalusa Falaya into a cave.

Kiliahote followed him to the cave entrance.

"Stay away," the sun warned.

Instead, Kiliahote kindled a fire and took it inside. Nalusa Falaya huddled in the dark, blending with the shadows so that Kiliahote could not see him. Again, he tried to eat the young man. Kiliahote wounded him with his fire, and Nalusa Falaya fell back.

"You are a smart boy."

"I am a man," Kiliahote declared.

"When you have sons, you will be a man," Nalusa taunted.

Kiliahote pounded his chest with his fist. "Soon."

"If your sons were the strongest, fastest, most resilient warriors, it would be great comfort, yes?"

"Oh, yes."

"I can make them that way."

Kiliahote was wary. "How?"

"Have you ever caught a shadow?"

"No."

"Because they are too fast. Have you ever forced a shadow to do your bidding?"

"Of course not."

"Because they are too strong. When the sun sets, do shadows die?"

"Shadows are always there."

"Because they are resilient. I can make your sons like the shadows."

Kiliahote was eager, now. Who better to make his sons like the shadows than a shadow monster? "What must I do?"

"It is simple. You must willingly give me a place to live. I will stay there for as long as I need. When magic returns to the world, so shall I."

The home Kiliahote shared with his wife would soon be filled with children. "I do not have much room in my house."

"I will not take up space in your house."

Kiliahote was doubtful again. "Will I have to build you a home?"

"Nothing must be built for me."

Kiliahote scratched his head and looked about the cave. "Can you live here?"

Bright eyes shone in the midst of Nalusa Falaya's shadow. "Yes. But you must say it."

"Say what?"

The shadow's voice was patiently slow. "You must say, 'I, Kiliahote, allow you to live here.'"

"Because I defeated you?"

"Yes, that is it. Give me permission."

That was simple, after all. Kiliahote spread his arms wide and said, "I, Kiliahote, allow you to live here."

Nalusa Falaya shrunk until he was a black shiny speck the size of a maize kernel. The kernel flew into Kiliahote's chest, piercing the skin and burrowing into his heart where his life blood flowed. The seed touched Killiahote's blood with every beat of his heart so that shadows whispered through him and his offspring. His sons were mighty warriors, and his daughters brave, as were their sons and daughters. But each first born carried a shadow in their heart; a curse that passed through generations; a monster awaiting rebirth.

I stared at Dad, speechless. It had never occurred to me that I'd gotten a double dose of the magic gene: one from each parent. Dad smiled a knowing, disappointed smile that I hadn't seen in years. "I'm an only child, just like you. My mother was the oldest of five children, and her mother, Noni, was also the oldest. I've spoken with my cousins and my uncles, no one is suffering from nightmares about turning their loved ones into ash then eating them."

Those must have been interesting conversations.

"You and I are the only firstborns still alive. When you told me you had Earth magic, I hoped I was mistaken. I wanted this to be mental illness instead of Noni's story come to life. But, what you have." He swallowed, and his eyes darkened. "It's stronger than what lived inside me. It conquered my own shadows."

"Lived." I found my voice. "Are you sure it's gone?"

He nodded. "You took it all."

I'd eaten every bit of my dad's curse and licked my fingers afterward. Now, I was the sole carrier of a shadow monster's seed. Mac would not be pleased.

CHAPTER NINETEEN

"The bad news is, the lingering black magic in my blood is actually the essence of a shadow monster that's probably trying to take over my body and regain its place in the world of magic. Good news, I haven't wanted to suck the magic out of you for nearly three days." I shook my head. Nope, that didn't sound right at all.

I tried again. "There's a monster living inside me, but right now he seems content." Maybe. "Okay, here's what happened. I—"

Mac emerged from the train bathroom and glanced around. "Are you talking to someone?"

"Nope, just . . . singing." It didn't matter how much I practiced, I couldn't tell him my dad's story.

"You sing?" Mac grinned as he stuck his travel kit inside his duffle bag. "How delightful and unexpected."

"Only in private," I rushed to add.

It had been two days since Dad dropped the bomb shell that I was cursed by the seed of shadow monster. He looked well rested when he and Mom saw us off at the train station before they left for home, too. They held hands and shared quiet smiles, back to the parents of my childhood. Now, *I* couldn't sleep.

Unlike the ingots, Mac couldn't just remove my monster and everything would be normal. The shadow monster was a part of me, and I needed to control it; but I couldn't bring myself to tell Mac. I wanted him to focus on finding Josiah/Cynddelw, then we could worry about Nalusa Falaya. 'One monster at a time' became my new motto.

"Before we get back into the storm, we need a list of allies," Mac announced, sitting in a tiny armchair and picking up a notebook off the table beside him.

"You won't need paper for that. There's you, and there's me."

And I was only sure about me half the time.

"Nonsense." He shook a pen at me before putting it to paper. "Be positive. I count Dr. Trotter, Mrs. Holt—." He paused as I snorted at the name of the woman who'd declared my magic was 'wrong.' Even though she'd proved right, I didn't have to trust her.

"She might be stuffy and irritating, but she's committed to the safety of the magical community, and she has connections. She'll want to stop Cynddelw," Mac promised. "I also have three friends in the city who are Magics: an elemental mage, a shifter, and a metal mage."

"Metal mage?"

Mac looked up with a grin. "Yes, he has amazing control over virtually anything made of metal, even guns and bullets. There are exceptions, of course, and spells that block his power but it's extremely useful."

A memory tickled the back of my mind. "Does he live in Brookside?"

"Yes! How did you know?"

Rifleman. "Josiah lives in Brookside."

"Oh. And what about you?"

"Where do I live?"

"Who are your friends we can rely on." He waited, pen poised.

I stared helplessly. Josiah used to be—not a friend—but someone I trusted and relied on, at least. I worked regularly with no one, and considering the depths this M-kes conspiracy seemed to run through, anyone could be against me. All I could think of was, "D.J. Chadar." She'd helped me kill the basilisk and escape M-kes headquarters. That made her loyal in my opinion.

"And?"

I shook my head. "I don't trust anyone else."

Mac looked down at his list, uncomfortable, just like anyone would be when someone admits having no friends. He cleared his throat. "Well, Dr. Trotter likely knows a few Evolutionaries who will join our cause."

"Which is what? Convince everyone else to remove their ingots, and put an end to Cynddelw's, aka Josiah's, Evolutionary magic-draining fun?"

"That sums it up, yes. What about Graves?"

"I don't trust him, either."

"Yes, but if Josiah—who you did trust—is not Cynddelw, then

Graves' determination to find him and his apprehension of you put him at the top of my suspect list. Plus, the bodies you described were in his custody. Maybe Graves found the murdered Eliminators because he knew exactly where he'd left them. He could be using the bodies to frame Doyen Hightower because he sees him as a threat."

"Maybe. But Josiah is just as suspicious. He ordered me out of town and away from Sophia who might give him away. He didn't want me talking to Provost Allen who has concerns about the disappearing Eliminators. Josiah cleaned out the cursed ingots silo—including Cynddelw's *Roc Fuil*—and knocked me unconscious. Plus, his house was crawling with Sophia's minions who are clearly out to get me. Why isn't he at the top of your list?"

"Because I trust your instincts, and you thought him worthy, once, which is obviously a rarity for you. Some of those suspicious reasons you listed are also the actions of someone who doesn't want you in danger."

I snorted and averted my gaze to the floor. The little flicker of hope his words kindled in my chest was hard to smother.

"Dr. Trotter also trusts him, and Trotter's a smart man. Why are you so quick to believe Doyen Hightower—a man you trusted with your life—is Cynddelw?"

I compressed my lips, trying to keep the truth bottled inside, but I couldn't hold it back. "Because he's a Magic, which means he knew I was and didn't tell me. He betrayed me. I was wrong to trust him. My instincts are shit." There, I'd said it with only a mild sting behind my eyes.

"That's difficult to overlook." Mac surprised me with agreement. "But he might have good reasons. Promise that before you do something you'll regret, like hack him with that katana, you'll give him a chance to explain."

"I never hack." I crossed my arms and turned to look out the window where trees passed by at a dizzying speed. "I won't kill him unless he tries to turn me into a golem."

"We'll get Cynddelw—whoever he is—to reveal himself, then we'll learn the truth."

"How?"

"By dangling something before him that he can't resist. What are your feelings on playing the bait?"

*****

D.J.'s apartment was so close to M-kes headquarters that the desire to look over my shoulder became a persistent itch on the back of my neck. I stood in the shadows of the building across the street and tried to sink as far as possible into the hood of my jacket. It rained just heavy enough to slick the pavement and keep most people indoors. In the half hour I waited there, only five individuals walked past—and just one noticed me. He moved to the other side of the street.

I shrugged to feel the reassuring weight of my katana then remembered I didn't have it. Mac had convinced me it was too distinctive for Kansas City. I should have faked another panic attack, but leaving it behind hadn't caused such an emotional reaction this time. Maybe Jun's influence faded, which worried me. Or maybe my purpose evolved, and I didn't need my safety katana.

I waited one more minute, listening for noises and looking for any late-night movement. I crossed the street, passed the building entrance without slowing, and rounded the corner. After casually checking for witnesses, I ran and jumped against the brick wall, vaulting farther up to grasp the slippery fire escape. At the same time, I braced my feet against the brick building and eased the ladder down in a controlled, quiet fall that brought me perpendicular to the wall before I swung my feet down and climbed.

When I reached the platform, a window below me opened. Despite my best effort, someone had heard the grating metal and stuck their head out to investigate. A shaggy head emerged, felt the rain drops, and ducked back in. Yep, the rain saved me some trouble.

I crept past two more windows to D.J.'s dark apartment. The windows of old buildings were easy to open for anyone who made the effort. I stood in her bedroom a minute later.

It was small, neat, and cute—just like its owner. The pale blue walls and white, eyelet bedspread were a little too sweet for my tastes, but no one cared about my opinion. I moved out of the bedroom into the living/dining area divided from the small kitchen by a waist high wall.

That D.J. wasn't home, yet, surprised me. She should have been on patrol shift this week which ended at 2:00 a.m. I'd arrived at her building at 3:00. Either I'd miscalculated, or her schedule had changed.

I tried to find a clue to her whereabouts, but nothing caught my attention. The lamp table held no mail. No boots sat by the front door. Her milk hadn't expired. At least the fresh food told me she wasn't missing—and that she ate better than me. She had poor tastes in weapons and footwear, though.

I almost missed the flashing light of an answering machine. Answering machines were fickle technology, brought out of retirement when Atlas wreaked havoc on digital storage. They didn't always work during peak Atlas hours, either, but the message would stay there until a time you could listen to it. Atlas still radiated electrical menace, but I pushed the button, anyway.

"Miss Chadar." A nasal voice sounded from the speaker. "We need you to return to headquarters, ASAP. An Erymanthian infestation in the West Bottoms requires all available Eliminators."

An invasion of giant boars—yikes. D.J. had probably heard the message as she walked in the door and turned right back around. I found a pen and note pad in the lamp table drawer. After scribbling a quick note telling her where to meet me, I put it in the fridge with her milk. Mac could have thought of a cleverer place to hide it in plain sight, but I was the muscle of this operation, not the brains.

I left through the self-locking door, seeing no one until the ground floor stairwell when a skinny man sitting on the steps asked me for a cigarette.

"I choose quicker methods of self-destruction," I answered and walked back into the rainy night.

Slipping into a steady pace, I had time to think: a dangerous activity some might say. I needed clothes, weapons, and money from my apartment. I'd been gone nearly a week. Surely any surveyors of my place were few to non-existent—or even called to the West Bottoms like D.J. I only needed ten to fifteen minutes.

Mac and I had split up in Kansas City. He'd gone on to Leavenworth alone to get the horses and talk to any allies near his home—though he'd promised not to go to his house for now. After that, he'd find his Kansas City friends and get a message to Dr. Trotter. Our rendezvous was tomorrow, so I had plenty of time to get in trouble and get myself out of it, too.

I couldn't have snuck into my building except the security guard argued with a shabbily dressed man who wanted to come in from the rain. I backed kindness to the homeless, but my goal was invisibility. I slipped behind them and quietly entered the stairwell. After reaching the third floor, I left the stairs and took the Da Vinci elevator to the thirtieth.

My hall was silent in the early morning hours. The few Evolutionaries who lived here still worked or crashed in their beds. A frisson of déjà vu shook me when I reached my door.

With my ingots gone, the scent unique to Josiah nearly overwhelmed my senses. A mix of burning wood and fresh outdoors, it reminded me of a spring campfire. I wondered if he was still inside, then I saw the bloody hand print on the door jamb.

"Damn it." I opened the door and crossed the threshold with zero caution.

Electricity wrapped around me. The jolt shocked every pore, stealing my breath until black edged my vision. I fell to the floor, gasping. My muscles were mush, refusing to rearrange themselves from awkward angles. I managed to move my eyes from the floor and see a ward burn electric blue before returning to a translucent shimmer.

"That son of a bitch." I pushed my hands against the floor with just enough power to roll to my back. He'd warded my apartment. *Mine.* As I lay there waiting for my heart rate to normalize, I pictured various forms of torture. Cynddelw or not, Josiah Hightower would pay.

I probably had less than ten minutes before anyone who spotted my entrance came running with help. Keeping a hand on the wall, I got to my knees, took a deep breath, and rose to my feet, legs shaking. I only stumbled twice on my way to the bedroom.

On autopilot, I changed my clothes and zipped on my favorite, black suede boots. Then, I stuffed a duffle bag with clothing and moved on to the bathroom. When I walked out, I focused on my bed for the first time and stopped mid-stride.

I only made my bed after I changed the sheets. After that it was a disaster until the next laundry day, but not this kind of disaster. The comforter bunched up on top of the bed, forming a foot high, U-shaped wall. All of the pillows piled around the outside and kept the wall from collapsing. The sheets swirled like a whirlpool inside the hole.

Bending down, I inhaled and received a nose full of Josiah. It took a moment to accept that Josiah had been in my bed as I stared at it.

When I pictured him shirtless and sleeping, my nerves tingled like I'd walked through the ward again.

I went to my closet and jerked the door open. A backpack that didn't belong to me sat there beside a pair of large black sneakers. Anger effectively erased my ward hangover. "I'm going to kill him. Mac can't stop me."

Grabbing my bag, I stomped down the hall to The Dungeon. Two swords that weren't part of my collection lay across the low table where I cleaned my blades. Cursing under my breath, I took my traveling weapons roll from the corner and unrolled it with a snap of my wrists. After inserting a few knives and an extra sword into the nylon sheaths, I rolled it back up and hung the strap across my chest so that it settled where my katana should be. It was a comforting weight.

My last stop was the kitchen, for my empty stomach, and because I wanted to know what else Josiah had violated. I checked my chocolate stash first where inventory matched memory. He wasn't a total idiot, then. He'd drunk only one of my strawberry beers—probably too fruity. Half of the food I'd purchased just before going rogue was gone. I threw a sandwich together and used my fury to eat fast.

On the island sat a notepad with a list in Josiah's handwriting:

half gallon of OJ, half gallon of "milk," three apples, four carrots, half pound of chicken breast, one loaf of bread, one leather recliner

Displaying tally marks and updates, it was clearly a replacement list for my food. My anger deflated slightly, even though he questioned the authenticity of my milk. My jaw halted mid-chew as the entire list registered. I went to the living room.

"My chair." My voice choked on disbelief.

The ward must have fried my senses because I'd walked right past it. It had caught fire and burned halfway. The remaining leather was brittle, its edges blackened. The stuffing and underlying wood frame were also charred. The rug underneath looked undamaged, and the sprinklers had never engaged. He'd ruined my *favorite* chair.

A large brown boot box from Connor's Tannery held the place of pride on my coffee table. I slowly lifted the lid, and my breath caught. I ran a finger along treated skin: shiny black with iridescent red and gold veins threatening to catch fire like my chair apparently had. They were knee high riding boots with adjustable, double buckles at the calves and flexible soles—the most fabulous boots ever.

"Jerk," I whispered.

A magic-sucking, Evolutionary murderer wouldn't buy a girl fire frog boots for staying out of his way. He had to know I hadn't kept two-thirds of my promise, anyway. Even though they sat beside the destroyed chair like a bribe, it was difficult to stay mad. I wanted to hug the box to my chest and take them with me, but they'd be safer in my closet. Seeing the evidence of Josiah in my room again filled me with frustration and stranger feelings, but I didn't have time to ponder my ambivalent emotions. I should have left the building by now.

I was at the open door of The Dungeon when the floor to ceiling windows shattered, and three bodies flew into the room. They'd picked the one room with window coverings to tangle up in and which also held my personal arsenal: not smart. Two wolf heads emerged followed by a new creature that might have been a caiman. So, the varied species worked together, now. At least Sophia didn't do the same thing over and over, expecting different results. That would be crazy.

Four more creatures swung on ropes through the windows and landed on the writhing black curtains. Before the new arrivals got their bearings, I picked the heaviest, most Medieval sword from my wall and shoved the tip through the thick damask curtains close to the caiman. Dodging a scaly fist, I grabbed a loose end and ran around the curtains' victims, winding the fabric tight. Broken glass crunched under my boots, and a variety of grunts emitted from under the curtains. I threw an elbow at a snout and ducked a beak. Sophia had pulled out all the freaks this go-round.

I drew my single-edged, military knife then drove it through the material and deep into the practice mat beneath it. The entire process took less than fifteen seconds, but the rest of the motley monster crew found their feet and focused their various claws and teeth on me.

I slipped my travel roll off my shoulder and rammed one end into the furry gut of a primate-tiger hybrid. Swinging the roll, I nailed an eagle head. The absurd, bird-headed elephant crumpled to the ground. Sophia should have used the thicker elephant skull and an eagle's body. Hmmm, maybe not.

All my swinging brought me to the table where I dropped the

travel roll beside my duffle bag and pulled Josiah's swords from their sheaths. They were matching Chinese blades similar to my katana: light and sharp. As the remaining three beasts tried to surround me, I held off the one on my right with a figure eight pattern and amputated a reaching paw on my left. Before the claws hit the floor, I diagonally sliced the exposed belly from hip to shoulder.

My next victim slipped in sour-smelling intestines and fell to its knees. Normally, I'd stab it through the heart, but I wasn't familiar with the anatomy of a pachyderm. I left it to slip in gore while I dropped my right sword and lunged with my left at the complacent creature still standing. It jerked away from my blade too late. The edge grazed a rib before the tip met the strong muscle of an ape's heart and pierced it.

The final creature rested on hands and knees in a pool of guts, ready for execution. It felt unfair as I swung my right sword down to behead him, but I reminded myself that all of its various bodies had died before. Sophia's sick experiments brought any pain it felt. I left the three still struggling in the curtain cocoon.

I dropped the swords—Josiah could clean them himself—and picked up my bags. I surveyed the mess in The Dungeon and realized I should have just kicked them all out the window. Now my apartment would stink.

I leaned out the shattered window to a light mist and seven ropes dangling from the darkness above. I bit my lip. There could be a dozen more creatures waiting for me on the roof, but there could be more out in the hallway, too. If I went back through that ward, I'd be incapacitated for at least a minute: plenty of time to die, more than once.

Opting to face the unknown while conscious, I threw both bags over my shoulders and climbed. I slipped on the wet rope once, banging against the building and hearing a cry of alarm beyond the mirrored window. If a monstrous horde didn't greet me on the roof, security might. Yet all was quiet when I reached the top.

Solar lights blinked red though low-flying planes no longer passed over the city. Aside from the hiss of light rain and a distant rumble of thunder, the night sounded empty. I was halfway to the access door when it banged against the wall. Sophia must have used up her supply of beast freaks, because the four men who ran onto the roof were human. And blue.

"Shit." I didn't want to kill any Enforcers, but judging by the weapons they pointed at me, they didn't feel the same way. I knew two of them and the others were familiar but not allies. At least with Waya, I'd have a chance at negotiation. Where was he?

I let the bags slip off my shoulders and held up my empty hands.

Then Sophia entered, her white teeth gleaming. "Shoot her."

"Wha—." An arrow sunk into my right shoulder. Immediate cold spread down my arm and across my chest. Another arrow grazed my thigh. A third missed me when I fell to my knees. My physical bond with Atlas ripped away. *Silica*. They shot silica arrows at me.

I picked up my duffle as a shield and ran in a crouch toward the edge of the roof. Using the ropes to bust through a window on a different floor was my best chance of escape. The arrows didn't completely bombard me, so maybe their goal wasn't my swift death.

"Stop her!"

Growling, I ripped the arrow from the fleshy part of my shoulder. Atlas' magic rewarded me. The silica tip was smooth and round, without notches. I didn't have time to wonder about the humane arrows before two Enforcers flipped over my head to block my path to the ropes. I used my bag to stop a blade. The sword tip poked through to graze my side. A twist of the bag ripped the sword from the Enforcer's hand. I gathered magic for a forceful backhand and sent him flying. Another arrow hit me in the arm.

"Arrgh." I yanked it out.

The second Enforcer lunged with his baton. He was deadly with the knives still sheathed on his belt, but he didn't use them. Determined to return the favor, I held back, too, despite the growling monster in my soul.

I fended him off with the bolt shaft, but he effectively backed me to the others. Then another bolt whistled over my shoulder and nailed him above the clavicle. Jerking backward, he dropped the baton to reach up to the arrow.

"Hey!" His blue skin darkened slightly, but his feelings appeared hurt more than anything. He left himself wide open. I just had to shove the bloody arrow I held right through his eye or throat and he'd be out of my way. But I didn't want to kill him. Right?

The shadow monster roared in protest, but I squelched him. "Not now."

I dropped down, toppled the Enforcer with a leg sweep, then ran for the edge again.

Sophia screeched, "Use the zip guns!"

While made of plastic to lessen Atlas' interference, zip guns were inaccurate from more than a few feet away. They also backfired often. No one obeyed immediately, and I didn't slow down as I grabbed my weapons bag.

One of her brutes argued. "I thought we weren't killing her."

"She'll live long enough."

"But—"

"Do it!"

A silica bullet pierced my thigh, and another bit into my trapezius. I couldn't yank these out like I had the arrows. Damn, Sophia made better zip guns than she did monsters. Just five more feet to the ropes, but my vision blurred and my heart raced painfully. My legs gave out and I fell face first.

Rolling to my back, I held up a hand. "Wait!" My voice was weak, but the shots stopped.

"Shut up!" Sophia ordered.

I struggled to speak between gulps of air. "Why are Enforcers following Dr. Bennet's orders? Where's Graves?"

"Jacobs, go get her."

With a burst of energy, I rose to my knees and lunged sideways for the repelling ropes. My hand grasped one just as silica slammed into my chest, right above my implant scars. I couldn't take the pain. The poison found my bloodstream and pumped its curse through my body. I slumped against the wall. Arms slid under my knees and shoulders to lift me off the roof.

"Just stop fighting, Bochs," Jacobs whispered. "You're not even who she wants."

I tried to speak, but my throat constricted. I knew my skin turned blue while the silica tainted my veins to black. If Sophia didn't remove it soon, I'd die. I didn't want to be the shadow monster who couldn't defend herself against the sexy scientist.

The metal door banged against concrete again. "Stop this, now!"

Jacobs' arms tensed. Provost Allen sounded impressively pissed. I wished I had the strength to lift my head and look.

"Provost Allen, what are you doing here?" Sophia's voice sweetened in an instant.

Allen's stayed angry. "What are you doing?"

"I'm not killing her. If she doesn't suffer, he won't come."

A crack of thunder boomed, shaking the building.

"You see? It's working! Just a little longer." Sophia spoke eagerly, like an enamored cultist.

"You're killing her," Allen snapped. Firm footsteps moved closer.

"We have a deal, Provost Allen."

White light filled the sky, and the roof shook. I thought I was finally dying, but Jacobs reacted, too. He fell to his knees and dropped me. More thunder roared, impossibly long, rattling my teeth. Above the noise, Sophia joyfully shouted. "He's coming! Get ready! Jacobs hold her near the edge. He needs to see her!"

Jacobs picked me up again.

"Wait!" Allen yelled.

Heels clacked rapidly on cement, faltering when a flash of light rocked the roof. Sophia's hard nails gripped my arm and more than silica revulsion churned in my stomach. A sharp blade pierced my chest. I jerked.

"Hold her still, Jacobs."

Steel squeezed my torso as panic did the same to my heart. The blade bit deeper, and I whimpered, having no strength to fight her. She removed the blade, and stuck her fingers in the wound. I groaned, and tried to squirm away. Jacobs made a gagging sound that I heard through his chest pressed against my face.

"Suck it up," Sophia ordered him.

Blood and tissue squelched as her fingers searched, but the pain moved beyond me. After a final tug, her fingers slipped out. My heart immediately slowed. My lungs took in their first decent breath in several minutes.

As the black faded from my vision, I saw Sophia holding the bloody bullet high, offering it to the sky. "I took the worst out! She lives and bleeds! Come get her."

"You are an imbecile," Allen said somewhere behind me.

Thunder crashed in agreement.

I stared at the bullet, and a thought occurred to me. If I could control the magic Atlas pushed at me, maybe I could control the silica, too. The other two bullets were cold weights, pushing death to my blood more slowly than the one above my heart had. I concentrated on them to see what would happen, but the clouds beyond Sophia solidified into a massive shape and distracted me. I shook my head, trying to see straight.

"What the hell?" Jacobs breathed.

"You see the giant bird, too?" I whispered.

The clouds exploded, and a bird the size of a bus hurtled toward us. The breast was blood red with the feathers lightening to orange then yellow at the tips of its wings and tail. A beak that could rip all of Sophia's monsters in half opened wide, and a screech like the tearing of giant sheets of metal filled the air. Even from hundreds of yards away, I felt the intensity of its electric blue eyes. Lightning crackled from their depths and cut a line across the roof between us and the rest of the Enforcers.

"That's what you wanted to piss off?" Jacobs dropped me and leapt across the smoking crevice the lightning created. He joined the other Enforcers running for the door. So much for the badasses of M-Kes.

Sophia threw her arms up in jubilation, ignoring her fleeing minions. "All that delicious power! Come join me, and I'll help you use it! The army we make will conquer all!"

I'd never seen a mad scientist. I really hadn't given the term much thought until now. Sophia's hair whipped wildly in the wind as she grinned, and her bloody hands raised in tribute.

Oh, shit. Blood. It had taken me long enough. "Is that Cynddelw?"

The perfectly pressed pants a few feet away creased as Allen crouched to look me in the eye, his face curious. "Where did you hear that old name?"

I laid back on the concrete, sorry I'd spoken. "I read it somewhere."

"Can you stand? We need to get off the roof."

I ignored him. The thunder intensified as Cynddelw drew closer to accept Sophia's sacrifice: me. Mac's book hadn't shown any pictures of birds, but it could be one of Cynddelw's golems. Allen grabbed my bloody hand, but let go to study his wet fingers.

"Wait," I whispered, closing my eyes and rolling to my side to remove my throbbing back from the concrete.

I focused on the magic, small and dwindling, but still present deep inside me. I fed it the energy I had left and pushed it toward the silica invaders. Sweat rolled down my face. The slug in my leg wriggled through my muscle. A few seconds later, it rolled onto the concrete, sounding louder than the thunder to my ears.

"Yes." I barely heard Allen's voice through the magic pounding in my head. "Keep going."

Hard little hands grabbed my shoulders and jerked me to seated. Sophia's crazy eyes flashed. "Come over here."

She tried to drag me, but my weight proved too much for her, and I didn't cooperate. I focused on that final piece of silica in my upper back.

"Allen, help me, and we'll let you live."

Allen didn't reply to Sophia's offer. His face was as dark as his scarlet dress shirt. I thought he might hit her, until a line of precise lightning slashed between the two feet separating us. It threw all of us backward. A screech so violent I had to cover my ears pierced the smoke. I saw Allen's shiny, unmoving shoes beyond the smoking gash. Sophia groaned beside me, holding her head in her hands.

Time to get this last bullet out and vacate the premises. It sat close to the surface already. A few seconds of effort, and it fall from my back. I stood. The toxins left my body and the glorious rush of Atlas returned. I didn't try to stop the glow or the exhilarating build-up of power.

"*Sceadu*." The whisper caught my attention. Allen sat, his face delighted. "You are *Sceadu*."

"I don't think so." Half Earth mage and half shadow monster, my body was already crowded.

A blast of wind hit the roof as lightning spread out with innumerable branches. The thunder seemed to roll from deep inside the building, shaking it until I thought it would fall apart. A shadow loomed with powerful wings pushing against a constant current of air. Cynddelw was on us.

My giant bird-appropriate weapons remained rolled up in the bag lying several feet away. I doubted the throwing knives in my boots would do more than annoy him. Not a single rooftop garden existed that I could terrify into defending me. The shadow monster might fight off Cynddelw, but it could defeat me, too. I pushed against the beast flexing its claws inside me, not desperate enough to use it, yet.

Two smoking chasms, Provost Allen, and a large set of bird talons blocked me from the rooftop door. The repelling ropes were a short sprint away. I jumped over Sophia and ran for the roof's edge.

In the middle of a calculated leap meant to take me behind the safety of the wall to grab a rope, two punches in my back sent me twirling off course. For a breath, I faced the roof with one foot balanced on the edge. I helplessly fell backward in slow motion as Allen shouted, reaching for me. Sophia laughed in mad scientist fashion, holding a plastic zip gun. That bitch shot me in the back.

Silica quickly poisoned my battered body again, and my muscles refused to obey me. I tumbled head first over the edge. The faces of Sophia and Allen appeared, growing smaller with each nanosecond that I approached the ground. Over their heads, a pair of angry, electric eyes rushed toward me, shooting lightning to my soul until my breath left me. Darkness stole my consciousness.

CHAPTER TWENTY

A hot knife stabbed me in the back and twisted around, looking for my heart in the wrong place. My weak scream didn't mirror the rage I felt. Someone growled, and the knife dug deeper. I squirmed, pressing my face into softness only to find my nose filled and my air cut off. I struggled, grasping empty space with my hands until my head was lifted, turned sideways, and held there.

I inhaled a glorious lung full, but the growling and digging continued. A voice entered the weird hell where I found myself. "They're too deep. You've got to push them out."

I whimpered like a coward. Tired and confused, if I hadn't died then I was in the clutches of a mage trying to bleed me. The hand holding my head in place smoothed my hair. The voice softened closer to my ear. "I only have two hands, baby. You have to help. I didn't rescue you so you could die on my couch."

I forced my eyes open, but I could only see a swirl of magical light and silica darkness. The darkness steadily grew. He was right. If I wanted to pay Sophia back for shooting me, it would help if I lived. I focused past the blood pouring down my back and the poison spreading through my veins, grabbing that core of magic once again. This grew tiresome. Mac's next project should be a silica vaccine.

I found the cold bullets between my shoulder blades and pushed on both of them at once. I understood the process, now, knowing how to stream my weakening magic and make it effective. The giant holes dug into my back helped them slip out.

"Good, *nizhoni*, good," he whispered.

Once the bullets left, warmth and exhaustion weighed my limbs instead of poison. A soft cloth wiped my entire back, and I yawned. "Did you call me Zamboni?" My words slurred with fatigue.

"Shhh." He dabbed something cool and soothing on my wounds

then lowly chanted more words I didn't understand. This time the darkness comforted, like a fleece blanket wrapping around me. I rode his chant, and it carried me to slumber. I dreamed of a giant chicken wearing fire frog boots and shooting chocolate truffles out of its eyes.

*****

The first thing I saw was one of my boots on a dusty, wood plank floor, crumpled in a position in which I would never leave it. A set of bare toes hung a foot above it. I wriggled them just to make sure they belonged to me. My lower leg, hanging out of a blanket, was still clad in jeans. Cool air touched my bare back.

I tucked my chin to see the rest of me. The blanket scrunched at my waist, and I laid face down on top of my shirt which still covered my shoulders but was cut up the back. I couldn't see the two itchy, unreachable points between my shoulder blades. The arrow wounds on my arms were red and half-healed.

Another breeze slipped across my back, raising goose bumps and ruffling my hair. I looked around the room furnished with two oversized, brown armchairs and my temporary bed, the couch. The vaulted room intended for more furniture dwarfed the three pieces. Textured, burnt orange walls were faded and cracked. Directly opposite me, a wall of windows and glass doors let in fresh, cool air and lots of sunlight. I wondered how long I'd slept this time.

Pushing to my knees, I let my ruined shirt fall off. My bra was undamaged. I tended to choose dark undergarments for that reason. Blood I couldn't see probably stained the comfortable, black cotton— which made it undamaged, in my opinion. A raw, jagged scar from Sophia's knife peeked over the top of my bra. I shuddered at the memory of her fingers digging into my chest.

I got up, happy to feel strong legs supporting me once again. The doors opened onto a large, rock patio, and I walked through them. To my left sat a three-storied mansion of brick with a four-car garage and a drive that sat on a thirty-foot retaining wall above a pool and cabana. It had been a long time since anyone maintained that pool full of cloudy water. Something sinuous swam beneath the surface before disappearing below a layer of green scum.

I turned around to look at the house where I woke. Terra cotta walls rose high, crumbling in a few spots but relatively intact. The roof was hacienda-style, red tile, and the windows arched to compliment it. Even run-down, this was an impressive neighborhood.

I moved to the patio's edge, but didn't trust the wrought iron balustrade enough to lean on it. The carnage of a great fire spread out below me. Mansions, office buildings, apartments, and businesses were charred ruins. Terraced gardens held the skeletons of shrubbery and the ash of long-dead foliage. Once colorful, mosaic fountains were black and full of debris. My eyes followed the swath of burnout for over a mile to the Broadway Bog with its flowering vines and carnivorous mud.

Now, I knew where he'd brought me. The Briarcliff Dragons were some of the first monsters to invade from the West, and they'd roosted in one of the swankier neighborhoods in the northern suburbs. The dragons brought destruction and terror to the Northland for years until a team of Evolutionaries finally eliminated them right before I came to Kansas City. Their deaths caused an inferno that permanently damaged everything in a one-mile radius. Scientists had blamed some kind of dragon virus for the lack of recovery. It was magical, instead.

A floor board creaked behind me.

"I thought only ghosts and monsters lived in Briarcliff." I kept my eyes on the city skyline.

"We do."

After a deep breath, I faced Josiah Hightower. All the anger that had consumed me to the point of nearly attacking Mac didn't return. Regardless of what he was—and it was scary—he'd rescued me from death and helped me heal. AND, he'd bought me fire frog boots.

He looked like he'd slept less than I had the past week. Those jeans didn't fit as closely, either. Not that my eyes lingered on the waist band riding so low that brown skin peeked below his plain white t-shirt. Nope, I looked at his arms where long rows of half-healed gashes ran down both—probably the cause of the bloody handprint on my apartment door.

He studied me, too, mirroring my wariness. His eyes roamed from my face to my bare chest. Where Mac would have blushed and looked away, Josiah focused on the healing, red wound.

When he looked back up, he broke the silence. "You cut your hair."

I'd opened my mouth to counter whatever he said but snapped it shut, not expecting my appearance to be his first topic. I touched the ends of my hair. "I was told it was too conspicuous."

His lips tilted at one corner. "It was."

More silence. Josiah always had a purpose when he spoke. His short answers and obvious statements confused me. He should have yelled at me for coming home when I knew it was dangerous. I acted strangely, too, because I'd been furious with him just a few hours earlier.

A flash of memory tingled my cheeks. Had he called me 'baby'? A different question popped out of my mouth. "How many different places have you crashed in this week?"

He shrugged. "I come here often, not just to hide. I enjoy the solitude. I only went to your place for a couple of days, right after Waya reported that you were in Leavenworth, and the Enforcers quit trying to find you in your closet." He moved inside, and I followed. When he sat on the couch and looked at the spot beside him, I stayed standing. I'd discovered a new reason to fear Josiah. My armored heart demanded distance.

A phantom smile briefly touched his lips. "Are you mad?"

Not anymore—not about my apartment. "I was. Then I saw your list and found the boots. How did you burn my chair?"

He stretched his long legs out and stared at his bare toes. "It was a sleeping accident."

"You start fires in your sleep?"

"Only when I'm stressed. And it hadn't happened since I was a kid." He seemed embarrassed—another rarity for Josiah. His soft gray eyes revealed exactly what he stressed over.

I looked away. "Oh, well, I was afraid you'd say my fire frog boots started a fire. They're beautiful, by the way, thank you."

"Considering you dropped yourself right back in the middle instead of staying away, I shouldn't let you keep them."

He teased, mostly, but anger gave me the courage to look at him. "I belong in the middle. You shouldn't have kept me out."

"It's my job to keep you out." He believed that one.

I unclenched my jaw. "You kept me from the truth."

"It's not that simple, Andee."

"Really?" I pulled my bra down enough to show my ingot scars. "This was very simple."

He bent forward and put his face in his hands.

"Ignoring me never makes me go away."

Silence.

"Okay, we'll come back to that. Why are you hiding? It can't be because Johnson was found in your backyard. You were gone by then."

He leaned back and dropped his head against the couch. "I was investigating all the missing Eliminators. Which is my job," he added, lifting his head enough to look me in the eye. "For over a year, large numbers of Eliminators and Enforcers have gone missing from different M-kes headquarters. Poking my nose around drew attention. I was attacked the night I left your apartment. After I left the basilisk's silo, it happened again, and again the next day. I decided to disappear and stop making myself such a great target."

"If you hadn't knocked me flat at the silo, I could have helped you."

He scowled. "I didn't want you involved. I wanted you gone."

"Well, you managed to make me think you were the bad guy, which made me determined to come back and kick your ass, instead."

He threw out his arms. "One little tap to your chest and you lose all faith in me? I've been hiding Eliminators for weeks, now. Half of the missing are actually safe. Johnson would have been safe, too, but he didn't stay where I put him." He shook his head. "I suggested you leave town instead of hiding you myself because I knew you'd be stubborn and cause trouble." He sighed and stared at the ceiling. "You're still causing trouble. I knew the boot thing wouldn't work."

"I'm not causing trouble, you are. I only accept that you're not the villain because you didn't drain my blood to make a monster while I was helpless."

He straightened. "How could I possibly be the bad guy? I had to swoop in and save your dumb ass. You didn't even have your precious katana last night. What were you thinking?"

"I was thinking I'd go into *my* apartment and get some of *my* things. If someone hadn't left a ward on my door that sucked up my energy, I wouldn't have climbed to the roof to get out."

"My ward didn't let you pass through?"

"Oh, I got through—after it zapped me and turned me into a pile of mush."

He frowned and put his elbows on his knees, resting his chin on both fists. "I guess a detecting ward automatically stuns, too. Hmmm. I'd never used one before."

"Detecting ward?"

"I wanted to know when someone entered your apartment. I showed up last night because I felt you cross it. Did the effects last long?"

"A few minutes. Shouldn't you try new things at your place instead of mine?"

Josiah rolled his eyes.

"So, you didn't show up as—as whatever you are—because Sophia was trying to form an alliance with you? You know I was some kind of sacrifice, right?"

He crossed his arms and sunk deeper into the couch. "You weren't a sacrifice. You were a hostage. Sophia isn't the one killing Evolutionaries. She wants to use my power to give those weird monsters life."

A short laugh escaped me. She really was a Frankenstein. "What does she use now?"

"Storm fairies. They're small and weak, and she depletes dozens of them just to power a couple of creatures. I think she's run out."

Ha, there were small fairies. Take that, Mac. "Depletes, as in kills?"

He nodded slowly. "I was already investigating that when the Eliminators started disappearing. I've worked very hard to hide what I am, even from other Magics, but somehow Sophia knows."

Josiah had spread himself thin being secretive and stoic instead of asking for help. I pictured him flying around Kansas City with a maniacal Sophia on his tail—literally. A shadow covered the scene, and shriveled Evolutionaries fell from the sky. "Did Sophia focus on you after you started investigating the missing Evolutionaries?"

"Yes." Our eyes met in dramatic communication. "You think whoever is killing my Eliminators told Sophia what I am to distract me?"

My Eliminators. I needed to remind myself how responsible Josiah felt for all of us—not just me. I focused on the bigger problem. "His name is KUN-thool, spelled C-Y-N-D-D-E-L-W. He's an Ancient blood mage who can make monster golems from the magical blood of his victims."

Josiah looked disbelieving, at first. Hearing the summary out loud sounded pretty ludicrous. He tilted his head back and forth a few times to weigh my information then shrugged. "That explains your basilisk. I did read your report before I disappeared. And the ogres I killed that night turned to dust; but after the silo, it was Sophia's creatures that attacked me."

Cynddelw had decided not to waste any more golems on Josiah and sent Sophia after him, instead. I almost felt sorry for him. Except, he would have had help from more than me if he'd just been truthful. "You think it's someone in M-Kes, don't you? Do you trust anyone?"

"I trust you."

His words brought surprising sadness. "No, you don't." He opened his mouth to argue, but I waved him off. "Do you think it's Graves?"

"Maybe. Graves is a Magic, but he pretends he's not. Allen, too. I thought they made themselves appear older to avoid the suspicion of other Magics, but I guess at least one of them is an Ancient."

"Graves found me at your house and tried to keep me in Enforcer Interrogation. I only escaped because Sophia wanted me, too."

"I heard." He smiled slightly. "I also heard you beat on Waya's pretty face."

He was still getting information from someone at M-kes, probably Jeff. He hadn't asked me where I'd been, and I had to wonder how much contact Mac maintained with Jeff, too. "What is your brand of magic, exactly?"

Josiah frowned. "It's complicated."

"That seems to be your theme song."

"I'm mostly thunderbird," he admitted, looking like he expected laughter.

I didn't find it funny, at all. After I removed my jaw from my chest, I found my voice. "You're an indigenous god?"

"No, no." He flashed his old, dazzling smile.

I tried to quell my fluttering heart by crossing my arms over my chest and squeezing.

"You can't think that way, anymore," he continued, oblivious to his smile's effect on me. "People used to explain the talents of powerful Magics by calling them gods. It seemed to be the Greek answer for just about everything. They'd make you a goddess of war for sure."

I huffed, but I was a little flattered. All women like to be acknowledged now and then.

"What are you, by the way? I showed you mine."

"Earth mage," I answered, face completely straight.

"You are not."

"I am." I released the hold on my magic and sent it beyond the patio where I found a cluster of choke weed. I encouraged it to rise above the patio railing then to the doors. Several tendrils stretched out, wrapped around the door handles, and pulled them closed. I let them shrink away and disappear: all behind my back.

"That can't be all." He stared at me a full minute, but I kept the monster locked away. "You still don't trust me, then."

Damn right, I didn't. I wasn't satisfied with his answer, either. He'd said *mostly* thunderbird. "How does it work?"

His brows raised.

"I mean, you're a good-sized guy and all, but how do you become a two-ton bird?"

"Magic, Andee, you should get that by now."

"Were you in bird form when you burned up my chair?"

His eyes lit up and he rubbed his face to hide another smile. "No. I don't have to take the form of a thunderbird to use all my magic."

All the pleasure his amusement stirred inside me disappeared as a disturbing thought formed. "Are there others who, you know." I waved at him. "Turn into mythical creatures?"

"Sure." He raised his brows, inviting me to continue.

I pushed my lips together and sat on the floor, concentrating on my socks and boots.

"What is it?"

I zipped my boots up and hugged my knees before I answered. "Do you think I ever killed someone who I thought was a beast?"

"Ah." He relaxed into the couch with half a smile. "They're Magics, not morons. No human would be dumb enough to cross your path in beast form."

I opened my mouth for another question and felt cold air on my back again. If I started the next conversation, I needed more layers. "Do you have a shirt I can borrow?"

Josiah reached behind him and grabbed a folded black shirt from the back of the couch. Guess he'd left that for me, earlier.

"Thanks." I studied it.

"You don't like black?"

"It's fine, but I've ruined a lot of borrowed shirts lately. Don't expect good things." I stood, put it on, then paced in front of him.

"Are you cold? I can get a sweatshirt or build a fire."

I shook my head and kept going.

Resignation darkened his voice. "What else?"

I put my hands in prayer position and tapped them to my lips. He stood and came close enough to stop my pacing with a hand on my shoulder. Keeping my hands where they were, I looked in his face, wishing I still trusted him.

By appearance he was hard, but I'd always interpreted that as solid, dependable. He possessed a warmth that made me comfortable, like his gray eyes were smoky instead of cloudy. But maybe I'd read him wrong. He had to be pretty cold to ignore the struggle of people just like him.

His hand stayed on my shoulder as he stared into my eyes, and a smile widened his pretty mouth. "Green. I always wondered what color they'd be."

Always wondering meant he'd always known what I was. I shrugged off his hand and walked to the patio doors. "When you were born, how did you avoid the Evolutionary hunt?"

He stayed quiet; probably deciding what to reveal and what to keep secret. The longer he waited, the heavier my heart became. "I'm going to tell you something that no one else, knows."

I turned around, hoping my eyes lit with my scorn. "Sharing supposed secrets will get you nowhere."

"My parents are two of the most magical beings on Earth. They knew exactly what I was at conception."

"Hold on." The lies already filled the air. "You're older than me. Your parents' magic genes have to be dormant."

"Not for Ancients."

Oh. Dear. God. I backed up until a door stopped me. "I thought Ancients were rare."

He frowned at my retreat, but he didn't follow. "Most Ancients don't want to be recognized, but there are plenty of them. My parents woke about thirty years ago and started a family. I have four sisters and three brothers."

Josiah was the product of two Magics powerful enough to sleep through the magic drought. I had no words. All the feelings for him I thought I'd squelched became insignificant. They shrunk into a tiny ball of never-going-to-happen and burrowed deep into my soul. This man was officially off limits.

He continued, ignorant of my silent vow to never touch him. "My parents are reclusive elitists. I didn't meet my first Evolutionary until I was fifteen—didn't even know what one was. They have no interest in New Magic. They've allied themselves with pockets of Magics who have the ancient memories and a few are Ancients, themselves. They think Evolutionaries are products of black magic, and they practically disowned me when I applied to be a warden at M-kes."

"Why did you join M-kes?"

"Evolutionaries felt wrong to me," he admitted, and I stiffened. He held out a placating hand. "I wasn't so sure about the black magic theory, though. Then, a couple of years ago, I got hold of some ingots before they were inserted. They reeked of a black curse. I thought, maybe, the ingots did create the Evolutionaries."

"They block our magic! They're killing us, Josiah." I started pacing again. The hungry shadow monster fed on my emotions, digging his claws deep inside me. I might not keep him chained this time.

"I know. I know that, now. I had to work my way to doyen and carefully select my allies before I learned that much."

"So, how long have you known the truth about us and kept it to yourself?" I seethed now. My skin grew hot. The calming breaths wouldn't come. I put my hands on my head and closed my eyes. I glowed a few seconds then controlled it.

"Andee?" I felt him move toward me.

"Stay away." If I didn't look at him, I could calm down. I forced the air through my nose, imagining its journey to my lungs.

"Andee, someone extremely powerful is behind this. They have so much influence that they've got the government detecting, tagging, and controlling Magics. That means they can have war declared on Evolutionaries if we're not careful. Not all Magics are like you and me. Most of them are low-level mages, seers, weak compellers. They're not fighters, and they're not powerful. We're still out-numbered. If war is waged on us, it will be genocide."

I didn't want him to be right. I refused to accept the sense of his words. Daring to look at him, I said, "It's genocide, now."

"I know, I know." His shoulders dropped, and he shook his head. "The rush and decapitate strategy won't work with this monster. We have to be patient." His voice was patient, too, full of sympathy that I ignored. "I do think I'm close to knowing who it is, though. If we can find out who kept that silo full of cursed ingots, we might find him."

I nodded stiffly and brushed past him, headed for the hallway and hopefully the front door. Despite my acceptance of his words, he was just too close. If I didn't get out, my control would crack and he'd see the real me.

"Where are you going?"

"I have someone to meet."

"I'll come with you."

My monster would love that. "No, thanks." If Mac got a message to Jeff, then Josiah knew where to go. "I'm sure you'll show up, anyway. Thank you for the help. And the shirt."

"So, you think I've let you down? Is that it?" The hurt in his voice bounced off the reinforced wall around my heart.

I stopped at the double, elaborately carved doors. He stopped, too, keeping his distance. When I'd asked how long he'd known about 'us,' I'd really meant 'me.' It hurt that he hadn't cared enough to make me an exception. He hadn't trusted me to join in his fight. I wasn't special. Not to him.

I finally looked him in the eye. He saw my monster gathering below the surface and stepped back.

"You have to support someone before you can let them down, Doyen Hightower."

I wanted to take it back as soon as I said it. I was unfair and should have said so, but I left, instead. Maybe hurting him would keep him at a safer distance. He didn't follow me through the overgrown garden and out the broken, rusty gate.

Most of the surrounding houses were burned up or crumbling. Just a few random homes like Josiah's had been spared by the Briarcliff Dragons. I'd have to walk at least a mile to Riverside and find a ride into the city to meet Mac. The sun shone in my face as a long rumble of thunder shook the ground beneath my boots. I kept walking.

CHAPTER TWENTY-ONE

A building more abandoned than the Mother Ship couldn't be found in Kansas City. Once an entertainment venue called the Sprint Center, it resembled a steel and glass sphere that a giant sat on until permanently elongated. It stood conveniently near the concrete and steel 'beacons' of Bartle Hall. In the early years of Atlas, thousands of people mistook the Sprint Center for a spaceship that would carry them to Atlas to reunite with their Creator. They had migrated to it, camped out in it, fought in it, and eventually, committed mass suicide in it. Not even vagrants came near the place. No building in Kansas City held more dark, disturbing vibes than the Mother Ship.

So, that's where I met Mac.

The remaining stadium seats surrounded us in the vast, shadowed oval. They were silent sentries, leaking all the terror, anger, and violence they'd soaked up. It collected in a heavy cloud of despair. The Mother Ship was a horrible, broken place from the busted windows to the blood-stained, concrete floor. Even if someone suspected we hid inside, they'd hesitate to barge in looking for us.

I shrugged into the reassuring weight of my katana that Mac finally agreed to let me carry. Standing beside him, I studied the three men in front of me. Mac had brought friends, and I'd met one of them before.

Rifleman smiled at me, nodding his shiny bald head. "Hello, darlin'."

"I guess you're the metal mage." No wonder his aim had been so unrealistic when he'd shot at Graves and the Enforcers.

His light blond brows wriggled, and he held out his right hand. "My name's Connor."

I shook it and moved to the other two hands stuck out in greeting.

"Cain," the tall dark-haired man, said.

Rick was the shorter blond man with freckles and a cheerfully round face.

Mac nodded at the other two. "Rick is an elemental mage and Cain is—uhm."

Cain narrowed his dark eyes at Mac before turning to me. "I am a shapeshifter. A *pure* shapeshifter, choosing whatever form I wish. I'm pleased to meet you." He sounded polite, but his eyes roamed over me in a calculating manner that felt like he memorized my form. His innocent gaze met mine.

"If I meet myself on the street, I'm more likely to hit her than strike up a conversation."

Cain threw his head back and laughed.

"I wouldn't risk it if I were you." Mac warned him.

"She's a spitfire," Connor agreed.

"Violence taints her, Mr. Cain, I would be very careful." I knew that voice. Connor and Rick parted to let in my newest, least favorite person in the world: Mrs. Holt. Two men followed her, wearing long swords at their waists. Long swords! Maybe Provost Allen could convince them to duel with him. Their pinched faces were so like hers that they had to be related.

She looked around the hollow arena with arched brows. "The setting seems a bit ambitious for our gathering."

"Mrs. Holt, thank you for coming and bringing your brothers." Mac nodded at the men. "Dunstan, Gerald."

"Mr. MacDuggan." Her voice echoed about the hall as she pitched it to make sure we all heard her. "If Cynddelw has returned, then as a descendant of Merlin it is my duty to involve myself in this affair. I shall hear your plans."

Mac said she had connections. He'd also said Merlin was unreachable and unhelpful.

I forgave Cain's rude appraisal of me when he scoffed. "Merlin? That's got to be so diluted it's worthless. You might as well claim kinship with Moses."

"Moses was a Magic?" I whispered to Mac.

"Don't embarrass yourself, lass."

Okay, then.

Mrs. Holt's nostrils flared. "Excuse me, Mr. Cain, but my family kept careful record for millennia. Each alliance was planned with magical families so that our genes remained strong and pure."

Cain rolled his eyes. "Cain is my first name, lady. Sounds like you're sugarcoating incest, to me. And don't lecture me on the purity of your magic. As a pureblood shapeshifter, I needed a straight line of magic from both sides of the bed."

Mrs. Holt reared back with a gasp. "How vulgar! Mr. MacDuggan, I am offended."

"Yes, yes." Mac stepped between them. "So sorry, Mrs. Holt. Cain, let's save the genetics argument for another day. We have work to do."

"We're here, Mac! Don't start without me!" Dr. Jeff Trotter hurried in with three nervous men behind him and one young Indian woman. "I've convinced a few to join me."

I recognized the men as Eliminators. A familiar ax protruded over the shoulder of a handsome one with Persian features overlooked when his skin was blue. "Nice to see you, Lajani. Where's Valdez?"

He shook his head. "He wasn't interested."

Then the young woman waved at me, and I did a double take. Her skin was golden brown and her eyes dark, but the grin stayed the same. "D.J.!"

"Hi, Andee." She gave me a hug.

I surprised myself by hugging her back. "You got my message and already removed your ingots?"

"No, I haven't been home since yesterday morning. Things got tense at M-kes after you left, and Provost Allen wanted to meet with me. I skipped out and stuck to Dr. Trotter just like you said. He told me about the possibility of the ingots being cursed, and I talked him into taking them out for me. We recruited these guys, yesterday."

She'd talked someone into something, hmmm. I looked at Mac, but Mrs. Holt spoke. "A compeller; a very strong compeller. What is your name, my dear?"

"Davita Chadar, but everyone calls me, D.J."

"Well, Miss Chadar, you are most impressive." She took the time to sneer at me, as if I should care that she approved of someone else. No surprise that Mrs. Holt judged a Magic by her color. "I cannot help but notice that Miss Chadar has only recently removed these tainted ingots, but her magic looks bright and pure. Why can't Miss Bochs rid herself of the darkness marring her magical aura, Mr. MacDuggan? Too weak?"

Mac frowned, but I answered. "Even a healer can tell that I have Earth magic. Maybe something is wrong with *your* magic."

She and both her brothers turned red-faced. I'd managed to offend them more than Cain's baby-making talk. "She's an abomination, Mr. MacDuggan. We cannot trust her to act honorably."

A little ball of fury named D.J. unleashed beside me. "Andee has saved me and countless others with no reward for herself. She defines honorable."

A slow clap sounded from the dark, floor-level entrance. "Nice, D.J., I second it."

Jeff jumped in front of D.J. and the three Eliminators with him. "It's Waya! Run!"

"Wait," I said, eyes on Waya's emerging form. "He's alone." Waya hadn't been with Sophia and the other Enforcers at my apartment. Plus, he wasn't stupid enough to take on five rogue Eliminators, alone. As he entered completely, I saw why he acted alone.

He walked straight to me, his smile wolfish despite lacking fangs. I hoped everyone else was enthralled as I struggled not to drool. It shouldn't be possible for Waya to be sexier, yet here he was, an ingot-free, walking orgasm. His goatee and brows looked even more devilish against his swarthy skin. He stopped close enough to assault my nose with pheromones and capture me with eyes the color of dark chocolate sprinkled with toffee chips. Not fair.

"I can't believe you took them out," I whispered.

He tilted his head toward me, as if every word I said mattered to him. "I trust you, Andee." It's odd, the words different women need to hear. Some want declarations of love or beauty, forever promises, but that sentence sunk into my heart deeper than any of those words could have. Waya had acted on what I told him because he trusted me.

"I'm glad." I meant it.

Mac cleared his throat, and I did the same, trying not to blush as I made introductions. Waya's nearness flustered me more than ever. The predatory gleam in his beautiful eyes didn't calm me.

"How did you find us?" Mac asked.

Waya nodded to Jeff and the huddle of Eliminators. "I followed them."

Jeff sputtered, turning red. Mrs. Holt's voice smothered Jeff's protests. "Why do you shield your magic, Mr. Waya?"

Waya smiled at her, but she just turned sourer. She lacked a libido, no doubt. "I'm not."

"I can't see it," she insisted. "Are you an illusionist?"

"I don't think so. I'm new to this magic thing but—" Waya's clothes ripped to pieces as his muscles bulged. He gained a foot of height. Black fur erupted all over him. His limbs elongated, and claws burst from canine hands and feet. I looked up from his feet to see a giant wolf head full of sharp, inch-long teeth. "I think I'm a werewolf." Fangs garbled his speech.

Mrs. Holt focused on him with suspicion. "Lycans, Mr. Waya, were nearly eradicated during moon magic."

"Yes," Mac said. "They experienced horrible persecution by Normals." He grinned. "You're quite rare! Fascinating."

Mrs. Holt sniffed and turned to me. "And what about you?"

"I'm not a werewolf."

"Mr. MacDuggan says you are an Earth mage, but I see little green in your darkness. Show us."

"What do you expect her to do, Gwyneth? There's not a plant in sight." That was one of Mrs. Holt's brothers, sounding bored.

I separated myself from the group, backing up at least a dozen feet. During my hiatus in the Enchanted Forest, I'd discovered that Earth magic didn't just involve what grew in the dirt. It encompassed the Earth, itself. I gathered magic to me, letting it saturate my pores until I glowed like a beacon. I concentrated on the rock beneath my feet. Unlike plants, rock eagerly obeyed me. Mac claimed it was because rock had a ponderous, indiscernible movement, and magic gave it a chance to be fast.

I didn't care about its reasons. All that mattered was that two seconds after I ordered it to form a wall around me, the concrete floor trembled and split. Giant slabs of rock rose around me, forming a jagged, ten-feet-tall circle.

Waya laughed and D.J. gasped.

"Well done, Andromeda." Mac sounded like a pleased teacher.

I closed my eyes and sighed with pleasure at my sudden solitude. Behind the walls I didn't have to prove myself to anyone, see Mrs. Holt's angry glare, or wonder why Waya's charms had such a strong effect on me.

"You can come out now, darlin', we won't hurt you."

I studied the top of the wall. A column of rock pushed under my feet would raise me dramatically, but something whispered that I could fly. That couldn't be right. I concentrated until sweat beaded on my brow, and fire bellowed in my chest. The whisper grew loud and eager: *fly like the shadows*.

The rock in front of me turned black, and my body lightened. Vapor swirled around me, then I rose in a blink to stand on top. Complete silence filled the building like I was a lonely gladiator in an empty Colosseum. Gray people stood surrounded by darkness, but my eyes could make out every detail.

"That is not Earth magic!" Mrs. Holt screeched.

I was a smoky mirage—swirling shadows in the shape of a human. I pushed the roaring magic out, struggling to expel a power that wanted to sink further into my soul. It left me trembling but solid again and almost normal, except for the web of black lines that covered my skin. I saw in color, at least.

I gulped air, recovering from the rush.

"She is tainted with darkness, Mr. MacDuggan. I demand an explanation."

Mac stayed quiet, his eyes troubled as he studied me. I never told him about Nalusa Falaya. If anyone deserved an explanation, he did, but not with Mrs. Holt around.

I stared at her as I forced my body to balance. The lines disappeared. "You can't see Waya's magic, at all, and you have no idea what brand of Earth magic I am. You're the one who's tainted."

Her eyes flashed, and a yellow glow brightened her skin. "You are an abomination!"

I unsheathed my katana and pointed it at her, ignoring her brothers who drew their weapons. "Call me that again and my sword will have its way with you."

The magic summit went downhill from there. Cain tossed a few rude comments at Mrs. Holt and laughed with Waya. She refused to be in the same room with me any longer, and I happily left. Mac coordinated this operation, anyway.

On my way out, I stopped behind him. "I'll explain, later."

He nodded curtly, without looking at me. I wasn't his star pupil, anymore.

*****

I liked to look out at the city while thinking. It was a habit rooted in the excellent view my apartment provided. So, instead of hanging out in a dark hospitality room like a typical shadow monster, I chose a part of the window-walled lobby closed off by a collapsed section of ceiling. Glass littered the floor, crunching under my boots as I skirted ripped, dusty chairs and sectionals where excited patrons had once awaited concerts, figure skating, and basketball games.

I stood before two large, intact panes of glass while a breeze lilted through the empty spaces on either side of me. On the street below, more glass sparkled in the afternoon sun to light a path away from the depressing building. Beyond the Mother Ship's shadow, a few businesses and an apartment complex struggled to be relevant. The front of the complex held a banner declaring monster-proof walls and the first month's rent waived. A couple of tenants in the parking lot worked on an old Dodge Dart that probably wouldn't start again without magic.

It wasn't the happiest place to contemplate my situation, but I didn't have better. I made a mental list of questions.

Who had removed Waya's ingots? Not Jeff, because he'd feared Waya when he arrived. Not Sophia, because the Enforcers she'd had with her the night before still had blue skin and purple eyes. She wouldn't see the advantages in Waya and not do the same with the rest of her minions.

Why couldn't Mrs. Holt see Waya's magic? The darkness she saw in me existed. I didn't know much, but a werewolf seemed straight forward. If he covered it on purpose, why? And could he teach me to do it?

Most important, who was Cynddelw? Deep down, I hadn't suspected Josiah though he'd wounded me in vulnerable places. It wasn't Sophia, either. Her monsters weren't golems, and she obsessed over Josiah too much to be an experienced, patient Ancient.

Doyen Graves was patient. He also held a position that helped him hunt the Evolutionaries he needed and drain them dry before claiming he'd found them that way. Allen had been suspicious of him, and last night the Provost had been suspicious of Sophia, too.

Broken concrete and glass rattled before a wave of sexy spice and leather surrounded me. I inhaled it with a smile even as I worried that his scent made me giddy. "Good, I have some questions for you."

Waya wasn't a werewolf, anymore. He wore a pair of dark jeans and a clinging, red t-shirt that belonged to someone less muscular. "Cain?" I nodded at his clothing.

"Yep, he's a prepared shifter." He leaned carelessly against a divider, ignoring the twenty-feet drop below the space at his back. "Where did you come up with the phrase, 'My sword will have its way with you'? I've never heard that one."

I actually blushed. What the hell was wrong with me? "Oh, I, uh, read it somewhere." Probably a euphemism in a romance novel. Waya smiled, and my heart fluttered. Get your hormones in line, Andee, geez. I took a deep breath like I tried to tame the shadow monster then focused on my earlier line of thought. "Who removed your silica?"

"I asked Sophia, but she tried to convince me that I needed a replacement, instead. I broke our association and found a starving surgeon with no ethics." His answer came easily enough, but his face hardened. Something about Sophia made him angry.

I opened my mouth to ask about it, but he smiled and took a step toward me. He raised his hand to my hair, letting his fingers brush my cheek as he brought a little piece of ceiling insulation out. "That's better," he murmured.

My stomach flipped like a silly teen's. I concentrated on the tip of his nose, found nothing sexy about it, and managed to continue. "Do you think Graves is the one killing Evolutionaries?"

"Yes."

I looked into his eyes and saw sincere conviction. And pure sex. Damn it, back to the nose. "Why can't Mrs. Holt see your magic?"

"I'm not sure. Maybe because of this." He pulled off his t-shirt. So much for staring at his nose. After finishing my scan of hard abs and caressable shoulders, I finally saw what he meant. Over his ingot scars was a dark purple infinity symbol.

"How did you manage a tattoo?" My finger traced it before I realized I touched him.

He inhaled sharply and put his hand around mine. Surely I imagined the tremble of his fingers before they squeezed. "I'll show you later, if you like." His head bent to bring his mouth a breath from my ear. "It has more benefits than just hiding from that obnoxious woman."

I looked over his shoulder, smiling as his warmth caressed my skin. Then a shiny red SUV with the sleek lines of a sports car but the height and tires of a truck crested the horizon. It drove past the shops and the apartments with the now-gawking car mechanics and stopped at the edge of the Mother Ship's shadow.

My hand stayed in Waya's while I moved closer to the glass. He turned with me, sliding his other hand across my back to circle my shoulders. Josiah stepped out of the vehicle and strode toward the cursed building as if the ghosts inside were friends of his.

"He won't understand," Waya said.

I wanted to run to him and explain my side of things before Mrs. Holt sunk her claws into his opinions of me. I feared Waya had it right. Josiah suspected evil worked inside me. That was why he didn't trust me. Waya stood beside me because he *did* trust me. We were misfits together, Waya and I—lovers of shadows who danced on the edge of darkness. A thunderbird born to Ancients flew too high for my reach.

"People like Hightower and Mrs. Holt, they see everything as dark and light. She can't see your benefits because your darkness is all she cares about. Hightower is the same, Andee."

I thought of all the chances Josiah had as my warden to confide in me, to encourage me to look higher. Even as my pulse quickened with the nearness of Waya, my heart felt heavy with the knowledge that Josiah didn't think me worth the truth.

Waya gently turned me away from the window and brought one hand to my cheek. His touch melted the frost in my heart, and I forgot about everything but his chocolate eyes. "Did you know I can see your magic?"

I shook my head, then leaned into his strong hand. He smiled. His eyes turned the color of melting truffles. "It's beautiful. No one here respects your power. They think this darkness in you is something that needs to be fixed. It's a part of you, Andee. It makes you dangerous and gorgeous." His lips brushed mine then he whispered, "And irresistible."

My body instinctively closed the small space between us, melding to his as his arm circled my waist and pulled me even closer. I slid my hands up his powerful biceps and around his smooth, strong shoulders. His hand on my face pushed into my hair. His fingers massaged the nape of my neck as his tongue delved in to taste what I eagerly offered.

Every move I made was a mindless attempt to get closer to him. His kiss pushed me deeper into desire where thinking was overrated and feeling was everything. His mouth broke away and slid along my jaw to nibble on my ear. "Come with me."

It struck me as funny, throwing some cold water of reality onto me, though not enough to stop me from touching him. "I will," I answered. "It will take more than a good kiss."

He groaned and pushed an unmistakable erection against my hip. "I mean leave this place and run with me. Leave these people who don't appreciate you." He ran hot kisses down my throat to the collar of Josiah's borrowed t-shirt. Discomfort flashed through me— the pain of knowing I behaved rashly, that I betrayed myself. I pulled away.

Waya held on, sliding his tongue underneath the oversized shirt and across my chest, teasing me back to irresponsible bliss. His lips moved along my skin as he spoke. "They can handle Graves without you."

He slipped my saya strap over my head, and the katana thudded on the floor. His hands caressed my back, then snuck under Josiah's shirt. I shied away, but the touch of his fingers on my bare skin brought mindless reactions back to the forefront. I squirmed close as he unhooked my bra. His fingertips lightly danced along my ribs.

Grasping his head, I brought his mouth back to mine and captured his erotic growl. My breasts filled his palms. His thumbs brushed my nipples in circles, coaxing them to eagerly stand up and demand more. I hadn't wanted this when he walked in, but now it felt like a century of longing finally fulfilled. A cloud of passion smothered my doubt.

He yanked the shirt and bra over my head, then grasped my hips and lifted me up. When he closed his mouth over one breast, I gasped then bit my lip to keep more from escaping. I hadn't experienced intimacy in too long, and the desire it inspired rolled through me with overpowering waves. My legs wrapped around him, squeezing until I forced a gasp from him, too.

He laughed and lowered me to reach my mouth, nipping my bottom lip playfully before melting me with another long kiss. His forehead rested against mine, and his hands squeezed my ass. "Come with me?"

I frowned, catching my breath before I spoke. "Why? You're ruining a really nice moment." Unless it wasn't that nice for him. Insecurity replaced the lust pumping through my blood. I tried to separate from him, dropping my feet to the floor.

His arms quickly enclosed me, squeezing my breasts against his chest. He kissed my nose in a cute fashion that didn't suit him. "Because I know what you think of me. I'm trying to prove that this isn't all about sex for me. It's about you, Andee. I want you to trust me." He kissed my forehead and left his lips against my skin as he said, "Like I trust you."

I relaxed against him. I'd already decided to throw out my inhibitions about him and just do what I wanted. I wasn't interested in a suddenly honorable Waya. It didn't fit with my goal of saying, 'Screw you,' to control and everyone who demanded it.

"We need to get out of here before Mrs. Holt convinces them all that you're dangerous. You and I will be fine together. Without them." He trailed his fingers up my spine and kissed me again. "Then I'll have all the time I need to make you as crazy as you make me."

It was an attractive offer, mainly for the reasons that his wandering hands promised. But it also reminded me what I stood to lose if I let loose like I wanted. If Waya had changed, so had I. The decision brought clarity to my surroundings, like I'd been dreaming.

I gently separated us to arm's length with his hands on my hips. "Okay."

"Really?"

"Yes." I bent down to grab my clothes. "But we have to see this through first."

"What?"

"Mrs. Holt isn't the only one we'd be leaving behind. I care about D.J., Jeff, Mac, even the others I barely know. We have to stop Cynddelw and find out who is poisoning Evolutionaries with silica. Then, I'll gladly run away with you."

I held my breath as he silently studied me. If he'd really changed, he'd help me and reap the benefits later. It was all I could do not to run my hands over that mouth-watering body and demand he finish what he started.

"Fine." He reached for his shirt.

Happy again, I pulled Josiah's shirt over my head as Waya walked over to me. "We'll have to do this the hard way." A blade flashed, stabbing me with silica in the chest he'd kissed just minutes earlier.

I might have screamed. Darkness instantly blinded me, and my legs gave out. Waya caught me, held me close, and jumped through the window.

CHAPTER TWENTY-TWO

My face almost touched the ground—true ground, smelling of soil, plants, and renewal. My arms stretched behind me, numb as I sat on my knees in an uncomfortable bow. Normally, someone would have to be pretty stupid to stab an Earth mage then toss her onto the actual Earth, but I'd proven myself a much better monster than mage.

I hadn't wanted an honorable Waya, and he'd delivered. My lips still swelled from his passion while my chest throbbed from his knife. Had he betrayed me for Sophia, Graves, or both?

I sat back on my heels. A dense forest surrounded a clearing the size of a football field. Knee-high purple, white, and yellow wildflowers filled the space in patches, half-obscuring my view of a dry rock fountain in the middle, twenty yards away. What looked like a reflective survival blanket covered something inside.

A shadow passed over the far corner of the clearing. I searched, but only wispy clouds dusted the dark blue sky above me. I felt, rather than heard, a distant rumble. The hazy pink and orange of dusk hovered over the western trees. The ground shook again, like something large shifted its weight in the forest.

I met resistance when I raised my hands. Manacles encircled my wrists. The chains connected to rings driven into wooden posts standing six feet apart so that my arms couldn't meet in the middle. If a giant ape crashed through the trees, I was in deep shit.

Judging by the way my skin cooled and tingled when I rubbed my wrists inside them, the manacles were silica. Silica's not particularly strong. I jerked on one and gasped as icy needles pierced my wrist, sending shockwaves up my arm. When the black spots cleared from my vision, I carefully raised one hand to study my bond. The inside of the manacle appeared smooth.

"The spikes only come out when you're naughty."

I couldn't express my rage coherently just yet, so I glared at the beautiful, betraying bastard, instead. Waya smiled, sauntered over, and crouched in front of me. "You see." He touched the manacle with a finger. "When you apply force, spikes come out. The more you struggle, the longer they get. And if you were to say, rip them off with one powerful jerk, well, your hands will pop right off, too."

Anger churned inside me, and I reached out with my magic. The needles returned, shocking me all the way to my chest. "Ahhhhh!" I fell forward.

"They don't like that, either. The stronger the magic, the more painful the penalty."

I stared at him. I expected my anger to grow and seethe, but instead, a black pit of sadness widened in my heart. He'd tricked me completely. I'd believed he wanted my trust, maybe even my love. It took losing those things—or the appearance of them—to realize I needed them.

I dropped my gaze before tears stung my eyes. "Why are you doing this?"

The trees rustled to my left, and a pair of expensive, pressed pants entered the scene. "Do not take it personally, Andromeda. It is his nature to seduce and deceive."

Provost Allen was the Ancient? He did have an accent. And all those weird rocks. And an undeniable love for the color of blood. If it wouldn't have cost me a hand, I would have slapped my forehead.

He gave Waya a hard look. My seducer stood, dropping his head in a surprising show of deference. Allen curled his lip. "An incubus will do all in his power to seduce his prey. Although." Allen took Waya's place in front of me and gently poked the healing wound in my chest, clicking his tongue. "He still had to damage you."

"Incubus. What about the wolf?"

Allen looked over his shoulder, as if giving Waya permission to speak.

"Someone in the room must have thought I was a werewolf, so I became one." His voice lacked all its usual, sultry arrogance.

"Whatever it takes to seduce his prey, an incubus can give the illusion of it," Allen agreed.

Like trust. Waya had played my need to be trusted. Tears pricked my eyes again, and I sneered to hide them.

Allen smiled. "All those monsters you've killed. I never dreamed a single incubus could take you down."

I looked to Waya: an incubus sent to seduce me into Allen's custody. But he hadn't, not really. My heart lifted. I hadn't been a slave to my desires and made a fool of myself. I'd resisted a freaking incubus.

Allen's brows lifted. "Why are you smiling? You do realize he is a demon?"

I smiled bigger. "Absolutely."

"I'm not a demon," Waya said.

Allen shrugged, keeping his back to Waya. "So, the incubi are Magics mislabeled by ignorant Normals. Your ancestors should have been more careful with their conquests."

"He didn't conquer me. He had to stab me."

"I wasn't really trying," Waya argued behind Allen.

Allen gave a very modern eyeroll then looked over his shoulder. "Bring my questing beasts."

Waya scowled, but he left through the trees.

Allen studied me like an interesting fish in his aquarium. "Did you suspect me, at all?"

"Nope." When he grinned, I decided to add, "You looked a lot bigger in your pictures."

His expression soured. "Scribes. No matter how much chaos you bring to their world, they still portray power with physical attributes. I used my beasts and cunning to control half of Britain for centuries. Women sought me. Kings obeyed me. All feared me."

Great. I was the captive of a blood mage with a little man complex. "I heard a lot of past tense."

He grasped my shirt and pulled me to my feet. I smirked the second he realized I looked down on him. He let go, but I stayed standing, hoping the blood would circulate back to my feet.

"I will have power again, Andromeda. I have built half an army from the other cities I visited, and Kansas City proved more fruitful than any. I was delayed by the interference of Hightower and Graves, but I will win." He ran a finger down my cheek, and I resisted my gag reflex. "Hightower tried so hard to keep you off my list. Did you know he hid reports of your greatest achievements? He altered your academy scores and deleted your Source Expedition membership. All of it to make you look weak and mundane. He even tampered with your basilisk report, but since I watched through the basilisk's eye that night, my interest was already piqued. Miss Chadar filled in the blanks for me the next day."

Josiah hadn't tried to keep me from interfering. He'd tried to keep me from dying. He'd probably thought if he clued me in, I'd do something crazy like get myself captured in order to . . . oh. He did know me well. "Damn him."

Allen laughed. "I know. He is infuriating. He has no idea what you are, my dear. I would not kill *sceadu*. Not immediately."

"Why do you call me that?"

"*Sceadu* is an old word for shadow. I suspected something dark in you when you touched my *malus molaris*, and it made you warm. I didn't see you were *sceadu* until last night. I am a perceiver as well as a blood mage. I helped Waya avoid detection by other perceivers with the clever tattoo. The ink is made from Atlas dust, but I can't claim complete credit for the idea." He unbuttoned his shirt to display a spare chest with a dull tattoo of Celtic circles. "We did the same with moon rock, ages ago, until we ran out of it. Back then it was iron that killed the magic in our bodies." He pointed to red lines mixed in with the circles. "I had to add an Atlas tattoo to be protected against silica. No more being stopped by puny bullets and knives. Even these manacles will not activate if the captive has an Atlas tattoo. Would you like one?"

Hell, yes. "No, thanks."

"It would be the first of many gifts, Andromeda. Did Waya tell you I let him live because he promised to bring you to me?"

I shook my head, hoping he didn't see hope spark in my eyes. Waya's precarious position might lead to his change of allegiance. I almost wasn't mad at him for choosing his life over mine.

"You have wasted years fighting for the weak, Andromeda. It is time to let someone else do that. Think of the power you could wield with the knowledge and paths I show you." His eyes traveled up and down my body, making me want to scrub my skin. "Think of the children we will make. So full of magic."

I stepped back as far as the chains allowed. "I'm sterile, remember?"

Allen tilted his head with a smile. "That side-effect should disappear in time."

"You're also a thousand years old. Will the side-effects of that disappear?"

He laughed until the veins throbbed in his forehead. Apparently only jabs at his stature irritated him. "I'm older than that, were I to bother counting. And yet, I am as old as I wish to be. I will show you." Before I guessed his intent, he slashed my forearm with a knife. He brought the shallow cut to his mouth and sucked my blood.

Bile burned the back of my throat. I was wrong before. Scrubbing my skin wouldn't help. It would have to be removed. Removed and purged.

Allen lifted his head, his hair now black, and his face smooth and firm like a man in his twenties. He licked his lips, and my stomach protested. "Your blood is full of invigorating magic." He ran his finger along the healing cut, pulling up the last drops and touching them to his tongue. "You would make a magnificent golem. It is such an honor to be immortalized in a powerful beast."

"Immortalized? Your beasts aren't so hard to kill."

Allen's eyes narrowed. "With golems, you get out what you put in. Though I admit, I invested four Evolutionaries in that basilisk. What I could make with you . . ." He clasped his hands and touched them to his mouth. "But my new assistant, Waya, has pointed out how useful you could be as you are, and I am forced to agree. But if *you* will not agree." He leaned into me, and I arched away. "Then you will force my hand in the opposite direction."

"That wasn't the plan," Waya called from beyond the trees. When he appeared, his transformation was so extreme that he had to speak again to prove his identity. "You said if she wasn't interested in your offer then you'd let her leave with her promise to stay away."

"I cannot do that."

I should have been involved in this bartering for my life, but I couldn't draw my eyes away from the nude incubus. Waya's skin glowed like carved obsidian in firelight. His ears were large, flat, and pointed at the tops like a nocturnal hunter. The tattoo on his chest blazed deep purple, and his large eyes flashed crimson. Fangs not visible earlier, now hovered over his chin. Two-inch claws protruded from the ends of long fingers and toes.

He had an expression I never expected from Waya: insecurity. "I have to take my true form to get Allen's beasts to follow me. What do you think?"

I heard the truth through his casual voice. Waya didn't like his new, magical self. I let my eyes drop purposefully to where he was endowed like a fertility statue. Waya disgusted me, and I didn't mean visually. Turned out, betrayal served as a giant bucket of ice water, even with an incubus.

However, as long as I'd known Waya, he'd been someone else's flunky. If I stayed friendly, I might convince him to be his own man and take me with him. I tried a sensual smile. "You're distracting."

He relaxed and laughed.

"True form? How did you learn to hide it as an Evolutionary?"

"Incubi do not transform until they reach puberty," Allen answered. "Waya was already subdued with silica by then. He only learned of his magic yesterday, though like all of you, he could unwittingly use some of it as an Evolutionary."

"You were one of those annoying kids who answered everyone else's questions in school, weren't you?"

Allen looked startled, then confused.

"King Arthur didn't teach him any manners," Waya chimed in.

Allen sneered. "Arthur was an idiot."

I rolled my eyes to Waya. "Now look what you've started."

He smiled, then frowned as he realized what I tried. He broke eye contact with me, turning to the trees where three strange beasts crawled out. They had snake heads, leopard torsos, and lion-like legs that tapered into deer hooves. The size of large dogs, they slunk low to the ground, moving like komodo dragons. One opened its serpent jaws, and the sound of twenty barking Chihuahuas came out.

"What the hell are those?"

Allen moved to pet the head of the barking snake with feet. "They are glatisant or questing beasts; a childhood favorite of mine born from a dark tale of incest and violence. They make excellent sentries."

"Sounds like your parents made poor choices with bedtimes stories."

Waya stifled his laugh.

"I thought you'd borrowed some of Sophia's freaks," I told Allen.

"Sophia." He spat her name like a curse word. "She actually thought she could get Hightower to spark her creatures to life. I destroyed the rest of them along with her."

I didn't like Sophia, but those words dropped like cold rocks in my gut. "You killed her?"

"Of course. I told her to lie about the basilisk dust you brought, then she tried to blackmail me. After that, she nearly killed you, just when I discovered what you are. I was—" He waved a hand and glanced back at Waya for help.

"Pissed." He offered the answer in a flat voice. Her death couldn't have been any later than the night before. Waya's allegiance change was very new, and he didn't appreciate the elimination of Sophia.

"Yes," Allen nodded. "She had great knowledge of magic, but she had none of her own. I tried to turn a few of her beasts into golems, but they had no magic, either. Pure science." His lips pursed like science was a pile of basilisk dung.

I wondered if my shadow monster never reared its head when I fought Sophia's creatures because of science. "What about griffins?"

Allen's brow puzzled. "Griffins?"

"Are they magical or just creatures?"

"Ah. They are made *with* magic, but they possess none of their own just like the rest of the beasts born in the black magic cradle of volcanoes. It is what many Magics foolishly believe Evolutionaries are."

"Because you tricked them with your cursed ingots."

Allen's eyes widened. "Me? Oh, no. The stifling of new Magics on this continent started before I arrived."

"Why did you come here?" I couldn't help my curiosity. A Dark Ages bad boy crossing the ocean to the modern world fascinated me.

Allen shrugged. "Europe bored me. The other waking Ancients were the same old adversaries. I wanted a new challenge."

"Why guard a silo full of ingots?"

"I was—what is the phrase—holding them for a friend. They also provided excellent cover for *Roc Fuil*."

"Then who—."

"I hate to interrupt this weird lecturing of a woman you've chained like a sacrifice, but one of your barking snakes is missing."

Allen rounded on Waya. "What?"

"He never answered my call."

Allen knelt by the three creatures and rubbed their spotted sides. "Where is he my beauties? Where is our friend?"

Now all three of them barked and I really regretted the loss of my hands. Allen closed his eyes and lifted his chin like he listened for something. Then he stood, grim faced. "I cannot feel him. I will search. You watch her." At the clearing edge, he turned and added, "From a distance." He disappeared.

Waya stared after him with true distaste. He hadn't respected Doyen Graves. I doubted he'd respected Sophia, and he certainly didn't respect Allen. If I played it smart, maybe I could turn things around.

"He doesn't trust you." Subtle. Very smooth.

Waya huffed and grabbed a bag sitting at the base of the tree. "Nice try, Bochs. I'm not helping you." He pulled some clothes from the bag, and his body fluidly changed back to the bronzed martial artist I recognized. I struggled to look away from his perfect ass, but I needed to keep my wits which meant no drooling.

After putting on a pair of jeans and a t-shirt, he came to stand a few feet away with his hands in his pockets. A smirk marred his mouth. "You could have helped yourself, though." He pulled a piece of paper from his pocket and dropped it at my feet.

It was the note I'd left for D.J., telling her to come to the Mother Ship. "Damn it, who looks in a fridge for notes?"

"I was hungry."

An eerie howl carried through the trees, and the three glatisant sitting near the fountain whined. Allen wouldn't leave me with Waya for long, but I couldn't figure out how to get a foothold in Waya's twisted conscience. "Why did you stop?"

"Stop what?"

"You're an incubus. When we were, you know, why did you stop?"

A slow smile spread across his face, and he dug his hands deeper into his pockets. "Afraid you didn't do anything for me?"

"You're an incubus, soooo no, not really."

Red lit his eyes before he laughed it off. "I was in a hurry. We can finish later, if you like."

If I were good at this, I'd play his ego and pretend I couldn't wait for more. Waya studied me. "You would have fought going farther, Bochs. I can see it in your face."

"You're wrong. Until you stabbed me, I was ready to do anything with you." Unfortunately, this was true.

He slowly shook his head. "Except leave. As soon as Hightower found out we were both missing from the little meeting he'd come looking for you. We had to get out of there." His eyes dropped to my chest then darted to the trees. "I'm sorry I stabbed you." He sounded sincere.

"Josiah's not that interested in my welfare," I argued, but it rang hollow.

"Please, Bochs, everyone knows he wants you. It's why Sophia was so intent on capturing you. She knew he'd come running to save you." His face darkened when he said her name. It took me a second to recognize the pain in his eyes. Waya had cared for the mad scientist.

"Did you try to talk her out of her plans?"

"Of course, I did." He paced in front of me. "I told her that something else was going on—that we needed to pay attention to these disappearances and the dead bodies. She was so damn obsessed with her freak monsters."

I inserted my sympathetic addition. "Then she inconvenienced Allen, and he killed her for it."

"Yes."

"And now you're working for him."

He stopped and raised a finger in my face. "No. I work *with* him. When I've learned all I can from him, I'll leave."

"Sure. After you help kill me. You know, I always thought you were a decent guy, Waya—a bit of a womanizer, but in retrospect, that's understandable. I'm disappointed."

He backed away. "He's not going to kill you, Andee." He didn't believe that any more than he'd believed Josiah didn't care about me.

"If he really thought he could convince me to join him, wouldn't we be in his office having a glass of wine? Allen knows I won't go for it. That's why I'm chained up in the forest where no one will hear my screams. He planned to kill me from the beginning. You were his tool to get me here."

Waya turned his back on me. He walked toward the center of the clearing and the stone fountain.

"I'll remember your betrayal as he drains the blood from my veins."

Waya paused and angled his chin over his shoulder. He opened his mouth but clamped it shut as Allen strode from the trees.

"Asshole," I growled under my breath. Thirty seconds more and I might have had him.

Allen surveyed me from a distance, then gave a satisfied nod. "You refrained from ravishing her. Excellent work."

And people accused me of reading bad romance.

"I'm not one of your beasts," Waya snapped.

"Not yet!" I yelled.

Waya glared at me, but Allen waved me off. "Ignore her. I could not find my fourth glatisant, so I must assume something happened to him. I need you to check our perimeter defense, then bring the others to me. We must work fast."

Waya hesitated.

"Go!" Allen barked.

Even though he left, I thought I might have an ally in Waya— especially if Allen kept treating him like a peon. My being Cynddelw's captive was almost Mac's original plan. Too bad no one knew my location, and my only possible back-up was a verbally abused incubus.

"Do your arms hurt, Andromeda? It won't be long. I need Atlas one last time, then we can leave Kansas City together."

He needed Atlas to kill me. I'd be leaving as something worse than a shadow monster. My eyes raised involuntarily to the clear sky, and I wondered if Josiah and the rest had noticed my disappearance. I'd left my katana on the Mother Ship's floor. Mac, at least, would see that and know I hadn't left by choice. His track record said he would support me until it killed him.

Allen walked to the reflective blanket and yanked it with the flourish of a showman to reveal a large volcanic rock. The questing beasts barked appreciatively, but I was unimpressed. Of course *Roc Fuil* sat under the blanket.

"Tonight, Atlas' path brings it the closest it will be until the next cycle." Allen strolled around the volcanic boulder, one hand hovering over it. "With the magic I store in here added to Atlas, I will have the power to make five, strong golems."

Allen removed his shirt to display the graceful, lean muscle of a duelist's body. He pressed his palm against the boulder and the red tattoos on his chest pulsed with life. His skin looked even younger, fresher.

"Five golems?" I had enough magic for five?

"Yes." He pulled his knife.

For the first time, panic seized my heart. I'd faced death countless times. I'd pictured dying in both heroic and tragic fashion. But I'd never dealt with the fear that my blood would be used against others. I could think of no escape as Allen came closer. The best I could do was lose my hands and fight him with my legs until I collapsed.

I gathered courage to yank free of my bonds, but he stopped before me and cut himself. Letting the blood pool in his palm, he chanted. The blood formed a sphere that glowed and floated above his hand.

It was slightly mesmerizing, but also confusing. "I thought you used my blood."

His devilish smile widened in the red glow of his blood globe. He circled me, letting blood drops fall to the ground while he chanted. When he completed his circle, he was middle-aged with salt and pepper hair. He tossed his blood globe above my head where it spread into a sheer red dome that surrounded me. I didn't know much, yet, but I had a feeling blood wards were strong.

Fear for myself evaporated, replaced with new anxiety as ten Evolutionaries followed Waya into the clearing. I yelled. "Get out of here! He'll kill you!"

None of them moved. Allen raised his brows, wiping his bloody arm with his shirt before dropping it and leaving me. They finally looked our way, but they saw nothing but Allen. His blood ward blocked me from view and hearing, but I could hear and see everything.

"Provost Allen, what's happened? Are you injured?"

"I am alright, but my friends." He held out his arms. "I need your help."

He was the most disgusting monster, yet, keeping the helpless pretense as he led them to slaughter. I jumped angrily toward the ward and got a shock that sent me to my knees.

"First, I have learned that your ingots are poison. Will you let me take them out? It will only hurt a moment, then you'll be free. Free and strong."

The Evolutionaries looked at each other, not willing to answer. The belief that the ingots saved our lives was a difficult one to overcome. We'd all held it since childhood.

The questing beasts moved from behind the fountain to skulk around the Evolutionaries. Three wolves the size of motorcycles emerged from the forest, silently joining the circle of beasts. The Evolutionaries took defensive postures, facing outward.

"They will not hurt you," Allen placated. "I control them. Allow me to remove your ingots, and you can control them, too."

What a sack of shit. I could barely fight the urge to rip free of my manacles. There had to be a better way. The ground trembled beneath my feet, so strong that my chains rattled. For a second, I thought my magic broke free with my anger, but there was no pain. It wasn't me.

Allen looked up; so I did, too. Black clouds highlighted with red rolled across the sky. The last time a freak storm formed on the horizon, a giant bird rescued me. A flutter of hope lifted my spirit. Allen threw his arms behind him and screamed at the sky. He sounded just like—

Five griffins burst through the trees, screaming in answer as they flew high to disappear in the clouds. Well, Josiah could handle five griffins, no problem.

Allen screamed again, and ten more griffins flew into the storm. Their screeches floated to my ears when I could no longer see them. Fifteen griffins. He hadn't lied about the army of golems he'd built. My hope dwindled.

The Provost persona discarded, he stalked to the Evolutionaries staring at him like he'd grown an eagle head. His skin glowed red in the twilight. Slicing his arm again, he joined the beasts circling the Evolutionaries. This time, a translucent ward formed, and he and his pets stayed inside.

Allen grabbed the woman nearest him, pushed her to her knees, and sliced her ingots free with two expert strokes. I couldn't hear her scream, but I saw it and the reaction of the others who tried to help. Allen's beasts kept them at bay while he continued his barbaric surgeries.

Atlas' magic pushed so hard on Allen's ward that the pressure built in my head. The ward brightened with heat as magic fought to enter it and fill the magic-starved Evolutionaries. Allen forced it to wait with his blood ward. He probably thought bringing them all to the magical forefront at once would disorient them and give him an advantage. Right now, the beasts crowded inside gave him all the help he needed.

Waya watched, his face unreadable. The ingot removal would go quicker with his assistance, but Allen left him outside. When it was finished, most of the Evolutionaries looked exhausted. A few lay unconscious. Allen thrust his bloody hand through his ward, shattering it to let magic rush inside.

The screaming and thrashing faded to white noise as I focused on Allen's hand. His blood broke the ward. His discarded, bloody shirt lay just a foot outside my prison. I had no weapons, no tools, no hands. I searched around my feet and found one scrawny tree branch.

A roar filled the clearing. A giant, at least ten feet tall, stood among the group of fledgling Magics. His skin was the color of frosted glass. Silver hair shimmered to his shoulders and sparkled in tufts on the backs of his massive arms and legs.

Allen laughed. "A frost giant! Magnificent!" Then he darted behind the still confused giant and threw two slim knives into his back. The giant screamed and fell to his knees. He tried in vain to reach the blades as his body shrunk and his skin flickered back to Evolutionary blue. That bastard perceived their specific magic then paralyzed them with silica before they could adjust.

Keeping my arms as still as possible, I stretched one foot out and caught the branch with the toe of my boot. The journey of the branch to the edge of the ward went excruciatingly slow as I listened to the screams and moans of my betrayed colleagues. My leg stretched as far as it would go in a half split when the branch reached the ward. I tried to scoot a little farther, slowly pulling my chains to their limit.

The tiny leaf on the end touched the ward wall and burst into flame, burning up instantly. I hung my head, more frustrated than ever that Allen couldn't hear me curse him. Not even Josiah's ward on his house had been that vicious. Angry tears stung my eyes as I stared at Allen's shirt.

Then a pair of bare feet stopped beside it, and a hand picked it up. Waya studied the shirt with a deep crease between his brows. He looked right at me, seeing nothing. Clutching the shirt, he turned to Allen's carnage then faced me again. "We'll barely have a minute."

He thrust the shirt into the ward wall. It cracked like an eggshell, and the pieces exploded in a shimmer of red that hurt my eyes. Allen cried out and fell to his knees, grasping his head.

Before the remnants of the ward disappeared, Waya stood beside me. "Hold still."

Instead of messing with the intricate manacles, he grabbed one of the rings, planted one foot against the pole, and pulled it from the wood. He yanked out the other one, grabbed my arm, and dragged me toward the forest edge. We were three feet from cover when the sound of yipping glatisant closed in, and Allen roared. "Waya!"

CHAPTER TWENTY-THREE

"I have to go back, Waya. You know I can't leave them."

We were literally up a tree while he worked the hidden locks of my manacles. His dark head stayed bent over my wrists, and his mouth stayed shut. Finally, he looked up, his eyes luminous despite the lack of light deep in the forest. "There are a dozen more dire wolves roaming this forest, plus a corps made up of trolls, chimera, griffins, a giant twice as tall as you can imagine, and a few things I've never seen before. I released you so we could go down fighting, Andee. No one's getting out of here."

I didn't think the situation so awful. I'd managed to strangle a glatisant with one of the chains still attached to me. Waya had ripped the head off one and torn the other in two. Fun fact: incubi are scary strong. Any other beasts Allen had sent hadn't found us, yet.

Waya kept working until metal clicked and one manacle fell off my wrist. It thudded on the ground below. A few moments later, the other followed, but instead of thudding, it clinked twice.

"Ouch!"

"Shhh."

"Oh, no." I dropped off the branch and landed in front of two shadows that should have been in defensive postures but stood like paralyzed deer, instead. "Mac?"

"Andromeda!"

"Andee!" D.J.'s cheery voice didn't fit our surroundings.

"How are you here?" I asked.

"Well, the despicable Waya obviously took you by force. Your blood was on the floor, and you left this." Mac handed me my katana. The situation brightened. An angelic choir sang in my head as the saya settled between my shoulder blades.

Waya cleared his throat and dropped beside me, looming with

menace.

"You can't really be offended by the truth," I told him.

D.J. jumped back with a squeak.

"It's okay. He decided to stop Cynddelw, too." Actually, I thought he planned to run for it. He'd earned the right to do as he chose, in my opinion.

D.J. picked up their story like an excited teen relaying the latest gossip. "After we realized you were kidnapped, Doyen Hightower forced Mrs. Holt to fly with him to search the city for your magic signature. She didn't want to, but I swear to Atlas, lightning shot from his eyes, and he told her it wasn't a choice."

A small thrill ran through me, but I pushed it away. "I hope everyone else is here and you have a plan. Cynddelw, AKA, Allen is a half mile away making new golems with Evolutionaries while the army he controls watches."

D.J. gasped. "Provost Allen?"

Mac was unfazed by the announcement. "The plan was to find you, send a signal, and get out."

"The two of you are a team?" That was strategic planning at its worst: a healer and a cute, sweet-talking pixie.

"We're all in pairs, moving toward the middle where Mrs. Holt last saw your magic." D.J. said. "Except Doyen Hightower. He's the distraction."

I looked to Mac. "Where's BOR?" A team with her made a little more sense.

"She's guarding the horses. We left them on Wornall Road."

Wornall Road meant we were in Loose Park. Even before Atlas inspired an unruly nature, Loose Park boasted enough size for a lake, tennis courts, and a famous rose garden. The horses could be a long run away.

"I'm surprised you managed to get in," Waya said. "The creatures patrolling the woods won't let you slip by a second time."

D.J. sniffed. "I compelled three trolls to ignore us. I think I've got it."

"You had to use a lot of magic on those trolls, lass. I don't know how much more you can do, tonight. You say Allen controls them?"

"Yes," I answered.

"Hmmm." Mac pondered, so we all waited. "Has anyone seen him make a golem?"

Waya's voice pitched low. "I saw him try. With Sophia's creatures. He'd just removed my ingots and thought I was unconscious."

I wondered if Sophia's lifeless body had been there, too. My distaste for Waya had gradually transformed to pity in the last half hour. He'd joined Allen because he saw no alternative but death. Maybe he *wanted* to go down fighting with me.

"Good," Mac continued. "Now think closely. Did he have to use some of his blood in addition to that of the creatures?"

Waya straightened and a hint of red sparked in his dark eyes. "Yes. He used a few drops with each one."

Mac clapped his hands. "There's our plan. His blood bond is how he controls them. All we have to do is kill Allen, then his golems will die with him."

Simple, yet oh, so complicated. For starters, we had to deal with the four beasts swinging through the night, heading right for us. "Incoming," Waya announced, stepping between Mac and the creatures that tree-hopped like monkeys. They swung from branch to branch so fast that I couldn't judge their size and build.

"A light would be nice!" I yelled before I jumped to meet a shadow that could have had poisonous suckers on its arms for all I knew.

I heard Mac mutter before a bright, white globe rose above us. I hit the first creature with my feet. It rolled back, but another landed in front of it. They looked like chimpanzees with red leathery skin instead of hair. Inch long teeth snapped at me, and blood red spike covered its skull.

"Go," D.J. commanded one monster in a voice that filled my head and sunk into my bones. The creature screamed and ran into the darkness.

Waya had his knives, slashing and advancing until he pinned a creature against a tree and finished it off. I deflected a clawed hand then kicked a knee, bringing the screeching monkey forward to pierce its heart with my katana. The remaining beast was too close to Mac who blocked D.J. and all her compelling glory.

I sent my magic to the bushes behind them. The branches grew, surrounded the creature, and yanked it inside before it could pounce on Mac. After a moment of thrashing, the bush stilled.

"You used your magic in a fight!" The globe lit up Mac's pleased face.

"Of course, I did. That's what you keep nagging me about. Turn the light out before you attract more attention."

"Oh, cripes." He extinguished it. "That light was the signal. Everyone else will go to the rendezvous instead of continuing to the middle."

"Damn it, MacDuggan." Waya raised his arms and crossed them on top of his head, looking skyward.

"Hey." D.J. jumped to Mac's defense. "She asked for a light, and he gave her one. Leave him alone."

"I'm a nocturnal incubus, I don't need a light. And since she's some kind of shadow monster, I doubt she needs one, either."

I glared at him. "Waya—"

"Shadow monster?" D.J. whispered.

"Incubus . . ." Mac was thoughtful. Not good. "Is that how he—"

"Shut it, Mac." I welcomed the darkness, now, since my cheeks grew hot.

"Right. Sorry." He paused, but he couldn't possibly be finished. "The shadow monster came from your father, I take it?"

"Yes. It's not as bad as it sounds—usually." I sighed and put a fist to my forehead. "We don't have time for explanations. Just meet everyone, tell them what's happening, and get to the clearing quickly. Waya and I will hold them off. Once we're back in his sight, Allen will probably pull all his creatures in, and you'll get there faster."

*****

I hadn't really expected Waya to come with me. He was no hero, and whatever moral code had led him to help me escape, it hadn't been strong enough to keep him from betraying me in the first place. As we moved stealthily like good creatures of darkness, I shot glances to my right, expecting his absence.

"Why do you keep looking at me?"

"You're noisy."

He huffed. "That's your heavy breathing, not mine."

As we drew closer to the clearing, smoke twined around the trees, and light flickered through the leaves. Large bodies crashed in the foliage nearby, but we melded with the shadows of the forest, eluding Allen's beasts. When we reached the edge, we stopped and watched.

In the spot where I'd been chained, two ponderous ogres fed tree branches to a large bonfire. Dire wolves and chimera surrounded the Evolutionaries slowly dying from silica poisoning, though Allen would help them along soon. Allen had a saber strapped to his waist and stood on top of *Roc Fuil* staring into the lightning filled sky. A scream filled the night. Allen convulsed violently before two griffins fell from the clouds, hit the ground in front of him, and turned to puffs of dust.

Ha! Josiah was kicking griffin ass.

"Why hasn't Hightower joined the others?" Waya wondered.

"Allen's been killing Josiah's Eliminators for over a month. He won't leave until this is over."

"Right. How could I forget he's just like you?"

I wouldn't fall into that trap, but I wouldn't guilt Waya into helping, either. "Look, Waya, you probably knew deep down that Allen wouldn't let me live, but I understand why you made the deal. In the end, you righted the wrong. We're good. You can leave, and I won't hold it against you."

"That's what you expect, isn't it? It just makes me want to stay, more. In fact, I can't wait to start."

He jumped up, his clothes ripping as he took his natural form. Power radiated from him, and his eyes gleamed red. After a clawed salute to me, he turned toward the clearing but hesitated. "I stopped because it was wrong."

"Killing monsters is wrong?"

He looked over his shoulder, his red eyes somehow sincere. "Earlier you asked why I stopped kissing you. I was using my magic on you. It was wrong."

"Oh." The gratitude that lightened my heart was strange since he'd decided stabbing me in the chest with a silica blade wasn't wrong, but it existed none the less. "Thank you."

He nodded, then cleared a waist-high bush with a standing jump. I smiled and drew my katana. Killing monsters was *not* wrong.

We fought our way to the group of helpless Evolutionaries. Working with Waya proved easier than I expected. Anything big I saved for his capable hands while the quicker opponents met my katana. Allen screamed, growled, and whatever else he needed to call in the troops. Just as I'd predicted, beasts vacated the forest to surround us. Hopefully Mac and D.J. had a clear path to the others, now, so Waya and I wouldn't die waiting for reinforcements.

"Make your wall." Waya panted a few feet from me as he struggled with a troll that looked like a seven-foot Gecko with tusks.

"What?" I dropped to my knees and shoved my katana into the belly of a leaping wolf, letting the blade rip the length of him before jerking it free.

"Push a rock wall up around them." He grabbed the troll's head, twisted, and jerked it off. "I'll watch your back."

Trust Waya with my back? I looked in his red, murderous eyes, wondering what possible reason he would have for lying this far into the fight. I glanced at the Evolutionaries dying on the ground, then I locked eyes with Allen. He grinned and ran for them. I had no choice but to trust Waya.

I sheathed my sword and knelt down to put my hands on the ground. Boulders rumbled below the creatures circling the Evolutionaries. The Earth cracked, sending the beasts tumbling away from their victims. I took a deep breath and forced more magic into the ground. A tower of rock rose to cut Allen and his golems off from the Evolutionaries. For now, my co-workers were protected within the circular wall.

"Climb it!" Allen screamed and jumped on the back of a wolf, slapping it with the flat of his blade.

A group of the red chimps scaled my wall. I squeezed my eyes tight again and found seeds burrowed deep. I fed them my magic, forcing them into vines that grew to cover the wall and sprout giant thorns that gouged the flesh of the climbing beasts. My arms trembled, and sweat poured down my face as I pumped more power into nature. The vines grew around each monkey, wrapping them in thorny ropes that squeezed like pythons until dust puffed through the cracks.

"Ooh, nice." Waya complimented behind me, then he grunted and the goat body of a chimera flew over my head. The thorns on my vines impaled it, then it squealed, jerked, and disintegrated.

A griffin fell on the rock wall. It rolled down to land beside Allen and exploded, covering him and his wolf mount in red dust. His face mottled with fury, he pointed his sword at me. "I will enjoy stealing your life and making you the most hideous beast on Earth!"

Waya laughed. "Taunting just motivates her."

Allen turned his snarl on him. "Your death will take longer, treacherous demon."

Waya's ruby eyes brightened. "Not a demon, asshole."

Allen charged, focusing his vengeance at the incubus beside me. A horde of creatures approached from our left. Waya moved to stand back to back with me. I went against everything I'd learned about fighting monsters and closed my eyes, hoping I had enough magic left to even our odds.

Thunder crashed. I didn't know if the thunderbird shook the ground or if my magic did as I wrapped it around the slabs of rock resting below the Earth's crust. The rock shot from the ground and sent a few monsters airborne. The clearing became a maze of boulders and rock towers. I'd made it harder to get to us, at least, but Allen and his sword charged a few feet away. It would take Waya and I, both, to defeat a sword-master blood mage—maybe more than both of us.

"Hold on!" I shouted to Waya, and I focused everything below our feet. We leaned into each other to keep our footing as a slab pushed us up to loom twelve feet above a furious Allen. Lightning lit up the clearing, and three charred griffins dropped at the base of our tower.

Allen looked like he might self-combust before he finally released a scream. "Draco! Draco!"

Trees on the far side of the clearing fell as a massive, blue dragon head pushed them away. It opened its mouth and hurtled an ear-ringing screech through the clearing. A scaly, blue and green body followed the head. As the dragon stood well above the forest, it unfurled a set of leathery wings spanning half the glade.

"*Áfær!*" Allen raised an arm to the sky. "*Ábradwe sé fugel!*"

I doubted his words meant: go greet the thunderbird and give him a kiss. The dragon dropped back on its massive haunches then shot into the clouds.

I angled my chin up to scowl at Waya. "You didn't say anything about a dragon."

"I've only known Allen was the evil mastermind for one day! He didn't show me everything."

I studied the Ancient blood mage, wondering if I could jump far enough to land on the wolf mount's head and decapitate Allen at the same time. Three cracks sounded, and Allen flew backwards off his wolf. Blood spurted from his chest then two more wolves joined his mount and hid him from view.

"That was a gun," Waya said, staring into the trees.

"Rifleman!" I waved as the metal mage walked out of the trees with one of Mrs. Holt's brothers.

All around the clearing, the rest of our magical group ran out and took on pockets of Allen's beasts. Even Mrs. Holt, who controlled a shield around a glowing, chanting Rick. A stream of wind whipped around them then twisted into a mini cyclone. It picked up two trolls, juggled them, and tossed them into the forest.

Mac and D.J. ran out near the wall I had erected around the Evolutionaries. I met eyes with Mac and pointed to the wall before letting the vines recede in a small section near him. "Help the Evolutionaries behind the wall!" I shouted.

D.J. repelled two firedrakes moving in on the climbing Mac. As the mini-dragons rolled back through the air, a giant hellhound snatched them both between his massive jaws and shook them until they flew apart. The midnight colored hellhound with its bony back ridge and ram-like horns must have been the shifter, Cain.

"Don't kill any hellhounds!" I told Waya.

"The monsters aren't dying," he said.

He was right. According to Mac's theory, the monsters should have stopped when Allen died. A few bullets to the chest was probably too easy. We crouched on top of our wall, trying to catch a glimpse of Allen behind all the fur and snarling fangs. One of the wolves rose on his hind legs, yelping before falling behind the other two. The wolves barked and whined until a hairy sack of bones flew out and burst, dusting the ground.

Allen stood with a roar, looking taller and younger. His inhuman face held the angles of a wolf confined within his human skin pulled tight and grotesque. He'd sucked the life from one of his wolves to heal himself.

He used a knife to prick both arms then raised them above his head, letting the blood roll down his arms as he chanted. The blood spread to cover his head and torso in armor that looked like a painting of muscle anatomy. Only his angry eyes and the lower halves of his limbs were uncovered.

Before I had time to worry over his blood armor, a dark shape loomed on the horizon behind him. A giant twice as tall as the oldest tree entered the clearing. His face was shaped and knotted like a potato with eyes so small I could barely see their gleam. He roared, displaying an abundance of yellow, crowded teeth.

It would take a blade much longer than my katana to pierce his bare chest and find a heart. He wore a studded belt and leather pants, his feet bare. Leather bands circled wrists as thick as my horse. Long spikes protruded all around them in a shiny, deadly bracelet.

My heart dropped to my toes, and I looked at Waya.

He just shrugged his ebony shoulders. "I told you about the giant."

Allen pointed at me, and the giant bent at the waist to hear his commands. "*Ábir to mec séo bicce*!"

"Pretty sure that was about me," I said.

Waya nodded. "He kept calling Sophia '*bicce*,' too."

All battling had temporarily stopped with the giant's entrance which enthralled even Allen's monsters. Now the fighting renewed with increased vigor and clear attempts to move between the rock slabs I'd raised. No one wanted to get caught under giant feet while they tangled with trolls.

It would only take the giant four or five steps to reach us. Three scaly, dark blue creatures built like lean elephants without trunks joined the remaining two wolves and surrounded Allen. The giant stepped over them, and his pallid, hairy torso completely filled my vision.

Gunshots sounded again. The giant's ponderous step faltered. He rubbed his chest with one finger and smeared a trickle of blood before continuing. A few more shots cracked. The bullets bounced off his thick skull. One of his hands reached toward me.

"I'll climb to the top if you take the bottom," I said.

"Deal." Waya jumped off the tower. He landed with an acrobatic roll that brought him between the giant's feet. I saw him bite the Achilles before I leapt through the giant's clutching fingers. I vaulted off the bony protrusion of his massive thumb and barely cleared the spiked bracelet. Running up his arm felt like balancing on the spongy ground of the bog—if the bog was hairy and smelled of animal fat. I reached his bicep when the shadow of his other hand hovered over my head.

I stopped, crouched, and lunged to grab his middle fingertip. His hand began to curl around me. Swinging my legs toward his palm for momentum, I flipped up and onto the back of his hand as it closed. It brought me just a few feet from his neck, but I couldn't stay on my feet. I tumbled toward his wrist and grabbed the base of a bracelet spike with both hands. My legs dangled twenty feet above the ground as he tried to shake me off.

"Bochs!" Waya shouted just before a thunderbird screeched and dive bombed the giant's head. The dragon followed close behind, forcing Josiah to veer off and avoid a tongue of fire. Waya ran up the giant's leg, his red eyes locking with mine. "Hold on!"

"I've got this. Just distract him!"

One of Mrs. Holt's brothers bravely hacked at the Achilles that Waya bit earlier. The car-sized foot jerked and stomped, missing him by a toenail. He swung his sword again. Blood spurted, and the giant roared. Off-balance, the giant tilted backward, then righted himself before falling to one knee. The swordsman disappeared. I took a terrifying ride on the giant's wrist as he tried to catch himself.

I managed to swing onto the back of his hand just in time, but the rib-bruising landing still knocked the breath out of me. I bounced to the ground. Claws graze my skin, and Waya yanked me upright by my shirt. Beautiful air rushed into my lungs, and I gulped it. I stared into the fathomless pupils of an incubus. He hugged me and spun around.

We were knocked down, and something pierced my breast— painful but shallow. Waya's weight suddenly lifted. He rose rapidly away from me, attached to the giant's wrist by three spikes protruding through his abdomen.

"Waya!"

The giant flicked his wrist, and Waya flew into the tower we'd stood on moments before. Bones cracked, and his body dropped with a thud that punched my heart. The thunderbird called again, and the dragon's roar drowned him out.

Allen's laughter grated across my senses. Still armored, he completed a blood ward around himself and *Roc Fuil* while his beasts stood guard. Anger rolled through me in a white-hot wave, and I silently promised to meet him inside once I finished his giant.

I bent to the Earth and unleashed every drop of magic I had left. Cracks started at my fingers, racing to where the giant still knelt. I forced them wider, and one of his knees slipped in up to his hip. Then I closed the crack, squeezing his thigh until the rock buckled around him. His other leg stretched awkwardly behind him. He fell to his hands and screamed.

I jumped, holding my katana overhead. Puncturing the inside of his elbow, I depended on gravity to cut a slit to his wrist. He tried to swat me with his other hand, but I dropped out of reach. When his cut arm gave out, I leapt onto his shoulder, then to his back as he fell on his face. Standing between his shoulder blades, I saw the bulge of his jugular snaking up the side of his neck. I shoved my blade through it, up to the hilt, and ripped it away.

Hot blood showered me and ran into the crevices I'd created with my magic. The giant's shoulders jerked violently beneath my feet, and I dropped to my knees. The shaking continued, keeping pace with the spurts of blood shooting from his neck. When the blood ran out, the giant stilled.

It was a brutal kill. Even with Waya's sacrifice fresh in my mind, it gave me little satisfaction. I took a shuddering breath and knelt low in the relative shelter of his immense back muscles, gathering strength for the next round. A distant cheer and the happy bark of a hellhound acknowledged the fall of the giant, but clashes with the lesser monsters continued. I had to continue, too.

When the giant's body convulsed, I jumped off and ran before a mountain of golem dust could bury me. I ducked into a small canyon created by my resurrected boulders and tower, only to find it occupied.

"Waya." I fell to my knees beside him.

His skin no longer shone ebony. It was dull and gray, quivering as he struggled to breathe. The spikes had ripped holes in his torso, leaking blood, tissue, and life. Through the hole in his chest, I saw the bottom of his heart spasm. My own heart lurched with it. I didn't know how he still breathed, but his face registered nothing. A white hand patted his shoulder. I followed it up to the pale face of Mrs. Holt's brother.

"Gerald?"

"Dunstan." He barely hung onto consciousness. His other hand gripped his long sword. One of his legs twisted unnaturally. Beside him, long lines in the dirt and grass disappeared around the corner.

"You dragged Waya inside?"

Dunstan nodded.

"Thank you." I lifted his pants leg and saw that the bone hadn't broken the skin. "I don't have anything to brace it with. I'm sorry."

"It is . . . fine." The three words exhausted him.

I turned to Waya. No tourniquets or applied pressure would save him. I put my hand on his head, and his eyes opened. Only a thin line of red circled his enlarged pupils.

"Do incubi regenerate?" I asked.

His lips twitched, and a trickle of blood rolled from his mouth. I interpreted it as a no. I touched my forehead to his, squeezing my stinging eyes closed. "I'm sorry."

"Ssss—okay." His voice was almost gone, whispering on a trail to darkness that he would soon follow. "You . . . forgive?"

My immediate thought was 'no,' then I realized it wasn't true. He'd taken recompense too far in the opposite direction, giving his life for mine. "Yes." I kissed his mouth, the cold death of his lips releasing the tears I'd held back. "Thank you, Waya."

I raised my head to see him smile. Then the light left his eyes, and he exhaled one last time.

"I'll kill Allen," I promised and stood up.

A hand grasped my calf before I could leave. "Allen's sword will beat your katana," Dunstan whispered, then took a shuddering breath. "Take mine."

I looked at my katana, still covered in the blood of monsters and giants. My fingers tingled at the thought of not wielding it against my greatest opponent, yet. Closer inspection proved Dunstan's sword as more a longish saber than the medieval monstrosity I first believed. Its weight and length made it a better defense than my katana against Allen's saber. But the C-shaped guard curving over one side of Dunstan's hilt protected a right-handed user. I'd die adjusting my grip.

I squatted beside him, placing my hand on his shoulder. "Thank you, Dunstan, but I'll keep my katana."

He tried to sit up, his cheeks flushing. "His saber is longer." He paused for a desperate breath. "His hand is protected. You have no basket, no . . ."

"Shhh." I patted him. "I understand the risk, but I have to stick with what I know. Plus, I'm left-handed."

Dunstan collapsed, laying his head back and closing his eyes.

"Thank you, Dunstan."

Allen stood waiting when I emerged from the rocky crag. No beasts surrounded him. It was just Allen, his sword, and *Roc Fuil*. His eyes met mine through the shimmering ward, and he held out his hand, motioning me forward with his fingers.

Fire and lightning flickered through the clearing. The dragon flew close, trailing blood that sizzled on Allen's ward. The blue and green body crashed, and the boulders around me rolled. Bolts of electricity crackled, hitting Allen's ward with a force that staggered me.

The ward popped and flashed like an exploding generator, but when the energy disappeared, Allen's ward stood intact. He shook his fist with a laugh, then yelled at his dragon. A taunting cry emanated from the roiling storm clouds, and the dragon bellowed before shooting back into the sky.

Empty of magic and carrying a short sword into a long sword fight, I approached Allen's blood fortress. It was time to meet my first dueling monster.

CHAPTER TWENTY-FOUR

I was exactly where Allen wanted me from the moment he'd seen my shadows, but I didn't have an alternative. He hid inside a ward I couldn't break without a lot of time and knowledge I didn't possess. Mac hadn't emerged from my wall around the Evolutionaries, and anyone else with magic intelligence was busy not dying by golem. I had to give Allen what he wanted so I could at least get close.

Allen waved a hand, and an opening appeared before me. A wail rolled from the heavens, then he closed the ward behind me, and I heard only my heartbeat. I stepped over the three-foot fountain wall and into the monster's dueling pit.

He countered my circling walk, keeping *Roc Fuil* between us at the dried-up fountain's center. "I feel the blood pulsing through your veins; so much magic waiting for me. Did you know I can make you a shadow golem? You will hardly change."

I didn't answer, instead using his ego-speech-time to study him. He seemed closer to my height now with broader shoulders touched by dark hair curling out of his blood helmet. The helmet moved with his mouth like a latex mask. His eyes were unprotected, but the broad tip of my katana wouldn't get in far enough to kill him that way. The armor continued down his thighs, protecting his femoral arteries but leaving his knees to flex. His forearms and elbows remained exposed, too.

My plan hinged on his armor being like his ward: broken by his blood. I'd have to draw blood from his limbs and use it to chip away his armor. He still rambled about golems and glory while I pictured him as a giant weasel with one sharp, extremely long claw. I could kill a weasel.

Raising my sword, I jumped onto *Roc Fuil* and swung down at his shoulder. Allen deflected the blow, but it knocked him backward and shut him up. I hopped down and sliced at his shin. He evaded, parrying with a stroke that rattled my teeth when I blocked it. "You're fast," he said.

His sword was a glistening blur that I focused on, protecting my chest, then my hip, my arm, back to my chest. I finally resisted his blade with enough force to repel him a step. Just in case his armor was all-show, I sliced across his chest before his guard returned. My blade bounced and his smile widened. He looked comfortable. I already sweated.

I jabbed at his left side, purposefully leaving my right open. I crouched for a leap when his sword flashed toward me. I jumped up, catching the flat of his blade with the bottom of my boots. My weight pulled him toward me. I reversed my katana, using both hands to slam the hilt into his right eye before I hopped off his sword.

Allen screamed and dropped into a backward roll, then stood with his sword up. His right eye was distended and full of blood. I'd increased his motivation to kill me, but his lost eye raised my winning odds. Plus, I'd pricked his forearm with my blade. A small amount of blood smeared the edge.

I lunged at him, letting his blocking blade slide down so my sword edge grazed his side. It cost me as his sword tip bit deep into the outside of my shoulder, but a portion of his armor dissolved. His good eye widened.

My blade drew more blood from his ribs, but I had to parry a new onslaught from Allen's sword before I could hack at his armor again. I blocked an overhead blow and he let his sword slip off my katana. His blade dropped to my midsection while I still held my protection over my head.

I couldn't bring my sword back fast enough. My awkward dodge avoided his thrust toward my abdomen, but he still cut a gash in my hip that immediately soaked my jeans with blood. Then his edge caught my rib cage on the return. Now the entire right side of my torso burned and anointed the ground with blood. Allen forced me to circle *Roc Fuil* until I could skip over its top and retreat to the opposite side. It bought me a few seconds of recuperation before he caught up.

Our fight continued in the same fashion: onslaughts by Allen followed by my sneak attacks on his limbs to slowly disintegrate his armor. In his last pass, Allen missed with his lunge at my inner thigh.

I destroyed the right shoulder of his armor. If I could finish the rest, I'd get a shot at something vital. Except I got slower and weaker with every drop of blood I lost, and my magic was depleted. Not even the shadow monster bothered to wake up for this battle.

Allen tensed his legs, preparing for another attack that I couldn't handle. Then his eyes rolled up. He clutched his head with one hand but kept his sword raised. His blood ward shook, visibly warbling while a noise like a thousand tuning forks bounced off the walls. The roof bent inward when Allen's dragon landed on top. Slowly, as if the air were made of gelatin, the dragon slid down, leaving a massive smear of blood. The battered, blue and green body shook, then exploded.

The dragon remains swirled in numerous, small dust devils, agitated by the wings of a landing thunderbird. When his feet touched the ground, he melted into Josiah on his hands and knees. Blood covered his arms and face, but he raised eyes full of life to meet mine. Then his gaze darted to the side, warning me soon enough to block a cheap shot from Allen.

Fury over his lost dragon fueled Allen's offensive, and I barely protected myself in the attack. I found no openings to take advantage. My arms and back ached from constant blocking. Lightning crackled overhead, and thunder boomed through the ward as Josiah tried to break it. Then Dunstan's warning became prophecy.

In paralyzing slow-motion, Allen's blade bounced off my downward block and rebounded to slice my unprotected wrist so deeply that it severed all my tendons. My katana fell from my useless hand. I tried to catch the handle with my foot, hoping to kick it into my right hand, but I failed. Allen thrust his blade through my stomach.

Unbelievable pain boiled my insides, searing me with agony. I dropped to my knees, grasping my katana with my right hand, but I had no strength to raise it. His triumphant smile hurt more than my wounds. My blood leaked onto *Roc Fuil* as I fell against it.

"Yes!" Allen's shout reached through the thick cloud of pain and disappointment that enveloped me.

I opened my mouth, hoping for one last smart-ass comment, but blood gurgled through my lips and flowed down my chin. My blood covered Allen's rock, doing his work for him. He could have finished me off, but he dropped his sword and watched. Black crawled across my vision, and I closed my eyes, completing the darkness. Continuous thunder filled my head and rattled *Roc Fuil* beneath my broken body.

Allen sounded like he yelled under water. "She is mine, now, Hightower!"

I felt Josiah's answering burst of energy, but I had none of my own left. Cold filled my veins as the blood vacated. I wanted to see Josiah one last time, and tell him I was sorry.

The warmth tingling the fingertips of my half-severed hand surprised me. It traveled up my arm then across my chest. Opening my eyes, a tiny light pierced the death shadows. It grew until my vision cleared. I looked down at my hand, shocked to see tendons and nerves mending, skin growing. I glowed with magical overload. My hand burned, melding to the rock.

New pain filled my abdomen: tugs and flames that started deep and spanned out to leave cool comfort in their wake. My body strengthened, and new blood filled my veins. *Roc Fuil* was healing me.

"What? No! No!" Allen watched my wounds repairing. "Take her magic!" He put his hand on the rock next to my head. Fury sparked in his good eye.

My magical glow intensified, so great that my monster awakened, lapped up the abundance of magic, then rose to the surface for more.

Allen pounded the rock with his fist. "No! No! No!" Then he screamed with wordless rage and raised his sword in an arc that would hack off my head.

I couldn't move. *Roc Fuil* still held me. The shadows burst from my soul, pushed into my head, and demanded control. Having experienced death just a few minutes earlier, I gave into them. The rock released me. I raised my katana too late.

Allen's sword should have sliced my neck. The blade flashed before my face. It stirred the air. It stirred *me*.

My body was a gray cloud that swirled when Allen's blade passed through me again. The world around me shaded gray and black. Allen's armor shone—a black mass of tainted blood. His eye was a dark pool of insanity as he continued swinging his sword at my shadow.

I dropped to the ground, weightless and free, then I rushed between his legs and twined around his waist. Rising, I hovered behind him. The shadows hissed, and I grew heavy. When he tried to face me, my body solidified. I put my black lined arm around his shoulders, pulling him close. Instinctively, I sank my fangs into the exposed flesh of his shoulder, just below his armored neck.

The shadows spun beneath my skin and whispered in my head, encouraging me. My first thought was 'Damn it, Mac, I'm a vampire.' But I didn't drink Allen's blood. I tasted his magic.

Sweet, powerful magic filled me, expanding until thoughts of anything else had no place. Even the whispers quieted. It was just me and magic—and a fulfillment I never dreamed possible. I didn't stop until the well dried up.

The sound of Allen's body hitting the ground slapped my conscience. I raised a solid, glowing hand to my mouth. My body shook with an overload of power and panic at what I'd done. A black web covered my skin, the will of the monster enveloping me.

Allen weakly raised an arm toward his rock. His armor had dissolved, exposing a body so wrinkled and ancient, it bore no resemblance to his former self. He sighed softly, and his arm dropped. I'd stolen his youth with his magic. Surprise, then despair lit his eye before it slowly dulled.

The blood ward dissolved, and fresh air caressed my flushed cheeks. Just beyond the last shimmering fragments of the ward stood Josiah. His bloody chest heaved, and shock filled his wide gray eyes. He'd watched me turn into a monster and drink Allen's magic. His hoarse whisper carried to me like a punch. "Nalusa Falaya."

He knew my monster. I reeled and hugged myself as if stabbed again. Anguish clenched my stomach. Magic, heavy in my bones, begged for release. I carefully backed around *Roc Fuil*, hoping for distance before I lost control again and let the shadow monster use all the magic I'd taken from Allen.

With a standing jump, Josiah cleared the fountain wall and followed me. "Andee, stop."

"Just where do you think you're going?" Mrs. Holt appeared at Josiah's shoulder, barely ruffled after a battle with golems. "I saw what you did." She turned to address the incoming Magics. "Now, perhaps you will all listen when I tell you she's dangerous!"

I sheathed my sword and shook my head, afraid the mere act of opening my mouth might let the shadows loose. Light flickered from the still-raging bonfire that the ogres built an eternity ago. Shadows played on faces like torch-bearing villagers surrounding the resident monster.

"Our goal was to kill Allen," Josiah said to everyone, though his eyes stayed on me. "She did nothing wrong."

"She's unnatural and unstable," Mrs. Holt insisted.

Gerald came beside her, shaking his head. "She looked monstrous to me."

Mac and D.J. appeared, followed by a disoriented group of Evolutionaries turned Magics. They all looked ready to bolt if I twitched. Even Mac kept his distance, no pen and notebook in hand. I'd finally done something he couldn't paint over with optimism.

Mrs. Holt continued in a troop-rallying voice. "Where's Connor with the silica bullets? He can subdue her. Then we'll decide what to do."

"I'm not shooting her." Connor pushed to the front. "I was surrounded by wolves that turned to dust because she did her job."

Finally, Mac spoke. "Subduing her isn't necessary. She's not threatening anyone." But he didn't come any closer.

Mrs. Holt glared at me over her shoulder. "She threatened me, this afternoon."

"She can't be blamed there," Cain said.

"The strongest *malus molaris* on Earth just healed her and filled her with black magic. Why did it help her instead of Cynddelw?" Holt swept her glance across the group before answering her own question. "Because it found a stronger patron. Her power is dark, and it will taint her soul. If it hasn't already."

Murmured conversations and muted arguments began. I took the opportunity to slink toward the darkness of the forest. Josiah's eyes flickered my direction, but he didn't follow me this time. Even though he and Mac had spoken in my defense, neither of them stood bravely beside me. Everyone feared what I'd done, including myself.

Mac pushed to the front of the crowd to face Mrs. Holt. "We just need to study it. She'll learn control."

I met his troubled eyes and shook my head. I was done being studied. He could speak of control all he liked, but unless he'd experienced the shadowy desires churning inside me, he had no clue how to help me. I had to help myself, just like I'd always done.

"Mac." My voice trembled, drawing attention better than a shout.

"Yes?"

"Please bury Waya."

"Andee!" Josiah ran toward me.

"Sorry." I feared what would happen if he caught me. He knew my danger.

A little focus and release of my pent-up magic brought the grays of my shadow world roaring back. Stretching my body as thin as mist, I slipped through Josiah's hands. I rose until the shouts of alarm and Mrs. Holt's demands diminished to wordless mutterings. Now I couldn't hurt everyone I'd come to care for—and a few I didn't. I'd known friends were a bad idea.

I flew to the trees, my weightless shadow body flitting through the forest at a speed my corporeal body would find dizzying. When I reached Wornall Road, I saw Pegasus standing with the rest of the horses. I solidified my body and ran for him.

An ax sliced through the air in front of me, nearly scalping me before I dropped to roll beneath it.

"Bochs?" The curious voice of Lajani reached my ears. "Where's everyone else?"

I stayed in the crouch where my roll had ended. I had to keep my distance from anyone with magic until I got the monster back in its cage. "It's okay, Lajani. I forgive you for almost beheading me." Sarcasm had never equaled control for me more than tonight.

His ax dropped. "Sorry. You came out of nowhere. I just reacted."

I headed for Pegasus again. "Everyone else is coming. The monsters are dead. Cynddelw is defeated, and—well that's about it." He didn't need a complete update.

"Is something wrong?"

"Nothing a mug of hot chocolate and a bubble bath can't fix." I mounted Pegasus.

Far enough away that she wouldn't startle the horses, BOR's green eyes glowed. They followed my movements, but she never rose from her reclining position beneath a tree. I walked Pegasus closer to her. "Take good care of Mac."

Her eyes narrowed in answer. After I urged Pegasus away, Lajani came to stand beside her. She allowed him to rub behind her ears as he watched me ride off.

Darkness and Pegasus were the only allies left for me, tonight. He felt my urgency, carrying me to my apartment without arguments. I ran upstairs, planning to pack a few essentials and leave Kansas City as fast as Pegasus would take me. That the ward on my door was gone completely escaped me until I entered to Josiah standing in my foyer.

I tried to jump backward through my open door, but a streak of lightning slammed it shut, sizzling the doorknob. His angry eyes sparked and power pulsed from him like heat from the sun. Knots formed in my stomach, multiplying as they rose to my throat. My monster tried to claw through it all, feeling the magic Josiah emanated. I could barely speak. "How did you beat me here?"

His voice shook like a growl. "I'm a bird, Andromeda."

I nodded, fear flooding me with panic. He wouldn't let me get away. "I promise to take care of this. Please don't make me stay."

The storm in his eyes died. He shoved his hands in his pockets and looked away from me. A muscle in his jaw ticked. "I can't make you do anything."

"I'll work on control," I promised. "I'm going to my grandmother's cabin. People without magic don't tempt this monster inside me. It's still my body. I can—" My rambling stopped when he faced me again.

Sadness filled his eyes and for a moment his stoic mask slipped, revealing a vulnerable man. My hand raised to touch his cheek before I clenched my fist and forced it down. Josiah was still untouchable, no matter how much of himself he showed me.

"I'll leave you alone." Each word was a brick he laid back in place to guard his emotions once more. He looked away to take a deep breath before meeting my eyes again. "But you have to ask for help if you need it."

"Ok." He stared at me until I said, "I promise."

He walked past me to the door, hesitating an inch behind me. His head bent to mine and the warmth of his body calmed my lingering shivers of fear. In that second, I knew if I turned to him, he'd hold me. He'd face the monster with me. But if I lost control again and hurt him, it would end me.

On my temple, he placed a gentle kiss that I felt to my toes. "Stay safe," he whispered. Then he was gone.

I would come back. The shadows would not beat me.

I was Andromeda Bochs: basilisk slayer and giant killer. I took my father's curse and defeated an Ancient. I would conquer my shadows and wield them in this war to free Evolutionaries.

I was Andromeda Bochs: Shadow Monster.

THE END

UMBRA MAGIC

Andromeda Bochs: Book 2

Coming Spring 2021

It's been six weeks since Andromeda Bochs consumed the magic of an Ancient and dropped his shriveled, thousand-year-old body at her feet. No matter that he'd tried to kill her first—her shadow magic terrifies her. She doesn't understand it. She can't always control it. But worst of all, the power comes from a monster in her soul who doesn't like his hostess.

When her scientist friend, Mac, needs a bodyguard while he travels to Quartz Mountain in the Texhoma Desert, Andee is relieved to go with him. Bonus, there are shadow mages there who can help her wield magic like a pro instead of a toddler with a light-up sword.

But Andee's problems only multiply in the desert, and the Quartz Mountain mages are less than helpful. In fact, one of them gets into her head—literally. She wakes up in strange places, and her typical nightmares contain a new dialogue that chills her blood. A worried Mac calls in the man Andee prefers to avoid, Josiah Hightower.

Andee has declared the sexy thunderbird off limits, but her heart didn't get that memo. The son of powerful Ancients, Josiah's stone façade always cracks when Andee is near, but his is the only magic that can destroy the shadow monster inside her. She may never know Josiah's heart, because the next time she loses control will be her last.

ABOUT THE AUTHOR

Christina Herlyn grew up in Texas and Oklahoma but now lives in the Midwest where she earned a History degree from William Jewell College. She writes fantasy because dragons and witches wouldn't stay out of the perfectly normal historical novel she tried to write. Christina hates to read. (Ha! Just checking your attention span.) She worships the sun and exercises just enough to avoid being the first casualty in a zombie apocalypse. Her husband and three kids probably know she's a writer, but don't ask them to name her books. To be fair, don't ask her the names of her husband and children while she's writing. She'll get them wrong.

Made in the USA
Middletown, DE
17 August 2021

46174296R00161